P9-CBG-367

Confirm Or Deny

CONFIRM
OR
DENY

Graham Ison

ASBURY PARK PUBLIC LIBRARY
ASBURY PARK, NEW JERSEY

St. Martin's Press
New York

CONFIRM OR DENY. Copyright © 1989 by Graham Ison. All rights reserved. Printed in the United States of America. No part of this book may be used or reproduced in any manner whatsoever without written permission except in the case of brief quotations embodied in critical articles or reviews. For information, address St. Martin's Press, 175 Fifth Avenue, New York, N.Y. 10010.

Library of Congress Cataloging-in-Publication Data

Ison, Graham.
    Confirm or deny / Graham Ison.
       p.   cm.
    ISBN 0-312-03803-8
    I. Title.
PR6059.S6C66   1990
823'.914—dc20
                                          89-27064
                                            CIP

First published in Great Britain by Macmillan London Limited.

First U.S. Edition

10 9 8 7 6 5 4 3 2 1

Confirm Or Deny

Chapter One

Sir Edward Griffin walked through to Piccadilly before hailing a cab; it was good security to be circumspect when making visits about delicate matters, but it was the cause of deep personal regret that he was having to avoid telling anyone in the service what he was doing – even his deputy. The Home Secretary, however, had made it clear that he had no choice; he had been firm on that.

Perhaps even now he would be proved wrong, but he had to acknowledge that it was a vain hope.

It was made the more bitter that it had come at the very time he should have been retiring; at a time when he should have been giving little parties at the office for selected friends and colleagues. And being dined out by his own senior people, or indeed those at the place where he was going now, and having distinguished guests, the Prime Minister even, make complimentary speeches about him and his career and how much he would be missed. He wouldn't be, of course; no one ever was; he was enough of a realist to know that six months later he would have been forgotten – six weeks even!

Then there were all the things that he and his wife had promised themselves over the years. Some compensation for the long hours, the at-times-impossible tasks, the responsibility. His pension would not have been generous, not by industry's standards, but he had invested wisely and there would be enough to live on quite comfortably; enough to do the things he and Mary wanted to do.

There was the garden – he had great plans for the garden – and he could have spent a little money on the books he had always wanted to own; and have the time in which to read them. And then perhaps they would have gone to the occasional concert, and less frequently the opera – his love, or the ballet – Mary's. They were neither of them very keen on the other's musical interests, but had been married long enough, thirty years, to give in gracefully, and make allowances.

And then this. Just about the most serious dilemma that could arise. The Home Secretary had asked him to stay on. There was only one small crumb of comfort in that: at least he wasn't under suspicion.

But there was one caveat he had disliked, and that was why he was in this cab now, going where he was going. He had been tempted to refuse, to demand his retirement, but it would have made no difference; someone else would have been given the job, and then there was no telling what might have happened. At least this way he could retain some control.

'Westminster Abbey, guv'nor.' Griffin was aware that the cab had stopped and the driver was peering back at him through the open panel. 'You did say the Abbey – not the Cathedral?'

'Yes. Yes, I did. Sorry, I was day-dreaming.' Griffin alighted and handed over the fare and a tip, not too generous but enough – he never gave anyone cause to remember him if he could avoid it.

He waited until the cab had turned and disappeared into Parliament Square before crossing the road and walking briskly down Tothill Street. Again he was avoiding being noticed, as with his dress: anonymous fawn raincoat – his flasher mac was how some of his more irreverent staff described it – and he wore no hat.

He rounded the corner of Dacre Street and strode along its narrow pavement to the main entrance of New Scotland Yard; 'Back Hall' the policemen called it for a reason he could never understand.

As he pushed his way through the revolving doors a young man in a dark grey suit moved rapidly across from where he had been waiting in front of the Roll of Honour. 'Good morning, sir. Please come this way.' He paused. 'You have your pass, sir?'

'Yes,' murmured Griffin, opening his wallet to show the security guard. The guard didn't give it a second glance. It was like all the others, the familiar pattern: a photograph and the Commissioner's signature.

Griffin knew exactly where he was going in the building and was entitled to free access, but the young police officer escorting him was an added safeguard against anyone asking awkward questions.

They walked across the predominantly grey foyer and into the grey lift. Griffin pondered on its greyness: all grey in a place where the business was essentially black and white.

The lift stopped and started all the way to the eighteenth floor; anonymous people getting in and out, messengers with file-laden barrows, tea-ladies with urns on trolleys, and once a policeman in uniform looking strangely out of place in this world-famous police headquarters.

They emerged into a grey corridor, Griffin's guide nodding to a colleague in a glass-fronted office.

The secretary's office was like any other: a girl, a typewriter, tea-things, paper, clutter.

The young policeman said hallo to the secretary and tapped lightly on the open inner door of the Deputy Assistant Commissioner's office. 'The Director-General of MI5, sir,' he said.

Donald Logan skirted his desk, hand extended. 'Good morning, Edward.'

'Good morning, Donald. Thank you for seeing me at such short notice.'

Logan waved a deprecating hand. 'Come and sit down. Coffee?'

'Thank you – black, no sugar.'

Logan smiled. 'I know. Carol, two black coffees – no sugar in Sir Edward's.' He closed the door and sat down opposite Griffin in the group of chairs behind it.

Neither man was inclined to start the conversation. Both

knew that the secretary would be returning with the coffee soon. Logan guessed that Griffin's peremptory visit must be important: Griffin knew it was.

'England seem to be doing well.'

'I beg your pardon?'

'Cricket, Edward, the test.'

'Oh, yes. I'm sorry, I don't follow cricket.'

Logan laughed. 'I'd've thought it was a must for an establishment figure like yourself.'

Griffin smiled a taut smile. 'Like Drake playing bowls, you mean?' It was a simile that was peculiarly apt to him that morning.

'Something like that.' He moved slightly so that his secretary could put the tray of coffee on the table between them.

Griffin watched the door close again, and then glanced round the big double-aspect office.

'It's swept quite regularly – by your chaps,' said Logan, a half-smile playing round his lips. They both knew he wasn't talking about the cleanliness of the rich pile carpet.

Griffin smiled too. 'Sorry,' he said, 'but this problem's beginning to get to me . . . '

Logan sat, relaxed, waiting. He had known Sir Edward Griffin for some time and they got on well. It was not always an easy relationship, the one between MI5 and Special Branch, or the Security Service and SO12 as each was now known in that infuriatingly bureaucratic world of ever-changing terminology. Overall their objectives were the same, the security of the state, but the nuances varied. MI5 were acquisitive; to them, intelligence, however obtained, was paramount. To Special Branch, enforcement of the law brooked no compromise; nothing could be permitted to interfere with their duty as police officers. It occasionally soured the relationship on both sides, particularly at the lower levels.

With a light sigh, Griffin said; 'We've got a leak, Donald.'

'Oh!' Logan pursed his lips. 'You're certain?'

'There's an outside chance that I'm wrong, I suppose, and I hope to God I am, but . . . ' He left the sentence trailing.

8

Logan put his coffee cup down on the low table between them. 'I thought you chaps always consumed your own smoke?'

Griffin's glance wasn't malevolent, but it betrayed the bitterness he felt. 'I've no option. The Home Secretary has instructed me to enlist your help.' He stared bleakly at Logan's coffee cup for a second or two and then looked up again. 'Fully supported by the Prime Minister, I may say, who seems to think that Special Branch can do no wrong.'

On another occasion Logan would have made jocular capital out of that but not now. 'I see.' The policeman waited patiently, sympathising silently with the man opposite. It was no easy task to face up to the existence of a traitor in one's organisation, and there seemed no other construction which could be put upon what Griffin had just said. It was worse when you had to tell an outsider and ask for his assistance.

'We've had two operations go wrong recently. Well, in the last year. One you know about – the Nikitin case.'

Logan remembered it well. Last summer an 'illegal' called Ivor Nikitin had been found to be the controller of a young naval telegraphist at the Ministry of Defence. The combined operation between MI5 and Special Branch had been undertaken, as usual, in the utmost secrecy, but at the moment the trap was sprung it was discovered that Nikitin had disappeared. MI5's so-called sister service, MI6, had subsequently reported his return to a hero's welcome in Moscow. They had been left with the naval telegraphist, a pathetic twenty year old whose only rewards had been one hundred and twenty pounds, an expensive camera – and twenty-one years' imprisonment.

'But last month,' continued Griffin, 'a similar thing happened. This time an East German.'

Logan raised an eyebrow. 'When?'

'Two weeks ago.'

'I didn't— '

'No, you wouldn't have known about it. It was aborted before you were involved – unfortunately.'

'What makes you think it was a leak, Edward? It could

have been bad luck. After all it does happen, particularly in our business.'

Griffin shook his head slowly. 'The pattern was almost identical with the Nikitin case.' He paused reflectively. 'And it was the same team from my service who worked on it.'

'Well it would have been anyway, wouldn't it?'

'Yes, I suppose that's true,' he conceded, 'but coincidences like that alarm me, Donald. It only needs one of those damned investigative journalists to get the merest whiff and they'll be shouting KGB penetration from the roof-tops. Look what they did to poor Roger Hollis.'

Logan nodded. All the world knew the constantly recurring allegations about the former Director-General, knew also that his death had prevented him from defending himself, but hadn't stopped the rumour-mongers. 'Still, Edward, they're not suggesting you work for the Russians, are they?' It was said with a smile, a smile that Griffin did not return.

'No, Donald, they're not,' he said solemnly. 'Not yet, anyway. But if I'm not seen to take some action – some positive action – they'll accuse me of complicity soon enough.'

Logan half turned in his chair and stretched out his long legs, his gaze flickering across to the group photograph on the opposite wall – a photograph of stern-faced and moustached Special Branch officers in the First World War army uniforms they had worn when attached to military intelligence. One of them had relentlessly pursued Percy Topliss, the monocled mutineer, to his death; Special Branch officers were very good at tracking people down.

'Roger Hollis wasn't a spy,' said Logan comfortingly.

'I know that and you know that,' said Griffin. 'It's a classic case of Soviet disinformation. Our source has proved that to us beyond all reasonable doubt, but we can't broadcast it without prejudicing that source.'

'Exactly. Might this not be the same?'

A ray of hope appeared on Griffin's face, to be extinguished almost at once. 'A set-up, you mean?'

'Yes.'

'I'd like to think so. If you can prove it I shall be eternally grateful to you.'

'Well,' said Logan, 'supposing they wanted to cast suspicion on one of your officers. What better way to do it than to put down a few clues that'll lead you on, and then pull the plug at precisely the right moment, leaving your service with egg on its face.'

'I must admit I've thought about it – hoped if you like. All we got was some poor little sod of a leading telegraphist in the navy who had no money and a weakness for scantily clad young ladies. And he didn't get much of either.'

'They wouldn't have worried about him,' said Logan, 'as you well know. They'll sacrifice anybody to achieve their aims. They don't play cricket, you know.'

'Neither do I,' said Griffin, and Logan glimpsed a little of the steel that had caused the Prime Minister to appoint him to his present post.

'You have a plan?' asked Logan, determined to steer the DG away from his self-pitying reminiscing.

'Of sorts, yes.' Griffin paused, reflecting, realising that he was getting too edgy about the whole thing, to the point where he was now wondering whether he should even confide in the head of Special Branch. He plunged. 'We've got a double agent – here in London— '

'Are you sure?'

For a moment Griffin looked puzzled. 'She's seen at regular intervals; of course she's here.'

'I didn't mean that. The question was, are you sure that she's on your side? Always a risk with double agents, surely?'

Griffin laughed cynically. 'I see what you mean. Yes, as sure as we can be.'

'Go on.'

'My idea was to make her the subject of an operation. Use the same team as we used for Nikitin and Gesschner, and place the team itself under observation.' He spoke the last words softly. The whole thing was distasteful to him; he still couldn't come to terms with the proposition that one of his own officers could be working for the KGB. Logan raised a quizzical eyebrow and Griffin went on. 'The moment our double agent is alerted, she would tell us.'

'And you'd be no further forward than you are now,' said Logan, half to himself. 'Who's her handler?'

'John Carfax.'

'He's fairly senior, isn't he? She must be pretty valuable.'

'Vulnerable more than valuable. But she's useful.'

'But that would blow her cover for all time, surely? You'd either have to let her go – back to Moscow, I mean – or put her into cold storage. The first option might make her useful to SIS, but in neither case would she be any more good to you.'

'You don't make omelettes without breaking eggs,' said Griffin. He looked tired.

Logan pursed his lips. 'If we're to take this on, Edward, I shall leave it very much to the officer charged with the enquiry to make his own plans.' He didn't like the sound of Griffin's proposal at all. In his view, the Director-General was allowing his judgment to be clouded; there would be no profit in sacrificing a double agent. It seemed that Griffin was too close to his problem to be objective about it.

'Who will you give me – Frank Hussey?'

The DAC shook his head slowly. 'I propose giving you John Gaffney,' he said. 'You remember him?'

'Wasn't he the chap who was involved with that girl in Moscow – the ambassador's secretary?' Griffin frowned.

'Yes,' said Logan flatly. 'But he was promoted detective chief superintendent after that. He was the officer who investigated the murder of that girl whose body was found in France.'

'Oh yes, I remember that – or more particularly a rather painful interview with the Prime Minister,' said Griffin. 'One of several lately,' he added.

At the other end of the short corridor leading from the DAC's office, three young men and one young woman were perched nervously on chairs specially placed outside a door through which they were shortly to be admitted

12

for interview. They looked around. At the thermoplastic flooring, at the vinyl-covered utility boarding that formed the walls, and at the office doors. From time to time self-confident men entered these offices. Most were attired in dark suits, some clutching files, some nonchalant with hands in pockets; others were scruffily dressed in jeans and sweaters. Some would knock deferentially, straining for the summons to enter; some would just barge in, and occasionally the nervous quartet heard gratuitous and ingenuous insults, or snatches of laughter. Somewhere a telephone seemed always to be ringing.

They had all entered the building boldly enough, pro-ducing their warrant cards as proof of belonging, but by the time they had reached the eighteenth floor, some of the bounce seemed to have left them. They sat now, wondering. The three men, immaculate in best suits, occasionally fin-gered their collars or adjusted their ties. The woman, a girl of twenty-four, had dressed carefully and soberly in a navy blue suit, under which she wore a cream blouse, buttoned to the throat. Her black hair had been dragged back off her face into a bun at the nape of her neck. She had been warned that to be sexually provocative at the interview was suicidal. She could have been devastating in her appearance but had taken the hint, and intended to rely on her degree and her awareness of current affairs for success. On her lap, beneath her handbag and white gloves, lay a copy of *The Times* which she had read from start to finish on her journey to St James's that morning.

The men, occasionally shooting sideways glances at the girl's legs, engaged in apprehensive banter and exchanged whispered policemen's stories about arrests and senior offic-ers, but once in a while raised topical world events just to test how much the competition knew. All four wanted des-perately to become Special Branch officers, to cast off their blue serge forever, but the competition was fierce. They had heard that from an initial one hundred and thirty applica-tions, fewer than twenty were likely to be successful. The phrase 'many are called but few are chosen' kept running

13

through the girl's mind, and probably those of her companions too.

Each had reported to the office on arrival. That had been disconcerting. Coming from the uniform branch where rank was displayed on shoulders or arms, they found the plainclothes world difficult. Each had made the same mistake about the two men, both in shirtsleeves, who were seated in the office. One was about fifty, with distinguished features and greying, well-groomed hair; each of the candidates had addressed him as 'sir', only to be told that he was the sergeant, and that the youthful man opposite with the gaudy tie was the chief inspector.

They had all passed the entrance examination, or they wouldn't have been there, of course; it had been a testing amalgam of general knowledge and current affairs, and a project paper to which the invigilator, six weeks previously, had cheerfully told them there was no model answer.

They had heard stories about the interview, too. Selection board was the police term. The two senior officers who decided on the candidates' suitability were apparently, and disconcertingly, uninterested in arrests or views about community policing, and were just as likely to ask a question about the outcome of the power struggle in Nicaragua, or the effect of the star wars programme on the economics of the Common Market.

The chief inspector came out of his office and the candidates started to rise. He smiled. 'Sorry about this,' he said, 'but the president of the board's been called away. Everything's been put back half an hour. Better pop down to the canteen – get yourselves a cup of tea.' It was the standard police solution to any delay or crisis.

'I'm sorry to drag you away from your selection board, John, but something rather important has come up. Sit down.' The Deputy Assistant Commissioner stood behind his huge desk going through the morning ritual of lighting his first cigar of the day. He pointed at the cedar-wood box with his forefinger. 'For you?'

14

'No thanks, sir, too early for me,' said Gaffney.

'How's it going? The board, I mean.'

'Last day today, thank God. I think we'll manage to get fifteen or sixteen out of that lot.' Gaffney had spent four days already in the difficult task of selecting young police officers who had applied to join the élite ranks of Special Branch and now, towards the end, he was finding it heavy going. In his younger days, he had imagined that presiding over a selection board would be much less demanding than appearing before one, but since his promotion to detective chief superintendent he had found it to be a daunting task. By the end of the day, he would have completed a week-long series of fifty interviews in which he had asked the same questions over and over again, and received largely the same answers from candidates desperate to impress him with their suitability, and whose faces he now found it hard to recall.

'Sir Edward Griffin came to see me this morning,' said Logan, finally settling in the armchair opposite Gaffney. 'As a matter of fact he left only a few minutes ago.' As briefly as possible, the DAC went on to recount what Griffin had told him. Then he sat back in his chair with a half-smile on his face. 'I'm giving the job to you, John,' he said. 'What you have to do is to confirm or deny Sir Edward's suspicions.'

'Is this to be done in conjunction with Five, sir?'

'Certainly not. It's ours, lock, stock and barrel.'

'Well frankly, I'm not very enamoured of having a double agent imposed upon us. There's no way in which we can exercise any sort of control over a situation like that.'

Logan smiled. 'I thought you'd say that. In fact, I'd have been disappointed if you'd said anything else. I've told Sir Edward that the officer in charge of the enquiry will decide how to run it; otherwise we won't play. Now then – resources. What sort of team will you want?'

'That could be a problem, sir. Their people know a lot of ours, and if surveillance enters into it, that could be difficult. It's hard enough anyway, but if the target knows the bloke who's following him, then it's doubly difficult.'

'What d'you suggest then?'

15

'D'you remember Harry Tipper, sir, the DCI from SO1 who worked with me on the Penelope Lambert job?'

Logan nodded. 'Yes, I do.'

'I'd like to have him seconded; he'd make a useful deputy, and they don't know him.'

'I've got a better idea, John. We've got a vacancy for a DCI; I'll get him posted in.'

Gaffney laughed. 'I think you'll have a job prising him out of Commander SO1, sir. Harry's regarded as one of their rising stars.'

Logan scoffed. 'You leave Mr Finch to me, John. Don't forget the Commissioner's a former Special Branch officer, and I can play very dirty when the mood takes me. But what about the rest? Harry Tipper's only one man; you'll need more than that.'

'Depends on how many suspects we have to look at.'

'You may be able to have some control over that when you see Sir Edward.'

'You want me to see him?'

'Yes, of course. What you'll have to find out is how many of his people are involved, how many have been in the past, and what he bases his suspicions on. What's more, John, you'll make it quite clear to him, as I attempted to do, that you are in charge of the enquiry and it will be conducted in exactly the way you want it to be.'

'I was thinking that we might use some of those youngsters that I've been looking at this week, sir.'

Logan seemed doubtful. 'It rather depends what you want to use them for. I don't want them running before they can walk.'

'I was thinking of a crash course in surveillance. . . . '

'Well, it's up to you, but I don't think that Sir Edward's traitor – if there is one – will be that easy to catch. If he's a professional, and they all are – to a greater or lesser degree – they'll be on the lookout for someone following them the whole time. Anyway, perhaps we're jumping the gun. Until we know precisely what we're up against, we can't really make any arrangements. But Tipper's a good idea, and I'll see the

16

Assistant Commissioner this morning; get him transferred as soon as possible.' For a moment the DAC remained thoughtfully silent. 'It might be a good thing to pick a handful of new entrants, nonetheless, John. With a job like this you never know who you're going to need, or when you're going to need them. But select good ones – say four – and make sure that they're closely supervised.'

'Well I'll make an appointment to see Sir Edward as soon as possible,' said Gaffney.

'Let me do that, John. I sensed that Sir Edward was a bit huffy about me refusing to assign Frank Hussey to his job, but if a job's handed to us, I decide who runs it. Incidentally – and I don't really need to say this to you – make sure that you discuss every move with Frank, and that it's all carefully documented. If for any reason this thing should blow up in our faces, I don't want any finger pointed in this direction.'

It was a long walk from the door to the chair that had been placed in front of the table. Despite what the candidates thought, it was not a deliberate ploy; it was just the way the room was laid out, and that was dictated by its shape.

'WPC Lester, sir.'

'Thank you.' Gaffney nodded to the sergeant. 'Come and sit down, Miss Lester.' Well groomed, and probably got a good body under that rather severe blue suit; with her hair loose, and a figure-hugging dress, she'd look quite a stunner, thought Gaffney. Right now she looks as though she's applying for a job in a nunnery. No doubt some harridan had told her to dress down for the interview.

The young woman sat down and carefully arranged her skirt over her crossed legs; she declined to return Gaffney's smile. 'Good morning, sir,' she said, looking first at Gaffney and quickly at George Winter, the detective superintendent sitting with him.

The other advice she had been given about the interview was accurate, though; they weren't much interested in what she'd done in the police force so far. Nevertheless the first question was so disconcerting that she felt tempted to give up there and then.

'Tell me what you know of the politics of China,' said Gaffney.

'The politics of China?' She repeated the question softly.

Gaffney nodded.

'Not a great deal, I'm afraid, sir.' She had read the papers for weeks now, but couldn't remember anything significant about China. She knew all about the coup d'état in Cuba; was conversant with the latest Senate investigating sub-committee in Washington – but China . . .

'Second largest communist land mass in the world,' said Gaffney. 'Don't you think it might be useful to know something about it?'

'Well, yes, I suppose so, sir.'

Gaffney left it. But the next question was almost as bad. 'What do you think is the most serious thing that can happen to a commissioner of police, Miss Lester?'

'Corruption?' she asked tentatively.

'Mmm – if he himself is corrupt, then yes, I suppose so, but I was thinking more of his supervision of the force.'

'Losing the confidence of the officers under his command.' She said it triumphantly.

Gaffney appeared to consider that. He could think of one or two commissioners against whom that allegation could be levelled. What the girl in front of him didn't know was that he wasn't much interested in whether she got the answers right, but how she fielded them, how she stood up to the questioning. In most cases there weren't definite answers anyway; they were more discussion points.

'Supposing I was to say public order,' he said, throwing her a lifeline.

'Oh yes, of course.'

'Yes of course, what?' Gaffney smiled again.

'I should think that a breakdown of public order – on a large scale – would be more serious than anything else. In fact,' she said, only half sure that she was right, 'I think

18

that Sir Edmund Henderson had to resign because of public order problems some time in the 1860s.'

Gaffney, who had no idea whether she was right, at least gave her a few points for that. 'And what, then, do you think is the rôle of Special Branch in all this?'

At last she was on sure ground, and gave him the textbook answer of the job of the branch. Slowly she found her confidence, and her true character started to emerge. But it wasn't over yet.

George Winter now took over the questioning. 'This degree you've got . . . ' He tapped the papers in front of him with his glasses. 'A two-two in medieval history. What good do you think that's going to be to you in Special Branch?'

'Well, of itself, sir, perhaps not a lot, although history of any description will always teach us lessons for the future. What it does say is that I have a mind that can embark on an ordered course of study and absorb facts.'

'All my detectives have got that,' said Winter dismissively. 'Just so long as you don't think it's a passport to success.'

'Oh no, sir.' She did not like Detective Superintendent Winter.

'What's the difference between MI5 and MI6?' he asked.

'I'm afraid I don't know, sir.'

'Why not?'

'Well, they're very secret organisations.'

'There are books about them in my public library – probably in yours too. D'you belong to a library?'

'Yes, sir.'

'You'll find them around 327 in the Dewey classification. D'you know what the Dewey classification is?'

'Not exactly, sir.'

'It's the way they classify non-fiction books under subject,' said Winter. Gaffney smiled. The only reason old George knew that was because he had spent two months working in a library years ago as part of a totally futile surveillance operation. 'Have you bothered to find out anything about this branch?' continued Winter relentlessly. 'I suppose that because you're a girl and you've got a degree, you think that

19

you can just walk in and we'll fall over ourselves to take you. Is that it?'

'No, sir, that's not the case at all.' She could feel her colour rising and wished desperately that she could do something about it.

'Just another application, is it? What else have you applied for? Mounted Branch, River Police, Juvenile Bureau? Hoping for anything to get you off the streets?'

'No, sir.'

'"No, sir" – is that all you can say?'

'I've got a good arrest record—'

'Pah! That's no good, young lady. We don't go about arresting people up here. We're more subtle than that. You don't seem to have found out very much about what we do at all. Haven't bothered, I suppose,' he added dismissively.

Marilyn Lester decided at that moment that she had failed, and felt bitterly disappointed that the one thing she had wanted ever since joining the Metropolitan Police was about to elude her. She also decided that she wasn't going to give in without a fight. 'As a matter of fact, sir,' she said calmly, 'I have tried to find out what goes on up here. I have spoken to Special Branch officers when they've called in at the station, and a couple of your DCs live in my section house. None of them would tell me anything. You ought to be pleased about that.' Winter looked as though he was about to say something, but she carried on. 'Presumably you don't expect people like me to know all the answers, otherwise you wouldn't have to train them when you get them, would you?' She paused. 'Sir!' And that's that, she thought. You might reject me, but you won't forget me.

'Thank you, Miss Lester,' said Winter, and looked towards Gaffney.

After a gruelling forty minutes of questioning, Marilyn Lester was released from the interview, convinced that she had failed miserably. There was no rationale to the line that her two interrogators had taken, and she felt utterly drained. If she had been the crying type she would have been in tears, but as she walked back to the office, her only reaction was to mouth a very rude word.

'How did you get on?' The sergeant put a time against her name on the list in front of him and laid down his pen.

'Awful,' she said. 'Not a hope. I've never met such an unreasonable pair of self-opinionated bastards.'

'Glad you enjoyed it,' said the sergeant. 'See you next time, then.'

'You bloody well won't,' she said, and stormed out of the office.

'Well George? What d'you think?'

'She'll do for me, guv'nor,' said Winter. 'Got a bit of spirit, that girl.'

'Yes, I'm happy to take her,' said Gaffney. 'Got nice legs, too.'

'That question of yours about the politics of China is a bloody crippler,' said Winter. 'I wouldn't have any idea how to answer that.'

'Well you don't have to know in your job, do you,' said Gaffney, and they both laughed.

Chapter Two

Sir Edward Griffin had decided to meet Gaffney in one of the several clandestine rooms that the Security Service kept dotted about the Whitehall area, rather than go to Scotland Yard again, or have Gaffney come to his headquarters in Mayfair.

'Mr Logan has briefed you on our problem, I understand?'

'He has.' Gaffney leaned back in the austere government armchair that had clearly not been designed with relaxation in mind.

'And what are your initial conclusions?' Griffin was a little stuffy about all this. Apart from the indignity, to say nothing of the hurt pride, of having to enlist the help of the police, he was somewhat piqued that a detective chief superintendent had been appointed to oversee his highly delicate enquiry. He thought that the least Logan could have done was to give him the operations commander, Frank Hussey, deputy head of the branch.

'It's not going to be easy, as I'm sure you've already realised, Sir Edward, but I have to say that I am not at all taken with your idea of using a double agent as ... what shall we say, bait?'

'Oh?'

'You could well be replacing one leak with another.'

'Well I'm afraid that that's my plan, Mr Gaffney.'

'Sir Edward,' said Gaffney patiently, 'we are talking about the commission of a crime.' Griffin nodded, reluctantly. 'And I am afraid that the victim cannot dictate how that crime is to be investigated.'

'But this is entirely different—'

Gaffney shook his head. 'No it's not. If you had reported to the police that your house had been burgled, you would not then tell them how to go about catching the burglar. If you were that proficient at criminal investigation you would have caught your own burglar and not troubled us. The same goes for your traitor.' That was unfair really; Logan had already told Gaffney that Griffin had been directed by the Home Secretary to pass the matter over to Special Branch. 'Apart from anything else, if I'm to take this enquiry on, I shall need to make my own arrangements, otherwise I cannot keep control. For example I don't suppose for one moment that you would even allow me to meet this double agent of yours.'

'That would be out of the question. In any case, even I don't know her identity, other than that she's a woman.'

Gaffney shrugged. 'Well that would make it impossible from the outset. Unless I can brief the woman and eventually advise her when the trap is about to be sprung, I cannot be responsible for the outcome – which would almost certainly be a failure.'

For a few moments, Griffin stared across the room, deep in thought. He understood what Gaffney meant when he talked about keeping control; it was exactly what he was trying to do himself. But he was not happy about it. He was certain that if he had been left to use his own resources, he could have established who was the traitor in his service. It pained him even to think the word, but the Home Secretary had been quite brutal about it. 'If you've a cancer, Sir Edward,' he had said, 'the only answer is to get a surgeon to cut it out. And get one from Special Branch.'

'I understand what you're saying, Mr Gaffney.' Now it was Griffin's turn to be patient. 'But I would suggest that your simile of the burglary is not wholly apposite in this case. This is the Security Service; we are dealing with highly sensitive matters. I couldn't possibly sanction having policemen running about all over the place— '

Gaffney interrupted. 'If you'll forgive me for saying so, Sir Edward, I think that is over-dramatising it somewhat.

I'm sure that you are perfectly aware that, by the nature of their duties, Special Branch officers are extremely discreet – and trustworthy. Ask any Cabinet minister who is protected by our officers, from the Prime Minister downwards, whether they think we are tactful. And our officers don't make a habit of writing their memoirs.'

That was below the belt and it registered with Griffin. 'I didn't mean to impugn your people's reliability, Mr Gaffney, but I am unhappy about releasing this enquiry totally, and having no say in how it's to be conducted.'

'And that, Sir Edward, is precisely how I feel about it.'

Griffin sighed. He recognised an impasse when he saw one. 'In that case, Mr Gaffney, I think that I shall have to consult your DAC again before we go any further.'

Gaffney sensed that the interview was over and rose to his feet. 'As you wish, Sir Edward.'

With the natural caution of the senior intelligence officer, Sir Edward Griffin was guarded in what he said, even though he was speaking over the secure line which connected the headquarters of the Security Service to Special Branch. It had taken him some time to contact Logan, who had been diplomatically unavailable to the Director-General until Gaffney had returned and briefed him on what had taken place at the meeting.

It was an unsatisfactory conversation from Griffin's standpoint; it was immediately apparent to him that Logan's view had hardened since their initial meeting, and that the DAC was not going to give an inch. Furthermore, he derived little comfort from the policeman likening the situation to the siege of the Iranian Embassy some years previously. The allusion Logan had drawn was that when the police had asked the Special Air Service to storm the embassy for them, they had not then dictated how it was to be done.

Griffin suggested that they ask the Home Secretary to arbitrate, but Logan refused on the grounds that it was a matter of operational policing, and had nothing to do with the police authority, the rôle fulfilled by the Secretary of State in relation to the Metropolitan Police.

Logan had made it clear that he would accept the assignment on his terms or not at all; and that was something that he was prepared to refer to the Home Secretary. Although that had put Griffin in an invidious position, it was not an acrimonious exchange; more a discussion between two professionals, each of whom put his own view, albeit forcefully. Eventually Griffin agreed; in all conscience he had little option.

'Do it your way, John,' said the DAC. 'And now we've got that far, perhaps you'd tell me what your way is.'

Gaffney had given a great deal of thought to his task. The fact that the same team of intelligence officers had been used to investigate the activities of Nikitin and Gesschner, the two agents who had escaped almost at the very point of apprehension, did not necessarily mean that the leak – if there was one – would be found among the members of that team. If MI5 was like any other large organisation – certainly the police and Customs and Excise, in Gaffney's experience – it was very difficult indeed to keep anything secret. There would be quite a few other people, apart from the team, who would have legitimate access to details of an operation; that's where Gaffney's job was going to develop its complexities. There would undoubtedly be an element of hostility, too, and if that hostility bred obstruction or want of co-operation, a result was going to be even harder to achieve. But there were ways.

Logan listened carefully to Gaffney's plan, nodding from time to time, and once or twice pursing his lips. 'All right,' he said finally, 'but I want you to talk this through with Frank Hussey; his experience is valuable. And don't forget what I said: everything is to be logged, carefully; if anything goes wrong, I don't want any blame attributed to this branch. Understood?'

The slight, grey-haired man who stood up and shook

Gaffney's hand firmly, did not look like the Provost-Marshal of the British Army, but Gaffney had long ago learned just how deceptive appearances could be.

The suggestion of a frown settled on Brigadier Parker's face. 'We have met somewhere before, have we not, Mr Gaffney?'

'Yes, Brigadier. When you were APM London District. You invited me into your office for a drink after a Trooping. About five or six years ago; perhaps longer?'

'Longer. I left London District eight years ago. Time flies, doesn't it? Now sit down and tell me how I can help you.'

'Put simply, I want to borrow an army officer.'

The brigadier smiled. 'Any particular size?'

Gaffney smiled too. 'I'll have to let you be the judge of that. If I outline the specifications, so to speak, then you can advise me. I want an officer who is engaged in sensitive work – something that would be of value to the Russians – ideally one who is single, or divorced, who can drink, but hold his drink, and preferably in debt. In short, a drunken, impecunious womaniser,' said Gaffney.

'Yes,' said the brigadier after a pause. 'Well that covers about half the British Army.'

Gaffney laughed. 'I can see that military policemen are about as cynical as civil ones.'

'What d'you want him for?'

'Bait.' Gaffney went on to explain the delicate operation with which he had been tasked.

Parker listened in silence, a silence which continued for some time after Gaffney had finished. Eventually he said; 'You're not asking for much. Why did you pick on the army?'

'Discipline,' said Gaffney, simply. 'And because I don't understand the navy, and the air force are a bit new.' He smiled.

'Huh! And I suppose that you're going to tell me that I can't consult the Chief of the General Staff – or anyone else for that matter, because it's all so damned sensitive?'

'Exactly so, Brigadier.'

Parker moved his chair slightly and gazed briefly out of the window. 'Very well,' he said, turning to face Gaffney again. 'I'll see what I can do, but I make no promises. There is one other thing, of course. This officer, if I can provide one, will need to be fully protected. I don't want any officer finishing up in the dock at the Old Bailey when all he has done is to assist the state.'

'Of course not. It's my intention that he would be comprehensively briefed, and that everything he does to assist us is fully documented – in advance. The instructions would be signed by him and by me, and then kept in safe custody at Scotland Yard.'

Parker nodded. 'I have to admit, Mr Gaffney, that I'm not very happy about the proposal, but I can understand your difficulty. It would be unwise to use a civil servant for an exercise of this sort. All right. I'll do what I can, but I am making no promises; and I don't propose to rush it, however urgent you may regard the problem.'

Gaffney nodded his agreement. 'I quite understand that. It's a matter that needs to be resolved as soon as possible, but I don't intend to rush it either – that would be foolish. We've got to get it absolutely right.' He paused at the door of the Provost-Marshal's office. 'At the risk of insulting you, Brigadier, may I ask that this conversation be kept just between the two of us.'

Parker smiled and nodded. Gaffney knew that it would remain confidential, but the brigadier knew also that Gaffney had to say what he had just said.

The four officers stood up as Gaffney entered. 'Sit down,' he said. He had deliberately picked a room outside the Special Branch complex, some seven floors below it, in fact. There was just the chance that a member of the Security Service on a routine visit to SB would have caught sight of them, and remembered their faces.

Each of them had spent the last twenty-four hours wondering why they had suddenly been warned to report to

Scotland Yard at ten o'clock the following morning. It is in the nature of police business that they had been apprehensive, wondering what on earth they had done wrong. Their dilemma was not helped by the fact that, in each case, it had been their own chief superintendent who had given them the instructions personally, and advised them to tell no one else. Gaffney had emphasised to the divisional commanders that they should not tell the four who had sent for them; he knew the damage that wagging tongues could do in a police canteen.

Slowly, Gaffney gazed at them. 'You're probably wondering why you've been called up here,' he said. They nodded. 'I have decided to accept each of you into Special Branch, among others.' He paused to allow that bit of good news to sink in. 'But I have also selected you for a particular job.' The four looked pleased. 'And in case you think it's because you've got special talents, or are outstandingly brilliant, forget it. I've picked you because you're so bloody ordinary, and because your faces are not known to the people in whom we're taking an interest. As of now, you are detective constables for duty in Special Branch. But don't let that go to your heads. The job, as far as you are concerned, is extremely mundane. It will be boring, and will probably shatter all your illusions about Special Branch. By the time it's finished, you'll be sick of it, wondering why you ever volunteered.' He frowned at them. 'It certainly doesn't mean that you're budding James Bonds. Such people don't exist, and if any one of you steps out of line you'll be back in uniform so fast that you'll forget you've ever been here. Understood?'

There was a muted chorus of acknowledgment; they were beginning to wonder what they were getting into. 'May we ask what this job is, sir?' ventured one of them, an intense and slightly balding young man called Paul Bishop.

'No, you may not,' said Gaffney, 'because you're not going to be told. Then you can't tell anyone else.' He smiled at them. 'For a start, you will be going on a crash course in surveillance techniques – from tomorrow morning. You will be under the supervision of a very skilled detective sergeant. He will be

28

entirely responsible for you, and you will do everything he tells you without question. Under no circumstances will you set foot in this building again, or any other police premises for that matter, until I tell you— ' He broke off as Marilyn Lester half raised her hand. 'Yes?'

'I live in a section house, sir.'

'Then you'll move. Get a flat.' She looked concerned. 'Don't worry,' he said, 'we'll arrange it for you. What about you others? If I remember correctly, you're all married and live in your own places – yes?' They nodded. 'Bloody lucky,' said Gaffney. 'When I got married, I was stuck in police quarters for three years before we got somewhere of our own.' He'd still got somewhere of his own, but his wife had left him a year or two previously to set up home with a resting actor. 'Do not forget,' he continued, 'that you are detective constables on probation. One slip and out you go, and there's no appeal. Right, any questions?'

'How long is this job going to last, sir?' asked Cane.

'No idea. As long as it takes. It could be months – might even be a year, but I hope not.' He looked around. No one else said anything. 'Right, I'm now going to give you the address of a house in West London. You will go there at half-hour intervals, not in a bunch; sort it out among yourselves. Okay, off you go.' The new detectives stood up and made towards the door. 'Miss Lester.'

'Yes, sir.' The girl turned. She was wearing again the blue suit and flat shoes she had worn on the day of the interview, and her hair was still drawn back into a severe bun.

'You look like a bloody policewoman,' said Gaffney. 'For God's sake get something that looks a bit feminine. We like our girls to look like girls; and incidentally, there's no law against smiling up here. Got it?'

For the first time she smiled. 'Got it, sir.' Perhaps they weren't such a bad lot after all. And perhaps he wasn't such a self-opinionated bastard.

'His name's Armitage, sir – James Armitage, known as Jack.'

'Is he what you're looking for?' Frank Hussey lowered

his heavy frame into his chair and linked his fingers loosely on the blotter in front of him.

'Remains to be seen, sir,' said Gaffney. 'I've looked at his army records, but I want to do a bit of background digging of my own.'

'How long's that going to take you?' asked the commander.

'Not long – week or two at most, I should think, but he looks all right on what I've got.'

'Which is?'

'He's thirty-five, a major in the Royal Signals due for promotion to lieutenant-colonel very shortly.'

Commander Hussey laughed. 'If you don't succeed in cocking up his career for him.'

'Please don't make jokes like that, sir. He's divorced – about three years ago. He likes a drink, can hold it, and can stop any time he feels like it.'

'What were the circumstances of the divorce, John?'

'Incompatibility. He'd been married for about ten years. He was stationed in Singapore as a subaltern, and married a local girl – against everyone's advice apparently. They were proved to be right. It dragged on for a few years, then she went home to mum – couldn't stand Catterick it seems.'

'Know how she feels,' murmured Hussey. 'And since?'

'The divorce was a formality – all done by post, and set in motion by him. He was keen on some girl, even thought he might marry her but it fell through by the time the absolute came through. Since then he's had a few girl friends, but nothing lasting.'

'Why's that – not queer or anything, is he?'

'No. I gather that he suddenly liked the idea of being a free agent.' This time it was Gaffney who knew how he felt. After the initial shock of Vanessa walking out on him, he had to admit that he quite enjoyed his single state.

'Right, John – you'd better get on with it. But keep me fully informed. Every step.'

The rent of the self-contained flat in Battersea that Gaffney had taken was prohibitive. That in itself didn't concern him

30

because the Security Service would eventually foot the bill, but as a part of the fiction he was creating, it might have appeared beyond the means of Armitage, the army officer he was intending to install in it. His fears had been allayed, however, by Brigadier Parker, the Provost-Marshal, who had told him that it was not unusual for the army to provide such hirings for its officers.

It contained, in Gaffney's view, only the basic essentials. Apart from the two bedrooms on which he had insisted, it could only boast a small living room – with dining area – a kitchen and a bathroom. Gaffney just hoped that his proposed occupants would get on together; if they didn't, there wasn't much room for a fight.

He levered himself out of the armchair as the doorbell rang, and walked quickly to the front door.

'Name's Armitage.'

'I'm Gaffney, Detective Chief Superintendent John Gaffney. come in.'

Major Armitage was about an inch under six feet tall and looked fit, as though he had played just enough sport in his earlier years but had known when to stop. His dark hair was a bit longer than Gaffney would have expected in a soldier, and he wore a plain blue suit that could have done with a pressing. 'I suppose you want to see this.' Armitage held out his military identity card, but instead of looking at the policeman, allowed his gaze to run around the room, assessing. 'Nice little place you've got here. Costs you a few bob, I should think.'

'Not me – the firm,' said Gaffney, perusing the ID card and returning it. He was pleased that Armitage liked the flat.

'D'you mind if I see yours?'

'Not at all.' Gaffney handed his warrant card over for inspection.

'Name's Jack,' said Armitage, extending a hand and grasping Gaffney's in a firm grip. 'This is all a bit cloak-and-daggerish, I must say.'

Gaffney gestured towards an armchair, and the two men sat down. 'You been told anything about this?'

31

'Not a word,' said Armitage. 'Got sent for by the Provost-Marshal, no less, this morning, and told to get round here this afternoon. Been trying to work out what the hell I'd done wrong. Not every day you get hiked out of your office and told to meet a senior detective at some flat in Battersea.'

Gaffney had spent some time working out how he was going to put his proposition to Armitage, and was still apprehensive about the right approach. 'I'm attached to Special Branch,' he said, having decided to play openly with this man whom he was about to ask to risk at least his career.

Armitage nodded. 'Thought you might be. But I haven't been selling secrets to the Russians.'

'I know that; at least, as sure as I can be.' Gaffney smiled. He was pleased that Armitage had said that. 'But I'd like you to give the impression that you'd be willing to.'

'So that's it.' Armitage took a packet of cigarettes out of his pocket, and offered one to Gaffney.

'No thanks. I smoke the occasional cigar, but you carry on.'

'What d'you want me to do, then?' Armitage blew smoke towards the ceiling.

'To be the hare, quite simply. D'you think you might be willing to take it on?'

Armitage grinned. 'Depends what's involved.'

'Well it could ruin your social life for a start.'

'Come off it. I haven't got a social life – at least not at the moment. And you know that anyway, don't you? You'll have done a hell of a lot of background work on me before we got to this point.'

Gaffney nodded and smiled. 'Yes, we have, Jack. In fact we know an awful lot about you.

'Well then.'

'I'm not going to tell you the whole story. Firstly you don't need to know it, and secondly, if you don't know it, you can't tell anyone else . . . '

'I wouldn't anyway— '

'People have been known to talk in their sleep.'

'I sleep alone— '

'At the moment you do.'

Armitage sat up slightly, and grinned again, an open, boyish grin. 'Now you're beginning to interest me.'

'Well don't get too carried away. There's no guarantee, and it'll be in the line of duty anyway.'

'No less enjoyable for that,' said Armitage, and slumped back into his chair.

'There's a part I want you to play. I want you to put yourself about in the pubs around Whitehall for a start; that's where the talent scouts operate. Give the impression that you're a bit of a drunkard, a womaniser, and that you've got no money.'

'There's no play-acting about that, old boy. It's all perfectly true. But what d'you hope to achieve by that?'

'They are all what the vetting people call character defects, make you open to pressure – vulnerable.'

'Well the drinking and being short of money, certainly, but womanising's only dodgy if you're married, and I'm not.'

'You will be,' said Gaffney quietly.

'Now hold on a minute.' Armitage sat up straight. 'There's a hell of a lot I'll do for Queen and country, but I'm damned if I'm going to rush into marriage.'

'Not asking you to do that. We'll fix it up for you.'

'Oh?'

'You'll have this flat, and there'll be a wife in it. There will also be a valid certificate of marriage in the records at the General Register Office showing that you got married about two years ago. The registrar who married you is dead, as is one of the witnesses. The other witness will swear on a stack of bibles that he was present at your wedding. Okay?'

Armitage raised his eyebrows, and then leaned back in his chair. 'And who is this "wife" of mine?'

'A policewoman.'

'Oh Christ! I knew there'd be a catch in it.'

'Don't jump to conclusions, she's a good-looking girl. So good she'll sleep in a separate room.'

'I said there'd be a catch in it.' He lighted another cigarette. 'And the rest of it?'

'Not much more to it, really. We're hoping that eventually you'll be approached by someone – no idea who – and that he'll try to bring pressure to bear by offering you money, perhaps ply you with drink, and – ' Here Gaffney dropped his voice to a stage whisper. ' – and maybe even offer you women, of the loosest possible kind.'

Armitage laughed. 'Join the army and see the world. What am I supposed to do – go along with this guy, whoever he is? I mean, he's going to want some goodies, isn't he?'

'That'll be taken care of. Arrangements will be made to feed you some convincing but entirely false stuff that'll satisfy them, at least in the short term. By the time they find out it's duff, the job'll be over.'

'This sounds remarkably like a fishing expedition,' said Armitage, who had done the staff course at Camberley and had had the regulation lectures from an MI5 intelligence officer, masquerading as a Ministry of Defence official. 'Isn't that what you chaps call agent provocateur?'

'Yes,' said Gaffney with a smile, 'or more particularly, the defence lawyers do. But it's not what you imagine.' Armitage raised a quizzical eyebrow. 'And what's more, I'm not going to tell you what it is.'

'Didn't think you would. In case I talk in my sleep.'

'What d'you think of it so far?'

'Do I get time to think this over?'

'Do you need it?'

Armitage sat in silence for a moment or two. 'Not really, no. There's only one thing that worries me. I'm due for promotion to half-colonel shortly. Supposing this goes wrong and I finish up getting arrested for being a spy?'

'You will, but if you agree, all that we've discussed will be put down on paper, signed by you and me, and lodged at Scotland Yard.'

'Do I get a copy?'

'What would you do with it? Fold it up and put it in the tea-caddy?'

Armitage grinned. 'If you keep it, I've got nothing if the job goes wrong.'

'I'll lodge a copy with the Provost-Marshal if that'll make you feel better,' said Gaffney.

'Okay. I'll do it. When do we start?'

'When I tell you. It won't be for a week or two yet.'

'How do I keep contact with you? I can't very well drop into Scotland Yard to give you a sitrep.'

'A what?'

'Sitrep – situation report.'

'No problem there. Contact will be through your "wife".'

Armitage smiled. 'Of course. When do I get to meet this wife of mine incidentally?'

'When I've got her to agree to marry you,' said Gaffney.

Chapter Three

Only the bottom half of Commander Colin Finch's face was visible, illuminated by a green-shaded desk lamp which, with the profusion of potted plants in his office, helped to create its tropical ambience.

'I just heard you're nicking Harry Tipper off me,' he said, as Frank Hussey entered.

'Sorry, Colin, but we need him.'

Finch waved at a chair. 'I bloody need him as well; he's a damned good detective is Tipper.'

'I know.'

'Well can't you take someone else? I know you're short of decent coppers upstairs in that dream factory of yours, Frank, but bloody hell . . . '

'Don Logan's discussed it with the Assistant Commissioner and he's agreed.'

'Well I think it's a diabolical liberty, I'll tell you that straight. I'd just got Tipper lined up for a job that's coming off, and your lot have him away. It's not on, Frank.' He paused to blow his nose on a huge red handkerchief. 'Why him anyway?'

'Because he's good; you just said that. He did a job with John Gaffney not long ago; the girl whose body was found in France on the— '

'Yeah, I remember. Your blokes stepped in and took all the glory – once all the hard work had been done – and you got him mixed up with that funny lot you work with sometimes. He's never been the same since. What d'you want him for, anyway?'

'For good, Colin.'

'What d'you mean, for good?'

'He's being posted in; transfer in Police Orders. The memo went down to SO2 this morning.'

'Christ! What the hell's going on in this job these days? Supposing I went waltzing along to the Assistant Commissioner and spun him some fanny about desperately needing one of your blokes; you'd not be best pleased about that, would you? Anyway, you haven't answered the question: what d'you want him for?'

Hussey spread his hands. 'Sorry, Colin, can't tell you, but it is important. . . . '

'So's the job I was going to put him on. Gold bullion heist – but keep that under your hat. Another secret squirrel thing, I suppose, with your funny little friends in Funf. What do you do up there, apart from nick my detectives?' He pointed towards the ceiling, indicating the Special Branch offices thirteen floors above his own in the other building.

'How much service have you got now, Colin?'

'Thirty. Why?'

'Because you're getting crotchety in your old age; it's time you put your papers in.'

'Bloody right, it is, and I might just do it. I'm getting fed up with the way this bloody job's going lately. There's blokes getting shoved about all over the place. I have to have a head-count every day just to make sure I've still got the same number of officers. The bloody anti-terrorist lot had two DSs off me last week. Another prima donna lot, they are,' he muttered. 'I tell my blokes now: don't leave your chairs in case the music stops.' He plucked a dead leaf from the Devil's Ivy that spilt over the edge of his desk and dropped it into his waste-paper basket. 'When's all this happening, then?'

'Monday.'

'Monday! Christ, Frank, how d'you expect me to run this branch? How am I going to get him disentangled from his caseload in that time? He'll have court appearances; knowing him, he's probably got three or four Old Bailey jobs lined up. No, mate, it's not on.' He bent down to peer at Hussey from under his desk lamp. 'I'm acting DAC this week.'

Hussey grinned. 'So what, acting sir?'

'Means I've got direct access to the Assistant Commissioner, and in about two minutes from now I shall directly access him.'

'I sympathise with you, Colin, believe me, but this job's very important. You should regard it as a compliment that I want one of your officers to help out. Anyway, as I said, the Assistant Commissioner's agreed it.'

'Well he can just un-agree it.' Finch stood up. He was short for a policeman, barely meeting the minimum height requirement for the force; one of his taller colleagues had once suggested that he try some of the Baby Bio he was always putting on his plants.

'Well I wish you luck, Colin, but I think you're on a hiding to nothing.'

'And I suppose you're going to dump one of your cast-off DCIs on me are you?'

'Certainly not; I haven't got any to spare. But that's the bonus; you can promote one of your DIs.'

'Thanks a bundle,' said Finch.

'Mr Finch was not best pleased, sir, no,' said Detective Chief Inspector Harry Tipper. 'In fact, it's a fair assessment to say that he did his pieces.'

Gaffney laughed. 'Yes,' he said, 'I gathered there'd been a bit of a set-to down on the fifth floor.'

'I'm afraid I'm in bad odour with Mr Finch. He accused me of conspiring with officers unknown to get myself a transfer out of the firing line and into a soft job up here.'

'Soft job? I hope you didn't agree with him, Harry. There's nothing easy about what we've just taken on.'

'He did his best to put the kibosh on it, anyway. After Mr Hussey saw him, he tore off and saw the Assistant Commissioner.'

'And?'

Tipper chuckled. 'Got no joy there. Then he bumped

into the Commissioner in Back Hall and had a go at him.'

'He never did give up easily. What did the Commissioner have to say?'

'He told him it wasn't an invitation to a debate, it was an order. Then he asked Mr Finch if it was right he was retiring; but he said it with that usual half-smile on his face. I hope to God he has retired if I ever get back to SO1.'

'I don't think there's much danger of that, Harry. Once we lay hands on people, they tend not to escape.'

'Yes, well I suppose you need some good blokes to help you out from time to time. So here I am. What is it all about, this sudden move? Bit unusual, isn't it?'

'It's not the first time we've "sidewaysed" a real detective into Special Branch, Harry, and I have to say, without inflating your ego too much, that you quite impressed the hierarchy when you were working on the Penelope Lambert job.'

Tipper smiled. 'That was a tortuous job if ever there was one. Still, we got there in the end. But Mr Finch said something about a special job. . . . '

'Did he indeed? Well, I suppose he had to give himself a reason for losing one of his best officers.' Tipper smiled smugly. 'That's not my view, of course,' said Gaffney. 'By Special Branch standards you're just about mediocre.' He said it with a smile. 'But he's right; there is a special job, and it involves the Security Service. I'm not yet sure quite how we're going to play it, but I may need an officer who's not known to them as an SB officer.'

'And are you going to tell me what it's all about then, this special job, sir?'

'No,' said Gaffney. 'At least, not yet.'

'No, I thought not,' said Tipper.

The Commissioner had listened patiently and without interrupting while Deputy Assistant Commissioner Logan had outlined the task which had been imposed on Special Branch. He was not unfamiliar with the ways of the Security Service, and realised how much it must have galled them to bring their problems to the police, and to have been forced to ask for help.

'I don't have to tell you that you're playing with fire, Donald,' he said at length. 'And for that reason, you'll need to document every move with care.' Logan nodded. 'But then you'll know that anyway. MI5 will form a circle of wagons quicker even than the Flying Squad when the chips are down, but in their case, they've got many more influential friends, and they won't hesitate to use them if they think they're in danger – yes?'

'Yes, sir. I'm well aware of that,' said Logan quietly.

'Good,' said the Commissioner. 'And I'd appreciate a briefing from you from time to time. It doesn't have to be a regular thing – just whenever there are significant developments – but I'd prefer to hear it from you before I hear it from the Secretary of State.'

'Of course, sir. Incidentally, I may need additional resources occasionally – and quickly. I don't want to have to go through the usual channels; it would take too long, and would require too much explanation. . . . '

The Commissioner nodded. 'I presume that's why you grabbed DCI Tipper from Colin Finch,' he said with a smile. 'He's still smarting over that. I reckon you owe him at least a couple of bottles of Scotch.'

'No problem, sir,' said Logan. 'It'll go on the Security Service's bill.'

'Ah! Come in.' For a moment or two, Gaffney had failed to recognise WDC Marilyn Lester. She had taken his advice and transformed her appearance. She now wore, a white suit with a pale blue shirt, and her hair, which she had previously pinned in a tight bun, was clipped loosely back, softening her face. Her sheer stockings and her carefully applied make-up, which emphasised her eyes, combined to produce a sex appeal that had been deliberately suppressed when Gaffney had first interviewed her. 'That's more like it,' he said.

She seated herself in the same chair that Armitage had occupied, putting her blue leather shoulder bag on the floor beside her, before crossing her legs and carefully arranging her skirt.

'I make no excuse for telling you this,' began Gaffney, 'but now that you are a Special Branch officer, you will discuss the firm's business with no one, and that includes other Special Branch officers.' She nodded gravely. 'In a branch that contains nothing but detectives, you will find that they have a natural aptitude for trying to find things out – even when they don't need to know them – and they won't always ask you directly.' He paused to light a cigar. 'That, of course, is just general advice. In your particular case you won't be mixing with any SB officers – apart from me to begin with – until the case is over and done with. But just bear in mind what I've said. Is that clear, Marilyn?'

'Yes, sir.' She was still surprised that a senior officer should use her Christian name, but the more she saw of Special Branch the more she realised that it wasn't anything like the uniform branch she had just left.

'Now we come to your particular task in all this,' continued Gaffney, carefully rolling the ash off his cigar. 'I want you to play the part of an army officer's wife – and that entails living with him . . . ' He broke off, expecting some sort of outraged refusal, but he had underestimated her.

'Yes, sir,' she said, and waited, expressionless.

'But not sleeping with him. That all right, then?'

'Yes, sir,' she said. 'But perhaps you'd like to tell me just a little bit more about it. How far you want me to go, for example,' she added with an impish grin.

'Yes,' said Gaffney, and ran a hand round his chin. 'We are setting a trap for the Russians – or any other Iron Curtain country that takes an interest – and the bait is the army officer in question. The usual form is that they will try to get him in some compromising situation whereby they can blackmail him into parting with secret information. The one they usually go for is homosexuality; well that's out, but adultery is a good second-best, followed closely by drunkenness and indebtedness. Jack Armitage tells me that he's pretty good at all three.' He paused for reaction, but she just nodded. Either she was very professional, or she didn't believe a word he was saying. 'I'm not going to tell you any more than you need to know; any more, in fact, than I've told him.' It was essential in any espionage case to maintain as many water-tight compartments as possible, but every once in a while the enormity of being the only operational officer who knew the whole story frightened the life out of him. 'You will be his contact with me, and the least suspicious way in which we can do that is for you to live in the same flat as him, passing messages on to me. And the fact that you're masquerading as his wife will give them – whoever they turn out to be – the additional leverage to blackmail him. I know it's asking a bit much of you, particularly as you've only just joined us, but that, of course, is the very reason why I picked you; your face is unknown to the people we're hoping to trap.'

'But surely, sir— '

Gaffney held up his hand. 'I know all the questions you'd like to have answers to,' he said, 'but I'm not going to give them to you. Nothing in this branch is ever what it seems, and I'm afraid that you'll just have to make do with what I tell you.' He smiled to soften the sharpness of what he had said. 'And believe me, it will always be that way. Now, I shall quite understand if you wish to refuse this assignment . . . ' He leaned back in his chair and waited for her reaction.

'How do I make contact with you and when?' was all she asked.

'Before I leave here, I shall give you the telephone number of the ops room at the Yard; commit it to memory. There will be someone there twenty-four hours a day; you can ring any time, but don't make it the same time, and don't make it every day. Now there's one problem as far as you're concerned. You must never make those calls from this flat, which is the flat you'll be living in with Jack Armitage, because there will come a point when there is a tap on the line.' She nodded and looked round the sitting room with renewed interest as a young woman about to purchase her first home might have done. 'Secondly,' continued Gaffney, 'Jack Armitage will almost certainly be arrested at some stage. You must make sure, therefore, that there is absolutely nothing in this flat that connects you with the Metropolitan Police, because it will be searched – by the police; everything here must support the fact that he's in the army, and that you've been married to him for about two years.'

Her eyes widened. 'But surely— '

'Don't concern yourself with that,' said Gaffney. 'All the documentation's been taken care of; you will have a copy of your marriage certificate, and it'll be genuine. Once he's arrested, Jack Armitage will be in prison on remand. I don't know how long that will be for, but it will hit the Press, no matter what we do to try and stop it. That means that you'll be bothered by them. When that happens, we shall, quite properly, put a uniformed man on the door, so to speak. Don't let him – or anyone else in the job – know that you're a police officer. One of the reasons I chose Battersea for you to live in, is that you've never served here, but that's not foolproof. If anyone should recognise you, let me know immediately, and I'll deal with it. Any questions so far?'

She shook her head, slightly mystified, and smiled. 'This all sounds a bit like James Bond, sir.'

'That is one thing it is not. This is real, it's boring, and it could go wrong. We might all be wasting our time, but for reasons which needn't concern you, it is very important. All right, Mrs Armitage?'

She laughed. 'I suppose I'll get used to that.'

'You better had. It's what you've been for two years now.'

'I want you to meet your wife,' said Gaffney. He had telephoned Armitage as soon as he had got the girl's agreement to her part in the operation.

Armitage carefully appraised the woman detective. 'Well,' he said, 'I take it all back.'

'This is Marilyn Armitage, née Lester. She's a detective constable, and she has a degree in medieval history.'

'Among other things,' said Armitage. 'Hallo.'

'How d'you do?' Remaining seated, Marilyn Lester extended

a hand. Armitage was surprised how cool it was, and at the firmness of her grip.

'You both know what this is about,' said Gaffney. 'The operation will begin on Monday week. That'll give you time to get moved in and settled. Arrangements have been made for your personal belongings to be collected and then put together before they arrive here on the same van as the furniture. Then it'll look as though you've both just arrived from somewhere else, if you follow my drift.'

Armitage and the girl both nodded. 'What about expenses, sir?' she asked.

Gaffney laughed. 'That's one dead giveaway with a copper – they always worry about expenses. All the bills will be paid, but don't go mad. Remember that you're an army officer's wife, and this particular army officer is in debt up to his eyes.'

'And he's not joking,' said Armitage.'Incidentally, what about a belated honeymoon?'

'That's up to her,' said Gaffney casually. 'As far as the Metropolitan Police is concerned, I think we could run to dinner for two.'

'I must say that this is one of the best things to have happened to me since I joined the army,' said Armitage. 'Unbelievable.' He shook his head.

'I'm glad you're pleased,' said Marilyn, studying the menu.

'Well it's not every day that I'm detailed off to live with an attractive girl.'

'Oh!' She looked up. 'I thought you were talking about the free meal.'

'My dear girl— '

She closed the menu and laid it on the table. 'Now then,' she said. 'Can we get something quite clear from the outset? As far as I am concerned this whole thing is just another duty assignment. What we are doing requires us to appear to be man and wife. Appear to be! That does not include you sleeping with me, and it does not include you calling me "My dear girl". I'll settle for "darling" – in public, as that seems to be what most husbands call their wives, and that's what I shall call you, or "Jack", or "love", or whatever else comes to mind and seems appropriate. But don't read anything into it. The nearest we'll get to intimacy is what we're doing right now – talking in whispers across the table in a not-very-good restaurant.'

'Yes, ma'am darling,' said Armitage.

Chapter Four

'We have set the hare running, Sir Edward. It is now a case of sitting back and waiting.'

'What form does your hare take, Mr Gaffney?' Sir Edward Griffin was clearly unhappy about the way things were going.

'There is an army officer who, to use police parlance, is putting himself about in the Whitehall area. He has all the appropriate character defects that will make him an attractive proposition to the enemy, so it's merely a question of waiting to see what happens next.'

'Who is this army officer?'

Gaffney shook his head slowly. 'I'm not telling you, sir. For a very good reason – well two, really; at worst he could be put in jeopardy, at best the ploy wouldn't work.'

'But good God, Mr Gaffney, surely you don't think that I shall tell anyone, do you?'

'I have no idea, Sir Edward,' said Gaffney, blandly, 'but I'm not prepared to take the chance. You, I am sure, would do exactly the same in my position. . . . ' Griffin nodded; Gaffney was quite right. 'And in any event, you'll find out soon enough if all goes according to plan.'

'What do we do now, then?'

'Nothing! We sit back and play a waiting game. I should know before you do if the opposition shows some interest – although with your impeccable sources, it might just be the other way round.' He half smiled. 'Then, I presume, you will assign a team. That's when you and I will talk again, because I shall want to know who has been deployed. And incidentally, I shall want as much background on each of them as you can provide. That'll save my foot-soldiers a lot of unnecessary work.'

Griffin nodded miserably. 'I really don't see why you can't be more forthcoming, Mr Gaffney. I am the Director-General, after all.'

'Indeed, Sir Edward, and you don't know who your traitor is – otherwise we wouldn't be having this conversation. Until your renegade is identified, we cannot afford to take any chances – any chances whatsoever, sir.'

'Let me get you a drink.'

'Thanks.' Armitage pushed his glass across. 'Scotch.'

'I'm celebrating tonight.'

'On your own?'

'Yes, silly isn't it?' The man held Armitage's glass under the soda syphon and raised a quizzical eyebrow.

'Just a splash. What are you celebrating?'

'Landed a damned good order today.' He shot a sideways glance at the soldier. 'Computers, you know.'

Armitage took a swig of his whisky and groaned. 'Don't talk to me about bloody computers,' he said. 'I'm sick of 'em.'

'I didn't realise you were in computers. I thought you were a civil servant or something. Aren't you over there?' He cocked a thumb in the direction of the Ministry of Defence building.

'Yes – but it's "or something". I'm in the army, as a matter of fact.' He dropped his voice as though he had said too much. 'But it's not generally known, if you take my point?'

'Secret's safe with me, old boy. Seen you in here quite regularly – just assumed you were a pen-pusher. Name's Peter Dickson – with a C and a K, not an X.' He extended a hand.

'Jack Armitage.'

'Captain, I'd guess?'

'Major.' It was true that Armitage had seen Dickson in the pub, most evenings after work, and they had exchanged greetings from time to time, once even had a brief conversation about the test match.

'Look,' said Dickson, as if the thought had at that moment

47

come to him, 'I've just got a contract that's worth thousands, and I've got no one to celebrate with. I'm thinking of going on to a night club, or something. Why don't you come with me?'

Armitage laughed. 'There are two problems there,' he said. 'One is the little lady at home, and the other is money. I can't afford to go night-clubbing.' Inwardly he laughed at the thought of anyone describing Marilyn Lester as 'the little lady'. She was slim, and of medium height, and indisputably very attractive, but 'little lady' was not a term – with all that it implied – that anyone knowing her would have used.

'Put your foot down,' said Dickson with a laugh. 'Ring her up and tell her that war's broken out – sounds better than working late at the office. And as far as money's concerned – it's on me. Well on the company really – they give me a very generous entertainment allowance. Not that I don't earn it, of course.'

Armitage appeared to waver. 'I don't know, I'd half promised – ach, to hell with it. Why not? Work too bloody nard as it is.'

'Never know,' said Dickson, 'we might even do a bit of business over dinner.'

'I don't buy the damned things,' said Armitage, his eyes narrowing. 'Just use them.'

'Finish your drink, and I'll get a cab.'

'Not before I've made a phone call.'

Marilyn Lester was too much of a professional to respond to Armitage's call other than in the way a put-out wife would have done, half complaining, half disbelieving, and telling him that his dinner would be in the oven. It wouldn't, of course, because if Armitage's bait had been taken he could well be out all night. But you could never tell who was listening.

They entered a discreet doorway and descended a flight of richly carpeted stairs.

'It's actually a gambling club,' said Dickson. 'Not that I ever gamble – that's a mug's game.'

'Mr Dickson, good to see you again, sir.' The head waiter

hovered, clutching an armful of menus. 'A drink first, sir?' He nodded deferentially at Armitage and led the way to the bar area.

The service was impressive; the drinks waiter arrived the moment they sat down, and Dickson ordered a bottle of champagne without consulting Armitage.

Dickson had taken only a sip of his wine when he stood up. 'I thought a little female company wouldn't go amiss,' he said as the head waiter conducted two young women towards their table. He kissed them both on the cheek and then turned to Armitage. 'Jack, I'd like you to meet Tessa and Fiona.' Two more glasses were brought and they all sat down.

Dickson had obviously arranged for the girls to join him before he had invited Armitage to dinner; he certainly hadn't made any phone calls after they'd met in the pub. It was beginning to look promising, both from the professional point of view and, Armitage had to admit, from the social angle too. They were both good-looking girls, probably around thirty years old; Tessa was a statuesque brunette, and Fiona a willowy blonde.

They dined in a softly lighted alcove in the corner of the restaurant, Dickson maintaining a sparkling conversation, and often stressing a point by holding one or other of the girls' hands on the table. From time to time the conversation divided, so that Dickson was talking to Tessa, the brunette, with whom he obviously had a more intimate relationship, and Armitage found himself chatting to Fiona, clearly invited to be his partner.

'Do you live in London?' It was the first of a long series of questions that Dickson was to ask during the course of the evening, and which were so cleverly woven into the general conversation that Armitage might have missed them, had it not been for Gaffney's intensive briefing.

'Battersea.'

'Very nice.'

'It's not – but it's handy for the office. Just hop on a bus – damned sight better than driving; parking's a nightmare. What about you – d'you live in London?'

'Yes – not far from here, as a matter of fact.'

Both the girls refused brandy, but were content to drink more coffee while the men consumed theirs.

'Peter tells me you're in the army,' said Fiona.

'Yes, that's right,' said Armitage. He couldn't remember Dickson having mentioned it but assumed that she had been told when the date was arranged. That was interesting: Dickson had professed not to know what Armitage did for a living until their meeting earlier in the evening, and yet he had arranged for these two girls to join them for dinner. It was another indication that, at last, Gaffney's plan was beginning to work out.

'I've had an idea,' said Dickson, glancing at his watch. 'It's only eleven o'clock – why don't we jump into a cab and finish off the evening at my place – it's not far.' He looked at Armitage and grinned. 'You don't want to go all the way back to Battersea, do you, Jack?'

'Not a lot, no.'

'Well, there you are then,' said Dickson, and winked broadly at the two girls.

Armitage sensed the inevitability of the ploy before they reached the flat. It was palatial, but accorded with what Peter Dickson had told him about his income as a high-earning computer salesman.

'Sit down, Jack.' Dickson waved a hand towards one of the two settees that faced each other across a glass-topped coffee table. Armitage collapsed onto the cushions, and was joined by Fiona, while Tessa sat opposite and waited for Dickson. It seemed to be a well-rehearsed routine.

Dickson busied himself at the cocktail cabinet. 'Why don't you put some music on the stereo, Tessa?' he said. The brunette pouted and stood up, a little unsteadily; Armitage noticed that she knew exactly where the records were, and how to operate the stereo.

When Armitage opened his eyes, the sun was streaming through the curtains, but it was the movement of his blonde companion that had woken him. She sat now on the edge of the bed, her naked back towards him, groaning slightly and attempting to untangle her tights.

'What time is it?'

'Nine o'clock,' she said.

'Christ!' said Armitage and quickly swung his legs out of the bed, a movement he instantly regretted. 'I'm going to be late for work.'

'I shouldn't bother, lover,' said the girl, standing up and starting to get dressed. 'Surely the army can do without you for one day.'

Dickson, looking remarkably fresh, was sitting in the kitchenette, drinking a cup of coffee and reading the morning paper. He laughed when Armitage appeared. 'God Jack, you look awful,' he said.

Armitage grunted and helped himself to a cup of coffee. Of the brunette, Tessa, there was no sign.

Two days later, Armitage sat in an armchair at the flat looking at the photographs. It had been earlier that evening that he had known for sure that he had attracted the right person in Peter Dickson. The computer salesman had appeared briefly in the pub, bought Armitage a drink, and handed him an envelope. 'Put those in your briefcase,' he had said. 'They might amuse you. We might even have a little chat about them some time.' Then he had downed his drink and left.

They were certainly good, and secretly Armitage was quite proud of himself, although he was mildly irritated at not having detected the hidden cameras. He had glanced briefly around the bedroom at Dickson's flat when Fiona had led him in there, but had been unable to spot anything. Still, he had to admit that hidden cameras weren't meant to be seen, but he could see now, from the angle of the shots, that there were at least two installed in the room.

It had been an enjoyble experience, the more so because it was official and on duty, so to speak. Fiona had told him that she and Tessa were friends of Dickson, and had been invited to join them for a celebration – an invitation which they had received at lunch-time. She had also said, as girls like her always say, that she didn't make a habit of going to bed with strange men. Armitage had made the standard reply that there was nothing strange about him.

'What have you got there?' asked Marilyn.

Armitage debated whether he should show her the photographs, but decided that, as a police officer involved in the case, she was entitled to see them.

She studied them for longer than he thought was professionally necessary before handing them back. 'Good-looking girl, that,' was all she said.

'I think we may have scored,' said Armitage.

'Well you certainly did.'

Dickson was obviously a professional; he didn't mention the photographs at their next meeting, didn't even mention the dinner that had culminated in Armitage bedding Fiona, but that event and the record of it hung there, between them – an unspoken threat.

But he didn't hesitate the following evening. 'What did you think of the snaps, Jack?' He sipped at his drink and gazed at the range of bottles behind the bar.

'Very good.' It amazed Armitage that Dickson was now going to try and use them as a lever. Had it not been a part of Gaffney's elaborate plan, the attempt would not have got off the ground. Armitage was always mildly surprised that otherwise intelligent and worldly men should fall so easily to such a blackmail. Had he been a free agent and about to become the target for entrapment, he would have gone straight to see the brigadier and laid the photographs on his desk. That officer, he knew, would have called him all the names imaginable for being a fool. Then he would have picked up the phone to the Security Service and offered Armitage as bait. Which really, Armitage thought, was what was going to happen now.

'It was just a little joke, of course, Jack. I've done it to a lot of my friends.'

'Very amusing,' said Armitage. 'You've got the negatives, I suppose?'

52

Dickson nodded. 'Yes,' he said. He knew what Armitage did, knew also that blatant womanising and drunkenness of the sort he had indulged in would cause sharply raised eyebrows among the ranks of the humourless – and occasionally hypocritical – vetting officers who had it in their power if not to ruin, certainly severely to curtail the career of an officer engaged in secret work. 'As a matter of fact, Jack,' continued Dickson, moving away from the subject of the photographs, 'I've been transferred up north – on to the development side.'

'Oh really? When's that, then?'

'Quite soon. Mind you, when I say north, I don't mean far north. Just north of London – but too far to continue using this pub so often. Pity, just as we were getting to know each other.'

'Yes,' said Armitage. 'Shame, that.'

'I was thinking, though.' Dickson shot a sideways glance at Armitage. 'You might just be able to help me. It's a cut-throat business, computers. Always trying to keep one step ahead of the opposition, if you know what I mean.'

'Yes, I think so.'

'It's much more useful to us to get field reports – unbiased views, I mean. I know we do a lot of experimental work, testing other people's equipment to destruction, but that's not as good as knowing what the blokes who are actually using it think.'

'No, I can see that.' Armitage ordered more drinks. 'Well, I shouldn't think there'd be much harm in that. What d'you want to know?'

Dickson passed a piece of folded paper discreetly along the bar. 'There's one or two questions there, Jack.' He smiled. 'It would be very helpful, and you wouldn't find me ungrateful. After all, it would be a sort of business arrangement, wouldn't it?'

Armitage nodded. 'How do I get the answers to you, Peter?'

Dickson appeared to consider that for a moment. 'Well, as I said, I won't be able to get in here as often from now on, but I could make a point of being here, say a week today. Would that be long enough?'

'Depends what the questions are, doesn't it?'

Gaffney now had to work very fast. Immediately after Armitage had been presented with the photographs, Gaffney had enlisted the aid, once more, of the Provost-Marshal. Brigadier Parker had introduced him to another brigadier, Armitage's superior officer at the MOD. Although unavoidably widening the circle of confidentiality, it was essential that when Dickson's demands came, Armitage should be in a position to supply him with material which was both convincing, at least in the short term, and unlikely to damage the national interest. Already it was starting to get complicated.

As for Armitage, he had been surprised at the naïveté of the questions posed by Dickson and expressed the view to Gaffney, through Marilyn, that the Russians must know the answers already. Marilyn conveyed Gaffney's explanation that it was all part of the trap. Once Armitage had handed over that information, no matter how innocuous, he would have committed an offence. After that he had to keep on supplying under threat of betrayal to the police. Again Armitage marvelled at the stupidity of anyone falling for that. But he knew that quite a few had.

It proved to be true. When Dickson kept the appointment in the pub a week later to receive the answers to the questions, he straightaway handed Armitage another list as feeble as the first. This was followed by a request for a harmless print-out – nothing sensitive, of course. Then it got serious. A print-out showing the deployment of certain military formations was asked for. That demand was made at their last meeting in the pub.

'I shan't be able to get here any more,' said Dickson, whose relationship with Armitage had, over the weeks, changed imperceptibly from one of friendship to that almost of master and servant.

'Well how am I going to get it to you? I'm not going to put it in the post.'

'Damn' right you're not,' said Dickson sharply. 'D'you know Teddington Lock?'

'I know where it is – roughly, but – '

Dickson handed him an envelope. 'Destroy that when you've learned it – for your own sake, Jack. It shows a place near the lock, on the Surrey side, where you can leave it. It's quite specific.'

'When do I put it there?'

'You'll receive a card through the post. It will congratulate you on your recent success, and it will be signed "Alex". Put the negative of the print-out into an empty beer can, and leave it in that place at seven o'clock in the evening of the Thursday following.' Dickson handed Armitage a small package. 'That's a Minox camera and some film. Don't use it for holiday snaps, will you?'

'Will it take photographs of guys in bed with blondes?' asked Armitage acidly.

Dickson laughed. 'It's not very good for that. Now, is that all clear?'

'Yes.' The simplicity of it all worried Armitage, not because it was dangerous – he was acting under instructions – but because he was afraid that Dickson might know he was being set up; he was getting results far too easily.

'Incidentally,' said Dickson, impervious to Armitage's fears, 'you'll find a small sum of money in the place where you leave the film. Just a token of our gratitude.'

'Our gratitude?'

Dickson smiled. 'Yes,' he said. 'Me and the company I work for. Oh, by the way, the same system will operate the next time I've got some questions for you: I'll leave them at seven on the following Thursday evening, Okay?'

'The thing that worries me, sir,' said Gaffney, 'is that MI5 might not have bloody well noticed that there's a spy at the MOD, but more to the point that there is a Russian "illegal" in the shape of the man known as Peter Dickson, alias Alex.'

The use of that name had almost sent Gaffney into hysterics; it had been used by the Russians so often that they might as well have signed themselves 'KGB'.

Commander Frank Hussey turned to face his chief superintendent, the light from his desk lamp glinting on his horn-rimmed spectacles. 'What do we know of this man Dickson? Do we know he's an illegal?'

'No, sir – although it's fairly obvious, unless he's a cut-out. But I've done no enquiries at all. I thought it unwise in the circumstances. After all, officially I know nothing of this.'

Hussey sat staring at his blotter for some seconds before replying. 'This is one of those damnable situations where our duty to the rule of law intrudes on the practicalities of an intelligence-gathering operation. We can't afford to let it run on for too long. The sort of information we're feeding through Armitage is going to be sussed out as worthless sooner or later – sooner I reckon. If Dickson takes flight on those grounds, it'll be because he realises he's been set up. That we don't want. It would mean we'd have to start all over again, because MI5 wouldn't even get a sniff of it before he took it on his toes.'

'So what do we do?' Gaffney put his empty glass on the edge of the commander's desk and looked hopeful.

'We've got to make damned sure they know without letting them know we know,' said Hussey, pushing the Scotch bottle across the desk towards Gaffney.

'What about an anonymous telephone call?'

'You're joking?'

'No, seriously, sir. It's happened before. Supposing a member of the public sees Armitage poking about at this DLB on the towpath at Teddington, thinks it's suspicious and phones the police.'

Hussey looked doubtful. 'Who's your anonymous caller?'

'Me?'

Hussey laughed. 'Everybody in the branch would recognise your voice.'

'I could ring it into the local nick . . . '

Hussey shook his head. 'What and have the local CID

crawling all over your DLB looking for stolen gear? No, John, that would blow it completely. It'd be all over the MPD in no time; the average nick's about as water-tight as a leaky colander.' He paused in thought. 'Who's that WDC you've got holed up with Armitage?'

'Lester, sir – Marilyn Lester.'

'Get her to do it. Wouldn't be the first woman to inform on her husband,' he said with a laugh.

The problem with anonymous telephone calls is the number of them that the police get. Gaffney's one fear was that the Special Branch officer at the Yard who received it might dismiss it as not worth recording. And there was no way that he could check, supposedly knowing nothing of the operation. Nonetheless, Marilyn Lester, by now beginning seriously to wonder what the hell her new career was all about when her boss told her to make an anonymous call to her own branch, made her way to Teddington on the Friday following Armitage's drop. Gaffney had told her to do that so that she could describe accurately the area where she had supposedly seen these suspicious goings-on.

From a public telephone box – the third she had tried, the first to be working – she rang Scotland Yard and asked for Special Branch. Declining to identify herself, she told the officer who took the call what she was supposed to have seen, being careful not to use any jargon which might identify her as a police officer, and finishing up by saying that she thought it was a bit suspicious.

Fortunately for the whole plan, the officer recorded the call, mildly reproved Marilyn Lester for not having told them as soon as she had witnessed this strange behaviour, and passed it on to the duty officer at MI5.

Chapter Five

'I know that you set this up, Mr Gaffney, but it's become serious now. After all, there is a genuine "illegal" involved. Surely you can give me some idea what's going on.'

'Sir Edward, we knew all along that a genuine "illegal", as you call him, would become involved. That was the object of the exercise, wasn't it?'

'Yes, I know, but— '

'This case,' said Gaffney, interrupting, 'has got to break on your service in exactly the same sort of way that they all do. If you feed information to your assistant director, he'll wonder what the hell's going on. Where would you tell him it had come from? No, leave it as it is, sir. You can't have your cake and eat it. Which is more important: to catch yet another "illegal", who, let's face it, hasn't received any genuine information and won't, or to detect a traitor in your midst?'

Griffin remained silent. That last comment of Gaffney's had hurt, the more so because he knew it was true; but it was just as unpalatable for all that. Eventually he said, 'You're quite right, of course, Mr Gaffney.'

'We won't make it too difficult, Sir Edward, but I am going to need the names.'

'Of course. But I haven't been told of anything untoward yet. You know as well as I do that this type of information comes to us from all sorts of sources. Hodder will put the watchers on the DLB, and take it from there – I just hope that they don't tire of it before Dickson makes his next move.'

'There is a way we can accelerate that, although I'm loath to do it for fear of alerting Dickson, but Armitage – my man

58

– can send him a message if he wants to speed up the next drop, but he'd have to have a good reason. Frankly, I'd prefer to leave it alone for the time being.'

'All right,' said Sir Edward. 'Leave it like that at present, and we'll wait and see what happens.' He passed a hand wearily across his forehead. 'I'm a bit impatient, I suppose, but the sooner this whole distasteful business is over and done with the better.'

It was three weeks before Armitage received another greetings card which was Dickson's instruction for him to leave the next consignment of sensitive material.

The dead-letter box was a tree just off the towing path, and was difficult to keep under observation; which was probably why Dickson had chosen it. The MI5 team of watchers had surveyed the area thoroughly, and had managed to establish a number of observation posts, one of which was on the roof of a block of flats some four hundred yards away on the other side of the river. The major problem for the surveillance officers was that although Marilyn Lester, playing the part of the anonymous caller, had said that the strange goings-on which she was supposed to have witnessed were on the Surrey side of Teddington Lock, it was possible to approach it from either side of the river. There were thick banks of stinging nettles and brambles near the DLB which afforded not only reasonable cover for one of the watchers, but also tended to dissuade the inquisitive from poking about in the bushes, and were definitely discouraging to courting couples. Most of the watchers were, however, plainly visible, but gave the appearance of being there for an entirely innocuous purpose.

Armitage followed the same route as on his first visit, driving over Richmond Bridge and along the west side of the river. He had told Marilyn Lester that he would approach the DLB from the Teddington side, as he had done before, but there was no way that Gaffney, when he heard, could pass that on to the Security Service without their wondering how he knew. He just had to hope that nothing would go wrong.

Unlike the first time, traffic on this occasion was extremely light, and Armitage found himself near the rendezvous with twenty-five minutes to spare. He parked in Ferry Road and waited.

At five minutes to seven, he locked his car and walked casually over the footbridge, occasionally pausing to give the impression that he was admiring the view. He mounted the steps of the second bridge, crossed to the other side, and turned right. There were two or three young couples strolling along the towing path, arms encircling each other's waists and lost in their own private worlds, and three fishermen, spaced at intervals, gazing blankly into the water.

Armitage hesitated, acutely aware of his vulnerability; what he was about to do would be nerve-wrackingly obvious to anyone, he thought. Admittedly he had done it before, but he knew that this time he was being watched by people not in on the secret, and although he was only playing a part, the adrenalin was pumping, probably because he was as keen as Gaffney for the ploy to work, whatever it was. He stood for a minute or two watching an expensive motor cruiser, which had just cleared the lock, glide effortlessly up river, before finally deciding that he could wait forever if he was going to leave his information only when the towing path was completely deserted.

He walked swiftly to the same horse-chestnut tree as before and, without pausing, tossed the drink-can with its bogus secret contents into the opening in the trunk.

He strolled on for a bit before turning and slowly retracing his footsteps, oblivious – despite looking for signs of them – to the watchers who were reporting his every move.

Armitage was also unaware that his arrival in Ferry Road – along with the arrival of several innocent citizens – had been the subject of several radio transmissions, and that the time it had taken him to make his drop had been used by MI5 to station surveillance vehicles in position ready to house him when he moved.

Dickson, being a professional, was far more relaxed in his approach to the DLB. He appeared from the Kingston end of the towing path, sauntering along as though he had all the time in the world; a man out for an evening walk. Despite his professionalism, he did not realise that he had been under observation for the past hour, having on this occasion left a sum of money – an insultingly small amount as it happened – at the DLB; a deposit which Armitage, in his concern for discretion, had omitted to collect. During that interval – between leaving the money and returning to collect the drink-can – Dickson had walked into Ham, consumed a half pint of beer, and returned.

He sat now on one of the benches and read an evening paper, casually lowering it from time to time to look around. It seemed to be a glance in admiration of the view, but the watchers knew that he was looking for them. Nothing had occurred to suggest that he was under observation, but he was an extremely careful man.

Eventually Dickson folded his paper and wandered along the towing path once more. As he passed the tree his hand shot into the gap and retrieved the drink-can; he had previously placed an old beer crate, which he had found nearby, in the gap to ensure that Armitage's deposit would fall only just below the level of the natural fissure in the trunk. To any casual busy-body, looking inside, there would be nothing more than a crate and an empty beer-can; all too familiar detritus along the banks of the river. As Dickson grasped the can, his hand had brushed against the screwed up newspaper containing the banknotes, but he had decided against recovering it; to pause might arouse suspicion, and if Armitage didn't want the money, so be it.

Instead of hurrying away, Dickson now began to walk slowly back towards Kingston, occasionally stopping to look at the river, but in reality searching for anyone who might be taking an interest in him. Then he continued, unaware that the man who was 'following' him was actually ahead of him; a method of surveillance which required great skill and years of practice.

Armitage meanwhile drove carefully back to Battersea, deliberately not employing counter-surveillance techniques, of which, in any case, he knew little. Despite looking for them, he had not seen a single surveillance officer by the time he reached the flat at Battersea; that worried him, and it was only later when Marilyn told him that they had been there that he realised how good they were.

The watchers' leader had monitored the progress of Dickson and was convinced that sooner or later, he would get into a car. Consequently when he unlocked a Mercedes parked in Lower Ham Road and drove off, the mobile team were in place and waiting. By the use of a variety of vehicles, two-wheeled as well as cars and vans, they were able to tail him all the way back to his flat north of Oxford Street.

The operation had been a success; MI5 now knew who was giving the information and who was receiving it.

The record of the anonymous telephone call that Marilyn Lester had made to Special Branch had been passed to Geoffrey Hodder, a senior intelligence officer in the Security Service. It was one of dozens of snippets of information to come his way in the course of a working day, but this had certain hallmarks which had made it of interest. It was Geoffrey Hodder who had assigned the team which had witnessed the incidents at Teddington. And it was to Geoffrey Hodder that the report was sent the following morning.

He read the report thoroughly, accepting without question the efficiency of the watchers who had completed their task by following the two principals to their places of residence – known in the trade as 'housing' them.

Geoffrey Hodder, however, was not a happy man. Last summer, he had been in charge of an operation involving a man called Nikitin. Special Branch had been involved in that too. But at the very point where an arrest was to be effected, Nikitin had disappeared, only to be heard of months later when MI6 had reported his reappearance in Moscow. As if that were not bad enough, two months ago, an East German, Gesschner, had disappeared as well, just as MI5's operation was intensifying.

Hodder had five men in his section, and normally they

would have been deployed to investigate this new affair. But was one of them a traitor? Should he use someone else? That would look suspicious – that would be accusing them in an obtuse way, with no evidence whatever. Eventually he decided that he had no option but to use the same team, but this time he would make sure that not one of them, not even Patrick Hughes, his deputy, had the complete picture. It would be difficult, and it would involve Hodder himself in doing more than he would normally have done. But he could not afford to take chances – not this time. Not again.

There were enquiries to be made, nonetheless, and he allocated them piecemeal, not telling his staff why they were doing them or what the operation was about. In fact, he didn't even tell them it was an operation.

For all his distrust, of which, obviously, the team were unaware, the results came quickly, and he now knew that the two parties to the strange goings-on at Teddington were Major James Armitage and Peter Dickson. He knew their addresses and he knew where they worked. When he learned that Armitage was stationed at the MOD in a section that handled high grade material, and that Dickson was ostensibly in the computer business, he knew that he was about to trap another spy.

But that was in the future, and would involve all manner of careful preparations. What he had to do now presented no problem. 'I should like to see the Director-General immediately,' he said to Sir Edward's secretary.

'Well, Geoffrey, and what gloom have you for me today?' For once in his career, Griffin knew what was coming, would rather it wasn't, and knew that he was on the verge of having to make decisions that he would rather not have been faced with.

'It looks remarkably like an Official Secrets job, Sir Edward,' said Hodder in bored tones. It was not an indication of boredom; he always spoke like that. He opened the buff folder on his knee. 'What we have, sir, is an army officer – ' He looked up. 'Major at the MOD – high grade stuff, and a computer salesman who lives in a rather expensive flat off the Tottenham Court Road.'

'What do you have so far, Geoffrey?'

'Good old-fashioned dead-letter box – Teddington Lock. No idea what was passed over, not at this stage, obviously, but it looks to be a classic routine.'

'This army officer – know much about him?' Griffin wanted to make sure that the unthinkable hadn't happened, and that two jobs weren't about to erupt simultaneously.

'Major James Armitage – known as Jack. As I said, he works in a secret communications section at MOD Army.' Hodder glanced down at his notes again. 'Married to Marilyn Armitage, née Lester – housewife; they live together in a rented flat in Battersea. Been married about two years. He was formerly married to Annie Hsieh, a Singaporean— '

'Annie?'

'I presume that was the anglicised form, sir.'

'Presumably,' murmured Griffin. 'Go on.'

'We now have him under close observation, and we are of course liaising with the Ministry of Defence. He has access to some very sensitive stuff apparently. I tremor to think how the damage report will read. No doubt we shall all get a wigging from the Prime Minister for not having spotted him before.'

'No doubt we shall,' said Griffin with feeling. 'How did you spot him, incidentally?'

Hodder looked down at his feet. 'Anonymous telephone call made to Special Branch actually, Sir Edward.'

'Very scientific,' said Griffin.

Later that morning, Gaffney saw Sir Edward Griffin and received from him the names of the six MI5 officers deputed to investigate the Armitage affair. At the top of the list, naturally, was the name of Geoffrey Hodder.

'Mr Gaffney, I suppose there's no way that . . . '

'No way what, Sir Edward?'

Griffin shook his head gloomily. 'I was going to say, no way that we can make absolutely sure that this business doesn't go wrong this time.'

Gaffney leaned forward and picked up his coffee cup. 'That

would be something that we couldn't guarantee under normal circumstances,' he said, 'but it's hardly what we're about, is it? We have deliberately set this whole thing up with the object of tracing a leak. We must let it run naturally, otherwise you'll be faced with a similar problem next week, next month, next year . . . ' He took a sip of coffee and set down his cup and saucer. 'And next time it could be very much more serious, much more damaging. And all the time there would be that nagging doubt that someone in your organisation was betraying you.'

Griffin nodded. He recalled the words, the harsh words, of the Home Secretary: 'If you've got a cancer, Sir Edward,' he'd said, 'cut it out.' 'You're right, Mr Gaffney, it's just that . . . ' He let the sentence lapse, eloquent for what was left unsaid, and stared into space.

In the afternoon of the same day, Geoffrey Hodder called at New Scotland Yard by appointment, and saw Commander Frank Hussey, the operational head of Special Branch. He outlined what the Security Service had learned and made a formal request for police assistance.

Hussey assigned Detective Superintendent Terry Dobbs to oversee the enquiries from the Special Branch standpoint, and to liaise with MI5. It would be Dobbs and his team who eventually effected the arrests of Armitage and Dickson. It had to be done that way because MI5 had no powers of arrest, save those accorded ordinary citizens at common law. The police would also be responsible for the preparation of the case papers and their submission to the Director of Public Prosecutions who, in turn, would apply to the Attorney-General for his fiat to prosecute. One of the other things that Special Branch had to do was to acquire as much of the evidence as they could themselves, in order to keep the MI5 officers out of the witness box when eventually the prisoners were arraigned, usually before the Lord Chief Justice, and more often than not in Number Two Court at the Old Bailey – traditional venue for the hearing of espionage cases.

* * *

Terry Dobbs, in total ignorance of the plan which Gaffney had conceived and put into effect, set up an incident room. There was a hand-picked sergeant controlling the paper-work, and a number of experienced Special Branch detectives who had been involved in Official Secrets Acts prosecutions before. There were also a couple of young officers who were there simply to learn the trade, and who in the future would take the places of the more experienced as they were promoted and eventually retired.

The plan was very simple. A team of MI5 watchers and Special Branch surveillance officers would combine to keep round-the-clock observation on Armitage depositing and Dickson collecting. There were two likely problems, however. The location of the DLB might be changed. Gaffney would certainly learn of this from Armitage, but he had no way of passing it on without arousing suspicion among his own colleagues. Again, the DLB method of passing information might be abandoned altogether, and another substituted for it. But the watchers should learn of that by the simple expedient of continuing to watch both men. The only difficulty in those circumstances was likely to be one of evidence; if the information was sent by post, anonymously for example, there would be grave problems in supporting a charge against either man.

But there was nothing new in all this; it was something that spycatchers had to face every time they embarked on an investigation.

In the meantime, full postal and telephone intercepts were put on the two principals, and the Security Service bided its time.

'I've got a list of six names here, Harry,' said Gaffney. 'Each of them is an MI5 officer, currently engaged on an Official Secrets Act job.' He carefully aligned the piece of paper with the edge of his blotter and stared at it for some time. Then he looked up. 'And each one of them is under suspicion of having committed a similar offence himself.'

Detective Chief Inspector Harry Tipper pursed his lips and

whistled silently. 'Blimey, you do go in for the complicated stuff, sir. What's the evidence?'

'There isn't any, Harry. It's pure speculation. But I can tell you this: Terry Dobbs is handling the job from our side, and the whole thing is a set-up – pure fiction.'

'Oh dear,' said Tipper. 'I think I'd better go and have a lie-down.'

Gaffney grinned. 'There is a man called Armitage, an army officer at the Ministry of Defence. He's my bait, and it looks as though he's hooked a man called Dickson. Armitage has passed secret information – bogus information – to this individual, all under my control, of course. Both are under surveillance, and we're waiting to spring the trap.'

'Sounds horribly like agent provocateur to me, guv.'

Gaffney waved a hand dismissively. 'Don't worry about that; there are bigger fish – one bigger fish actually, in the shape of an MI5 officer.' He tapped the piece of paper on his desk. 'One of these, possibly.'

'How d'you know, sir? You just said there's no evidence.'

'I'm hoping to acquire some,' said Gaffney.

'But you must have some reason for suspecting them – or him.'

'Yes,' said Gaffney. 'Two similar jobs have gone bent in the past. The same team of MI5 operatives were involved on each occasion. Which leads me – and, I may say, the Director-General of MI5 – to the conclusion that one of them is working for the other side.'

'Reasonable,' said Tipper. 'So you've set him up?' Gaffney nodded, smiling. 'Christ! And I thought we were devious in mainline CID.'

'Ordinary crime is a bit different, Harry. A villain will always come another day. These characters are much too fly for that – apart from the Armitages of this world, the real Armitages, I mean, who just get taken for suckers. And they're dumped when they've outlived their usefulness.'

'But what about those six?' Tipper pointed at the list on Gaffney's desk. 'Are they all under suspicion?'

'Got to be, Harry. They were all part of the same team

– twice. On each occasion the controller, the spymaster, the contact – call him what you like – vanished, just as the forces of law and order were closing in. That is the only evidence – if you can call it that – that the Director-General has. Not much, is it?'

'It's sod-all, if you'll forgive the expression, guv'nor. So what do we do now?'

'Nothing.'

'Nothing?'

'We wait. Wait for Armitage to be arrested, and we wait for Dickson to disappear.'

'And if he doesn't?'

Gaffney held up his hands. 'God knows, Harry. We'll be left with egg on our faces, and a bit of squaring up to do. Major Armitage is entirely innocent, of course – working for us. But if we do land Dickson . . . Well, frankly, I don't know. That, I imagine, will be something for the DG to work out. It'll be all right if Dickson turns out to be an illegal— '

'A what?'

'An illegal. It's the term used for foreign agents who are in the country masquerading as something else.'

'You mean they're not official spies?' asked Tipper, grinning.

'Oh, you can laugh, Harry, but that's exactly what I mean. Every embassy has its spies, usually the military attaché. Everybodyy knows it, and everybody's reasonably happy. You can watch them like hawks; it's the illegals that give us head-aches.'

Tipper shook his head. 'Guv'nor,' he said with mock seriousness, 'why couldn't you have left me downstairs dealing with ordinary straightforward honest criminals?'

'If it's all too much for you, Harry, just say the word.'

Tipper laughed. 'I'll manage. But what do we do after Armitage is arrested – presuming, of course, that Dickson's taken it on the toes? Obo?'

'I'm not sure that observation is the answer, at least not to begin with. I think what we need is full background enquiries on each, but covert; none of them must know that he's under suspicion, let alone being investigated. It'll call for some very delicate detective work. It's distasteful in a sense, too, because almost certainly five of them are completely innocent – possibly all six. It might just be a horrible coincidence, but it's too serious a matter to overlook, because if it's true it won't go away.'

'And what if that proves nothing, which it probably will? What do we do next? Anyway aren't all these blokes vetted?' Gaffney nodded. 'Well if there was anything dodgy, aren't they supposed to have picked it up?'

'Supposed to,' said Gaffney. 'But they aren't looking for something specific – they're just looking for anything. What we'll be looking for is a crack, a blemish, the slightest thing that will tell us they're working for the Russians – or for that matter, the East Germans, the Poles, or any of the other Iron Curtain countries.'

'Some hope,' said Tipper.

'Oh, it won't be easy, and I'm conscious of the fact that if they are, we probably haven't got a cat's chance in hell of discovering it by plain footslogging detective work. These blokes are much too sophisticated – you've only got to look at the likes of Burgess, Maclean, Philby and Blunt to see that.'

'You've only got to look at the blokes who tried to catch'em,' said Tipper acidly. 'Couldn't catch a cold, half of them. They'll all tell you afterwards that they always had their suspicions, but they didn't do much at the time.'

Gaffney laughed. 'You're much too cynical for one so young.'

'Is there going to be any stage at which we can come out into the open in all this, sir?'

'Meaning?'

'Well if we're investigating bent coppers, we suspend everyone in sight; then we have them in and give'em a good talking to – under caution, usually.'

'What are you suggesting, Harry?'

'Supposing this thing comes out right. Armitage gets nicked official, and Dickson does a runner; can we move in then and interrogate these monkeys?'

69

Gaffney pondered on that. 'I'd never given it a thought. Launch a full-scale investigation, you mean?'

'Why not? To be perfectly honest, if we put surveillance on them, I reckon they'd spot it straightaway. After all, they're in the trade – sort of.'

'Would they spot it, though?' asked Gaffney with a grin. 'How often do you look over your shoulder when you're walking anywhere?'

Tipper laughed. 'Never, guv'nor. But then I haven't done anything wrong.'

Chapter Six

'Armitage received a greetings card yesterday morning,' said Geoffrey Hodder. 'It congratulated him on his "success", whatever that may mean. And it was signed "Alex".'

Terry Dobbs burst out laughing. 'Good God,' he said. 'Talk about tried and trusted methods. They've been using that name ever since the end of the Second World War.'

'Yes,' said Hodder, and looked blank. 'I suppose it's an intimation that there's to be another drop.'

'Thursday?'

'There's nothing to indicate that on the card, but there wouldn't be.' Hodder spoke in rather superior tones. 'But I think we ought to increase the effort.'

'How do we do that? We've got a heavyweight team on now.'

'Well at least alert them to the possibility that something's in the wind, so to speak.'

'What a good idea.' There was sarcasm in Dobbs's voice – a sarcasm that completely eluded Hodder; it annoyed him that these people from what was euphemistically called 'another government department' tended to overlook the fact that the police were carrying out investigations all day and every day. 'There's always the chance that they've changed the day or the venue, of course.'

'How? We've been intercepting their calls and their post.'

'Pre-arrangement. It might be Thursdays one month – Fridays the next. Or every twenty days – or three days after the card. Christ, Geoffrey, you know the drill as well as I do.'

Hodder nodded slowly and shrugged. 'We'll just have to be on the qui vive, that's all.'

* * *

'It looks as though an arrest is imminent,' said Frank Hussey. 'Terry Dobbs reckons it'll be this Thursday. Do you think you ought to let Armitage know?'

'No, sir. I advised him at the outset that he was likely to get nicked at some stage. I don't think it's a good idea to let him know now; we need his reaction to be as natural as possible when Terry Dobbs picks him up – for MI5's benefit, because they'll be there. It would be difficult anyway, MI5 having taps on the Battersea flat that he and Lester are living in; I have to wait for Marilyn Lester to ring me from a call-box, and she has to be damned careful in case they've put surveillance on her as well.'

'They haven't – according to Dobbs.'

'Thanks for telling me,' said Gaffney, and laughed. 'I was just about to say that Terry Dobbs'll kill me when he eventually finds out that I set this all up, but now I don't care.'

'Have you thought what you're going to do when Armitage is arrested, John?'

'Yes and no. I've told both Armitage and Marilyn to make sure the flat's clean – from our point of view, I mean. I've arranged that there's something incriminating for the MI5 blokes to find: camera, few photographic negatives – that sort of thing. But what concerns me more is what happens if Dickson's arrested. We've been working all along on the basis that when it comes to the crunch, he'll be gone. Supposing he hasn't? That'd knock the bottom out of Sir Edward's case, and would leave us with a nasty allegation of agent provocateur to contend with.'

'Bad luck,' said Hussey mildly. 'Armitage would have to be released – that goes without saying, and that means that Five would have to lose Dickson. Just have to hope that he's an illegal, here on false papers, then they could deport him. Think about it, John. We're expecting him to escape anyway. It comes to the same thing in the long run.'

'Yes, but wouldn't that leave Jack Armitage with a bit of a stigma?'

72

'I don't think so. The whole thing could be veiled under the guise of some complicated intelligence operation with international ramifications – you know the sort of stories they come up with. It happens all the time.'

'Does it?' asked Gaffney, not very hopefully. 'We'd have to persuade MI5 to go along with that.'

Hussey smiled. 'We can leave that to Sir Edward Griffin,' he said. 'He started the bloody thing off. I think you're worrying unnecessarily, John. All we do is release them both; Sir Edward can tell his blokes that it was part of a wider plan that didn't come off – or for that matter, did come off. It matters not.'

'I wish I had your confidence, sir.'

'Ah, but then you're not a commander,' said Hussey.

At ten past six on Thursday evening, the combined observation team assigned to Armitage had reported his leaving the Battersea flat. Strictly observing the speed limit – he didn't want to be stopped by the police at this stage – he drove through Wandsworth and along the Upper Richmond Road. Negotiating the centre of Richmond, he crossed the bridge into Twickenham, then followed the course of the river until he reached Teddington Lock. It was the same route that he had followed previously. Early once more, he parked again in Ferry Road and waited.

Meanwhile, the team concentrating on Dickson remained at the ready in the vicinity of his flat, north of Oxford Street.

Adhering strictly to the timetable, Armitage left his car and crossed the footbridge. This time he was more relaxed than before and made his way almost directly to the horse-chestnut tree and dropped his drink can into the slot in the trunk. With a quick glance round, he felt about for the screwed up newspaper, and stuffed it quickly inside his jacket; then he continued his stroll.

'I've got a couple of good shots of him, guv'nor,' said the voice through the earpiece of Dobbs's personal radio.

Dobbs raised his arm and spoke into the microphone

73

secreted in his sleeve. 'Thanks, Dick. Hang on there for the next one, will you.'

'Roger.' The voice of the photographer, lying flat on the roof of the block of flats in Strawberry Vale, acknowledged Dobbs's instruction, and settled down to await the arrival of Dickson.

'Are you going to lift him now, sir?' asked Francis Wisley, the detective inspector who was Dobbs's deputy in the case.

'Where's Dickson? What's the latest report?' The question was directed as much to Geoffrey Hodder as it was to Wisley; each was monitoring the radio transmissions of the other surveillance team.

'Still not left his place in town, sir,' said Wisley.

'What's his game, then? Don't tell me there's been a change of plan. Anyway, we're clear to nick Armitage, but we'll let him run a bit, just in case Dickson's playing a substitute today; just our luck, that'd be. You stay here, just in case, and I'll go and collect the galloping major.'

Taking a sergeant, a constable and one of the MI5 officers, Dobbs crossed the bridge, following the path that Armitage had taken a few minutes before. Dobbs knew exactly where he was; the rest of the team had taken care of that, and as he stepped down into Ferry Road, he was just in time to see Armitage's car turn right into Twickenham Road.

Dobbs had already arranged to have a marked police car standing by, and now tuned his car radio to the channel reserved for traffic division. As Armitage's car headed along Strawberry Vale and into Cross Deep, the white Rover, with its two blue lights on the roof, pulled out of Waldegrave Road. The first that Armitage knew of its presence was when he heard a quick burst of siren and glanced in his rear-view mirror to see the flashing blue lights. In common with most motorists in such situations, he glanced quickly at his speedometer before pulling into the kerb.

It was not, however, a member of the uniformed crew of the police car who approached him, but a man in plain clothes, accompanied by two others, who appeared beside his door and opened it.

'Major James Armitage, I am a police officer,' said Dobbs. 'Would you mind stepping out of the car, please.'

Armitage stepped out into the roadway. Although he had been expecting police action at some stage of the operation, the presence of the traffic car had confused him. Dobbs, however, knew that one of the more dangerous moments of policing was to attempt to stop a suspect vehicle when driving an unmarked police car.

'I have a warrant for your arrest for passing classified information to an unauthorised person,' said Dobbs. 'I must warn you that anything you say will be put into writing and may be given in evidence.' Armitage had heard the familiar sentence a hundred times on television, and had been expecting it ever since his first meeting with Gaffney when he had agreed to undertake the assignment. But it was still a shock. 'I shall now take you to a police station where you will be charged.'

Armitage wasn't quite sure what one was supposed to say in circumstances like this, and so he said the first thing which came into his head. Ironically it was what most people said: 'I think there must be some mistake.'

'I'm afraid there's no mistake, Major Armitage.' He hoped to God there wasn't; this bloke was pretty cool. And it was just possible that he had left a cache of obscene photographs in the DLB; Dobbs had known that happen before.

They drove the short distance to Twickenham police station to be greeted by a custody officer somewhat surprised that a Special Branch superintendent should be bringing in a prisoner.

'Turn out your pockets, Major Armitage,' said the sergeant.

Dobbs surveyed Armitage's belongings when they were laid out on the charge-room table. They consisted of the expected contents of a man's pockets: wallet, cigarettes, lighter, loose change, handkerchief, and in Armitage's case, a military identity card. In addition, there was a piece of screwed-up newspaper. Carefully, Dobbs spread it out; in the centre was one hundred pounds.

Dobbs smiled. 'Your birthright for a mess of potage,'

he said adapting the Genesis quotation. Armitage shrugged. 'Put him in a cell,' said Dobbs to the custody sergeant. 'I shall have him transferred to Rochester Row very shortly.' He turned to the sergeant who had been with him when the arrest was made. 'Where's the car?'

'Being brought in by one of the traffic blokes, sir.'

Dobbs nodded. 'Good. Have that transferred to Rochester Row as soon as you can. And you can stand guard over it while it's here; I don't want any of our uniformed colleagues putting their grubby hands all over it.' The custody sergeant frowned, but straightened his face as Dobbs turned to him. 'I shall leave my two officers here until Major Armitage is removed,' he said. 'In the meantime, he is to have no contact with anyone, and that means solicitors as well.'

'But, sir, PACE— '

'I know all about the Police and Criminal Evidence Act, skip, and I know also, as you should, that if I say no contact, it's no contact. If you get any press enquiries – and if you do, I shall mount a full-scale enquiry – you are to make no comment. You do not even admit to Major Armitage's presence in this nick. And that includes any enquiries you might get from our own Press Bureau. Understood?'

'Yes, sir,' said the sergeant.

That part of the operation had taken just over half an hour, and Dobbs, with the MI5 officer who had accompanied him, now made his way back to Teddington Lock. If things went according to plan, he would shortly have Dickson banged up alongside Major Armitage.

Aware that he was now back at the scene of events, Dobbs parted company with the Security Service man and sauntered casually over the footbridge from Ferry Road. Then he walked slowly along the towing path until DI Wisley caught up with him.

'One down and one to go,' said Dobbs. 'What's happening?'

'Dickson's on the move, sir, on foot,' said Wisley, 'but he's going to be pushed to make it here at the usual time.'

Dickson hadn't vacated the flat in which he had entertained

Armitage – and Tessa and Fiona – despite telling him that he had been transferred to somewhere north of London, a story which unsurprisingly had proved to be without foundation. The flat was in a block in one of the numerous little streets which nestled in the angle made by Oxford Street and Tottenham Court Road, and the watchers had been able to set up a couple of good observation posts near it.

Dickson was a skilled operator and worked on the assumption that he was being watched constantly. His counter-surveillance techniques were practised enough to give the impression that he was indecisive, and uncertain as to his precise destination. But that was only at the outset. Once he was satisfied that he was unobserved, he would carry on normally. Such was the expertise of the watchers that he had yet to discover their presence, but he still went through the drill.

Dickson emerged from the block of flats and stood, looking up and down the street. A dark-skinned couple, a boy and a girl, were strolling by on the other side. The boy's arm was around the girl's waist, and she was leaning into his body. Both wore students' uniform: dirty jeans and shapeless sweaters. A man with a briefcase walked swiftly in the opposite direction, eyes fixed on the ground; an office-worker perhaps, on his way home and heading for the tube station. Dickson watched dispassionately; they could be part of a surveillance team. He knew all about MI5 and they were good. But perhaps these people were what they seemed. He glanced at the parked cars, bordering both sides of the street, but there was no one sitting in any of them. He wouldn't have expected it. He looked for vans; they were the usual vehicles used by watchers, but there was none.

Finally the street was devoid of pedestrians – visible ones anyway – and Dickson set off at a slow stroll. He had to be careful. This particular day was special and he could not afford for anything to go wrong. There was no adrenalin pumping, just ice-cold reserve. He was fully in command of himself, and his years of training and experience had been brought into play to ensure the success of what he was doing. He had done it before in other countries and on other assignments, and had lived to do it again. He never took chances, although sometimes he had been forced into making sudden decisions, but every move had been planned carefully, as had the whole range of possible alternatives. Dickson would be a difficult man to catch. As a consequence, the entire journey was going to include every known twist of avoidance behaviour, which would make life very difficult for the watchers.

The combined resources of Special Branch and MI5 had amassed a formidable surveillance team, some twenty-four in all. The SB team, under the redoubtable Detective Inspector Dave Wakeford, were deployed on foot; so were some of the Security Service people, but they also had a number of vehicles, including vans, one or two cars, and three motorcycles. By a miracle they were all on the same radio network; some achievement, even in these days of modern communications. The control room was situated at the Security Service operational headquarters, but was monitored from New Scotland Yard in case urgent reference to police indexes was needed; and Detective Inspector Francis Wisley at Teddington had a personal radio linked into the operation so that he could alert Terry Dobbs when the target was approaching the DLB.

Dickson strolled into Rathbone Place and made his way casually towards Oxford Street where he turned right, apparently making for Marble Arch. The watchers deployed themselves carefully. All too often in the past they had encountered avoidance techniques and they were waiting for Dickson to do something designed to throw them. They weren't disappointed. When he reached Newman Street, Dickson paused at the traffic lights, looked around, and then crossed over. Then he turned to his left, retracing his route, but on the opposite side of the road. 'He's at it again,' said one of the watchers into his wrist microphone.

Dickson looked into one or two shop windows, then turned and walked to the kerb. He waited for some seconds, glancing around, before hailing a cab going towards Marble Arch.

This information was transmitted to control, together with

78

the plate number of the cab. By now the controller had Dickson's and the surveillance teams' precise locations plotted on a huge street map of central London. He noted that one of the motor-cyclists, call-sign Delta, was now waiting in Rathbone Place. 'He's yours, Delta,' said control, and repeated the plate number. Then he moved the magnetic disc bearing a large letter D into Oxford Street behind the red marker indicating the cab, and waited.

'He's done a U-turn,' said Delta. 'I'm right behind him.'

'Is that a woman?' asked Detective Sergeant Randle, the SB liaison officer.

The controller grinned. 'Sure is,' he said. 'Best motor-cyclist in the business.' He looked at the map again, and started to issue instructions to the radio operator to move the other mobiles to locations where they would be instantly available to take over from the girl motor-cyclist should the journey prove to be a long one; it was necessary to prevent suspicion being aroused. 'Well,' said the controller, stretching his arms above his head, 'it doesn't look as though he's going to Teddington.'

'Could be going to Waterloo to catch a train down there, I suppose,' said the Special Branch man, also looking at the map.

The controller nodded, non-committally. 'Anybody's guess.'

'Past Centre Point. New Oxford Street. Right into Shaftesbury Avenue. Delta over.' Then a little later: 'Naughty! He's jumped the lights, and across into Endell Street.'

The controller was at his map again, redeploying his mobiles. 'Beats me,' he said. 'What the hell's he up to?'

Meanwhile, Dave Wakeford's team of Special Branch foot-surveillance officers were swearing and cursing, and piling into a battered transit van that the DI had thoughtfully arranged to have parked in a side-street against just such an occurrence.

'I'm putting someone in to leap-frog you, Delta,' said the controller.

'Don't bother. The roads are too narrow. There are bits

of pavement sticking out in Endell Street; I nearly came off just now,' said Delta. 'Long Acre – Bow Street – past the magistrates' court . . . '

'How fitting,' murmured the sergeant with an irony that was lost on the controller.

'Right into Russell Street and stopping, Delta over.'

Wakeford and his team, having broken just about every traffic law on the statute book, were now only yards behind the lone motor-cyclist, and the transit braked sharply just before reaching the Russell Street turn. 'Out quickly,' shouted Wakeford, and the half of his team that were with him baled out and spread. He let them go. 'Control from Zulu One,' he said into his sleeve. 'He's into the Covent Garden complex, strolling. Get the rest of the Zulu team down here ASAP, over.' And he too followed Dickson.

Observing the movements of a target in a crowded area like Covent Garden is easier than it might at first seem. Provided that the watchers are stationed at strategic points, it is a case simply of handing the target over from one to the other; but the placing of watchers – if they are not to be noticed – requires great skill and experience. Dave Wakeford possessed both.

Dickson sauntered through Central Avenue, occasionally stopping to gaze into shop windows with no apparent purpose in mind.

'Control from Zulu Four. He doesn't seem to be going anywhere particular. Keeps looking at his watch; I reckon he's got a meet. Over.'

'Control from Zulu Two. Gone through the alleyway to the Henrietta Street side; still window-shopping. Coming back again. Gone through to the other side now – still looking at shops. Oh Christ, he's coming back again, into the centre. He's leaning over the railings now, looking down into the lower court – where the steak bar and the pub are.'

Dickson continued to wander aimlessly about the old market, looking in shop windows and poking around in the merchandise on the open stalls. He stood awhile in the centre, watching the accomplished performance of an accordionist who managed to combine his musical talents with some footwork that would have done credit to a Cossack. Dickson seemed engrossed in the show, but suddenly glanced up and carefully scanned the people standing on the other side of the ring of spectators, clearly looking for someone who was looking at him rather than at the accordionist. It was an old trick, and one with which the watchers were familiar; it was the man immediately behind Dickson who was watching him.

The control-room officers, and Dobbs and Hodder at Teddington, were now debating what Dickson was up to; it was well past the time that he should have made his collection at the DLB. Gaffney could have made an accurate guess, but prudence dictated that he and Tipper had to wait in silence – and ignorance.

'Now he's having a cup of coffee, lucky sod. I reckon he's waiting to make a meet, Zulu Five over.'

Dickson was indeed taking things easily, sitting at one of the tables in the centre of the complex, sipping coffee and reading an evening paper. But he was never relaxed; from time to time he looked around, shooting searching glances in unexpected directions. He could have been waiting for someone, expecting them and seeking them, but the team knew better; he was looking for watchers.

'We're on the move again, Zulu Seven over.' The transmission was backed by snatches of accordion music.

'Looks like back to Russell Street, Zulu Six over.'

'He's making a call from one of those phones in Russell Street; dammit, I can't get near enough to see what he's dialling, Zulu One over.' It was Wakeford back on the air.

There was a three– or four–minute pause, then: 'Zulu Six to control. On foot ... across Bow Street ... he's done a right into Catherine Street. Now into Aldwych, going towards Kingsway, on the north side. He's stopped. Christ! He's looking at the menu in the Waldorf Palm Court. Anyone got any money?' There was a pause, then: 'Panic off ... on the move again ... Zulu Six over.'

The controller started moving his mobiles yet again, conscious of the fluidity of the operation; none of the watchers, or the people in control, now believed that Dickson was going to Teddington.

Down at the scene of the DLB, Dobbs listened phlegmatically to the radio traffic. 'I'd love to know who he telephoned,' he said; it was almost a criticism of the team; in common with a lot of detectives, Dobbs always thought that he could do a better job than the blokes who were actually doing it.

'Delta, give location, control over.'

'Kingsway, near the LSE, facing south, over.'

'Zulu Four to control. He's crossed over to the south side of Aldwych. Still going east. . . Melbourne Place. Stand by, he's getting into a car.' The voice assumed urgency. 'It's a Sierra Ghia, blue in colour. I'll give you the number as soon as I can see it, Zulu Four over.'

'Control to Delta. Sorry, you seem to be in the pole position. I'll get someone else in place ASAP.'

'Roger. Delta out.'

Zulu Four came up with the car's number, and the Special Branch officer at the Yard immediately keyed it into the Police National Computer.

'Zulu Four from Handcuffs, are you sure about that number?' asked the computer operator.

'Handcuffs from Zulu Four – affirmative,' and Zulu Four repeated it.

'Well in that case, all units, you'll be interested to know that it's an electric milk-float. Registered keeper lives in Gwent.'

'Control from Delta. This is the fastest Welsh milk-float I've ever seen. Round Australia House . . . Strand going west . . . across the traffic. He's sussed me, I think. Jumped the lights at Melbourne Place . . . and again at Montreal Place . . . left onto Waterloo Bridge. Sod it, there's a bus in the way . . .'

'How unladylike,' said DS Randle quietly.

'I can't hold him . . . seventy . . . I'll try . . . Tenison Way roundabout . . . the Bullring . . . ' Then Delta went silent.

'Delta from control, receiving?' Still silence. 'Any other mobiles? Location?'

'Control from Echo. Just turning into Waterloo Bridge, but I'm in a van. I'll do my best.'

Then the air was filled with the call-signs of other units as they came up, converging on Waterloo Station. But still there was nothing from the girl biker called Delta.

'Control from Echo. Delta's come off her bike at Tenison Way roundabout. Hit a diesel slick.'

'Is she hurt, Echo?'

'She's torn her leathers, and she's a bit shaken up and bruised. She'll live, but I'm a bit worried about her mouth.'

'What's wrong with it?'

'Control from Echo. It's the language coming out of it.'

It had happened again. Delta's accident had occurred before the other mobiles, thrown into disarray by Dickson's sudden manoeuvre, had been able to catch up with their quarry. Despite an immediate circulation of all police cars in London and beyond, as well as to ports and airports, the car and Dickson had vanished without trace.

Down at Teddington, Dobbs turned to Hodder. 'Well that's that then. I fancy we've seen the last of P. Dickson, Esquire, or whoever he is.'

Hodder looked gloomy. 'I rather fancy you're right.'

'I thought your blokes were the surveillance experts,' said Dobbs savagely, seeking already to apportion blame. 'My blokes only went along for the walk.'

'I really don't know what can have happened.' Hodder looked unhappy, aware, now that a contact had escaped for the third time in succession, that there were likely to be some fairly high level questions and, doubtless, recriminations.

'Well there's no point in hanging about,' said Dobbs. 'He's had two hours to get here by fast car. He's not coming, that's for certain, Geoffrey. I suggest we open Pandora's box out there, and see what the bold major was leaving for him. If it's a box of chocolates we'll know we've uncovered a poofters' circle.'

'It's not funny,' said Hodder.

'I'm not joking,' said Dobbs.

Despite being conscious that it was a waste of time, Dobbs and Hodder eventually agreed to leave an observation team at Teddington until midnight.

Dobbs himself, deeming it too urgent to go looking for a justice of the peace, issued a superintendent's written order to search Dickson's flat, which he was empowered to do under the Official Secrets Act. He and a small team went through the flat thoroughly, but without much enthusiasm. They found the two hidden cameras, and some indications that Dickson had departed, but nothing else incriminating.

'Sod it!' said Dobbs, speaking for them all.

Once again a spymaster had evaded them.

Chapter Seven

'It's damnable,' said Sir Edward Griffin. 'Damnable!' He was pacing his office, backwards and forwards past the armchair in which Gaffney was seated. 'There can be no doubt, no doubt at all. I wish . . . I had hoped . . . ' He left the sentence unspoken. It was obvious that he would rather have been facing the comparatively minor problem of finding an excuse for taking no further interest in Armitage, and arranging for Dickson to be deported. Instead there was the certainty that someone in his organisation was working for the KGB.

'It must be evident to just about everybody in your service that something's gone badly wrong over this Dickson business, Sir Edward. It seems that he had no intention of going to Teddington; he must have been warned, either in advance, or told of Armitage's arrest almost as soon as it happened.'

'What do you propose, Mr Gaffney?' He sat down behind his huge desk and gazed at the detective across the broad expanse of mahogany, now devoid of paper. He had been convinced that this situation would not arise; thought that he would be able to go to the Home Secretary and say that the previous cases had been a coincidence; he was even prepared to admit to incompetence. But now he knew. The culmination of his career would be to preside over an enquiry to discover a traitor, and to admit that, under his stewardship, the Security Service, to which he had devoted all his working life, had been penetrated. His portrait would hang alongside all his predecessors, certainly, but in the years to come they would point him out for special notice, just as they did now to poor Roger Hollis, with his heavy eyebrows, and the half-smile which the viewer could interpret as guilt or innocence, according to what he thought.

'I think that a thorough investigation is the only way,' said Gaffney, 'and it cannot be done covertly; not in the end, anyway. I shall have to ask questions.'

'What sort of questions?' Griffin shook his head, slowly and hopelessly.

'What they do: their social life, their hobbies, their friends, who they mix with; that sort of thing.'

'But think of the embarrassment. You can't just go knocking on doors, asking questions.' Griffin considered the gravity of it. Gaffney was right. It was just not possible to make discreet enquiries about a thing like this. There was a limit to what could be learned, and all the time a subtle background investigation was going on, suspicion would hang in the air like a black cloud. Invisible fingers would point, not least at the Director-General himself. But then again, suppose it got out. There was a number of investigative journalists who specialised in poking their noses into matters of security, most of them ill-informed. The whiff of a suggestion that things were not quite as they should be in MI5 would bring them baying like a pack of unscrupulous hounds.

Gaffney smiled. 'We are a little more subtle than that,' he said. 'I don't propose to mount a full-scale operation all at once. We've plenty of time; the first stage will be to talk to Hodder and each member of his team. Then I shall move to a more thorough investigation of those who interest me. Some may not even know that they are being enquired into – may not be, in fact.' Gaffney paused. 'You may rest assured, Sir Edward, that I shall do my best not to compromise your officers. I am conscious of the possibility that at least five of them are above suspicion. Unfortunately, I do not know, at this stage, which five; with any luck it may even be six.'

Griffin raised his eyebrows. 'I'd like to agree with you,' he said, 'but I don't see how you can— '

'Disinformation?'

'In what way?'

'I suspect that the KGB have a pretty good idea of the way in which your service operates, as you are familiar with theirs. It may be that they have decided to rock your boat. Suppose they had decided to put in three successive red herrings – ' Griffin did not smile at the pun. ' – knowing how you would react, and then withdraw their man at the crucial moment each time, just to cast doubt on the probity of your officers.' Gaffney didn't really believe it, but he felt a genuine sympathy for the man opposite him.

'D'you really think so?' There was a sparkle of hope in Griffin's face, but it faded just as quickly. 'I'd like to believe it, but somehow I think it's too much to wish for.'

'Incidentally, Sir Edward, there is one other thing: some of your people may be a little reticent; they do tend to shelter behind the Official Secrets Act. I should like you to provide me with a letter authorising them to tell me what I need to know about these matters . . . '

Griffin nodded. 'Very well.' The words came out softly, as though he was unwilling to release them, and had fought to the last to prevent them being heard.

'What sort of order are you going to play this in, guv'nor?' Tipper handed the list of names back to Gaffney.

'I don't think it matters too much. The problem's going to be starting an investigation into one of them without alerting the others to the fact that something's going on. We'd have to be very lucky to pick the right one first time. And I don't suppose we shall.'

Tipper laughed. 'We should be so lucky. Well who d'you fancy for starters?'

Gaffney glanced at the list once more. 'Geoffrey Hodder.'

'Any particular reason?'

'Yes. He's the team leader; and I've got a nasty mind.'

Detective Superintendent Terry Dobbs sat silently as Gaffney told him the full story behind the arrest of Armitage. 'So there it is, Terry,' he said. 'I'm sorry about your big job.'

'Nice to know I'm trusted, sir,' said Dobbs.

The sarcasm was not lost on Gaffney. 'It's got nothing to do with trust, Terry. If you didn't know, you couldn't do anything but act naturally; that was vital. It's fairly evident that the KGB have got a snout on the inside; he's the one I'm after, not Dickson.'

'What happens to Armitage, then?'

'Nothing. When's he up again?'

'Five days' time, sir.'

'Let him out, then. Don't object to bail. Have a word with his brief; tell him that Dickson's done a runner, and Armitage's prosecution now looks doubtful.'

Dobbs laughed. 'Doubtful! It's a non-starter— '

'I know, but you don't have to tell him that.'

'The only thing that grieves me is how he must have been laughing up his sleeve when I nicked him.'

Gaffney smiled. 'He won't be laughing so much after eight days in Brixton,' he said.

'Have a nice holiday?'

'I think that everyone should spend eight days in there,' said Armitage. 'It's the greatest deterrent to crime I can think of.'

'It isn't, you know,' said Marilyn. 'If it was, the prisons wouldn't be full to overflowing.'

'You've no idea what it's like.'

'Oh but I have. I'm a police officer, don't forget. Just think yourself lucky that they didn't put you in Holloway.'

'Now that would have been all right,' said Armitage, smiling.

'Don't you believe it; they'd have brought you back here on a stretcher.'

The one policeman on duty in the Back Hall of New Scotland Yard was heavily engaged in conversation with an unkempt woman whose worldly belongings were in three plastic carrier bags grouped around her varicosed legs.

Geoffrey Hodder made his way round them to the desk and waited for the receptionist to finish a telephone conversation. She looked up and smiled.

'Chief Superintendent Gaffney, please. I have an appointment.'

'Which department?' she asked.

'Special Branch.' It was not unusual for Security Service officers to visit the Yard, or for them to be asked to call there to discuss some problem of mutual interest. In fact it was only a few weeks previously that Hodder had called to see Commander Frank Hussey to ask for help in connection with the arrest of Major Armitage. He presumed, when one of Gaffney's assistants had telephoned him, that it was in connection with that very case. He was a bit concerned about that. It wasn't going the usual course. Certainly to have released Armitage on bail was unusual, but he assumed that the police, who now had full responsibility for his prosecution, must have a good reason – or that the Director of Public Prosecutions had.

'The messenger will take you up, sir.' The girl replaced the receiver, signed his pass and handed it to the woman in the blue overall who had appeared beside him.

Gaffney was waiting in the lift lobby on the eighteenth floor when Hodder stepped out of the lift. He took the pass from the messenger, thanked her, and shook hands. 'Geoffrey, how are you?'

'Fine, John, thank you.'

Gaffney had decided that the normal stark furnishing of the interview room was unsuitable for what he had in mind. The table and the two or three hard, upright chairs had been removed and replaced with three armchairs. He would have used his own office, but there was no guarantee against interruption, particularly from the telephone.

'May I introduce Detective Chief Inspector Harry Tipper. Harry, this is Geoffrey Hodder, from Five.'

Tipper stood up; he noticed that Hodder had a weak handshake.

'I don't think we've met before,' said Hodder. It puzzled him; he thought he knew most of the senior officers in Special Branch.

'Harry's only just joined us,' said Gaffney. 'He's spent most

89

of his service being a real detective – investigating murders and suchlike. You probably remember the Penelope Lambert job; your predecessor, Hector Toogood, handled it from your side.'

Hodder nodded vaguely. 'Oh yes, of course,' he said. He didn't remember it at all.

'I've been tasked by Sir Edward Griffin to look into the disappearance of Peter Dickson.'

'Yes, it's very worrying,' said Hodder.

'Just to show you that it's all official and above-board, you'd better look at this, Geoffrey.' Gaffney produced a letter signed by the Director-General, giving him full authority to conduct his enquiries. He had taken the precaution of encasing it in a plastic sleeve, mainly because he knew that it was going to come in for a lot of handling, but also because he had learned in a previous case that it was a very good way of acquiring fingerprints without letting the handler know too openly what he was doing. Hodder skimmed through it and handed it back. 'You won't mind if Harry takes a few notes, will you?' said Gaffney.

Hodder waved a hand airily. 'Not at all.'

Gaffney smiled. 'It's always difficult to know where to begin with a job like this,' he said. 'Frankly, I don't really know what I'm looking for, Geoffrey.'

'A leak – from the inside, I should think,' said Hodder in matter-of-fact tones. 'It's what I'd be looking for; have been, actually.'

'Have been?'

'John . . . ' He sounded tired. 'It hasn't escaped my notice that this is the third time this has happened – and the third time when the same team, led by me, has been assigned to deal with it. How do you think I feel?'

Gaffney knew how he must feel, so he didn't bother to ask. 'What was the result of your enquiries?'

'Drew a blank. I'd trust the five chaps on my team absolutely. I know that sometimes you think the fellows in our lot are odd, but they're all damned good at what they do. Even Selby . . . ' He smiled.

'Why d'you mention him in particular?'

'Well he is a bit strange, I suppose. Looks a bit of a wimp, and people tend to think he's a homo.'

Tipper smiled at the old-fashioned description. 'And is he?' he asked.

For a moment Hodder stared at him as if giving the question careful thought. 'No, I don't think so,' he said at length.

'Shouldn't you be certain?'

'How can you be? If there'd been any evidence, he'd have been sacked.'

Tipper nodded and left it; it was a pointless discussion.

'How much did the team know? Was there anyone who knew the full story?' asked Gaffney.

'There wasn't a full story to know. All we had was the anonymous telephone call that a woman made; made to you, Special Branch, as I'm sure you know.' Gaffney nodded. 'We put the watchers on to it; they eventually saw Armitage do the drop, and subsequently, Dickson do the pick-up. They followed them and identified them both. They were under round-the-clock surveillance until the second occasion. That was when Armitage was arrested, but Dickson never showed up. It was almost the same with the last two jobs. I wondered if the DLB had been set up quite deliberately, with Dickson intending to wait somewhere, so that if he saw Armitage being arrested, he'd make a run for it. But that theory was destroyed: Dickson must have had prior knowledge. We now know he had no intention of going anywhere near Teddington that day; he'd already planned to escape. He must have been warned.' Hodder ran a hand through his soft, untidy brown hair. 'Believe me, John, I've puzzled over this thing – and the other two – until I'm left with absolutely nowhere to go.'

'Apart from your team, who else knew about this?'

Hodder leaned back in his chair, his gaze wandering up to the ceiling. Then he looked down again, straight at Gaffney. 'The DG, of course, and John Carfax, my boss.'

'How much did John Carfax know?'

'Just the bare bones. I didn't even give him the names;

he didn't want to know. I told him it was an army officer, and what I presumed to be an "illegal". He just asked me to keep him informed. It's usual.'

Gaffney was disconcerted. The Director-General had said nothing about Carfax being told. And the fact that he had not been given the names of Armitage and Dickson made no difference. If he was the leak, all he would have had to tell his KGB masters was that someone who was in contact with an army officer was about to be compromised. That would have been sufficient; they would have known who it was. But Carfax had been in the Security Service for years; must be close to retirement. Not that that made any difference, of course. The Russians were nothing if not patient – it was the peasant in them, thought Gaffney – and they'd been known to let a sleeper sleep for years before activating him, perhaps for just one job – or three!

'When did you tell John Carfax?'

'The day that your people were going to make the arrest, just as I was leaving for Teddington.'

'The day you thought that they were going to make the arrest; it was only an assumption that it would be the Thursday.'

'It had been a Thursday before, and Armitage had received a card. Yes, the day we thought it would all happen.'

'So you told Carfax that day?' Hodder nodded. 'Why then? Why not earlier?'

'I judged that to be the best time. It would have hit the Press very quickly; these things always do. It wouldn't have done for my master not to know. If I'd told him earlier, he might have forgotten.'

'Forgotten?' Tipper sounded incredulous. 'You're about to arrest a spy, and he might have forgotten?'

'He does have rather a lot on his plate . . . '

'Or did you perhaps think that he might have been the leak? This, as you reminded me, was the third occasion.' Gaffney spoke softly. He knew from long, hard experience that you never got anything out of an interrogation if you browbeat your subject. He had once been paid a great compliment

92

by a Hungarian whom he had interviewed years previously. 'Mr Gaffney,' he had said, 'I have been interrogated by the Gestapo, and by the Hungarian Secret Police, but I have told you more than any of them. D'you know why? Because you are a gentleman.'

'No,' said Hodder. 'I didn't think he was the leak. At least, not him specifically.'

'What does that mean?'

'It had happened twice before, John. I had this unnerving feeling that it might happen a third time. I don't know why, but I just did. I wasn't prepared to take chances. I kept more of it to myself than ever before; the need-to-know principle. It's bloody awful— ' He stopped and stared into space, and Gaffney noticed how ashen his face was; he was a man clearly under a great deal of strain. 'You suddenly realise that you're no longer trusting the people you work with. You start looking over your shoulder, and wondering. You start casting your mind back. I've conducted my own soul-searching post-mortems ever since those two other jobs – going back over them again and again in my mind. Each time wondering who I'd told – who'd perhaps got something about him that would make me mistrust him. You can understand that surely? It must be the same in your profession. Those trials you had in the seventies – the corruption; you must know what it's like?' He looked at Tipper. 'You particularly.'

'It happens,' said Tipper unsympathetically.

'John.' He looked back at Gaffney. 'You must know what I mean.'

Gaffney nodded. 'Yes, Geoffrey, I know what you mean.' He drew him back to the main topic of their conversation. 'Was there anyone else – anyone at all – who you told about this particular operation; never mind the others?'

Hodder stared moodily at his feet. It was silent in the room, but the wailing of a police car's siren rose above the hum of the Victoria Street traffic far below. Eventually he looked up. 'No, John, absolutely no one at all.'

'What about the watchers? They obviously knew.' It was Tipper, harsh and realistic, who posed the question. Gaffney realised just how shrewd a detective Harry Tipper was. He just sat there, a bland expression on his face, and then suddenly he posed a question that went straight under Hodder's guard. Except that this time it had no effect, because there was no answer.

'I thought of that, too,' said Hodder. The expression on his face had not changed. 'But it was a different team each time.'

Tipper was not prepared to let go. 'But they could have talked.'

Hodder looked suitably scandalised. 'They wouldn't,' he said.

'Oh? It was you who talked about looking over your shoulder and wondering who you could trust. Why wouldn't they have talked?'

Hodder looked stunned. 'You're right, of course.' It was as though he had to keep reminding himself of the sudden unacceptable infidelity of his own colleagues. 'The only thing is that they are so busy that they rarely have time to talk to each other. They're all over the place most of the time.'

'But it's possible. They don't have to talk to each other, do they? It only needs one of them. One of them and a telephone, and it's done.'

Hodder shook his head, only now seeing, as if for the first time, the endless possibilities that were being opened up by the policeman's ruthless probing. 'I suppose so. But I still say it's unlikely.'

Gaffney reached out for the packet of cigars which rested on the side-table next to the DG's letter. 'Geoffrey,' he said. 'It seems to me that you're saying that no one else could have known.' Hodder continued to stare at the floor at a point somewhere between himself and Gaffney, but said nothing. 'You've already admitted that you were careful to keep the whole story to yourself; that you told your team some details of the operation, but not all. You said that Carfax, even, was told only the outline, and that was on the day of Armitage's arrest – and Dickson's disappearance. Apart from the DG, the only other people to know, obviously, were the watchers, but you argue, not very convincingly I may say, against them being in a position to pass on that information. What you're really saying, Geoffrey, is that you are the only person from whom the leak could have come.'

There was now a discernible tension in the room. Hodder's expression remained unchanged and still he stared at the floor. After what seemed an incredibly long time, he looked up at Gaffney, vacantly, as if not seeing him at all. 'Yes,' he said eventually. He spoke softly. 'It looks like it, doesn't it?'

Suddenly Tipper weighed in, hard. 'Are you saying that you are the leak, the traitor, Mr Hodder? Are you admitting it?'

'No, of course not.'

'Well what are you saying?'

Hodder dithered. 'Well, I er – I suppose I'm saying that it looks bad.'

'Yes!' Tipper agreed. 'Mr Hodder,' he said pleasantly, 'as Mr Gaffney told you, I have spent all my service in the hard world of crime, investigating criminals.' He injected loathing into the last word. 'And a breach of the Official Secrets Act is just like any other breach of the criminal law. It's crime.'

'I know that.'

'I also know that criminals come in all shapes and sizes. From the East End of London, as well as from the finest public schools in the country, but at the end of the day it comes down to one thing – greed. Greed or intellectual superiority, usually misplaced, and sometimes ideology; although there's usually an element of greed in that, greed for power too.' He flicked an invisible speck of dust from his sleeve. 'How much did the KGB pay you? Or what did they promise you?'

Hodder was white-faced and aghast, his hands clenched around the wooden arms of his chair. 'They didn't. I mean, they haven't – it's not true.' He shot a despairing glance at Gaffney. 'John, you must know that.'

But Gaffney remained impassive, and Tipper carried on. 'I don't believe you, Mr Hodder, and I'll tell you what we're going to do, Mr Gaffney and I; we're going to put you under the microscope. We're going to examine your life-style, and everything you do or have done. We'll look at your wife, your friends; everything about your social life. We're going to examine your bank account with a fine-tooth comb, and we're going to find out where every penny came from. And we're going to discover what you spend, and where that comes from.' He leaned back in his chair. 'We're going to shake you until your teeth rattle, mister, and then we're going to hang you out to dry.'

Hodder was sweating now, and his fingers were intertwining; spasms of rapid nervousness. 'It's not me,' he said in a hoarse whisper.

'What d'you think, Harry?' asked Gaffney. He had returned to the small interview room after conducting the distraught Hodder to the main entrance of the Yard, and had sat down again opposite Tipper.

'Nah!' said Tipper scornfully. 'He's too bloody honest. A bent bastard would have said bugger-all and demanded his mouthpiece.' Gaffney wrinkled his nose. 'I tell you what, guv'nor,' continued Tipper, 'he wouldn't have the guts to nick a packet of aspirin if he was out of his mind with a migraine. I don't think he's our man.' He watched the smoke from Gaffney's cigar curling up towards the ceiling. 'If he is, he's a bloody good actor.'

'I think you're probably right, but the field's opening up already,' said Gaffney. 'It was too much to hope that the only people who would be in on it were the five on Hodder's team – and Hodder himself, of course. I should have realised that Carfax would be told, and that the watchers had to know . . . I don't know why I didn't think of that.'

'And the Director-General,' said Tipper.

Gaffney was learning not to discount his chief inspector's quiet observations. 'What about the DG?'

'Might he be the leak? And another thing; when he gave you the list of the six on the team, why didn't he think of Carfax and the watchers? One of two reasons: he's already made up his mind who's not under suspicion and ruled them out before they got to us, or he's shielding someone. Perhaps he is bent.'

Gaffney laughed. 'You're no respecter of persons, Harry. Are you really suggesting that the DG might be a KGB agent?'

'It's been suggested before, so I understand. Of course,' he continued in an offhand way, 'I'm new to this Special Branch work, but . . . '

'You're talking about Sir Roger Hollis, I suppose?'

'I suppose I am, sir,' said Tipper, smiling.

'What you're suggesting, Harry, is that the DG comes to the head of Special Branch and asks for help to uncover a KGB mole in his organisation, well knowing that he himself is that mole.'

'He didn't come voluntarily, from what you said. He was forced into it by the Home Secretary. That's what you said, wasn't it?'

'Yes, true.' Gaffney reflected on that for a second or so. 'Let's take that a stage further then. A couple of jobs go wrong. The DG is duty-bound to report it to the Secretary of State. Then, on instructions, he asks us for help and we set up another similar operation.'

'But he didn't like the way you did it, sir. You said that he wanted to put his own hare on the run.'

'You're right, Harry – a double agent.'

'Ample justification for it going wrong again. Suddenly his precious double agent goes bent – it's happened before, if snouts are anything to go by – and he holds up his hands in amazement. "That shouldn't have happened," he cries. Same result, but this time for a different reason. And he might just have instructed Hodder to keep it to himself, so that he could take all the blame when it did go pear-shaped.'

'You've got a devious mind, Harry, but I think that's stretching the imagination a bit far. Anyway, if the DG told him to keep it to himself, why didn't Hodder say so, particularly when you were being nasty to him?'

'Loyalty? Anyway, what other explanation is there, guv'nor? Christ, the bloody man admitted it. He sat here and said that no one else had the information he had. Even Mr Dobbs; he's still pissed off about having to let Armitage out on bail, even though he now knows why.'

Gaffney smiled. Detective Superintendent Terry Dobbs was indeed unhappy about the whole operation, and would be quite delighted at the prospect of an MI5 officer being arrested, if for no better reason than fouling up his big job.

'Well?' asked Tipper, 'Where do we go from here, sir?'

'We start what are known in the trade as in-depth enquiries. It'll soon be an open secret that we've interviewed Hodder, I should think – '

'D'you think so?'

'Doesn't matter anyway. We've got to start asking some direct questions some time. And I think we'd better start with the team. Find out if it's true that Hodder told them little or nothing – and while we're about it, Carfax, the watchers, and the DG. But the team first. I don't want to put anyone on alert if I don't have to. It'll be interesting to see if they all support each other about what Hodder's supposed to have told them or didn't tell them.'

'Why shouldn't they?'

'Misplaced sense of loyalty, perhaps. Hodder still can't bring himself to believe that there's a traitor in their midst. Trying to shield them, perhaps?'

'From what, for God's sake?' asked Tipper.

'Savages like you, I should think,' said Gaffney.

Chapter Eight

Grenville Jackson emerged from the entrance leading to the steps of the gentlemen's toilets and peered around the concourse of Waterloo Station. After a few moments of fruitless searching, he hurried across to Platform 15 and into the police office.

'Hallo, mate,' said the constable behind the counter, 'and what can we do for you this fine summer's morning?'

'There's a bloke locked in one of my cubicles, boss,' said Jackson. 'Been there an hour, I reckon.'

'Probably fallen asleep. Night duty copper more 'an like,' said the PC and laughed. 'Why don't you open it up – see what's happened?'

'Huh!' said Jackson. 'Last time I did that some bloke was injecting hisself. Got very nasty – very violent.'

'Yeah righto, mate, hang on.' The policeman put his head round the doorway into the back office. 'Fred, pop over to the gents' with old Grenville here, will you? He's got a bloke living in one of his cubicles. Probably have to get an eviction order, bleedin' state of the law these days.'

A heavily built constable emerged from the office, putting on his helmet. 'Come on then, mate,' he said. 'Let's go and have a look at your lodger.'

Together they walked across the concourse and down the steps. 'Which one is it?' asked the PC.

'This one here, boss,' said Jackson, pointing out a cubicle with the door closed and the little sign showing red.

The constable bent down and peered under the door. Standing up and replacing his helmet, he said, 'Well there's feet there all right, but his trousers aren't round his ankles. I

99

reckon he's kipping. Open it up and we'll have a look.'

The attendant unlocked the door and stood back. The policeman pushed it open and gazed inside. Slumped on the lavatory seat was a man with a plastic bag over his head. The policeman lifted the man's right arm and felt for a pulse. 'You've got a dead'un there, Grenville, my lad,' he said.

Jackson looked over the policeman's shoulder, his eyes rolling; the policeman spoke into his personal radio.

Ten minutes later the ambulance arrived, silently; there was no sense in rushing to pick up a dead body.

Together the body and the policeman went to St Thomas's Hospital where the casualty officer carried out his examination in the back of the ambulance. 'Dead on arrival,' he said. 'You can take him straight to the mortuary.'

The mortuary nurse, a businesslike woman in her midforties, stood in the centre of the room with her hands on her hips. 'Not another one?' she asked. 'That's the third this morning, and not half-past nine yet.' She walked across and peered at the corpse. 'Well at least he's clean and tidy. The last one was in bits – fell under a train. Oh well, let's get started. You the officer dealing, love?'

The policeman nodded and got out his pocket book. The nurse looked at him acidly. 'Well give me a hand,' she said.

Reluctantly the policeman laid his pocket book down, and he and the nurse started stripping the body. That complete, the two of them sat down at a small table next to the naked corpse and began the tedious task of listing the property; she for hospital records, he for police records, and subsequently the coroner.

'Found a name yet?' asked the nurse.

'Yes,' said the PC. He spread the contents of the body's pockets out on the table. 'On the cheque book.' He slid it over so that she could copy it. 'Plus one wallet, leather, containing twenty-five pounds in Bank of England notes, one Access card, one bank cheque card, membership card for the AA, quantity of corres, two one-pound coins, fifty-five pence silver, fourpence bronze, one yellow metal wristwatch . . . Hallo? What's that then?' He held up a laminated plastic card with a peculiar multi-coloured device on it. He turned it over. On the back was an instruction requiring anyone who found it to hand it in to a police station; there was also a paragraph drawing attention to a section of the Official Secrets Act. 'That's a pass for a government office,' said the policeman. 'Must be a civil servant.'

'It comes to them all, love,' said the nurse. 'No matter who they are.'

'What am I supposed to do with this, Sarge?'

The British Transport Police sergeant took the plastic card, turned it over, and then laid it on his desk. 'Dunno, mate,' he said. 'Ring the Met – they'll probably know.'

The station officer at Kennington Lane police station wasn't quite sure either. 'I could tell you what to do if it was property found in the street,' he said, 'but found on a stiff – that's different. If I was you, mate, I'd try Special Branch at the Yard.'

The sergeant on duty at Special Branch listened to the railway policeman's story and made a few notes. 'Describe the card,' he said, and made a few more notes. 'And the name, what's the name?' He wrote that down, too. 'Hold on, mate, I'll see what I can find out.'

The sergeant went next door, to the office of Detective Superintendent George Winter, who dealt with administration, and a thousand and one other things.

'Yes?' asked Winter, adopting the permanently harassed look that tended to put off most people who bothered him.

The sergeant explained.

'Well – what about it?' asked Winter.

'From the description of the card, sir, it sounds like a pass for Security Service buildings.'

'I should give them a ring then, ask them. Better still, go along to the commander – he holds a pass for MI5 – have a look at his.' Winter was clearly intolerant of what he perceived to be trivia.

The problem was explained to Commander Hussey who

took out his pass and showed it to the sergeant. 'Anything like that, is it?'

'It could be, sir, yes.'

'What was the name of this bloke they found?'

'Hodder, sir, Geoffrey Hodder,' said the sergeant, consulting his notes.

'Christ!' said the commander. 'Get hold of Mr Gaffney, as quickly as you can.'

Gaffney strode through the outer office, nodding to the DAC's secretary, and tapped lightly on Logan's open door.

'May I close the door, sir?' asked Gaffney.

'Yes. What's the problem?'

'Hodder, sir. He was found dead in a cubicle in the gents' at Waterloo Station earlier this morning. Looks like suicide. He had a plastic bag over his head.'

'I'd've thought he had more finesse than that,' said Logan. 'Do we know how long he'd been there before he was found?'

'No, not really. Lavatory attendant noticed the cubicle had been occupied for some time. He said about an hour, but he wasn't really sure – could have been there all night. They're quite used to it, apparently. Get drug addicts in there, and tramps kipping – that sort of thing. The railway police have got a statement from him, but it's not much good. I haven't seen it yet, but it's all a load of nothing; doesn't actually remember seeing him come in.'

'How did we get to know so soon?' asked Logan.

'Bit of luck, really. Railway police asked Kennington Lane what to do about the office pass. They didn't know, told him to ring us. Our skipper didn't know either, and finished up asking Mr Hussey. Of course he recognised the name.'

'Bloody hell,' said Logan. 'We're always impressing people by accident. Where's the body now?'

'On its way to Tennis Street mortuary, I understand.'

'Post-mortem?'

'Today – three o'clock, sir.'

'You going?'

'No – I'll probably send Harry Tipper – he's used to dealing with dead bodies.'

'Fine. Well keep me informed, John.'

'Yes, sir.' Gaffney paused with his hand on the doorknob. 'I've been thinking that we might use this to our advantage.'

'How so?'

'If we can keep the cause of death under wraps, surround it in mystery, we could perhaps make it an excuse for our enquiries into Sir Edward's leak. That would enable us to come out into the open and ask a few direct questions.' Logan looked doubtful. 'Well, sir, you remember the Georgi Markov business – the Bulgarian who was murderd on Waterloo Bridge by a bloke with a lethal umbrella?' Logan nodded. 'If we could hint that we might have a similar sort of job on our hands, it could be helpful.'

'Yes, that's a good idea, John.' He paused. 'But first of all, make sure that Hodder wasn't in fact murdered, won't you.'

'Well?'

'Usual carve-up, guv'nor.'

'Spare me the jokes, Harry.'

'No, seriously. Bloody pathologist was an hour late. Said he hadn't been told, or some damned thing.'

'Terrible,' said Gaffney, shaking his head. 'What did he say?'

'Asphyxiation compatible with deceased having placed a plastic bag over his head which, I may say, came as no surprise to any of us.'

'Harry.'

'Yes, sir?'

'I am right, there wasn't a note in his property, was there?'

Tipper sniffed. 'No, sir, nor upon his person.'

'That's typical,' said Gaffney. 'They can never do a bloody job properly. What was the pathologist's view?'

'Privately he's in no doubt it was suicide.' Tipper looked glumly at the ceiling before continuing in a monotone similar to that in which he normally gave evidence. 'Estimated time of death nine o'clock this morning – give or take. Which means that the late Geoffrey was an early riser, or stayed at the office overnight.'

'Why do you say that, Harry?'

'He lived in Surrey.'

'So?'

'He lived out in the country. Nearest station is Guildford, and that's about four to five miles away, and the fastest train from there to Waterloo takes about forty minutes.'

'I can see you've been doing some work.'

Tipper laughed. 'Not me, guv. Railway police came up with all that. Incidentally I gave them all the warning formula. Told them not to mention he was with MI5 – and not to talk to the press under any circumstances.'

Gaffney leaned forward and placed his arms on his desk. 'How in hell's name did they know that?'

'Some big-mouth clever PC recognised the address of this terribly secret Ministry of Defence establishment he was working at. Mind you, every cab-driver in London knows it too.'

'Terrific!' said Gaffney. 'That's all we need – a bloody spotlight to work under.'

Tipper smiled. 'It's all right, sir. I gave them all a friendly little lecture – and promised them five years under the Official Secrets Act if a word of it got out.'

Gaffney laughed. 'You do have a way with words, Harry.' He opened the bottom drawer of his desk and took out a bottle of Scotch and two glasses. 'I suppose there's no chance that he was murdered?' he asked thoughtfully, sliding one half-full tumbler of whisky across the desk towards Tipper.

'Murdered? What makes you ask?'

'The Markov job. D'you remember Markov, the Bulgarian who was jabbed with an umbrella?'

Tipper nodded. 'Yes. It was a platinum pellet doctored with . . . ' He paused. 'Ricin; it's a poison developed from the castor oil plant.'

'Well?'

'Too soon. Death takes much longer in a case like that.

And then it has the appearance of cardiovascular collapse, like a heart attack, perhaps two or three days later.'

Gaffney laughed. 'I can see you've done your homework, Harry.'

Tipper looked offended. 'I have investigated quite a few murders, sir,' he said.

'All right.' Gaffney raised a placating hand. 'When's the inquest open?'

'Tomorrow; Southwark Coroner's Court.' Tipper took a mouthful of Scotch and grimaced. 'Open and shut case, I should think.'

'Open, Harry, but not shut, not yet. I shall see the coroner, get him to open and adjourn for further police enquiries. And no evidence put in about cause of death at that hearing. We can then ask all sorts of people all sorts of questions, leading them to believe that we're conducting a murder enquiry. How's that grab you, Harry?'

'Blimey, guv'nor, you'll never pull a stroke like that.'

Gaffney smiled, a tolerant smile. 'One of the things you will eventually learn about Special Branch when you've been in it a bit longer, Harry, is that when they need to they can deploy some pretty powerful guns.'

'You will appreciate, of course, Sir Edward, that Geoffrey Hodder's death will greatly assist me.'

Griffin looked directly at Gaffney, a slight frown on his face. 'Really?' There was an element of disdain, an old-fashioned disapproval of talking about the departed in that way, certainly before a suitable period of mourning had been observed.

'Certainly,' said Gaffney cheerfully. He suffered none of the inhibitions that seemed to be affecting the Director-General. 'I am going to work on the basis that Hodder was possibly murdered – he wasn't, of course – which will allow me to ask a lot more questions without alerting people, particularly your people, to the fact that we're looking for a traitor.'

Griffin nodded and looked away. He much preferred euphemisms like mole or leak; the word traitor was too stark, too real for him. 'Yes, I see. Where are you going to start?'

105

'With Hodder. I want to get as much background material on him as possible. On the face of it, Sir Edward, he could be your man. Why else should he commit suicide? Guilty, wouldn't you say?' Gaffney didn't think that at all – not yet. If the evidence subsequently proved that to be the case, well so be it, but he had been wrong too often. But he posed the question to see what Griffin's reaction would be.

The Director-General shook his head. 'I'd never have thought so, but I have to admit that a man must have a strong reason for taking his own life – and that is a strong enough reason in my book.' He sighed, a sigh of sorrow; he didn't seem at all angry. 'What help do you need from me, Mr Gaffney – any?'

'Just a sight of his personal file, Sir Edward, please. That will give me a base from which to start.'

'Put the "Engaged" sign on the door, Harry, and come and sit down.'

'You ought to have it screwed on, guv'nor – it seems to be up there most of the time,' said Tipper.

'I've got Hodder's personal file from the DG.'

'Anything interesting?'

'Not really, just the bare bones. Funny thing, isn't it? There's a man's complete professional life.' He held up the slim manilla folder containing perhaps a dozen sheets of paper. 'That's him and all about him.' He turned his chair on its swivel base, stretched out his legs and crossed them at the ankles. 'Decent grammar school in the Midlands, then to university. Got a two-two in German, then into the army for his national service – commissioned in the Intelligence Corps.'

'What made them pick him for that?'

'God knows. There's nothing here to indicate any special talents. Probably just had vacancies that week. You know how the army works.'

'No!' said Tipper.

'But that was undoubtedly his entrée to MI5 which he joined in 1963. Married Elizabeth Barlow two years later, and they had two children: a boy in 1966 and a girl in 1968. All perfectly orthodox until 1978 – '

'What happened then?'

'He divorced Elizabeth and married a girl called Julia – Julia Simpson, she was twenty-five.'

'And how old was he, sir?'

Gaffney did a calculation. 'Thirty-six, coming up thirty-seven,' he said.

'Good for old Geoffrey,' said Tipper.

'Regular vetting clearances, including an extra one they put in after his remarriage, so the current Mrs Hodder's been cleared as well.'

'So where do we go from here, sir?' said Tipper.

Gaffney stood up. 'To use a well-known phrase, we go about our enquiries, Harry.'

Brigadier Parker smiled as he shook hands. 'Well, you've arrested one army officer,' he said. 'Don't tell me you want another one?'

'No,' said Gaffney. 'He'll do nicely, thank you. But I would like the records of one.' He sat down and opened his briefcase, continuing to talk as he did so: 'It's a Second Lieutenant Geoffrey Hodder, sometime of the Intelligence Corps.' He opened a file. 'I've got his personal number here somewhere. He was a National Service officer in the early sixties.' Gaffney extracted a piece of paper from the file and handed it to the Provost-Marshal. 'It's all on there,' he said.

Parker took the paper and glanced at it. Then he smiled. 'I don't suppose our records will tell you any more than you've got there, Mr Gaffney.'

'That's not enough.'

'No – I didn't somehow think it would be. What else d'you want?'

'Names,' said Gaffney. 'The names of his commanding officer, anyone who served with him. In fact, anyone who can tell me anything about him during his time in Germany.'

'Good God, man! D'you know what you're asking? You've seen army personal records before, I take it?' Gaffney nodded.

'The most you'll get is a couple of confidential reports – probably with indecipherable signatures. The chief clerk of the day will have scrawled on a few bits of paper, and if you're very lucky the quartermaster will have signed his eleven-fifty-seven.'

'What's that?'

'His record of clothing and equipment – if he's got one. Officers have to buy their own uniforms in the army, you know.' The military always seemed mildly irritated that senior policemen were issued with their uniforms free of charge.

'Lucky to have uniforms at all,' said Gaffney with the mock severity of a detective annoyed at having to pay tax on his plain-clothes allowance.

'All right,' said Parker. 'I'll do what I can. I suppose, as usual, you're in some tearing hurry?'

It took only forty-eight hours before Parker rang Gaffney, which considering the work involved was pretty good going.

'I've got three names. There may be more, but I somehow doubt it. I thought I'd let you have these to be going on with.'

'That's better than I'd hoped for,' said Gaffney.

'Two of them are out of the army now. One's a recently retired brigadier called Chapman. He was Major Chapman when he was your man Hodder's company commander. I've got an address for him – it should be right, it's where they send his pension.' Parker chuckled. 'The other one is called Withers. He was a subaltern along with Hodder, but he was a National Serviceman too, and left the army at about the same time. No idea where he is now, but I can give you full name and date of birth. Perhaps you can trace him. The third is still serving, Major Colin Sadler. He was a warrant officer class two in Hodder's unit at the time. He's stationed in Aldershot now.'

'Thank God for that,' said Gaffney. 'I felt certain he was going to be in the Falklands.'

* * *

108

'Hodder? Yes, I remember young Mr Hodder. As a matter of fact, I think he's in that picture there.' Major Sadler walked across to a battery of group photographs which occupied a large part of his office wall. 'That's him, there.' He jabbed at a face with a nicotine-stained forefinger. 'Second from the left.' He resumed the seat behind his desk and continued to play with a paper-knife. 'What d'you want to know about him? More to the point, why? In trouble, is he?'

'No, not unless you call being dead in trouble.'

'Oh!' said Sadler, and raised his eyebrows. 'No point in me saying I'm sorry to hear it; hardly knew the chap. Not seen him for – must be twenty-five years. What happened – he get murdered?'

'Why d'you presume that, Major Sadler?'

Sadler grinned. 'Stands to reason, doesn't it? Big shot down from the Yard. He's not going to have been run over by a bus.' The humour suddenly disappeared from Sadler's face and his eyes narrowed. 'Just a minute. Didn't he go to Five when he left the army?'

Gaffney nodded. 'Yes, he did.'

Sadler leaned back in his chair, very much the intelligence officer. 'You from Special Branch, then?'

'Yes, we are.'

'Right.' He pushed his hands down gently on the blotter as though doing some callisthenic exercise as a preliminary to the work to come.

'You asked just now if he was in trouble,' said Gaffney. Sadler nodded. 'Did you expect him to be? Or to put it another way – would you have been surprised if I'd said yes?'

Sadler laughed. 'Boys and men – boys and men,' he said. 'Twenty-five years ago I wouldn't have been surprised what he got up to, but now, well, he must have been getting on for fifty?' He looked enquiringly at Gaffney.

'Forty-six, forty-seven, yes. What did he get up to, all those years ago, Major Sadler?'

'Young officers, away from mother for the first time in their lives.' He shrugged. 'Bit of responsibility – not much,

109

but quite a lot of power, at least for a twenty year old. Army's like that, you know. I suppose it goes back to the Indian Raj – further probably. An officer is God. Got their own mess, their own servants – well, used to have.' He pouted. 'Which is why I can only tell you what I heard for the most part.'

'I don't quite— '

'I was a warrant officer then. Sergeants' Mess – all that. Never set foot in the Officers' Mess until I was commissioned.' He stood up and walked over to a cupboard. He put a bottle of whisky on the table and poured a measure into each of the glasses without asking. 'Wasn't much cop when I did,' he said. 'Much preferred the old Woes-and–Joes.' He reached across to the window-sill for a carafe of water which he banged on the desk in front of them. 'But young Mr Hodder was a bit wild, so I understand, but then we probably all were.'

'Which part of Germany was your unit in?' asked Gaffney, taking a sip of whisky.

'Berlin, old boy. A very good place to run wild in.'

'Doing what exactly – the unit I mean?'

'BRIXMIS.'

'What was that?'

'British Military Mission,' said Sadler. 'We used to go across into the eastern sector, almost every day. It was part of the agreement – still is, of course. Entitled to show the flag, which is precisely what we used to do. Never got anything out of it, mind you.'

'And Hodder went too?'

'Oh yes. There was either an officer or a warrant officer in charge. We usually took a Volkswagen with a bloody great Union Jack on it, and through Checkpoint Charlie we would go, drive around a bit – just baiting the Russkies, really – and then home to tea.' He dropped his bantering tone and leaned forward. 'To be perfectly honest it was a bit hairy. There were all sorts of things going on at that time. They'd just built the Berlin Wall, and there'd been the Bay of Pigs fiasco. There was the Cuban missile thing while we were there, as well. Frankly, we thought that war was going to break out any day; the last thing I wanted to be was on the wrong side of the wall when

110

it did. Come to that – either side of it, that near, anyway.'

'What sort of character was he – Hodder?'

'As I said, for the most part I can only tell you what I heard. But he liked his drink – and he liked the women. That's what I was told.' He was at great pains to emphasise that what he was telling them was second-hand. 'I heard stories of him whooping it up in the mess – getting drunk, that sort of thing. Mind you, we all did to a greater or lesser degree. Still, with Scotch at about ten bob a bottle – ' He broke off and looked across the room. 'I think it was anyway; it might have gone up to twelve and sixpence by then.' He shrugged. 'Either way, it was bloody cheap, and I reckon he took advantage of it. I've seen him looking the worse for wear in the mornings on quite a few occasions. And he liked the ladies. Not that there was any shortage, not in Berlin. Always out shafting some fraulein – so I heard.'

'He just did his National Service, I understand?'

'Yes. The CO – ' He flicked his fingers. 'Trying to think of his name . . . '

'Chapman?'

'That's the bloke – Major Chapman. Apparently he had some drinking chum of his, worked for Five. Got him fixed up. Sort of second best as far as the old man was concerned, I think. I gather he tried to talk him into staying on. God knows why – he was a very mediocre officer – Hodder, I mean. Anyway, what did happen to him? Did he get murdered?'

'Don't know,' said Gaffney blandly. 'That's what we're trying to find out.'

'Must have been something to do with a bird. Can't have been anything to do with his job; would never go out on a limb for the army, our young Mr Hodder. He can't have changed that much.'

'Brigadier Chapman?'

'Ah, you must be the chap from the police. Superintendent . . . ?'

'Detective Chief Superintendent Gaffney, yes.'

'Oh, sorry. Never can get the drift of police ranks. Come

in. You said on the phone that you wanted to talk about some fellah called Hodder?' He looked vague.

'I understand that he was one of your officers when you were at something called BRIXMIS in Berlin, back in the early sixties.'

'Yes . . . ' Chapman still looked puzzled. 'Think I recall the chap.' He waved vaguely at the armchairs. 'Don't happen to have a photograph of him, do you?'

'No. Well at least not one of him as he was then. But I've been told that you were instrumental in getting him a job with the Security Service when he left the army.'

'Ah, yes.' Chapman banged the arm of his chair with the flat of his hand. 'Got him. Right, what's he been up to?'

'He's dead.' Gaffney spoke in flat tones; he was a little weary of going through this explanation every time he started an interview.

'Oh, I see.' Chapman nodded, as though it was fairly routine for people he knew to have died. 'What happened to him?'

'His body was found in the men's lavatory at Waterloo Station.'

Chapman curled his lip slightly. 'Damned extraordinary,' he said. 'What was that all about, then?'

'That's what I want to know.'

'Oh, well fire away then.'

'I've been to see a man called Sadler who was a warrant officer in your unit at that time, Brigadier.'

'Sadler – yes, good man, Sadler. Got a commission, you know.' He spoke as though Major Sadler had been handed the greatest prize in the world. 'Not really officer material, of course, but a very good technician – very good. Still, the army's not what it used to be. There's a hell of a lot of good officers now who never went through Sandhurst, but he didn't quite fit in. Would have felt a bit uncomfortable in an officers' mess, I should have thought.'

'He's a major, now,' said Gaffney.

Chapman nodded. 'Mmm!' he said. 'Is he really? Well, well.'

'But it's Geoffrey Hodder I've come to talk to you about.'

112

'Yes, of course. Good young officer, Hodder. Very mature young man. Had a good education, too; degree in German as I recall. Don't know what the army was thinking of, sending him to Germany.' He said that with a wry smile.

'I've been told that he was a bit wild.'

'Who – Hodder? Shouldn't have thought so. No, he was a good mess member. Mind you, I have to say that I didn't live in mess myself; had a married quarter, you see, but from what I heard . . . '

'No wild parties then?'

Chapman looked mystified. 'What, in the mess?' Gaffney nodded. 'No, my dear chap, I think you must be confusing us with the RAF. Nothing like that in the Intelligence Corps.' He smiled tolerantly. 'Pillow fights – smashing up the furniture – all that sort of thing?' He shook his head and smiled again. 'Not the army – not any more. If ever,' he added.

'It's also been said that he had an eye for the girls.'

'Maybe so,' said Chapman. 'No idea, really. There was certainly plenty of opportunity.' He looked wistfully at the empty fireplace. 'Never heard anything, and I always prided myself on knowing what was going on. No, I would say he was a good officer. His intelligence reports were damned good, damned good – absolute model. As a matter of fact, I took a few examples of them with me when I went on the directing staff at the School of Intelligence – very good to show the students. I wanted him to stay on, take a regular commission, but he wouldn't have it. Said two years in the army was quite enough for him. Pity really – he'd have done very well. He knew the German scene, and was well up in current affairs. That's the way it should be for an intelligence officer, ideally, but quite frankly some of the chaps I got weren't really that interested – just wanted to get their two years done and push off. Just as well when they did away with National Service. I suppose you were too young to have done it?'

'Yes,' said Gaffney.

They traced Douglas Withers through his driving licence, and at his invitation, went to see him at his office off the

Tottenham Court Road where he was a senior partner with a firm of civil engineers.

Gaffney decided to try to short-circuit the weary explanation with which all his calls seemed now to be prefaced. 'I'm investigating the death of Geoffrey Hodder,' he said. 'I understand that you served with him in the army?'

'So it was him. I saw a bit about that in the paper. Didn't you find his body in a loo somewhere?'

'Waterloo, to be exact,' said Gaffney.

Withers smiled. 'I wondered if it was the same chap.'

'What can you tell me about him, Mr Withers? I realise that it was a long time ago, and for that reason may be of no value at all, but I have to explore everything.'

'I suppose so. I only had two years of it – intelligence-gathering – but I know what you mean. You collect a whole load of rubbish, and then throw away what you don't need, which is usually about ninety-nine per cent as I recall.' He pulled out a pocket-watch and stared at it.

'If you've got an appointment . . .'

'No, no. I've got to go out and look at a site some time, but there's no rush. Rome wasn't built in a day,' he said. 'That's because civil engineers built it.' He laughed at the old professional joke. 'Now then. Hodder. What can I tell you about him'

'Anything,' said Gaffney.

'Went to work for Five.'

'Yes, I know.'

'Very keen on placing his young men, as he used to call us, was Chapman – he was the CO.'

'Yes, I've been to see him.'

'Still alive is he? That's a surprise. I'd've thought he'd have drunk himself to death by now. I'll bet he offered you a drink before you'd been there five minutes.'

'No, he didn't actually.'

'Don't tell me he's sworn off it?'

'He's retired now – a retired brigadier.'

'Good God! And I thought he was lucky to have made major. Just goes to show, doesn't it? He was always trying

114

to get us either to stay on in the army or go to some civilian intelligence outfit, like Five or GCHQ. Tried it on me, as a matter of fact.'

'Not interested?'

'Not really, no. But I knew where I was going. I was going to be a civil engineer, and that was that. Old Chapman could never understand anyone wanting to do anything but his wretched intelligence work. But Geoff Hodder didn't know where he was going, and he fell for it.'

'Didn't know where he was going?'

'No. He'd come down from university with a degree in German. I remember that because he was very good – too good. He stopped me learning it. Used to go out with him and he did all the chatting. Saved me the trouble. The natives couldn't understand him half the time – he spoke high German. Thought he'd been to Heidelberg, not Hull.' Withers chuckled. 'But a degree of that sort's not much good as a qualification for a trade – not unless you want to be a schoolteacher or an international telephone operator – something like that.' He dismissed Hodder's educational qualifications with a wave of the hand.

'I've heard conflicting reports about his behaviour while he was in Berlin.'

'Oh? From whom – if you don't mind me asking?'

'Well I've seen Brigadier Chapman – ' Withers smiled. ' – and Major Sadler.'

'Sergeant-Major Sadler, you mean.'

'No, he's a major now, and still serving.'

Withers burst out laughing. 'That man's a cretin. They actually gave him a commission?' He shook his head. 'And what did Sadler have to say?'

'Said that young Mr Hodder, as he insisted on calling him, was a bit wild.'

Withers became serious again. 'Yes, well that's true, but then we all were. All that cheap booze. Quite frankly it's a wonder I've got a liver left at all.' He smiled at some lost memory. 'The excesses of youth. Hodder was no worse than the rest of us. We'd convinced ourselves that we were doing something terribly important out there – that an East–West war was imminent – and that we were the spearhead of the intelligence-gatherers. We weren't, of course. If the survival of the Western world had had to rely on what we served up, they'd have been in a parlous state, I can tell you. But we enjoyed ourselves – Geoff particularly.'

'In what way?'

'Oh, the usual – hard drinking, hard living. I don't think Geoff spent many nights in his own bed the whole time he was there. No reason why he should, of course. Berlin was the place for girls – girls and night clubs; they go together, really, and he had some gorgeous little dolly birds in tow when he was there.' He looked across the room. 'There was one he was very serious about. Now what was her name? Helga something . . . ' He shook his head. 'No – gone. I thought he'd finish up marrying her. She was a beaut. But that was him all over. Never could resist a pretty fraulein. Wining and wenching – that was our Geoffrey. Always being invited to parties – in the German community, of course.'

'Why do you say that – "of course"?'

'Always very popular with the Krauts, particularly the women. Strange that, because the men in the unit detested him. It was almost as if there were two sides to his character. At work he seemed to be bumptious and self-opinionated. I heard him described once as a jumped-up little prig by one of the sergeants. I wasn't supposed to, of course. But he had a point. It was a funny unit, nothing like the infantry or the armoured. There were only about ten of us altogether. Chapman, Hodder and I, Sar'nt-Major Sadler, and about six sergeants. Very top-heavy. I think all the sergeants were National Servicemen, and so were Geoff and I, of course. All doing the same job. The sergeants used to get a bit uptight with Geoff. Reckoned he was only a National Serviceman, same as they were, and he didn't have to throw his weight about. Roll on demob – two years and we'd all be out. I did hear that one of the sergeants threatened to sort him out in civvy street – when we were all out.'

'Don't remember who, do you?'

Withers shook his head. 'No – Perkins, Pogson? Some name like that. I didn't actually hear it said. It might have been a load of nonsense. Parsons – that was the name, but I can't remember anything else about him. We were all going to meet up ten years after we were demobbed. You know the sort of thing – see what we'd all done, how we got on? Never did though. People never do . . . Was he still with MI5 when he died?'

'Yes.'

'Amazing. Never thought he'd stick it. Was never any good at it, either. I thought that was a bit of a flash in the pan.'

'Brigadier Chapman thought he was brilliant. Said he used his reports as models.'

Withers laughed. 'They were bloody good fiction. He used to write all sorts of balls in his reports. Full of speculation: things like, I have been reliably informed, or, It is a widely held view that – you know the sort of stuff; all the jargon so beloved of the intelligence community. I think Geoff just caught on a lot quicker than the rest of us. We used to flog ourselves to death trying to find things out. He never bothered. That didn't make him too popular, either, because everyone in the unit knew it.' He paused. 'Except, it seems, Major Chapman.'

Gaffney was leaning back in his chair with his feet propped on the open bottom drawer of his desk. 'And what did you make of all that, Harry?'

'Bit of an enigma, our young Mr Hodder.'

'Certainly wouldn't have recognised him from the description that Withers gave us, but it's interesting that he was a ladies' man. That certainly fits in with his sudden divorce and remarriage. So what do we do next?'

Tipper was reclining in the armchair, a despondent expression on his face. 'I think we ought to see Mrs Hodder next, sir,' he said.

'Which one?'

Tipper thought about that. 'The first wife – before we see the second, and current Mrs Hodder.'

117

'Any particular reason?'

'It's chronological, ain't it? No, seriously though, I think we might get a bit more of the true Geoffrey Hodder from her – warts and all, so to speak. And her story of the divorce – if she's prepared to tell us. It'll be a useful yardstick for when we see Mrs Hodder the second.'

'If, as you say, she's prepared to tell us.'

'I should think she'll be delighted to recount all the sordid details – scorned women usually are.' Tipper sniffed loudly. 'There's only one problem . . . '

'Which is?' asked Gaffney.

'We don't know where she lives.'

'Oh but we do.' Gaffney reached out and picked up a piece of paper. 'Here we are – enquiry completed this morning. Mrs Elizabeth Hodder.'

Tipper took the piece of paper and studied it. 'What sort of place is this, then?'

'A flat in the centre of Godalming, I'm told.'

Chapter Nine

The flat in which Mrs Elizabeth Hodder lived was adequate
– no more than that. It was clean and carefully looked after,
but the curtains and the upholstery were worn, and there were
bare patches on the carpet. The woman herself looked tired
and strained, drained of all emotion.

'Would you like a cup of tea?'

'Thank you, yes – if it's no trouble.'

'It's no trouble.'

They heard her busying herself in the kitchen and spent
the five minutes or so it took her to make the tea, looking
around the sitting room. Standing on the television was a
photograph – the type they take at schools – of two children, a boy and a girl, the boy's arm unwillingly round his
sister's shoulders. There were no other photographs, none
certainly of Geoffrey Hodder, but then they hadn't expected
to see any.

She returned, poured the tea, and sat down in the armchair facing them, patiently, hands folded demurely in her
lap. 'You've come to talk to me about Geoffrey, I suppose.'

'Yes, Mrs Hodder, but first may I express my condol-
ences . . . '

'You needn't bother, Mr Gaffney. There was nothing
between us – nothing left at all.' The comment wasn't
bitter, just flat. 'My only regret is that the maintenance
dies with him. God knows what I'll live on now.'

Gaffney thought that an exaggeration. He knew that she
had a part-time job at the local hospital, had been trained
as a nurse before her marriage, and she was only forty-three
now. Her son was in the merchant navy, away at sea, and her

daughter, at twenty, two years younger than her brother, was a civil servant.

'I understand that you split up about ten or eleven years ago, Mrs Hodder?'

'Yes.' Again a flat reply. She was going to be a difficult woman to interview.

'Are you prepared to tell us about it?'

'Is it relevant?'

'I don't know. We are trying to establish why Geoffrey died.'

'Was he murdered then? You wouldn't be here if he'd committed suicide, would you – not a chief superintendent?'

'It's not that easy, Mrs Hodder. I don't know if you knew what Geoffrey did for a living?'

'I know he worked for MI5,' she said.

'He told you that, did he?'

'No. I worked there too. That's how we met.'

'I thought you were a nurse.'

'So I was, but I gave that up. It didn't pay enough, so I became a secretary at the Ministry of Defence. Then I got a transfer to the Security Service.' She looked vaguely past the two policemen, as though travelling back over the years. 'It was all rather ordinary. Never enough money . . . ' She laughed – a short savage laugh. 'When was there ever? Bringing up the children. It was no fun, believe me.' She just sat there, talking – whining almost – as if to herself. She was dowdy in an unfashionable dress that looked as though it had been bought from a mail-order catalogue six or seven years ago – probably had, thought Gaffney. 'And all because of that damned woman.' For the first time there was anger, a show of emotion, in her drawn face, mixing strangely with her obvious self-pity.

'What about her?'

She looked up sharply, staring at Tipper as if resenting his sudden intrusion.

'What do you mean: what about her?'

'Are you suggesting that she was wholly to blame?'

'Huh!' There was derision in the exclamation. 'Well you don't think it was my fault, do you?'

120

'I'm not suggesting it was,' said Tipper, uncharacteristically gentle for him. 'But was it your husband's?'

'Ex-husband! Late husband now, I suppose. Of course it was.' She thought about that. 'Men are so damned stupid,' she said vehemently. 'That trollop came along, flaunted herself at him and he went.'

'How did you know?'

'How did I know? Everyone knew; it was an open secret in the village.'

'But did you know they were having an affaire? I presume they were.'

She gave a short laugh. 'Oh yes, and I have the best evidence there is – these.' She pointed a finger towards her eyes, and Tipper noticed that her nails were bitten. She leaned back in the chair as though savouring the moment again. 'I got a phone call – from a woman, needless to say . . . ' The voice faded.

Tipper prompted her. 'Yes?'

She sat up slightly. 'This woman, whoever she was – I never did find out, which is a pity, really; I've never known whether to thank her or scratch her eyes out – just rang me and said that if I cared to go over to Julia Simpson's cottage I'd find my husband there.'

'And?'

'She put the phone down.'

'But you went?'

'Oh yes – I went. Didn't knock – just went in through the back door, which unwisely she'd left unlocked – or he had. Never very good at planning and taking precautions was Geoffrey. They were in bed – well on it, actually, which left nothing to the imagination.' She hesitated again, as if seeing it all in her mind's eye once more. Then she laughed. 'It was just the wrong moment for him – he was almost there. I said, "Hallo Geoffrey." I shall never forget the panic on his face. The fool waved an arm about as if trying to find a sheet or something to cover himself up with.' She lay back in her chair and started to laugh, a low chuckle that gradually increased until the tears were running down her face. Gaffney was afraid that she would start crying next – a sort of hysterical torture that she must have been through a hundred times.

But she didn't. She stopped as suddenly as she had begun, looked around for her handbag and took out a tissue, dabbing her eyes with it. She made no apology, just carried on talking. 'But it was that woman. She just lay there with her hands behind her head and her legs apart and said, "Hallo Elizabeth" – just that, "Hallo Elizabeth."'

'And that was that?' asked Gaffney.

'You could say that, yes. We slept in separate rooms until I found this place, and the divorce went through. He didn't oppose it – couldn't very well, could he? Next thing I heard was that they were married and the bitch had moved into our house.'

'Did you see anything of him again, after the divorce?'

'Occasionally. He had access to the children – one day a month. They were . . . what?' She pondered on that. 'Ten and twelve at the time of the divorce. He would come over here and collect them – take them out for the day, I suppose; I don't think he ever took them back to her: children weren't her scene. But that stopped when they were fourteen and sixteen. They stopped it – the children. Just happened not to be here when he came. He was quite annoyed about that – thought it was me, doing it deliberately, but it was them. They didn't want to see him any more. Jim went off to merchant navy school about then, and a couple of years later Petra got a job – they became independent very quickly.'

'How long had you known Julia Simpson?' He avoided referring to Hodder's second wife by her married name. 'I presume you did know her?'

'In a village that size you knew everyone. About a year, I suppose. That's when she moved in.'

'Where had she come from, d'you know?'

'No idea. I never particularly liked her anyway – none of the women did. Pretty, single woman; in her mid-twenties, I suppose she must have been. Most married women see a woman like that as a threat.'

'Did she have an affaire with anyone else that you know of?'

'I don't know; wouldn't surprise me if she had.'

'Why d'you suppose she picked on your husband?'

'Because he was there and he was willing.' She spoke in flat tones, objectively, as though she had been asked to comment on a liaison between two people whom she knew only casually. 'He was weak, you see – Geoffrey. Always had an eye for a pretty woman; couldn't resist them.'

'Had there been others, then?' Gaffney asked.

'Probably. It's a big advantage, having a job like his. Everyone, including his wife, accepts that he can't talk about it. It's a good excuse; you never know whether he's at work or at play. He wasn't much of a father and husband, that's for sure. Always morose and tired. The only thing he ever did for us was to provide the money; nothing else. More often than not he would come home, eat his meal in absolute silence, and then sit in his armchair, staring at the television. Then he'd go to bed. The next day it'd start all over again – nothing!'

'What d'you think, Harry?'

'If she looked like that when they were married, I'm not surprised he played around. Couldn't exactly describe her as sexy, not with the best will in the world, could you, sir?'

Gaffney laughed. 'Yeah, but she's been divorced ten years. That means she was only thirty-three . . . '

'Got nothing to do with it,' said Tipper dismissively. 'I've met birds of twenty-two with no sex appeal, and I've met women of fifty who're never short of a man. I've not met many of them, though – unfortunately.'

'This Julia sounds a bit of a man-eater, doesn't she?'

'Yeah – and cool with it. "Hallo Elizabeth" indeed.' Tipper laughed.

'We'd better go and see her, I suppose,' said Gaffney. 'Where's this place she lives?'

'Just off the Hog's Back – 'bout five miles from Guildford.'

'That's worth a few bob,' said Tipper as they turned into the driveway of the late Geoffrey Hodder's house.

'He probably picked it up quite cheap when he bought it,' said Gaffney. 'It was over twenty years ago.'

It was a neat house, predominantly white. White walls, white paint on windows and garage, and round the door was an enclosed glazed porch. The grass needed cutting, and the drive was thick with weeds, but there were one or two pleasant trees in the garden. Two dormer windows projected from the steep roof.

'Yes,' said Tipper, nodding, 'not a bad little drum.'

'Not so little, either,' said Gaffney. He looked for a bell-push, couldn't find one, and lifted the heavy brass knocker. The bang it made seemed to resound through the house.

'Christ!' said Tipper. 'Sounds like the opening to one of those Dracula films.'

The woman who answered the door was very attractive. Tipper reckoned that she was about five feet seven, probably in her mid-thirties; and her breasts were definitely meant to be noticed. Her short blonde hair was curly and tousled, and her ready smile revealed teeth that were white and even. 'Hallo,' she said.

'Mrs Hodder?'

'Yes ... ' She said it hesitantly, as though there were some doubt about it.

'We're police officers,' said Gaffney, and showed her his warrant card.

She smiled again. 'I'll have to take your word for it,' she said. 'I haven't put my contact lenses in yet. I suppose you've come about Geoffrey?'

They followed her into the sitting room and gazed round. 'This is a pleasant room,' said Gaffney. It was white, like the outside of the house, and the furniture was low, giving a feeling of relaxation.

'It is now. You should have seen it when I moved in. But Geoffrey let me go right through the house, redecorating. It took time, of course, and it cost quite a lot of money.' She shrugged her shoulders as though it was something excessively naughty to have done.

'I'm very sorry about your husband's death, Mrs Hodder.'

124

He had decided against telling her that he had known Geoffrey Hodder, had worked with him in the past. If she wasn't aware of his precise job it wouldn't mean much anyway, and Gaffney had always worked on the principle that you told no one that you were from Special Branch if you didn't have to.

'It was a terrible shock – terrible.' The smile vanished but she remained dry-eyed, thank God; Gaffney never quite knew what to do with weeping women, usually pretended it wasn't happening.

'You were Mr Hodder's second wife, I understand?'

'Is that relevant?' she asked. Strange that. Exactly the same response as Hodder's first wife had made when they had asked her about the divorce.

'It may be. We are making enquiries about his death.'

'I thought he had committed suicide.'

'What makes you think that?'

She looked genuinely surprised, and for the first time her composure seemed to slip. 'But surely . . . I mean, what else . . . you're not suggesting . . . '

'I'm not suggesting anything, Mrs Hodder. I'm investigating. But supposing, for a moment, he did take his own life, why should a reasonably successful man, happily married . . . '

He let the sentence fade so that it sounded like a question.

'Very happily married,' she said rather haughtily as though they were impugning her in some way.

'Why should such a man want to take his own life?'

She twisted her broad wedding ring and looked straight at Gaffney. 'It's a question I've been puzzling over ever since it happened,' she said.

'Did you come up with an answer?'

'No. No, I didn't. It's a complete mystery.'

'Would it have been anything to do with his work, do you think?'

'He never said so, never complained about problems or overwork, nothing like that. He was a civil servant, you know?'

'So I believe. In London, I think, wasn't it?'

'Yes. The Ministry of Defence. He never spoke about

it. I think it must have been a bit hush-hush.' She laughed infectiously. 'Actually it was probably something quite silly like keeping lists of how many nuts and bolts went into an aircraft-carrier, but you know what men are like – they always want to seem important, even in their wife's eyes – particularly in their wife's eyes.' She laughed again, girlishly, but Gaffney sensed that the brittle gaiety was artificial.

Gaffney looked round the room. It was not opulent, but it seemed above what he estimated an officer of Hodder's grade could have afforded, particularly as he was paying maintenance to his first wife, and supporting the children of that marriage – or had been in their earlier years. 'Did your husband have any money worries, Mrs Hodder?'

'No – well yes.' Gaffney put his head to one side, quizzically. 'Doesn't sound right, does it?' she said with a smile. 'What I meant was that he had his first wife to support, but I've money of my own.' She swept an elegant hand round the room, the chunky bracelet on her wrist jangling as she did so. 'I paid for all this, for instance.'

'Oh!' said Gaffney.

'You sound vaguely disapproving,' she said, 'but if a husband and wife share a home I don't see why she shouldn't put money into it as well.'

'I don't disapprove, Mrs Hodder. It's just that most wives can't afford to. So you can't think of anything that might have been playing on your husband's mind?'

'No, I really can't.'

'If you'll forgive me for asking, did the divorce upset your husband very much?'

'D'you mean did he have any regrets?'

Gaffney nodded slowly. 'More or less.'

'None – none whatsoever.'

'That sounds pretty emphatic.'

'Well of course. I did live with him, you know. His first wife was a bit of a dragon – no, that's not quite fair. She was domesticated – a mouse. Always worrying about keeping the house clean and tidy. Houseworked to all hours apparently. Left no time for the physical side of the marriage.'

'Did you ever meet her?'

'Oh, yes – a few times. The first time I met Geoffrey she was with him. It was a party at the Harrises' – Dick and Tina – just after I arrived here.'

'Where did you arrive from, Mrs Hodder?'

'Africa – does it matter?'

'Not really. What on earth were you doing out there?'

'I worked for a charity. My family were old Africa hands – I think that's the expression.'

'You were friends of the Hodders – Geoffrey and Elizabeth, I mean?'

'In a manner of speaking – well to start with. Elizabeth was a very uninteresting person – flat.'

'And one thing led to another and you and Geoffrey . . . '

She smiled. 'Yes – me and Geoffrey. Actually it wasn't meant to come to a divorce. To be perfectly frank I was quite happy with our arrangement; it could have gone on like that, as far as I was concerned. Funnily enough, I found Geoffrey a bit stodgy to start with. I think if anyone had said that I'd finish up marrying him, I'd have had a fit. Just goes to show, doesn't it. But I'm afraid it got out of control. Not to mince words, Elizabeth, er – "caught us at it" is the phrase, I think.' She didn't lower her eyes or look embarrassed, she just laughed. 'That was a day to remember. Poor Geoffrey – he was so upset . . . '

'I can imagine that Elizabeth was too,' said Tipper mildly.

It was the first time he had spoken apart from greeting her when they had arrived, and she looked at him with interest, as though she hadn't really noticed his presence before. It was an intense look; a look of appraisal that he found surprisingly discomforting, and he felt like telling her that he was married. Women like her worried him. One half of him fancied her; the other half said that she was bloody dangerous, particularly to a policeman, and particularly to a policeman who was married.

She ran her tongue round her top lip. 'Actually no – not at the time. She was very English. She just said "Hallo Geoffrey," and looked at me as though I'd just crawled out

127

of a piece of cheese. So I said "Hallo Elizabeth." Then she left.'

'Mrs Hodder – Elizabeth Hodder that is – said that she had had a phone call telling her where her husband was. Did you know that?'

'No – no, I didn't. It doesn't surprise me though. I'm afraid that in a village this size there's always someone willing to blacken a young woman's name – I think it's a cross between malice and envy.'

'Does that concern you?'

'You learn to live with it.' She leaned back in her chair so that her breasts strained against the satin of her blouse, and held Tipper's gaze long enough to make him feel uncomfortable again. 'I'm not being very much help to you, am I?'

Gaffney waved a deprecating hand. 'It takes time,' he said. 'I'm sorry that we had to intrude at all.'

At the front door she paused. 'There was one thing,' she said thoughtfully. 'I don't know whether it means anything, but about six months ago Geoffrey mentioned someone at work he was worried about . . . '

'Can you remember the name?'

She furrowed her brow. 'No – no, I'm afraid I can't.' She held her chin with one hand, cupping the elbow with the other.

'Would it have been Selby by any chance?' asked Tipper, mentioning that name only because Hodder himself had done so when they had interviewed him at Scotland Yard.

She shook her head, her gaze still fixed on the floor. 'No,' she said. 'I've never heard that name before.'

'What concerned him about this person?' asked Gaffney.

'I've no idea.' She looked at him, dropping her arms to her sides. 'He just mentioned him one evening – said he was a bit concerned about him, but then clammed up, almost as if he regretted having mentioned it at all. P'raps someone had stolen the tea money,' she said and giggled.

They don't call them village policemen now, probably because villages don't have a policeman to themselves any

128

more. These days they call them home-beat officers, or community constables, or some other grandiose title that those in authority hope will excuse the economy-driven reduction in operational manpower.

Consequently, Gaffney and Tipper had to drive a mile to the neighbouring hamlet. The police house was on the main road, but the constable himself was out.

'I'm Mrs Bates, his wife.' She was a youngish woman, perhaps thirty, no more. 'Can I help?' She was neat and tidy and had the confidence and probably the competence that went with the largely unrecognised but indispensable rôle of being the local policeman's unpaid assistant. It was a post that encompassed first-aider, midwife, counsellor, guide and secretary, and that was usually in addition to bringing up a couple of children of her own.

She led them through into the sitting room and, unimpressed by their rank, sat them down and made tea.

'Frank shouldn't be long, Mr Gaffney,' she said. 'He's only gone over to the farm about the shotgun certificate. Is it anything that I can help you with?'

'We are making enquiries about the death of Geoffrey Hodder, who lived at— '

'I know where he lived,' she said. 'It was Frank who took the message.'

'Did you know him?' Gaffney asked.

'Oh yes; him and his wife. Funny chap, he was. Bit antisocial. Friendly, mind you – always passed the time of day – but never seemed to mix: well not at first. Come to that, not at the end either.'

Gaffney smiled. 'You've lost me a little there, Mrs Bates.'

She laughed. 'Yes, I would have. It was the bit in the middle when he was different, when the scandal happened. That was a few years ago now, before we were stationed here.'

'Oh,' said Gaffney, 'I rather gathered you were here at the time.'

She smiled tolerantly. 'I was – Frank wasn't. Let me explain – ' Gaffney let her; she was going to anyway. 'I was born only a few hundred yards away from the Hodders' house. When I started work it was at Mount Browne, the police headquarters in Guildford. That's where I met Frank. When we got married, he stayed on in Guildford for a bit, then we got posted to Leatherhead – terrible place that, all one-way streets. We've only been here a couple of years, and now we're in the wrong place.'

'You don't like it here?'

'That's not what I meant. I mean that this house is in the wrong place – typical that is. There's hardly anybody living here, so this is where they put the house. Everybody lives down near the Hodders – a mile away – that's where the police house should be.'

'That's the police force all over,' said Gaffney. 'But you were telling me about the Hodders.' He gently nudged her back on course.

'Oh yes,' she said. 'That was quite a to-do. They love a bit of gossip round these places. Well they had plenty to get their teeth into then, I can tell you.'

'I understand that Mrs Hodder, or Julia Simpson as she was then, hadn't lived here very long?'

'No. I suppose it must have been about a year before – before the excitement, that is. She bought a cottage – Raven Cottage it was, only about a quarter of a mile from where she is now. She'd come from abroad somewhere—' She stopped, thinking. 'Africa, I think they said.'

'They?'

She laughed. 'The village gossips. You just have to keep your ears open round here, Mr Gaffney, and you hear everything. You'd be surprised what I pick up just going shopping. Particularly now I'm the PC's wife. They all want to tell me things. They know it'll all get back to Frank, but it's not the same as telling him direct – that'd be informing, you see. Funny sort of logic, but they are basically country folk.' She chuckled.

Gaffney shook his head and smiled, recognising how invaluable Police Constable Bates's wife must be to him. 'Do you know where in Africa she came from, Mrs Bates?'

'No I don't, but that was enough of a mystery for this

lot. I think they were prepared to cast her in the rôle of scarlet woman as soon as she got here. She'd have been about twenty-five then, I suppose. Good-looking girl – and she still is; have you met her?' Gaffney nodded. 'Living in a cottage by herself, and in the summer she'd stroll down to the village shop in very short shorts. Well that was too much for the busy-bodies, I can tell you. You could almost see them tutting away, and whenever the poor girl walked into the shop or the post office, they'd all stop talking and ignore her. I suppose they thought she was after their husbands. Well most of them needn't have worried. You've never seen such a dowdy lot. Mind you I'm rather glad my Frank wasn't here at the time.' She laughed. 'I think he might have taken a shine to her.'

'So how did she come to meet Geoffrey Hodder?'

'Well there are two groups down here, Mr Gaffney. There's the locals, live here and work here, and there's what we call the townies – they're the ones who drive off to Guildford in their big cars and catch the train up to London. Most of them seem to have working wives, too, who go with them. Now they're a different sort – worldly, you might say, and a girl like Julia Simpson wouldn't worry them – they'd know how to deal with her. There's quite a few young wives among them—'

'And don't they ever wear shorts?' asked Tipper.

'Oh, yes,' said Mrs Bates, 'but they're married. That's all right. I tell you, Mr Tipper, you've got to live here to understand the local culture. Still, won't be for much longer.'

'You're on the move then?' asked Gaffney.

'Frank's promotion's come through. He's going to Godalming as sergeant next month.' She was obviously proud of her husband. 'That'll be much better; I prefer living in a town.'

'That's where Hodder's first wife lives.'

'Oh yes, I know.'

Gaffney was beginning to think that he'd have saved himself a lot of time if he'd come to see the policeman's wife first. 'Did she have a job – go out to work?' asked Tipper.

'Now that was a bit of a mystery. She never let on. Always said she'd worked for one of those charities out in Africa, and let it go at that, as if she still did – sort of hinted that she worked from home, but never actually said precisely what it was she did.'

The telephone rang at that moment, and she stood up to answer it. 'I don't know where Frank can have got to,' she said, glancing at the clock. She listened for a few seconds and then said; 'No, you can drive unaccompanied if you've passed the test. If you're stopped just produce your provisional licence and your certificate of passing the test. You're welcome.' She replaced the handset and sat down again.

'You sound as though you know as much law as your husband,' said Gaffney.

'Should do,' she said. 'I think I tested him on just about every page of Moriarty when he was studying for promotion. Now, where were we?'

'You were telling me about Julia Simpson's job.'

'Oh yes. That's all I can tell you, I'm afraid. But you asked how she met Geoffrey Hodder. There's a couple called Harris – used to live in that big house at the end of the village. You've been up there, I take it?'

'Not to their house, no. We saw Mrs Hodder – Julia – this morning.'

'Yes,' she said, 'you would have done,' demonstrating again her knowledge of police procedure. 'Well the Harrises had a party. Had one every so often. Invited us a couple of times, but Frank always likes to stay at arm's length. Anyway they invited Julia, and that's where she met the Hodders. The Hodders were townies, of course – well half and half. Elizabeth used to go up to London until she had children. Then she stayed at home to look after them. The Hodders invited Julia to dinner a couple of times. Probably the worst thing Elizabeth Hodder ever did. Then one after-noon Elizabeth got a phone call telling her exactly where to find her husband. And she did.'

'Any idea who might have made that phone call, Mrs Bates?' asked Gaffney.

'Could have been any one of a dozen bitchy wives, but . . . '

'But what?'

'Well I've got a theory – no proof, mind, just a theory, but I reckon it was Julia Simpson who made that call. Just to speed things up, if you take my meaning. Knowing Geoffrey Hodder, he'd never have asked his wife for a divorce so he could marry Julia. But when Elizabeth found them in bed together, it was her who divorced him. And that was that,' she said with finality.

'You said that the Harrises used to live in the village, Mrs Bates.'

'Yes. They moved about a year ago. Dick Harris's job took him up to Welwyn I think it was. It was too far to travel every day. I think he tried it, but it was too much.'

'You don't happen to have their new address, do you?'

'Yes, of course.' Mrs Bates walked through into the office, returning moments later with a piece of paper. 'There you are, Mr Gaffney. Phone number's on there, too.'

Mrs Bates's husband came walking up the path as they were at the front door. He'd already taken note of their car and had identified it as a police vehicle. He looked at the two visitors.

'Detective Chief Superintendent Gaffney, Metropolitan,' said Gaffney.

'Anything I can do to help, sir?' asked Bates.

Gaffney laughed. 'I don't think so, thank you, Mr Bates. Your wife is a mine of information; very useful to you, I should think. And she makes a good cup of tea.'

Bates laughed. 'She does that, sir.'

'Oh,' said Gaffney, pausing at the gate. 'Congratulations on your promotion.'

'That Hodder woman intrigues me,' said Tipper, pulling into the fast lane of the A3.

'Yes,' said Gaffney. 'I noticed that you couldn't take your eyes off her boobs.'

Tipper laughed. 'Yeah, that too. But she didn't seem to be too cut up by the demise of her beloved Geoffrey, did she?'

'Difficult to tell. Grief affects different people in different ways.'

'Only if there's grief there to start with.'

'What are you suggesting?'

'Don't really know, sir, but there was something. D'you think that Hodder had money? A private income, or investments; that sort of thing?'

'We can certainly find out. I'll get one of the skippers to do some digging.'

'I don't understand why she married him,' said Tipper. 'He wasn't exactly my idea of a stud – and she's a good-looking bird. What was the attraction?'

'Perhaps he was a good performer,' said Gaffney, but looked as though he didn't really believe it.

'Yeah, maybe. It's not the sort of question we can ask Mrs Hodder though, is it? Either Mrs Hodder.

Chapter Ten

The outside of the block of flats where Selby lived in Fulham, but which he preferred to call Chelsea, was ordinary. Gaffney knew to the last penny how much Selby earned, at least from his employment as an intelligence officer with MI5; but given that he was unmarried and had budgeted his resources carefully, the décor and the furnishings were not excessive, although the Bang & Olufsen audio equipment would have set him back a few pounds. There was always the possibility that he had a private income – a legitimate one, that is – as a few of these fellows seemed to have. Some, too, were connected with the aristocracy; MI5 seemed to think it a form of water-tight vetting to recruit the kinsmen of the titled, although Gaffney could think of a few peers who had gone astray in their lives.

'We are here,' said Gaffney, having introduced himself and Tipper, 'in connection with the death of Geoffrey Hodder.'

Selby did not react. 'Rather strange to conduct your enquiries at my home rather than in the office, isn't it?' he asked. His face wore a supercilious sneer, but Gaffney was to learn that it was a natural and constant expression.

'I conduct my enquiries where and when I see fit, Mr Selby,' said Gaffney curtly. 'A suspicious death is not something to be treated lightly.'

'Suspicious? I thought he committed suicide.'

'What makes you think that?'

'Well he wasn't murdered, was he? And it wasn't an accident.'

'You seem very sure, Mr Selby. If we were as sure as you are, we wouldn't be bothering to investigate his death.'

135

'Well it might have been something to do with his work,' said Selby. 'But of course,' he added airily, 'you will appreciate that I can't discuss that.' He waved a dismissive hand.

'Oh, why's that?' Gaffney realised that he would have to keep himself on a very tight rein; Selby was a man he could easily take a dislike to.

'I'm afraid my profession is covered by the Official Secrets Act. You should know that. It's a question of need to know.'

'My job's covered by the same rules,' said Gaffney quietly. 'But if it makes you feel any better, read this.' Gaffney handed him the DG's letter of authority, the same letter he had shown Hodder as a preamble to that interview.

Selby read the letter, then handed it back without saying anything. He looked uncomfortable, but Gaffney could not decide at that stage whether it was because he had something to hide, or was merely the natural reticence of the MI5 officer, many of whom wouldn't even tell you the colour of their toilet rolls for fear of breaching some security regulation.

'I know, of course,' said Gaffney, putting the letter to one side, 'that Hodder led the team responsible for the Nikitin, Gesschner and Dickson cases, and that in all three cases the hostile contact evaded capture; in the Dickson case almost at the point when he was to be arrested. I'm also aware, Mr Selby, that you were a member of that team, and were therefore concerned in those investigations – from the MI5 point of view.'

'From every point of view,' said Selby sarcastically. He was one of the very few within the Security Service who resented their having to enlist the aid of the police to effect an arrest.

Gaffney decided that a little taunt would not go amiss, just to remind this objectionable young man that he could get away with so much and no more. 'Where were you recruited for the Security Service?' he asked. He knew the answer, but wanted Selby to tell him.

'Cambridge University.'

Gaffney nodded slowly, the trace of a wry smile on his face. 'Oh, I see,' he said.

Selby stared malevolently at Gaffney. It was the sort of snide jibe that he had had to contend with from his colleagues ever since joining MI5. The knowing smile, the whispered aside, the sudden burst of laughter and the conversations that stopped when he entered an office, from among those who knew all about the Apostles, that pre-war gang of traitors and homosexuals. Fifty years or more ago, and still Selby had to contend with that legacy, the principle that because he was unmarried and had been to Cambridge, he must be tarred with the same brush. His effete appearance didn't help, the half-bored, half-sneering expression, the upper-class drawl that he had so carefully nurtured as a youth, and which had now become so much a part of his character that it wouldn't go away.

The background music stopped. It was only then that Gaffney noticed it; noticed it because it had stopped. Slowly Selby rose from his armchair, carefully uncoiling himself as though to move quickly might break something. He walked across to the stereo unit, gently removed the compact disc from the little drawer, and put it into its plastic box.

'You're a music lover?' asked Gaffney.

Selby lifted his head slightly. 'Not all music,' he said condescendingly. 'That was Monteverdi.'

'*Coronation of Poppaea*, wasn't it?' asked Tipper.

Selby's eyes widened as though he hadn't heard the comment properly, or that he had imagined it. 'Yes,' he said.

'Thought so,' said Tipper. 'I prefer his madrigals and motets, personally.' He said it casually as though he was giving an opinion on a heavy metal pop group.

Gaffney shot a sideways glance at his chief inspector, nearly as surprised as Selby had been. But Gaffney knew policemen better, knew the extraordinary flashes of knowledge that the most unlikely of his colleagues displayed from time to time.

Selby paused, uncertain quite what to do next, and his hands moved aimlessly in front of his body as though operating some invisible diabolo. Then he switched off the stereo and sat down again.

'You're not married.' It was a statement, not a question.

'No,' said Selby flatly. 'Is that important?' He spoke defensively, about to make an excuse, then thought better of it.

'Might be.'

'I don't see how.'

'No, you probably don't,' said Gaffney, a bite in his voice. Again, he cautioned himself not to lose his temper with this self-cultured aesthete, whose languorous sprawling pose clearly radiated disdain for the two policemen, and sent a signal which said that he was much too clever to be caught out by such people.

'How much did you know about the man known as Dickson?' It was Tipper who spoke, his harsh cockney voice cutting through the comfortable cocoon in which Selby existed, and contrasting sharply with his last comment about Monteverdi.

It clearly jarred him and he sat up slightly. 'Er – only what we were told by Geoffrey.'

'Geoffrey?' Tipper knew, but he didn't like untidiness. Didn't like the snooty Christian-name world in which Selby operated either.

'Geoffrey Hodder – the team leader.'

'The team leader who was responsible for overseeing this job – and the two before it that went wrong?' It was a ploy of Tipper's. He knew fine that Gaffney had said all that, but was giving the impression now that he hadn't heard, or that he wasn't very bright. In juxtaposition to his comments about Monteverdi, it left Selby wondering what sort of individual he was. And that in Tipper's book was very useful.

Selby nodded miserably, and Gaffney smiled inwardly. He was glad he'd picked Tipper for this job – he was much too nasty for the Selbys of this world. He glanced at Selby again; he looked as though he was going to cry.

'And what did Hodder tell you?'

'Just that Armitage – Major Armitage – was believed to be passing material from the MOD to a hostile agent.'

'Nationality? Did he mention nationality?'

'No – not in as many words. We all assumed that he was

138

IC – er, Iron Curtain,' he added nervously. He wasn't sure
about Tipper. He looked a bit uncouth, and yet he wasn't,
well not wholly; but above all else, Tipper frightened him.
He was unorthodox; not the sort of Special Branch officer
he normally had dealings with. And he knew about Special
Branch; of course he knew about them. That frightened
him too. These were the men who went in where MI5
dare not, secure in the knowledge that they had the full
force of the law behind them. There was clearly something
not quite right in all this. They'd come here talking about
poor Geoffrey's death, and suddenly they were talking about
Nikitin, Gesschner and Dickson.

Abruptly it came to him; it was a witch-hunt. They were
out for blood. They suspected a mole – a traitor. Why else
would they deploy a chief superintendent, aided by this nasty
chief inspector? He wondered if he should ask for his solicitor,
dismissed it immediately; that would make him suspect, tell
them that he was panicking inwardly. There was no privilege
attached to working for MI5 when the chips were down – not
these days. He remembered what had happened to Bettaney,
and the shock waves that that had sent through the office.
The disbelief; and the comment of one long-service officer
who had boasted quite openly that it wouldn't have happened
in the old days, then added, with a glance at Selby, that the
service seemed to be recruiting a different breed these days.
Selby had taken it personally, reacted too quickly, and said,
'Not like Burgess, Maclean and Philby, you mean?' It had
been a mistake. Openly smirking, someone had pointed out
that admittedly they were Cambridge men, but had been
MI6 not MI5.

'What was your part in all this?' asked Tipper.

'Very little, actually.' Normally he wouldn't have undersold
himself, would have boasted a bit, but now it seemed politic
to play down his part.

'How little?' Tipper was relentless.

'Well nothing, actually.'

'I see. You were involved, I suppose. We haven't been
misinformed?'

139

'I was briefed, along with other members of the team, but it was fairly straightforward. Real textbook stuff, as a matter of fact. Straight drop at a DLB – er, dead-letter box— '

'I do know what a DLB is,' said Tipper. 'Why were you briefed then, if you were going to take no part in all this?'

'For afterwards.'

'For afterwards?'

'Yes, after the arrest. I mean, the Armitage fellow would have been no problem. Just some poor guy with no resistance to a bribe, or whatever— '

'Or a loose woman,' said Tipper. 'So your job was to enquire into Dickson and his activities, was it?'

'Yes. There'd be a tremendous amount of background work to be done. Always the chance of others involved, you know. And there'd be the damage report to prepare . . . '

He tried to imply that these were the academic aspects – the esoteric – that mere policemen could not possibly be bright enough to deal with.

Tipper was unimpressed. 'So you were the junior hand – the dogsbody, so to speak?'

Selby studied his right hand for a moment or two, a delicate artistic hand that looked almost too frail to support the heavy signet ring on the fourth finger. 'I suppose so, yes,' he said.

'Were you involved in the surveillance on Dickson?'

'No. The watchers took care of that.' And not very well, thought Gaffney, but said nothing. 'Geoffrey briefed them.'

'But surely there were some enquiries made?'

'Of course.' Again the accentuated sneer.

'What sort of enquiries?'

'The usual checks. We confirmed where he worked, how old he was, where he was born – that sort of thing.'

'And where was Dickson born?'

'Australia, as a matter of fact.'

'Confirmed?' Tipper's questions came fast after the answers, giving Selby little time to think. He was an expert interrogator was Tipper.

'Not yet.'

'Meaning?'

'We're still waiting for ASIO.' He saw Tipper's raised eyebrows. 'Australian Security Intelligence Organisation.'

'I've got a pony says it doesn't check out,' said Tipper.

Selby looked genuinely puzzled. ' A pony is criminal slang for twenty-five pounds,' said Tipper casually. 'I suppose you sent them a letter?'

'Not exactly – we did it through our liaison.'

'Oh!' There was a wealth of sarcasm in that single word. 'All in all, then, you didn't know a great deal of what was going on?'

'Geoffrey did tend to play it close to the chest.'

'Why do you think that was?'

'Standard practice in the office, I'm afraid.'

'Who else was part of this little team?' Gaffney took up the questioning again, now that Tipper had softened Selby up a bit.

For a moment or two Selby said nothing, trying perhaps to recall the names, maybe wondering whether he should tell these two policemen even if he could remember. 'Apart from Geoffrey, there was Douglas Craven, Patrick Hughes, Jim Anderson and Fred Weston.'

'Seems a lot.'

'You never know how something like this is going to develop. It's easier to shed extra guys than take them on halfway through. Anyway, they each have their own skills – cyphers, handwriting, locks – that sort of thing.'

'And you – what's your speciality?'

'Languages. I have a degree in modern languages, and I speak Russian – fluently,' he added, preening himself slightly.

'And you will all have discussed this job among yourselves, presumably?' asked Gaffney.

'Good Lord, no – that would have been most improper.'

Gaffney didn't believe that for a moment; that was just a formal denial. 'Who, out of the six of you, would have known most about this job? Well, the five of you – you can leave out Hodder.'

Selby pondered on that for a while. Eventually he said; 'Patrick Hughes, I suppose.'

141

'Why him?'

'Well he's – was – Geoffrey's unofficial deputy.'

'And what's his particular qualification?'

'Nothing really – he's a mathematician.' He said it as though it was not the sort of thing one mentioned in polite company.

Gaffney thumbed through his pocket book. 'Lives in Twickenham, I believe.'

'I have no idea,' said Selby, as though he couldn't conceive of anyone living in Twickenham.

'What was your impression of Hodder after the disappearance of Dickson?'

'My impression of him?'

'Yes, Mr Selby,' said Gaffney impatiently. 'What was his demeanour like? Did he say anything – react in any way?'

'Oh, I see.' Selby spoke in a tired way and passed a hand across his forehead. Gaffney noticed that there was a bead or two of perspiration there. 'If anything, I suppose he was a little more withdrawn than usual.'

'Was he normally a withdrawn individual, then?'

'He was never very communicative.'

'What I'm trying to get at is whether the failure to capture Dickson, particularly after the previous two failures, had got him down to the extent that he might have committed suicide—'

'So he did commit suicide.'

' —Or on the other hand, whether someone had decided to remove him in the most forcible way possible.' Gaffney had continued as though Selby hadn't spoken.

Selby looked startled, a quick show of fear that he too might be vulnerable. 'Why should anyone want to kill Geoffrey?'

'That is precisely what I am trying to determine.'

'But surely you must know how he died.'

'Not yet, no,' lied Gaffney. 'There are tests to be carried out. No doubt you remember the Markov case – the poison pellet fired from an umbrella? Took quite some time to establish the cause of death in that case.'

Selby looked appalled. 'But surely . . . ' He relapsed into

silence, stunned by the concept that anyone working in the cosy little world of MI5 could actually be killed because of what he did. MI6 maybe, but MI5 . . .

'Well look at it this way,' said Gaffney. 'Do you really see Geoffrey Hodder as the sort of man who would commit suicide in a public lavatory on Waterloo Station? Drunks, tramps and drug addicts maybe, but a senior intelligence officer of MI5?'

'I presume, from what you were saying just now, that Patrick Hughes will have taken over where Hodder left off?' It was another of Tipper's straight-to-the-point questions.

'Er – yes, I suppose so.' Selby nodded vaguely.

'In that case we'd better talk to him.'

'What's the betting he's on the phone to Hughes right now?' said Tipper with a chuckle, as they walked back to the car.

'Not him, Harry. He'd be bloody terrified that we'd see that as conspiracy. He might look stupid, but he's got enough sense to have worked out that the hunt is on. What's more, he'll probably think that we've got a tap on his line. No, he'll just curl up into a foetal ball and stick his thumb in his mouth.'

Gaffney and Tipper had discussed Selby at some length. Tipper's mainline CID background had led him to believe that an unmarried, effete individual like Selby must be, as he put it, 'as queer as a nine-bob note', but that was not helpful. Contrary to popular belief, homosexuals do not automatically become traitors; the official view is that they are more susceptible to pressure. Or they used to be; nowadays, Gaffney wasn't so sure.

'He certainly didn't give anything away,' said Tipper, 'except that he was terrified. You could almost smell the panic.'

'There's too much at stake, Harry. Anyone in the Security Service knows the going rate for spying, in any form, and twenty-five years in the nick is too high a price to pay.'

'I don't think he's got the guts to go bent.'

'Don't you believe it. Very few of the people who betray their country seem to have the stomach for it. One of the things we have to deal with in Special Branch is the ideologically motivated traitor, and that produces some very strange characters. Selby wouldn't have much physical courage but if he thinks he's right in his views it produces a gritty sort of determination to stay with it. And he's got all the hallmarks of a closet socialist.'

'Too much for me, guv'nor,' said Tipper with a shake of the head. 'What do we do now?'

'I'm afraid there's only one thing for it. Plain old-fashioned, tedious detective work.'

'Now that I do know something about.' Tipper sighed.

Gaffney leaned back in his chair and lighted one of his cigars. 'But that will take time.'

'We've got plenty of it.' Tipper paused. 'Haven't we?'

'Yes. There's no hurry, unless another similar job comes up, and the same thing happens all over again. If it does then we'll get some of the backwash too.'

'What about Armitage? That's blown out, hasn't it? We can't just leave him, can we?'

'I don't see why not,' said Gaffney, smiling. 'He's locked up in a flat in Battersea with an attractive girl – what's he got to complain about?'

'What are you going to do then? Run through the list?'

'I think so. We'll interview the rest of Hodder's little chums – see what they've got to say for themselves, then stop and survey what we've got. Unless we have a lucky break, we'll probably have to interview them all a second time, but as you said, we've got plenty of time.'

'Don't forget the Harrises, sir – the people who introduced Hodder to his second wife. They could afford us an outside view of the relationship – and the man: Hodder, I mean.'

Gaffney looked thoughtful. 'Yeah – but I don't want to get confused. Let's do the team first.'

'Right, but where – their place or ours?'

144

The table and chairs in the room at Security Service head-quarters which Gaffney had been assigned were standard government issue, spartan grey tubular steel and heavy-duty plastic. Gaffney was not sure whether that was an advantage to his enquiry or not. The one drawback was that his interviews would be conducted on the subjects' home ground. He had considered Scotland Yard and dismissed it as a trifle melo-dramatic, and he had shied away from local police stations on security grounds and the fact that, although he and Tipper might regard them as suspects, he didn't want them to think of themselves as such – at least not yet. Some of the wives did not, in all probability, know what their husbands did for a living, so that ruled out the sort of homely interview they had had with Selby. And that left the headquarters of MI5; not entirely satisfactory, but at least he had Tipper to offset any feelings of superiority that the members of the late Geoffrey Hodder's team might have derived from being in familiar surroundings.

Almost the first thing that Patrick Hughes told Gaffney and Tipper was that he had a degree, which caused Tipper to comment later that the only people who talked about their degrees were people with degrees that weren't worth talking about. Hughes also adopted a languid superiority that implied that he didn't rate policemen too much, even Special Branch officers.

Gaffney explained the purpose of the interview: that he and Tipper were investigating the death of Hodder. Hughes remained apparently unmoved by the demise of his boss, sitting with a half-cynical smile on his face.

'I shall be glad to help you, Mr Gaffney,' he said, a statement which left Tipper convinced that that was the last thing he would do. 'I presume it was suicide?'

Again the casual and convenient presumption that Selby had made, that Hodder had done away with himself, and by impli-cation, the sooner forgotten, the better. Again Gaffney made the same counter: 'What makes you say that?' he asked.

'What else could it have been?'

145

'He could have been murdered. It's a possibility that I am not dismissing.'

Hughes smiled lazily. 'Oh, I wouldn't have thought so.'

'Why do you say that? People do get murdered, you know.'

'Yes, I know, but who could possibly have wanted to kill Geoffrey? He was such a quiet unassuming fellow.'

'The Russians?'

That startled Hughes, but then he smiled again. 'Now that is being a bit melodramatic, surely?'

'Is it? You know that he had been trying to find out where the leak was?'

Hughes shook his head in puzzlement, still the sarcastic smile on his face. 'I'm sorry, I don't quite follow . . . '

'I think you do,' said Gaffney. 'I'm talking about the somewhat rapid departure of Peter Dickson – at the very moment that he was going to be arrested. And, as you well know, that followed the similar disappearance of Nikitin and Gesschner.'

Hughes shrugged his shoulders. 'These things happen.'

'What things? Unexplained deaths – or jobs that go wrong?'

'Cases that don't come to fruition.' Hughes leaned back and crossed his legs, managing to look relaxed and comfortable in a chair that didn't encourage either. 'I mean, we can't get it right all the time.'

'Once in a while wouldn't hurt, though,' said Tipper acidly.

'I would remind you that two out of the three cases to which you allude also involved Special Branch. Can you be sure that the problems could not have been attributable to your own people?'

Gaffney wasn't going to rise to that. 'Thank you, Mr Hughes,' he said icily. 'I was aware of that. How much did you know about these cases in advance?'

'If you'll forgive me for saying so,' said Hughes, 'we seem to have progressed rather rapidly from talking about Geoffrey Hodder's death to recent and current operations. You will know that I can't possibly talk about those things – even to Special Branch.'

Gaffney handed him the Director-General's letter.

Hughes made a great show of taking out his glasses, wiping them with his handkerchief, and putting them on. Then he read the letter, appearing to give great attention to Griffin's signature, as though it might have been a forgery. 'Mmm!' he said, and handed it back.

'Well?'

'Hardly anything in the Dickson case. A little more of the other two, but not enough to be able to give any useful information to a foreign power.' He said it with a supercilious drawl.

'Who said anything about giving information to a foreign power?' asked Gaffney.

Hughes tensed slightly. 'Well that's the implication, isn't it?' He realised that he might have said too much.

'Not the implication, Mr Hughes – your inference.'

He spread his hands. 'Er – well, I assumed that was why you were making these enquiries.'

'Well you assumed wrongly,' said Gaffney. 'As I said just now, Mr Tipper and I are investigating the death of Geoffrey Hodder. However, if you have some information to volunteer about possible leaks within the Security Service, you are, of course, free to make a statement.'

'No, it's just that I thought . . . ' Which was exactly what he hadn't done; he lapsed into silence.

'I understand that you were Geoffrey Hodder's deputy?'

'Yes.'

'You would have known more about these cases than any other member of the team, then. As much as Hodder?'

'Who suggested that?'

'Peter Selby.' Gaffney decided it was time to get them fighting among themselves.

'Oh!' said Hughes in an offhanded way. 'Well he would.'

'What's your view of Selby?'

'D'you think he had something to do with Geoffrey's death?'

'I'm the one asking the questions,' said Gaffney.

'He's an insufferable prig,' said Hughes mildly. 'Thinks he's a damned sight more important than he is. Quite frankly,

147

I never knew why Geoffrey entertained him on the team. He was bloody useless.'

'He tells me that he is a linguist of some merit – a fluent Russian speaker, he said.'

'Quite possibly. Personally, I've never heard him speaking Russian, so I wouldn't know. I think he spends most of his time reading *Pravda* – not a great deal of good when you're trying to discover if the animal rights movement is a left-wing front organisation.'

'Huntsmen wear red coats,' said Tipper jocularly, and was rewarded with a withering glance.

'Frankly, and between ourselves,' continued Hughes, as though Tipper hadn't spoken, 'I think Selby's a raving poof.'

'Nevertheless, it seems likely that as Hodder's deputy, you would have known more about these operations than the others.'

'The first two, certainly: Nikitin and Gesschner. But not Dickson and Armitage.'

'Why d'you think that was? Why didn't Hodder tell you, or didn't he know either?'

'I can't answer that, can I?' said Hughes with a trace of sarcasm in his voice. 'As he didn't tell me, I couldn't possibly know whether he knew or not.'

'Let me put it another way,' said Gaffney. 'With the amount of knowledge that you had about the Dickson case, could you have overseen the operation?'

Hughes gave that some thought. 'Probably not,' he said at length.

'So we must conclude that Hodder didn't tell you everything?'

'I suppose not.'

'Why?' Gaffney gave him no time to answer. 'Can I make one thing clear, Mr Hughes. I am investigating Hodder's death, and anything else that may have a bearing on it – like Nikitin, Gesschner and Dickson. I am not here to indulge in verbal gymnastics.'

Hughes sat up slightly, recognising that he had been rebuked. 'No, I suppose that he didn't tell me everything.'

'Then again, I ask you why not?'

'He was desperately worried. This business of losing two in a row – Nikitin and Gesschner – really got to him. And when Dickson vanished, well that was really too much. He got snappy – bad-tempered with his staff – and that was something I'd never known him do before. I tried to talk to him about it, but he wouldn't even discuss it. He said it was his problem, and that he would solve it. I told him that I was there to help, but he said it again: it was his problem.'

'He expressed no views about it?'

'None. But I've been in the service long enough to know that he must have been having misgivings about someone here.'

'Have you any idea who?'

Hughes looked round the room, seeking inspiration. Eventually he shrugged. 'Not really, no. Where do you start?'

'Selby?'

Hughes smiled. 'He's the obvious choice, but quite frankly he's too obvious. It'll probably turn out to be someone who any one of us would least have suspected.' He paused. 'If there is anyone! I'm not yet convinced that it's not one horrible coincidence.'

'Was there any sign that Geoffrey Hodder might have been having domestic difficulties at all?'

'No . . . ' The word was drawn out, pensive.

'You sound doubtful.'

'I was about to say no positively, but then I remembered that he's on his second marriage. Funny that.'

'Why funny?'

'Well he wasn't the sort of chap you could ever visualise having been through the courts.'

'Through the courts?' Gaffney knew what he meant, but was a little tired of this self-important poseur's affectations.

'Yes – divorce, and all that.'

'What do you know of his divorce?'

'Very little. It happened just after I came here. I heard them talking about it, but I didn't know Geoffrey then. He was just a name. But afterwards – after I got moved to his section – I wondered. You can't keep anything secret here – funny that, isn't it, considering the nature of our trade – and it was the talk of the office, how old Geoffrey had shed his dowdy little wife and married some tantalisingly sexy creature who'd appeared in his village. There was some story that he'd been found in bed with her – by his wife, no less.' He laughed at the prospect that anyone could be so careless.

'Yes, but more recently. Had he had problems lately?'

'Not that I know of. But I suppose if you've got a sexy young wife you're always worried that someone else is . . . well, you know.'

'That brings us back to the professional side of his life, then – '

'Something that may have made him commit suicide, you mean?'

'At the risk of repeating myself, Mr Hughes, I am by no means satisfied that he did commit suicide. But supposing for a moment that he did, do you think that he was sufficiently concerned about the failure of recent operations to take his own life?'

'Well I wouldn't have done, that's for sure – not unless it was my fault, and I was the one about to be caught out.'

'You mean that if you had been a traitor – if you had been passing information and suddenly you realised that you were about to be arrested?' Gaffney wanted to get it very clear.

'Absolutely, old boy,' said Hughes jovially. 'Certainly wouldn't have done myself in because of some admin balls-up.'

'But it couldn't have been, could it – not an admin balls-up as you so graphically put it? For three "illegals" to decamp just as they were about to be compromised is not an administrative matter. In my book it means that someone has passed infor-mation – sensitive information about operational matters of the utmost importance. You, as an intelligence officer of some experience, would agree with that, wouldn't you, Mr Hughes?'

Somewhat reluctantly, Hughes nodded. 'Yes,' he said.

'That then takes me to the next stage. Was there anything, anything at all that you can think of, that would make Geoffrey Hodder's death an advantage to the other side?'

Hughes smiled wearily. 'At the risk of underselling our little firm,' he said, 'no, there isn't. To be perfectly honest, and you know this anyway, we only exist to counter: to counter espionage, subversion and sabotage. By and large, we're a threat to operations, not to lives. If there's a problem, they remove themselves, not us – unlike our cousins across the river.'

'Like Nikitin, Gesschner and Dickson appear to have removed themselves, you mean?'

'Exactly so.'

Chapter Eleven

Gaffney shook hands with Douglas Craven, whom he had not previously met, and introduced himself and Tipper. 'We are making enquiries into the death of Geoffrey Hodder,' he said bluntly.

'It was a terrible shock to all of us,' said Craven, 'but I didn't realise that the police were going to make enquiries.' He looked from Gaffney to Tipper and back again.

'I can assure you, Mr Craven, that we are by no means satisfied as to the cause of death. I am here because of the delicate nature of Geoffrey's work, but Detective Chief Inspector Tipper is here from the CID – and he has been positively vetted,' he added, correctly interpreting Craven's look of alarm. The members of MI5 worried about such things. The allusion to Tipper belonging to the CID was meant to imply a possible murder enquiry. It was not untrue, of course – Special Branch is an integral part of the Criminal Investigation Department.

'Well what happened? All we've heard here is that he was found dead. I just assumed that it was natural; I think we all did.'

'What makes you say that? He was only forty-seven. Had he been ill?'

'Well, no – not as far as I know. Occasional day off here and there with a cold – that sort of thing.'

'Why then should you think it was natural causes?'

'I don't know really. I suppose we wouldn't like to think it was anything else. He's not the type of chap to commit suicide.'

'That's a fairly downright statement. Would you ever expect anyone to commit suicide?'

'No, I suppose not, but Geoffrey I most certainly wouldn't have thought . . . '

'Had it occurred to you that he may have been murdered?'

'Murdered!' Craven's eyes opened in astonishment.

'I'm not saying that he was, Mr Craven. I'm just asking whether you would have been surprised if that had been the case.'

'Well of course. I can't imagine anyone wanting to murder Geoffrey Hodder.'

'As the result of something done in the line of duty, maybe?' Gaffney's questioning was casual, conversational, and that made what he was saying unreal.

Craven appeared to be making a positive effort to think that one out. Eventually he said; 'No, frankly, I can't, but I suppose in our line of business it's always a possibility.'

'Why?' Gaffney knew what the answer would be.

'We are up against the KGB – and similar organisations.'

'Never happened before, though, has it?'

'Not to my knowledge.'

Gaffney moved his position slightly, regretting the hard chairs. 'Let's talk now about the three operations in which he was involved recently – and yourself, I believe.' Craven frowned. 'I'm talking about Nikitin, Gesschner and, more recently, Dickson.'

'Yes,' said Craven flatly.

'You'll be aware, naturally, that on all three occasions, the contacts – the three I've just mentioned – disappeared at the very moment that they were about to be arrested. Actually in the case of Gesschner – ' He corrected himself, 'some time before. That case hadn't even been referred to Special Branch.'

'Yes,' said Craven again. 'Those were very worrying events.'

'That's putting it mildly I should think. It must have caused some concern in the service.'

'Yes, it did. The first time it was put down to bad luck – the sort of thing that happens occasionally. The second time was a bit unnerving, but the third . . . ' He left the sentence uncompleted.

'Was there an enquiry?'

'Sort of.'

'Sort of?'

'John Carfax went through all the papers and then spoke to each of us informally.'

'And what were his findings?'

'I've no idea – it wasn't an official thing.'

'Sounds a bit slap-dash,' said Tipper, familiar with the searching enquiries usually conducted by the police Complaints Investigation Bureau that went on for months and left nothing that hadn't been examined thoroughly.

Craven looked hurt. 'It's the way we do things in the service,' he said.

'What do you think went wrong?' Again Gaffney's quiet questioning got them back to the core of the enquiry.

For a while Craven didn't answer. Then, reluctantly, he said, 'It looked very much as though someone had spoken out of turn.'

'You mean there was a mole in your organisation,' said Tipper brutally.

'In all honesty,' said Craven, 'I don't think any of us wanted to face up to that possibility.'

'But surely,' said Gaffney, 'it's the only logical answer?' Slowly, Gaffney's questioning was pulling Craven down from the esoteric world in which he lived and operated to the stark reality of traitors and sudden deaths.

'I suppose so,' Craven admitted.

'How well did you know Geoffrey Hodder?' asked Tipper.

Craven looked puzzled at the shift in questioning, as though having to adjust to the fact that these two policemen were here to enquire into his boss's untimely death. 'I worked with him on an almost daily basis for – what – two years, I suppose.'

'Yes?'

'I got to know him quite well in that time, although . . . '

'Although what?'

'He was a very private person – never said much. Didn't give

154

anything away about himself, if you know what I mean.'

'Not exactly – no.' Tipper wanted details.

'Well he never talked about himself. Never mentioned his family, or domestic things. Most people working together will bore everyone else with trivia, like burst waterpipes, or their children's illnesses – that sort of thing. But Geoffrey never mentioned anything like that. He seemed to live in a vacuum; very much the technician.'

'Did you ever meet socially?'

'Good heavens no!'

'Why so emphatic?'

'Firstly, I suppose, because he was my boss,' said Craven, 'and secondly you never felt you could ask him – couldn't imagine him sitting round your dinner table or spending a night at the theatre. Pity really, because he always gave the impression of being a lonely man.'

'Was he happily married?'

'As far as I know, but he never mentioned his wife. I suppose he had one.'

'Yes, he did,' said Tipper. 'Children?' Tipper knew the answer to that, too.

'No idea – he never mentioned any, but then I've already said that he never discussed domestic things. To be perfectly honest I only knew that he lived in Surrey because he was late for the office one day, and seemed to feel that he owed us an explanation. It was a meeting that he'd arranged, and he wasn't there. He came in and said something about trains from Guildford being delayed. That's all he said, and then looked as though he wished he hadn't.' Craven hesitated. 'He was very self-effacing, you know; the epitome of a Security Service officer. Very mild-mannered – bland features. You never quite knew whether he was there or not. Eminently forgettable is, I suppose, the best way of describing him.'

'Do you think that he could have worked for the KGB?' It was a stark, ruthless question that Gaffney posed.

'Good lord, no – absolutely out of the question.'

'You seem very certain,' said Gaffney. 'Why?'

Craven wavered a little before coming up with an answer

that was not really an answer at all. 'Well, he was . . . he was too English!'

Gaffney smiled to himself. They always got it the wrong way round. He recalled a lecture he had attended in his early days as a Special Branch officer when one of his seniors, who had been involved peripherally in the arrest of Gordon Lonsdale, talked about the reaction of the spy's neighbours. They could not believe that the friendly Canadian business man they knew so well could have been a Russian spy. What they should have been asking was how KGB Colonel Konon Molody could have duped them into believing that he was a friendly Canadian business man.

'I have been asked by your Director-General,' said Gaffney, changing the drift of the interrogation yet again, 'to look into the apparent leak that resulted in the escape of Nikitin, Gesschner and Dickson, and that will necessitate some fairly probing questioning.' Craven nodded. 'Setting aside the first two for a minute, what exactly did you know of the Armitage – Dickson case?'

'Very little. Geoffrey briefed us – Selby, Patrick Hughes, Jim Anderson, Fred Weston and me – but told us very little— '

Tipper touched Gaffney's arm. 'May I?' he asked. He knew the dangers of interrupting at a delicate point in an interrogation, but Gaffney nodded.

'I noticed just then that when you were listing the other four members of the team you referred to each by his Christian name and his surname – except for Selby. Why was that?'

Craven looked momentarily flummoxed. 'Er – I don't know really.'

'Do you not like Selby?' Tipper persisted.

'No, it's not that, it's just that I don't know him awfully well.'

'I'm beginning to think that none of you knew the others awfully well.'

'No, that's not true. But Selby's different.' Tipper bit back the obvious retort. 'He's not married, and his interests are different. He has strange tastes, and— '

'You mean he's a snob.'

Craven looked pained, but eventually admitted it. 'Yes, I suppose so.'

'And?'

'Well for one thing he used to boast about his Cambridge education, as though he was the only person in the world ever to have been there and got a degree. He probably was the only one in his family.'

'Bitchy!' said Tipper.

'It's true. I got sick of him going on about it. I went to Sandhurst, but I didn't find it necessary to tell everyone. And he never hesitated to tell us when he'd been to a concert, or to something that he thought was a bit above the rest of us.'

'Did he ever boast about women?' asked Tipper mildly.

Craven appeared to give that question some thought. 'No,' he said with some naïveté.

'Was he a queer, then?'

Craven appeared stunned by the question. 'I don't know. Why do you ask?'

'Very simply,' said Tipper, 'because I'd like to know.It may have some bearing. Generally speaking it is easier to apply pressure to sexual deviants who are in sensitive posts than to other people. It has happened before, you know.'

'Yes, I know. I'd never thought about it, to tell you the truth.'

'You're married, Mr Craven?'

Craven smiled. 'Yes,' he said. 'But you'd know that, wouldn't you. I married when I was in the army in Germany. My wife's name is Anna, née Kurz – illegitimate daughter of Sophie Kurz of Paderborn. And every time I've told that to a vetting officer, his eyes have lighted up.'

Gaffney laughed. He had been wondering whether Craven had a sense of humour, but now it looked as though he had. 'I'll bet they did. Children?'

'No, unfortunately, but that's a genetic problem which we're trying to do something about.'

'Let's go back to the Dickson case. You said that you were briefed by Geoffrey Hodder, but that he told you very little.'

'That's right. It was almost as if he was afraid to tell anyone anything. They tend to get a bit like that in the Security Service after a few years. They're terribly secretive about things which aren't secret at all. I suppose it becomes a habit. But on this occasion, Geoffrey was worse than usual. He really only gave us a very sketchy outline. It was something like the fact that there was an army officer suspected of passing information and that there might be an arrest very soon.'

'If that was all there was, why did he bother at all?'

'It was a courtesy more than anything else, I think, and he wanted to make sure that we weren't tied up in anything else when the job broke.'

'Well he'd know that anyway, wouldn't he? He was in charge of the section, after all.'

'Yes, that's true. I must say that I found it a little odd, because on the previous jobs he'd always been fairly forthcoming – giving us a bit of background, even about things that weren't to affect us directly. But this time – well, it was as though he'd been told to keep it to a minimum because of what had happened last time – the last two times.' He corrected himself and paused. 'He certainly looked as though he was under a lot of strain. I wondered whether he'd been spoken to about it – you know, by the DG or someone like that.'

'What's your speciality, Mr Craven?' asked Gaffney.

Craven looked uncertain. 'My speciality?'

'I understand from the enquiries I've made, that each of you is specialised in some way.'

'Did your informant happen to mention that his speciality was modern languages and fluency in Russian, by any chance?' Craven smiled.

Gaffney laughed. 'I never disclose my sources, Mr Craven.'

'It's not that clearly defined. We can always find someone who can come up with the answers. As far as I'm concerned, I suppose I could have found my way through the labyrinth of military organisation – speak the language, if you like – but only on this Armitage case. Anyway, there are quite a few ex-services people here. Of course, you do have a few real specialists – locksmiths, code-breakers, that sort of thing – and I suppose that the Arabists would want to be seen as experts; they always regard themselves as a race apart.'

'Fred Weston's the name. They tell me you want to see me. Mr Gaffney, is it?' He was over six feet, and broad-shouldered, with a bluff, round face that made him appear more like a farmer than an intelligence officer, and he had entered the room with his hand outstretched. 'We've met before.'

'Yes – John Gaffney.' It was a firm grip that Weston had. 'And this is Harry Tipper.'

'Pleased to meet you.' Weston sat down and held up a stubby pipe. 'D'you mind?' he asked.

'Please do.' Gaffney took out his packet of cigars and lighted one.

'I suppose you're here about Hodder and the Dickson business?'

'D'you see a connection, then, Mr Weston?'

'Call me Fred. No, I don't see a connection. Just assume there has to be one, that's all.'

'I'd better show you the DG's letter of authority— '

Weston held up his hand. 'Don't bother. I'll answer your questions.' He laughed. 'We've got no bloody secrets left here. One or two more won't hurt.'

'How well did you know Geoffrey Hodder, Fred?'

'Well enough. We've both been in the service for donkey's years. Mind you he was typical of the old school – wouldn't give you the time of day till he'd checked it with the DG for clearance.' He chuckled. 'I'm a bit different. Seen it all before. The panic and the looking over shoulders; the ad hoc conferences in the corridor – all that. Get fed up with it, tell you the truth. I'll be glad to retire.'

'When will that be?'

'Another ten years yet, God help me. Unless I can get early retirement.'

'We spoke to Douglas Craven this morning. He said that Geoffrey Hodder kept himself very much to himself.'

'Yes, well he would with Craven – jumped-up little pillock.'

'I take it you don't like him?' asked Gaffney with a smile.

'Don't like him or dislike him, as a matter of fact. He's just there – a bloody nonentity.' Weston fiddled with his pipe and replaced it in his mouth. 'He's typical of the new breed. Started off in the army, but didn't get anywhere. Comes in here thinking he knows it all – lording it about the place just because he was an officer. Me – I was a corporal in the air force. National Service.' He blew a cloud of smoke into the air. 'This business with Geoff – what happened there? Commit suicide did he?'

'Why do you say that?'

'Well he was dead worried about this Dickson thing. Mind you, he'd been worried before that, what with Nikitin and – ' He paused. ' – the East German, er – '

'Gesschner.'

'That's the fellow. I think he felt some personal responsibility for them going off course.'

'Was he justified in thinking that?'

'Search me. He was in charge, so I suppose he felt something. But you can worry too much in this job. Then there was his home life . . . '

'What about it?'

'He'd been divorced, you know.'

'Oh?' Gaffney pretended he hadn't known that.

'Oh yes. Quite a to-do by all accounts. Bit messy is the expression, I think.'

'How did you know that? Did he tell you?'

Weston smiled and shook his head. 'No, not Geoffrey. But you hear things, you know. Always been a bit of a listener, me.' That came as a surprise to Gaffney; Weston had done nothing but talk since he had entered the room. 'Hotbed of gossip, this place. You hear these little chits of typists nattering in the lifts and in the canteen. Well in our job you get into the habit of eavesdropping – bit like your business, I suppose.' Gaffney wasn't sure whether that was flattery or condescension, took it for the former, with a leavening of ignorance. 'You know what it's like. Somebody knows somebody whose auntie lives in the next village. Only trouble is it gets a bit distorted – send three-and-fourpence, I'm going to a dance, sort of set-up. But by all accounts, wife number one caught him in bed with she who is now wife number two.' Weston stopped to laugh – a deep rumble. 'I must say I find it hard to believe of old Geoffrey. Still they say there's a bit of Hyde in all us Jekylls.'

'Wouldn't that have affected his vetting, though?' asked Gaffney.

'Not really – gave it a hiccup; a bit of a murmur, as you might say. May even have cost him a promotion, but you can't tell.'

'Do you think Hodder could have been the mole?'

'No!'

'You seem firm on that?'

'As firm as I can be. I look at it this way. If you're giving away the firm's recipes, you aren't going to look as worried about it as he was, not unless you're a bloody good actor, are you?'

'Unless he was under pressure.'

'Unlikely in this business. We all know the rules. If you slip up – you know, moneywise, or a bit of adultery – and get caught at it, you see the DG and confess. You might lose your job, but it's a bloody sight better than losing twenty-five years of your freedom. Leastways, that's the theory. We all know the way the Russians work – Christ, we should. Know the sort of pressure they exert – seen it dozens of times. Still – ' he paused, ' – there's always one, I suppose. But Geoffrey Hodder – no, I don't somehow see him as a mole. Course that's not much help to you, John, is it? You've got to have evidence.'

Gaffney nodded. 'Yes, I'm afraid that hearsay, helpful though it can sometimes be, is not really of much assistance in the long run.'

'Well if there's any way I can help . . . ' Weston sat upright on the hard chair, knees apart and hands resting lightly on them; it gave him the appearance of a large, friendly bear.

'Have you any ideas? Who would have known enough – who could have been the agent?'

'We can all speculate, but that's no help. No, John, quite frankly there isn't anyone.'

'What about Selby?' It was Tipper riding his favourite hobby-horse again.

Weston shifted forward, placing his elbows on his knees and loosely linking his fingers between them. 'I'll be quite honest with you,' he said. 'I think Master Selby's a bloody queer, and I don't like queers. But frankly I don't think he's intelligent enough to be a mole.'

'But he's a Cambridge graduate . . . '

'You don't have to be intelligent to get a degree,' said Weston. 'Just a slogger. And I should know – I've got one.'

'What in?' asked Gaffney.

'Geography,' said Weston, and then he grinned. 'That's how I know my way about.'

'But surely, if Selby's a homosexual, he'd never have got clearance.'

Weston grinned again. 'Don't you believe it. I've known a few – here what's more.' He waved a hand airily around the office. 'But it's another thing to prove it. And it doesn't follow that just because you aren't married you're queer. It worries them though. I was single for seven years between marriages, and they started to look at me a bit askance. That wasn't too bad; it was when the other unmarried blokes started looking at me I really got the wind up.' He rumbled his deep laugh again. 'I think it worried Geoffrey a bit— '

'What, your not being married?'

'God no – Selby not being married. I think that's why he never told him much. Never trusted him – and neither do I, but in my case it's probably because I hate his guts, pompous little prat.'

Chapter Twelve

Jim Anderson was down-to-earth. He was forty years of age, had a normal wife and two normal children. 'I heard you'd been talking to people in the office,' he said. 'About these jobs that have been going wrong, is it?'

Gaffney nodded. 'Yes,' he said. 'Is there anything you can add?'

Anderson shook his head glumly. 'No, not really. I suppose you must think there's a mole in the outfit somewhere.'

'What do you think, Mr Anderson?'

'Well I must admit it looks a bit that way, happening three times, but I can't immediately think of anyone – but then you never can, can you?'

'How much did you know of the last operation, the Armitage – Dickson affair?'

'Not much. Nothing had really happened – then suddenly it had all gone haywire – over – finished.'

'What did Geoffrey Hodder tell you?'

'Only that there was a job on, that was about all. We were really on stand-by, just in case. There's nothing abnormal about that. You get these things every so often. Half the time nothing ever comes of them, and frankly I thought that's what had happened this time. I was quite surprised to hear about the arrest, but again that's not unusual. After all it's you blokes who take care of that side of it for us, isn't it? I wasn't sorry, really. There are times I get fed up with this job. 'Fraid I can't develop the wild enthusiasm the others manage. You'd think they were all James Bonds, the way they scuttle about whispering in corners, or being terribly secretive as though they're doing something frightfully important. And what is it at the end of the day? In nine cases out of ten it's a load of rubbish. I don't mean the spy jobs of course – I'm talking about garnering odd snippets of information, and when you analyse them it's nonsense.'

'You sound a bit disillusioned, Mr Anderson.'

'Not really, no. But there are times when I wish that this lot wouldn't take themselves so damned seriously. They ponce about late at the office with bits of paper; you'd think that this country was on the verge of revolution to hear some of them talk. All I want to do is get home. D'you know I'm trying to rebuild my kitchen? I'm swinging the whole thing round, putting a run of cupboards right along one wall, and putting the sink-unit under the window with a— '

Gaffney held up his hand with a smile. 'I'm sure you have a lot to do, Mr Anderson, but can we just get back to the point.'

Anderson laughed, and ran a hand round his chin. 'Sorry,' he said. 'One of my passions, DIY; that and jazz.'

'What we're trying to discover,' continued Gaffney, indicating Tipper with a sweep of his hand, 'is why Geoffrey Hodder should have died.'

'That was a bit of a shock. I must admit that he'd looked a bit off colour lately— '

'In what way?'

'Difficult to say. I suppose he'd been a bit introverted – more so than usual; never very forthcoming was Geoffrey, but I never thought he was the sort to take his own life. That is what happened, isn't it? Nobody seemed quite sure.'

'We don't know.' Gaffney perpetuated the myth. So far he had found that the suggestion of a mystery about Hodder's death had a sobering effect, made people sit up and take notice, and wonder. 'The main reason for our being here is to investigate Geoffrey Hodder's death.'

'But I thought you were investigating the leaks.'

'What leaks?'

Anderson looked around helplessly. 'But everyone knows—'

'Knows what?'

'You said you were here to enquire into the leaks.'

Gaffney shook his head. 'No, Mr Anderson. You raised it. You asked if I was here about the jobs that have been going wrong. That's the phrase you used, I think. I just nodded. But perhaps there's a connection. What do you think?'

'They're a nervous bunch here at the best of times,' said Anderson, 'but when things like that start happening, they get to looking over their shoulders – we all do, I suppose – wondering. You start to ask yourself questions, and stop trusting each other. It's pretty demoralising. You look at people, thinking that it might be him – or her.'

'What d'you think of Selby, Mr Anderson?'

'Why d'you ask about him, in particular?' Anderson looked sharply at the detective.

'No reason,' lied Gaffney. 'He was a member of the team, that's all.'

'Well I'll be quite frank with you, Mr Gaffney, I don't like him. He's a pompous arse; thinks he's so much better than everyone else. Well it doesn't cut any ice with me. There are a few like him here. Just because they've had a superior sort of education they think they can lord it over everyone else.'

'Is that the only reason?'

'Yes – that and the doubts I've got about his masculinity.'

'You mean you think he's homosexual?' asked Tipper.

'Yes – not to put too fine a point on it.'

'Why do you think that?'

Anderson seemed puzzled by the question. 'Well, you've only got to look at him to see that he's a bloody pansy.'

'He's been positively vetted.'

'Pah!' Anderson dismissed that. 'So were Burgess, Maclean, Philby, Blunt, Blake . . . ' He counted them off on his fingers. 'And there are plenty more – you know that, Mr Gaffney.'

Gaffney had to admit that he had a point. 'But if there had been any proof of homosexuality, he wouldn't have been cleared – wouldn't be here, in this job.'

'I wouldn't bank on it. You know how the system works. Anyone who's refused clearance can ask for a hearing by the three wise men – the Security Tribunal. Then the vetting people have to put up or shut up. I tell you, Mr Gaffney,

165

they've got to have a cast iron case before they'll risk it.'

'I'm afraid that that still doesn't make Selby a homosexual.'

'He's not married, though, is he.'

Gaffney smiled. 'A lot of people aren't married. That doesn't necessarily make them queer, does it?'

'No, but he's effeminate as well – and he likes weird music.'

'So does my chief inspector; but how did you know?'

'How did I know what?'

'That he likes early music?'

'He's always bragging about it, boasting – giving the impression that he's superior to everyone else.'

'What you're really saying is that you don't like him, and because he looks down at you, you've decided he's a poof. That's it, isn't it?'

'No – not at all.' But Gaffney knew that that was probably the reason. Anderson was an ordinary sort of chap, doing what he saw as an ordinary sort of job. He couldn't abide the gratingly arrogant airs of educational snobs like Selby. The simplest way of dismissing them was to describe them as homosexuals. Gaffney thought he might be right, but for entirely different reasons.

'Did you get the impression that no one likes our Mr Selby, Harry?'

Tipper nodded. 'I don't bloody well like him either, sir.'

'However, just because he is universally disliked does not, of itself, give us any reason for assuming that he's a mole.'

'No,' said Tipper. 'Pity, that.'

'What we've really got,' said Gaffney, looking at the window and noting that the venetian blinds needed cleaning, 'is a bloody great load of nothing.'

'That's certainly how much most of them seemed to know in advance about this latest job.'

'The irony of it is that the only bloke who apparently knew all about all three jobs is Hodder – and he topped himself.'

'QED!' said Tipper, sinking down into Gaffney's easy chair and staring at the ceiling.

'Pardon?'

'Perhaps that's the answer. Two jobs go wrong. A third comes up – that's a stumer. You set it up, but he doesn't know that. But straight afterwards you have him up here and give him a going over. Result: goes home, panics, and tops himself.'

Gaffney laughed. 'Great! But just supposing what you say is right. He's working for the Russians, and warns them off in the first two cases. After the second one he knows the heat's on. What would you do, in his place? You'd tell your masters to cool it for a bit, wouldn't you. If they'd got a man like Hodder placed in MI5 they wouldn't want to sacrifice him for a twopenny-ha'penny job like Armitage – Dickson. If – and it's a big if – if he was a plant, he'd have been there for a long time – a sleeper.'

'Could they have turned him, guv'nor?'

'I doubt they'd take the risk, Harry. A long-term sleeper is the best bet. With a plant – in a place like Five – they'd never have known whether he was doubling, and the Soviets aren't terribly keen on being had over.' He sighed. 'Perhaps the answer lies in his private life. From what we've heard from his colleagues, he doesn't sound the type of man to get involved in some village sex scandal, and yet Mrs Bates, the PC's wife, seemed to have all the facts at her fingertips. And then there's what the army said about him being a womaniser.'

'Yeah, but everybody's human, guv'nor, and if a woman like Julia Hodder made a play for him I shouldn't think she'd have met much resistance. She certainly wouldn't from me, I can tell you.'

Gaffney laughed. 'I'd sort of worked that out for myself, Harry.'

'So what do we do now? See the Harrises?'

'Yes, Harry, I think we do.'

The Harrises lived in an elegant house on the outskirts of Hitchin. Dick Harris explained that he had been promoted about fifteen months previously, and transferred to the firm's offices at Welwyn Garden City. The journey from Surrey had

proved too tiring and time-consuming, and somewhat reluctantly he and his family had moved to their present house.

'But you intrigue me,' said Harris as they settled in the
spacious sitting room. 'Why do the police want to talk
to me?'

Gaffney had telephoned him earlier in the day but had
declined to tell him what his enquiry was about, although he
had assured him, as the police always had to with law-abiding
citizens, that he had done nothing wrong. Gaffney had particularly wanted to talk to Harris's wife as well; consequently
it had had to be an evening visit, something which pleased
neither Gaffney nor Tipper, but which they shrugged off as
one of the constant inevitabilities of police duty.

'I think you should offer our guests a drink, Dick,' said
his wife.

'I'm sorry . . . ' He started to get out of his chair.

Gaffney stayed him with a gesture. 'No, thank you very
much.'

'Coffee, then?' Tina Harris was not going to give up.

'I don't want to put you to any trouble,' said Gaffney.
What he meant was that he wanted to get home as soon as
possible.

'It's no trouble,' she said, 'it's already on. It'll only take
a couple of seconds.'

'I want to talk to you about Geoffrey Hodder,' said Gaffney,
when they were finally settled with cups of coffee.

Harris laughed. 'What's old Geoffrey been up to?'

'He's dead,' said Gaffney.

Harris placed his coffee cup carefully on a side-table.
'Good God!' he said.

His wife put her hand to her mouth. 'How awful. What
happened? Was it an accident?'

'No,' said Gaffney, 'it was not.'

They waited for him to elaborate, and when he didn't,
Dick Harris asked, 'You don't mean he was murdered?' He
could think of no other reason why a detective chief superintendent from Scotland Yard should have wanted to come
and see him.

168

'I don't know, quite simply, Mr Harris. That is something I have been asked to find out.'

'Well what happened?' asked Tina Harris again.

There was no secret in that; it had been in the newspapers, albeit a brief article, and Gaffney was vaguely surprised that the Harrises hadn't spotted it. They looked like people who read newspapers. 'His body was found in the public toilets at Waterloo Station.'

'God Almighty!' said Harris, and shook his head.

Tina Harris stood up and poured more coffee without enquiring whether anybody wanted it. 'Poor Julia,' she said. 'I must give her a ring.' She paused, looking at Gaffney. 'I suppose that's all right?'

'Perfectly all right,' said Gaffney.

'And you think he might have been murdered?'

'At the moment we don't know. The pathologist is not entirely happy about the cause of death. They're very careful people, pathologists, and until he's satisfied, he won't say. In the meantime, I have to treat the death as suspicious.' He spread his hands. 'Of course, it may well turn out to be innocent; what I mean is, he may have committed suicide.'

Harris looked thoughtful and then shook his head slowly. 'I was about to say I wouldn't have thought so,' he said.

'But?'

'But, on second thoughts, I'm not so sure. He wasn't a very happy man, you know.'

'You knew him quite well?'

'We both did. We lived there for about, what, ten years?' He looked at his wife for confirmation.

'Yes, all of that,' she said. 'We actually knew his second wife better than his first.'

'She must have arrived in the village at about the same time as yourselves, then.'

'Yes. Julia bought Raven Cottage. Nice little place. She had money of her own. Well, I presume she had.' Dick Harris took up the story again.

'How did you meet her?' asked Gaffney.

'We held a house-warming – we love giving parties – and

we invited just about everyone in the village: well, our sort of people, if you know what I mean.'

'He sounds an awful snob, doesn't he?' said his wife casually.

'You know what I mean, darling.'

'And Julia Simpson was one of your sort of people?' asked Gaffney.

Tina Harris smiled tolerantly. 'Have you met her?' she asked. Gaffney nodded. 'Well,' she continued, 'you'll have seen why Dick thought she was one of his sort of people.'

Harris looked embarrassed. 'It was more a case of feeling sorry for her,' he said.

'I gather from what I've heard so far that you two were instrumental in bringing Geoffrey Hodder and Julia together,' said Gaffney.

'I suppose we were, in a way,' said Tina Harris. 'Quite innocently, of course. Actually, Dick's quite right; we did feel sorry for her. She'd arrived in the village on her own, and there's no doubt that she's an attractive woman; you'll know that as you've seen her. You could see the women shielding their menfolk protectively.' She glanced at her husband, but he avoided her gaze. 'She must have been about twenty-five or so then, when she first arrived there, and I suppose you could say that she flaunted herself a bit. In the summer she would stroll about in very short white shorts.' She laughed. 'It was evident that she was being pretty well ostracised by most of the women, so when we decided to have a party, we invited her – more out of devilment than sympathy, if I'm honest – just to see what the reaction would be. On reflection it wasn't a very clever thing to have done,' she added wistfully.

'And what was the reaction?'

'Oh, very polite; a bit stilted, I suppose; but then we were new as well.' She flicked her long, brown hair off her collar and leaned back in her chair. 'It was rather amusing, really, watching the wives watching their husbands. The moment any of them spoke to Julia, the wife would home in very quickly.' She paused and looked again at her husband. 'Except for . . . what was her name, Geoffrey's first wife?'

'Elizabeth,' said Gaffney.

170

'Yes, of course. Yes, except for Elizabeth. She didn't seem to worry, but then you only had to look at him to see why.'

'Oh?'

'He was the classic example of the domesticated, henpecked husband. I got the impression that he wouldn't have dared step out of line. Ironic, isn't it?'

'You mean that Elizabeth was overbearing?'

For a moment or two the Harrises looked thoughtful, weighing up the question. 'Well – ' they both said together. Tina smiled and gave way.

'The best way of describing her was coarse,' said Dick Harris. His wife nodded. 'It was her very coarseness that made him appear afraid of offending her,' he continued. 'It wasn't so much that she might have taken him to task, but that she would do so in a coarse way.'

'I can vouch for that,' said Tina Harris. 'I'd only been talking to her for about five minutes. There was quite a crowd there— '

'Cost a bloody fortune,' said Harris, interrupting.

His wife ignored him and carried straight on. 'I was trying to pair everybody off – in my mind,' she added hurriedly, and smiled. 'And I asked her who her husband was. She pointed to Geoffrey, who was actually talking to Julia at that moment, and said, It's him over there. I nodded and she went on, saying something like, Talking to that hussy – makes you laugh, doesn't it? Then she said, He'll be no good to the likes of her – he's no good to me. Then she held up her little finger, and said, That's about the size of it.' Tina Harris was clearly embarrassed at repeating the story, but obviously thought it relevant enough to make the effort.

'That about sums her up,' said Harris. 'That was the way she used to talk. She was dowdy, too. I don't mean scruffy – she was immaculate – immaculate but unimaginative . . . ' He paused, then: 'Even if Elizabeth had worn exactly the same clothes as Julia, she wouldn't have looked at all attractive. It's difficult to describe, and it's odd really, because she had quite a good figure. Mannish, that's the

171

word. The one thing that Elizabeth Hodder didn't have was sex-appeal.'

'So the first temptation that appeared and he was off?'

Harris nodded. 'So it seemed, but frankly I wouldn't have thought that he had the guts.' He took a cigarette case from his pocket and offered it to the two policemen before lighting a cigarette for himself; his wife obviously didn't smoke. 'I think that's the mistake that Elizabeth made. I reckon that she was actually challenging her husband, daring him, and that's why she invited Julia Simpson to dinner. I honestly don't know why Julia accepted; I wouldn't have thought that she could possibly have fancied old Geoffrey, not in a million years; not her type at all. Strange really, the way things turned out. I suppose it was the first hand of friendship that had been extended to her. Apart from our party, of course.'

'Did anyone else invite her to dinner, or to parties?' asked Gaffney.

Tina Harris laughed. 'They didn't really have the time. It was fairly evident to casual observers of the social scene that something was going on between Julia and Geoffrey. How Elizabeth didn't find out I'll never know.' She reflected on that. 'Perhaps she did, and didn't care. Maybe the sexual thing between her and her husband was her doing and not his. She might have been quite content to let him have a fling with young Julia, knowing that he hadn't the guts to walk out on her. Not a great decision maker, Geoffrey.'

'I understand that Elizabeth got a phone call one day,' said Gaffney.

Tina Harris looked puzzled for a second or two, then she smiled. 'Oh, *the* phone call, you mean? Yes, that put her on the spot. All the while she knew but didn't know, if you see what I mean, she might have been happy to let it run on. But once she'd got that phone call, she either had to follow it up, or display the fact that she didn't care. Well, no woman likes doing that, and her problem was that she didn't know who the caller was, so she didn't know who else knew. Tricky, that. There was only one thing left for her to do if she was to retain any dignity, and that was to confront them.'

172

Tipper, who had been sitting quietly and making the occasional note, looked up. 'Who d'you think made that telephone call, Mrs Harris?' he asked.

Tina Harris glanced at her husband. 'Julia, without a doubt,' she said. 'I think she did it as a way of getting back at Elizabeth for her coarse remarks and her innuendoes about Geoffrey. It was a strange sort of revenge: knowing for certain that Elizabeth knew that her husband was being unfaithful. I don't think that Julia thought it would ever come to divorce, though; but it did, and she was stuck with him. They got married soon after that, and Elizabeth pushed off somewhere; I don't know where . . . '

'Godalming,' said Tipper.

Tina Harris nodded. 'But Geoffrey was a changed man. He'd stop and chat, and was much happier than I'd ever seen him before.'

'And what about Julia?' asked Gaffney, 'Did she seem happy with her lot?'

'I don't know, really. She didn't seem to change. Still the bright vivacious girl she'd been when we first met her. What was more to the point, she was accepted. The women started talking to her. She'd become one of them, you see. Married, and no longer a threat, I suppose. Apart from anything else, I don't think they much liked Elizabeth. Funny creatures, married women.'

'True!' said Harris.

His wife laughed and switched her gaze back to Gaffney. 'We got to know her a lot better after that. They would come to our parties, and she and Geoffrey came to dinner a few times; and we went there.'

'How did they behave?'

'To each other, you mean?' Gaffney nodded. 'Oh,' said Tina Harris, 'blissfully happy, or so it seemed. Geoffrey very attentive; Julia very loving. It seemed a perfect match.'

'Seemed?'

'As far as one could tell, yes. It's always difficult to assess other people's marriages. Only the partners really know what it's like, but on the surface theirs appeared to be okay.'

173

'Did Julia ever talk about herself?' asked Tipper. 'Mention anything about her past life? All we've learned so far is that she suddenly appeared at Raven Cottage one day, and the story goes on from there.'

'As much as anyone ever does,' said Harris. 'She mentioned one night over dinner that she'd been brought up in Nigeria – at least her early life – first three or four years, but that she'd been back since.'

'What had her job been? Did she mention that? Was she qualified at anything?' asked Tipper.

Harris shook his head. 'No, don't think so. She did say that she'd been working over there, with a charity, I believe. It came up because we were discussing a news item that had been on television that evening – something about floods, or a famine – and she mentioned that she'd been there, had worked in the area helping to distribute relief. It was only a fleeting reference, then someone went on to talk about something else. Not really the sort of thing to chat about over dinner – the starving millions in Africa – particularly when you're just opening your fourth bottle of Côtes du Rhône. . . . '

Gaffney did a bit of mental arithmetic. 'You must have lived there for about nine years after they got married, before you moved up here; would that be right?'

'That's about right, yes,' said Harris.

'And did the marriage seem to go along in much the same way as it had started? No deterioration, apart from the sort of settlement you get once the novelty wears off?'

'Not even that. They seemed to be as happy the day we moved as the day they got married. Why d'you ask?'

Gaffney ignored the question, appearing not to hear it. 'Did Geoffrey ever mention his job? Did you know what he did for a living?'

'Never,' said Harris. 'I don't think I can recall him ever talking about it the whole time we knew them.'

'I think he was a civil servant,' said Tina Harris. 'I asked Julia one day. I forget now why I asked; it wasn't nosiness. I think we'd got some tickets – ' She stopped. 'I remember,' she said, looking at her husband. 'It was when you got those

174

tickets for Ascot, d'you remember, from Frank Jamieson?'
Harris nodded. 'We asked them if they could come. Actually
I asked Julia, asked if her husband could get a day off mid-
week. It was then she said something about his being a civil
servant, and that it was always very difficult. We went on our
own eventually.'

'They had two cars, though,' said Harris.

Gaffney raised his eyebrows. 'Is that significant?'

'It is if he was a civil servant. Civil servants don't get
company cars.'

'I think she must have had money of her own,' said Tina
Harris. 'Don't forget she'd bought Raven Cottage when she
arrived, and sold it again when she got married. I don't think
she was short of a pound or two.'

'You haven't asked me about enemies,' said Harris.

'Enemies? Why, did they have any?'

'I don't think so,' said Harris.

'Well why . . . ?'

'I thought you always asked if people had enemies when
you were investigating a murder.'

Gaffney laughed. 'I didn't say I was investigating a murder,
but in my experience, Mr Harris, people are not generally
killed by their enemies. They are either murdered by complete strangers, or by people they know rather well. However, it
could well be that Geoffrey Hodder committed suicide, as I
said earlier.'

Harris shook his head. 'I still can't see Geoffrey as a
suicide,' he said. 'Not married to Julia. She wouldn't have
pushed him to kill himself, although she might just have
killed him in bed.'

'Dick!' Tina Harris sounded scandalised, but Gaffney reckoned that she had done so for his benefit; she looked quite a
sexy woman herself.

Harris laughed. 'These gentlemen are policemen, darling.
They don't shock easily.' He looked at Gaffney. 'That's right,
isn't it?'

'Yes,' said Gaffney in resigned tones. 'I'm afraid there's
very little left either to amaze or excite us.' He eased himself

out of the deep armchair with some difficulty. 'We've taken up too much of your time,' he said. 'Thank you for talking to us.'

Harris closed the front door as the two policemen walked down the driveway, and turned to his wife. 'Can't say I'm surprised,' he said, 'if he did commit suicide.'

'Nor me,' said his wife.

'I don't think they were telling the whole truth, guv'nor,' said Tipper.

'Nor do I,' said Gaffney, 'but I don't know why they weren't. It was almost as if they'd rehearsed it; it was too polished. I think they must have heard about it from someone.'

'Didn't want to get involved, perhaps; the usual cry of the law-abiding, stalwart citizen.'

'Involved in what? A suicide?'

'They think it's a murder, and I think it comes as no surprise to them; which is interesting, but probably totally irrelevant.'

Chapter Thirteen

John Carfax was a rotund man. He was balding, and wore heavy horn-rimmed spectacles with wide arms that pressed into his fleshy head. His suit needed cleaning and his waist-coat was too short, permitting an expanse of striped shirt to be pushed out above his waistband by a stomach that had refused to accept the strictures of a suit bought originally for a lesser figure.

He returned the Director-General's letter of authority to Gaffney. 'I have to say, John, that I disagree with the DG. A few years ago an investigation into the service's activities by an outside agency would have been unthinkable.'

'Perhaps a few years ago it would not have been necessary,' said Gaffney mildly.

'Mmm, maybe so.' Carfax sniffed. 'Nevertheless,' he said, 'I find it distasteful and . . . still unnecessary.' He laid his podgy hands on his desk top and examined his fingernails. 'There is nothing to investigate. Naturally, I have looked into it; there's nothing to discover.'

'I heard that you'd conducted an enquiry of sorts.'

'Oh? Who told you that?'

'Who told me doesn't matter, but I understand that you were satisfied with your findings?'

'No, I was not, but the plain fact is that I was unable to find out more.'

'Have you any private thoughts about it? For instance, Geoffrey Hodder, whom I interviewed just before his death, maintains that he told no one the full details of the Dickson affair, and that, I gather, included you.' Gaffney looked searchingly at the other man.

'YYes,' said Carfax. 'But even in an organisation like this one, people do have to be told certain things. The merest indication that an army officer was involved would be sufficient information for the KGB to act upon.'

That interested Gaffney; it was the conclusion he had reached when Hodder had told him that he had given those bare details to Carfax. And now Carfax himself was saying the same thing; not that it took too much working out.

'When did Hodder tell you about Armitage and Dickson?'

Carfax thought about that. 'About fourish, I suppose, just as he was leaving for the venue at Teddington.' He leaned forward and thumbed through his desk diary. 'I thought so,' he said. 'I remember it now, I was outside the DG's office, talking to Cutty Wilson – ' He glanced up. 'Cuthbert Wilson is head of— '

'Yes,' said Gaffney, interrupting, 'I know Cutty. What happened, exactly?'

'Hodder drew me to one side and told me that he was just off to Teddington with your people to arrest an army officer and, hopefully, the contact.'

'What did you do then?'

'Rejoined Cutty and went into the DG's office. It was a heads of department meeting; we were there until about a quarter past seven.' He raised his eyes to the ceiling. 'Bloody meetings,' he said. Then he beamed. 'So you see, John, I couldn't have told anyone, if that's what you're thinking.'

'Cutty didn't overhear any of this?'

'Certainly not. That's the way we work here; but I must say, John, that I think you're clutching at straws.'

'Didn't you find that all rather strange? Hodder sidling up to you in the corridor and whispering that he was just off to arrest a spy. Wouldn't you, as his boss, have expected to be told much sooner, and be given the full details?'

'Not really, no.' Carfax leaned back in his chair and stretched, revealing even more of his ample stomach. 'Hodder was a strange fellow, of course. . . . '

'Why "of course"?'

'He was a dark horse – '

178

'An admirable quality for an intelligence officer, I should have thought.' Gaffney smiled.

Carfax ignored that; he was a serious-minded individual. 'I knew Geoffrey for ...' He paused, calculating. 'Nigh on twenty-five years, I suppose; and yet in all that time, I didn't really know him at all.'

Gaffney thought that there would be no harm in revealing a little of what he had learned already; it might prompt the reticent Carfax into saying more. 'The chaps he was in the army with said that he was a bit of a live wire.'

'Really.' Carfax spoke flatly.

'He lived quite a high life in Berlin apparently. Always drinking, and out with women most of his spare time.'

Carfax knitted his bushy eyebrows together into a tight frown. 'You surprise me; doesn't sound like the Geoffrey Hodder I knew.'

'Or didn't know.'

'What?'

'You said that you didn't really know him at all.'

'Yes, true, but even so. If a man's an alcoholic, it shows.'

'They didn't suggest that he was that; just said that he liked a good time.'

Carfax nodded gravely. 'Wouldn't surprise me to hear that he was a bit of a Jekyll and Hyde character. He was positively vetted though – naturally.' He said it as though it was utterly foolproof, yet both he and Gaffney knew that it was far from being so. 'His divorce came as a tremendous shock to us.'

'I suppose you'd have known his wife? His first wife, of course.'

'Went to the wedding. Well we all knew her, those of us who were here at the time. She used to work for the service. In a secretarial capacity, of course.' He added the last sentence with some disdain; there was a clear demarcation in his mind between officers and the rest. 'Pleasant enough girl.'

'Did you ever meet his second wife?'

'No. I don't think anyone did – not from the office, anyway. I suspect that no one would have known about it,

179

but he had to declare it for vetting and that sort of thing.'

'Was he a womaniser?'

Carfax appeared to give that some thought. Eventually he said, 'No. No, I wouldn't have thought so.' Then he added, earnestly, 'That sort of thing's frowned on in the service, you know.'

Gaffney suppressed a laugh. 'I've no doubt; but does that stop it?'

Carfax considered the point with some care. 'Probably not, but it does tend to blight one's progress.'

'Let me frame it another way. Did you have any reason to suppose that Hodder had liaisons with other women?'

'No.' Carfax shook his head, and for the first time during the interview allowed a wintry smile to cross his face. 'Not him.'

'And yet,' said Gaffney, 'we know that he did have an affaire, with Julia Simpson, whom he later married. If he'd done it once, surely he could have done it again.'

'Oh, I think that was rather different. In my opinion, his first marriage was a mistake. She wasn't really up to much. As I said, she was a secretary. Ran after him by all accounts. Interesting that, now you mention him being a bit of a live wire. Up until his marriage – his first marriage – he was quite an amusing fellow; quite bright and lively. Mind you, he was much younger then; but marrying that girl, Elizabeth Barlow she was then, seemed to put years on him. Never the same after that.'

'What was she like – Elizabeth Barlow?'

'Strange girl. Been a nurse, I understand, but came into the service via the Ministry of Defence. Apparently nursing didn't pay very well. Always a bit dowdy; clean and smart, but never attractively turned out, if you know what I mean. Don't really know what attracted him to her. I must say it took everyone by surprise when he announced his engagement.' He shook his head. 'Never can tell, of course; I suppose she must have had something.'

'Money, perhaps?'

'Good Lord no. Well I just said that she left nursing because it didn't pay enough. Why d'you ask?'

'The house the Hodders lived in must be worth nearly a hundred and forty thousand. Seemed a bit high when you look at his rate of pay.'

'Yes, I suppose it does – now. But Geoffrey bought that house years ago, very shortly after he came out of the army; before he was married even. Wish I'd done the same thing. It was about the only bit of foresight he ever showed.'

'That sounds as though he wasn't very good at his job.'

Carfax took off his glasses and pinched the bridge of his nose. 'Frankly no. That's not to say that he was inefficient. He was adequate, but somewhat pedestrian. Never had any flair, if you know what I mean.'

'Why did he get promoted then?' asked Gaffney. He could imagine the sort of annual confidential report Carfax had written on the hapless Hodder.

Carfax spread his hands. 'These things happen,' he said. 'Because someone is reasonably capable of doing the job they have, people automatically think that they'll be able to do the next one up. Doesn't always work. In fact, sometimes it goes the other way. A chap who's not much good will shine when he's pushed up. Probably happens in the police, doesn't it?'

Gaffney nodded; he could apply that description to quite a few of his colleagues. 'He'd reached his maximum then, would you say?'

'Quite definitely. As a matter of fact, I wasn't too happy with his performance; intended to speak to the DG about it and get him moved.' He leaned forward as if to impart a confidence. 'My view of this Dickson business and the two before it, is that it was due entirely to Geoffrey Hodder's inadequacy. Personally I don't think there's a leak; just bad staff work. You've got to think it through, you see, John. One case goes wrong – Nikitin. That could be a leak. But three in a row; no one would take a chance like that. It's the opposite of what it seems. Three times is too much to indicate a traitor; no agent in the world is going to take that sort of risk of exposure, because everyone's going to suspect immediately . . . '

'That's one way of looking at it, I suppose, but it still doesn't explain Hodder's death.'

'Oh, my dear fellow, that could be explained in a variety of ways.'

Gaffney leaned back. 'Go on then.'

'Well he's got a flighty young wife— '

'I thought you'd never met her.'

Carfax looked pained. 'I am an intelligence officer of some considerable experience,' he said. 'One picks these things up.'

Gaffney gave him that. 'All right,' he said, 'but what has that to do with it?'

'Just imagine that she's playing around. It would make him a laughing stock in that village where he lives. Very serious fellow was Geoffrey; he couldn't bear that. Imagine the reaction; people sniggering behind his back. No.'

'I don't see what that has to do with his death. Are you suggesting that she killed him?'

Carfax's eyes widened. 'Is it suggested that anyone killed him? Surely he committed suicide?'

'Everyone I've spoken to automatically jumps to the conclusion that Hodder took his own life,' said Gaffney. 'But they are then unable to suggest any good reason. You're suggesting that he did so because his wife was playing around with other men.'

'Well it's happened often enough in the past.'

'I don't think so. I think you're confusing it with murder committed to take one side out of the eternal triangle. You've already dismissed that; and so, incidentally, have I.'

'Then perhaps he feared exposure.'

'Of what?'

'These three jobs going wrong.'

'Oh come now,' said Gaffney. 'You can't be serious. If everybody who was no good at his job committed suicide, the world population would plummet overnight. In my experience, inefficiency is more often than not rewarded with promotion.' He looked hard at Carfax. 'What did you learn from your investigation? Is what you're saying a result of what you discovered?'

182

'Not really, no. I didn't learn very much at all; probably no more or less than you have done.'

'Which was what?' Gaffney was beginning to tire of this cat-and-mouse conversation.

'Very simply that Hodder seemed to tell no one any of the details; at least nothing very much – '

'But enough,' said Gaffney. 'As you yourself said, the mere indication that an army officer was involved would have been sufficient, if that information was planted in the right place.'

'True, yes true. But d'you not see the difficulty – for us as investigators, I mean . . . '

Gaffney was mildly amused that Carfax had not aligned himself with the suspects. 'What do you mean?'

'All you need,' said Carfax patiently, 'is a public telephone box and the right number to ring. It's untraceable.'

'And is that the conclusion you came to?'

'Only because of the absence of any alternative. We're dealing with seasoned intelligence officers here. They know the tricks of the trade, so to speak. They are not going to arrange clandestine meetings with Russian agents in Kensington Palace Gardens, are they now? No, of course not.' He answered his own question. 'A quick telephone call and the damage is done.' He held up his hands in an attitude of surrender. 'It's as simple as that,' he said.

Not to Gaffney it wasn't. 'What form did your enquiries take?'

'Asked the usual questions. How much did you know? Who told you? Who did you tell?'

'And you were satisfied with the answers?'

'Case of having to be,' said Carfax. 'What else can one do?'

It was a good question; and it was one that Gaffney had been asking himself ever since he had been assigned the enquiry. Short of massive technical and physical surveillance, there was little more that could be done; even then it might produce nothing. Unless, of course, you got very lucky. 'What's your view of Peter Selby?' he asked, deciding on a change of tack.

Carfax smiled. 'No one seems to like him,' he said. 'But it's his unfortunate attitude, I think. He's a very capable officer. He does have this rather supercilious approach that tends to rub people up the wrong way, but he's utterly reliable. I'd stake my reputation on that. Trouble is that Hodder and people like him don't trust him; think he's homosexual . . . '

'And is he?'

'Good God no.'

'How can you be so sure? And don't say vetting,' added Gaffney with a smile.

'Oh but I do say vetting,' said Carfax. 'They're a little more particular with chaps like him— '

'Like him?'

'Thirtyish and single; particularly when they're working for the Security Service. I'm quite satisfied that he is heterosexual – and loyal.'

Gaffney shrugged. 'If you say so.' He was prepared to take Carfax's word for that. He didn't like Selby personally, but he did not have the same downright view of his sexual proclivities that Tipper seemed to adopt.

'Did Geoffrey commit suicide, by the way?' asked Carfax.

'Don't know. I'm still not satisfied, and I'm awaiting the outcome of further tests – and enquiries.'

'I hope he did,' said Carfax.

'That's an odd thing to say.'

'Not really. Suicides happen but imagine the publicity if one of our people got murdered. . . . '

Gaffney nodded. 'Yes, I can quite see that,' he said. 'Especially if he was killed by a jealous husband.'

Gaffney looked at the clock as the phone rang. 'That'll be her,' he said to Tipper. Three or four days after their visit to Hitchin, Gaffney had received a telephone call from a hesitant Tina Harris. She was going to be in London, shopping, the following day and asked if she could see Gaffney. He had arranged for her to call at the Yard.

'Would you have her brought up, please,' he said to the receptionist, and replaced the handset.

A few minutes later Mrs Harris appeared in Gaffney's office. 'You remember Chief Inspector Tipper?' he asked, as he offered her a chair.

'Yes, of course.' She smiled briefly at Tipper as she sat down and arranged herself. She looked much less confident than when they had last seen her, even allowing for the overawing effect of Scotland Yard, and played nervously with the strap of her handbag.

'This business of Geoffrey Hodder,' she began. 'It is rather important, isn't it?'

Gaffney smiled comfortingly. He had deduced that whatever Tina Harris was about to tell him had taken some fortitude. 'Yes, Mrs Harris. Unexplained deaths are always regarded by the police as extremely important,' he said quietly.

For a few seconds she sat in silence, still wrestling with herself about the wisdom of having come to see Gaffney at all. Gaffney let her sit, knowing that having come this far, she would tell him in her own time why. Finally she looked up. 'I'm afraid that my husband and I weren't entirely honest with you the other evening,' she said.

'I see.' Gaffney tried not to make it sound like an admonition. 'In what way?'

Again a silence while she summoned up the courage to say what was on her mind. 'About three years ago, my husband had an affaire with Julia Hodder.' She spoke flatly, her face emotionless.

Gaffney smiled. 'Why didn't you mention it the other night?'

'I suppose we would have done it we'd had time to think about it. But it's a bit embarrassing, and neither of us had the nerve to raise it – I suppose that's the truth of the matter. It's not taboo; we talk about it quite openly, even joke about it. You may think it's silly, but I could hardly have mentioned it first, and I suppose Dick didn't say anything in case it embarrassed me. Even so, I tried to prompt him.'

'And does your husband know that you're here now?'

'No – but I shall tell him I've been to see you.'

'How did you find out – about the affaire, I mean?'

'I had a letter – from a well-wisher.' She half smiled. 'These things happen in villages, you know. They're very parochial.'

'And what did it say – this letter?'

'Just that – that my husband was having an affaire with Julia Hodder, and I ought to know. It was actually signed "A Well-wisher" – I thought that sort of thing only happened in books.'

Gaffney nodded. 'So did I. What did you do?'

'I burned it.'

'Is that all?'

'Oh no. I had it out with Dick. It was all very civilised. I just told him that I'd had this letter, and I asked him if it was true.'

'What did he say?'

'He admitted it – to my surprise. I'd honestly thought that it was a piece of malice, without any foundation. But he said he had – called it more a wild fling than an affaire. Then he asked me if I wanted a divorce.'

'And what did you say to that?'

'I laughed, and asked him where he would go. Then I told him not to be so damned silly.'

'And?'

'He promised never to see her again.'

'And did he keep his promise?' asked Gaffney, and then added, 'I'm sorry to have to ask you that.'

She gave that some thought. 'Yes, I think so.' She spoke pensively. She'd probably never asked herself that – deliberately.

'Mrs Harris, forgive me for asking this question, because I know that to come here obviously took some courage on your part, but why did you think it important?'

She didn't react to that, looked neither surprised nor annoyed. 'Because I don't think the Hodders were as happy as they made out. It stands to reason, doesn't it? If they were idyllically happy, why should Julia have had an affaire with my husband? And if she had an affaire with him, how many other men did she have affaires with?'

'Do you know of any?'

'No, I don't, but there are other men in other places, aren't there? It didn't have to be one of our neighbours. There's another thing too. If my well-wisher wrote to me, she could have written to Geoffrey Hodder as well.'

'You say she.'

'I'm sorry – I don't quite— '

'The well-wisher – you referred to the well-wisher as she. Did you know who it was – that it was a woman?'

She shook her head and smiled. 'No. I just assumed it was a woman. Men aren't that petty, are they? It's the men who have the affaires – it's the women who complain about them.'

'Yes, Mrs Harris, but for every man who has an affaire, there's got to be a woman. . . . '

For the first time she laughed. 'Yes, I suppose so. I'd never really thought of it like that. Perhaps I've been missing something.'

Gaffney studied her and decided that he wouldn't mind having an affaire with her himself. 'When we saw you and your husband the other evening, your husband said, first of all, that Geoffrey Hodder wasn't a very happy man, but later he – and you, if I remember correctly – described him as blissfully happy. Was that a slip of the tongue?'

'Yes and no. Once the trauma of the divorce was out of the way and he married Julia, yes, he was very happy. But after about a year he seemed to decline into his old introverted self. Perhaps Julia was playing fast and loose even that early.' She looked around Gaffney's office, at the group photographs of his courses at the Detective Training School, and a later one from the Police College. Then she looked back at him, brow furrowed. 'The thing that's puzzled me all along, Mr Gaffney, is why on earth Julia should have married Geoffrey at all. She was an attractive woman; still is. She could probably have had any man she wanted. But why him? He hadn't got any money – well nothing to talk of; he must have been supporting Elizabeth and the children. He certainly wasn't good-looking, and he was quite a few years older than her. None of it makes sense – not to me, anyway.'

'Well, as you said the other night, Mrs Harris, only the partners to a marriage know all about it. There must have been something.'

'Yes, I suppose so.'

'Is there anything else you want to tell me, Mrs Harris, anything that you can remember?'

She remained in thought for some seconds before saying, 'No, I don't think so. I do hope that I haven't wasted your time?'

'No, not at all. I appreciate your having come; I know it must have taken some soul-searching.'

She smiled and held out her hand. 'Goodbye,' she said.

'What are we going to do about Jack Armitage, John?' Hussey put his hands behind his head and leaned back in his chair.

'I think we've got to leave him on ice for the time being, sir,' said Gaffney. 'He's not coming to any harm where he is.'

'Depends how our WDC's treating him,' said Hussey with a chuckle. 'He might be desperate to escape.'

Gaffney shook his head. 'It's anybody's guess with that one,' he said. 'She's a very deep young lady. But seriously, we're not a great deal further forward. Selby concerns me, but I don't think we've uncovered a spy; he's not devious enough.'

'Are any of them at the end of the day?' asked the commander.

'Don't know,' said Gaffney. 'We only know about the ones we catch. For all I know, this wimp-like attitude of his might be a pose, just to put us – and everyone else – off the scent. Incidentally, I'm going down to see Julia Hodder again, see what we can make of her the second time round. She was having it off with a neighbour, I've discovered.'

'You taking Harry Tipper?'

'Not this time. He'll be mortified, but I'm taking a woman

188

officer. Surprising what another woman will see that'll completely escape a man.'

'Good thinking, John. We have to admit that at times we don't know all the answers, except for commanders, of course.'

Claire Wentworth was a tall, slender girl of about thirty. She looked like a young business woman, but with a few extras, which was probably why she was a detective sergeant in Special Branch. 'You wanted to see me, sir?'

'Yes, Claire. Sit down, and I'll try to condense into a few minutes what is developing into a rather complicated enquiry.'

'I see, sir,' she said when he had finished. And then with a smile: 'Actually, I don't see at all, but I think I've grasped the main points.'

'Don't worry,' said Gaffney. 'With any luck, you'll pick it up as you go along.'

Gaffney had telephoned Mrs Hodder and made an appointment to see her. He did not say that he would be bringing DS Wentworth with him, however, and he presumed that Julia Hodder had dressed to be attractive to two male officers, one of whom she thought would be Tipper, whose appraising glances she had noticed last time. She was wearing the short white shorts that Mrs Bates, the local policeman's wife, had described, and a shirt that was knotted under her breasts to reveal a bare and sun-tanned midriff. Her smile vanished when she caught sight of the woman officer.

'This is Detective Sergeant Claire Wentworth, Mrs Hodder,' said Gaffney.

'Do come in,' she said, the smile returning to her face, but now a little artificial.

She led them into the sitting room and they sat down. Julia Hodder decided that she would ignore the woman detective and sat in the centre of the settee facing Gaffney.

'I understand that you had an affaire with Dick Harris,' said Gaffney without preamble.

189

Julia Hodder tensed slightly; she now understood the presence of Claire Wentworth. She laughed, but there was a falsity about it. 'Whatever makes you think that?' she asked.

'His wife told us,' said Gaffney simply.

The smile vanished again. 'It's true,' she said coldly, 'but quite frankly I don't see what it has to do with you, or anyone else for that matter.'

'Mrs Hodder.' Gaffney spoke quietly, gently almost. 'I am investigating the death of your husband – and one or two other matters which need not trouble you – ' She frowned at that. ' – and any information concerning his private or professional life could be relevant to that enquiry. Until I am satisfied that these things have nothing to do with his death, then I am entitled to ask and will ask.' Gaffney sat back in his chair, playing his old game of waiting for her to speak. The silence usually forced the people he interviewed into saying something.

At last she spoke. 'It seems much worse now that Geoffrey's dead; it makes the underhandedness seem even more deceitful. But I was desperate, Mr Gaffney – I don't know if you understand that. I'm a normal healthy woman, with normal healthy appetites.' She glanced at Claire Wentworth's left hand, hoping to find a wedding ring, at least an engagement ring. It was bare. There would be no sympathy there, she thought, wrongly. Claire smiled to herself and crossed her legs, the sun from the French windows catching the sheen of her stockings. Julia continued. 'Geoffrey neglected me – just that. It was driving me mad. I began to wonder what was wrong with me. I don't think I'm an unattractive woman . . . ' She paused, seeking agreement in Gaffney's face, but he just sat there, listening. 'The Harrises were good friends; I suppose that makes it worse. I didn't want to do anything to hurt Tina – Mrs Harris – ' Gaffney nodded. 'But it happened. There was nothing either of us could do about it. I wasn't particularly proud of going to bed with Dick – I just couldn't help myself, even though I knew we were deceiving both Tina and Geoffrey . . . '

With the intuitiveness of a woman, Claire Wentworth

interrupted the conversation. 'Mrs Hodder, do you mind if I use your bathroom?'

'Of course not, my dear,' said Julia, a little too gushing. 'It's the first door on the left at the top of the stairs.' She waited until the policewoman had left the room, and then leaned forward confidentially, both feet on the floor, arms loosely folded across her bare knees. 'It's embarrassing to say this in front of another woman,' she said, 'but I need men – I can't live without sex. You do understand that, don't you, Mr Gaffney?'

'I think so. But surely, to have an affaire with someone who lived in the village was taking a risk – particularly after what happened the last time?'

'The last time?'

'I gather that your liaison with Geoffrey, while he was still married to Elizabeth, was something of an open secret around here.'

She shrugged. 'People don't choose to be what they are, to feel what they feel. You don't criticise someone who suffers from asthma, do you? You sympathise. So why criticise someone who is over-sexed?'

'That sounds a pretty callous way of putting it.'

'I don't know if you've ever had an affaire, Mr Gaffney,' she said, which surprised him by its boldness, perhaps because it contained the hint of an invitation, 'but once you embark on it, callousness becomes second nature. You get devious, and the occasions when you feel any pangs of conscience get less and less. You can make what you like of that, but it's true.' She was still sitting forward, an earnestness in her pose.

'Did your husband know?'

She leaned back, slowly sliding her hands up her legs until they rested at the tops of her thighs, her fingers spread. 'I don't think so. He never taxed me with it, if that's what you mean.'

'Do you think he would have mentioned it, even if he'd found out?'

She shook her head, so that the curls of her blonde hair bounced. 'No.' She smiled. 'I don't think so. I'm sorry to

191

say that Geoffrey was a very weak man, which is probably why I got him into bed in the first place. He hated rows. Even when I complained about him not making love to me, he didn't flare up.' She looked up very slowly, her blue eyes fixed on Gaffney's. 'He just apologised, and said that he was very tired these days. But that was what I was complaining about. He was always too tired or too busy.' She raised her arms above her head until they were gripping the back of the settee, revealing a little more of her midriff. 'Does this really have anything to do with Geoffrey's death?'

'You tell me, Mrs Hodder. Supposing he had found out about you and Dick Harris. You say he hated rows, and he'd already got one divorce behind him. Perhaps he wanted to hold on to you whatever your shortcomings.'

'Shortcomings?' She bridled at that.

'I mean your other affaires.' That was pure guess-work, but based on his assessment of her, it seemed likely.

She relaxed, a smile of cool appraisal on her face. 'You seem to have been finding out an awful lot about me. I thought it was Geoffrey you were investigating . . . ?'

'Not exactly, Mrs Hodder; it is his death I am investigating, and any surrounding circumstances which may have had a bearing on it.'

'And am I a surrounding circumstance?'

'You were his wife, and your behaviour may have had something to do with it.'

'I've had other affaires, yes,' she said after some time. 'What of it? Lots of women do. It's so utterly boring, being stuck here. Geoffrey spent an awful lot of time at work, you know. I had to do something.'

'Might he have been having an affaire? After all he reneged on his first wife.' Gaffney didn't think that that was the case at all, but he wanted to penetrate the ice-cool reserve of this woman opposite him.

She brought her arms down and linked them round her knees, a little too tightly. 'He wouldn't,' she said. 'He wouldn't have dared.' But she obviously hadn't thought of it before.

Claire Wentworth came back into the room and smiled at Julia Hodder. It signalled an end to frankness.

Gaffney stood up. 'Thank you for your time, Mrs Hodder. You've been most helpful.'

'I don't know about helpful,' she said, smiling. 'Candid perhaps.' Gaffney noticed that she stood close to him, much closer than was necessary, and he got a waft of expensive perfume. 'If you think I can possibly help you again, please do come down.' The invitation was clearly directed at Gaffney alone; it was as if the woman sergeant wasn't there.

At the front door she held out her hand. 'Goodbye,' she said, and he noticed her reluctance to relinquish the grasp. Then she nodded briefly at Claire Wentworth.

'And what did you think of her?' asked Gaffney on the journey back.

Claire Wentworth laughed. 'I think she's what's called a man-eater – she was certainly dressed to eat one today.'

'That's because she wasn't expecting you – she thought that Mr Tipper would be coming with me again. Quite disappointed, wasn't she?'

'Did she say anything useful when I went upstairs, sir?'

'Not really. She just said, in more graphic terms, that she was sex-starved.'

Claire laughed again. 'I doubt that. She's the sort of woman who only has to look at a man and he's hooked.' She looked sideways at Gaffney. 'As a matter of fact, sir, I think she rather fancied you.'

'Really?' asked Gaffney, concentrating on the road. 'I take it you did your usual survey upstairs?' He had discovered, some years previously, the value of a woman officer when questioning women.

'She had quite a collection of good-name toiletries in her bathroom,' said Claire. 'Bath oil, soap, talc, body lotion, toilet water – the full works. I reckon there must have been about two hundred quid's-worth of the stuff. You don't buy that out of the housekeeping a civil servant gives you.'

Gaffney whistled softly. 'Interesting.'

'I had a quick look in her bedroom, too. There was a ticket from a refrigerated fur store stuck in the dressing-table mirror. That means an expensive coat; you don't put rabbit fur into store. And there was a bottle of very expensive perfume to match the stuff in the bathroom.'

'Yes,' said Gaffney, 'I caught a whiff of it when we were leaving.' He negotiated a roundabout before speaking again. 'I'm still puzzled by her relationship with Harris. It was taking a risk, especially with all those wives just waiting to point a finger.'

'There might be an explanation for that, sir – desperation. The Hodders slept in separate rooms; single beds, too.'

'That's interesting,' said Gaffney.

'And I reckon she's a nympho,' said Claire. 'She'd run after anything in trousers – or better still, without them.'

'You're probably right,' said Gaffney, 'but I still feel uneasy about her.'

'If I were in your shoes, sir, I think I would too.'

Chapter Fourteen

'D'you know what I think, guv'nor?' asked Tipper.

'What?'

'I reckon she's a West End tom; high-class stuff. None of your Shepherd Market "short time, luv" routine, but a discreet society sort of bird. And Mrs PC Bates said she worked from home; all a bit vague. That would explain the perfumery and the fur coat that Claire turned up; they all have that sort of gear.'

Gaffney nodded. 'Well I'd expect an ordinary detective like you to know all about the insalubrious side of life. But why marry Hodder? He's not exactly the answer to a girl who's used to the high life, and I'd be surprised if his take-home pay reached seventeen grand a year.'

'Respectability. If she ever got pulled, she could always claim that she was a civil servant's wife, and it was all a terrible mistake. Or admit to having a bit on the side, with a knowing wink; but not for profit.'

'I'm doubtful, Harry. If she'd got form for tomming, she'd never have got clearance, or rather Hodder wouldn't have done when they did his up-to-date vetting when he remarried.'

Tipper scoffed. 'She wouldn't have form, not for that sort of tomming, guv'nor. They never set foot on the streets. Go everywhere by taxi; best hotels, private apartments. You never catch'em at it. Look, she's on the end of a telephone, and some rich bloke rings her up and books her for the night in his London flat. Next morning, he puts her in a cab and gives her a little present – a monkey, probably— '

'A what?'

'Oh, I'm sorry, sir,' said Tipper heavily, 'I keep forgetting I'm in Special Branch now. Five hundred pounds.' He grinned. 'But how are you going to prove it?'

'With difficulty, I should think.'

'Dead right.'

'But if that's the case, how did she explain away her absences to Geoffrey?'

'Perhaps she didn't bother. Look at it like this: we weren't able to ask Hodder himself about his married life, and the chances are he wouldn't have told us anyway. And she wouldn't have given anything away either. It was only when you got a cough out of Mrs Harris that her old man had been having it off with Julia that we knew that everything wasn't quite what it seemed. What we don't know – and what we won't be told – is whether Dick Harris paid for the pleasure. Don't forget that he's a well-heeled company director. It's a funny thing, but blokes like him will confess to having had a bird on the side, but they seem to think it's some sort of slur on their masculinity if they have to admit that they paid for it. Life's a funny thing, isn't it?'

Gaffney laughed. 'You weave a nice tale, Harry, and it's the most plausible so far.' He patted his pockets, searching for his lighter. 'It could explain his suicide, I suppose.' He stared reflectively through his cigar smoke. 'If he'd found out that she was a call-girl. . . . '

'He's not going to top himself though; kick her out maybe.'

'Anyone else might, Harry, but he's thinking about his job, and his vetting, and the publicity if it came out; these blokes worry about things like that all the time. Think of the headlines: "My life as a prostitute, by MI5 officer's wife". No, Harry, it would be a good enough reason for him. But there's not a scrap of evidence.'

Tipper looked mildly disappointed. 'I still don't think he'd do himself in because of it. It's not his fault if he accidentally married a whore, is it?'

Gaffney shook his head. 'I reckon he was a bit of an enigma, particularly when you think about the stories we heard from the blokes who were in the army with him. You wouldn't have thought it was the same bloke.'

'People change.'

'That's very profound, Harry; but you're right. That outfit he worked for has a strange effect on some people; they start looking over their shoulders. Eventually they get frightened of everybody and everything. And having a flighty young wife doesn't help, either; she must have exhausted him, or tried to.'

'Well one thing's certain, sir, we aren't going to find out by sitting here speculating. What d'you reckon, a few background enquiries? I'll take that on if you like.'

Gaffney nodded slowly. 'All right; but you know, Harry, I think we're clutching at straws here. Let's face it, Hodder tops himself, and he does it after the third job he's been in charge of has gone wrong. If that doesn't indicate guilt, I don't know what does.'

'He's not going to run the risk of grassing on three jobs in a row, guv'nor; that'd be a dead give-away.'

'Funny thing,' said Gaffney, 'that's what Carfax said, and I suppose there's something in it. Somehow or other we've got to get to the inside of this man Hodder; until we do we aren't going to find the truth, or the leak. To be honest, I don't think that having a wife who puts herself about is the answer.'

'Well let me see what I can turn up, sir.'

'Okay. You might be able to get some help from the vetting people, although they're a bit funny about releasing any of their stuff; all highly personal and confidential, but the fact that Hodder's dead now might make a difference.'

'No thanks,' said Tipper. 'I've met some of them; my old guv'nor's in that lot, and he was as thick as two short planks. No, I'll do it myself, then I'll know it's done properly.'

'Where are you going to start, Harry?'

'From right here, and work backwards.'

'There's only one problem. You'll never be able to make local enquiries in the village where she lives; not and get away without her knowing.'

Tipper gently pulled down one of his lower eyelids with a forefinger. 'I know a few tricks, guv'nor; stand on me.'

There was an air of confidence about the way that Caroline Farrell strode into the room. Gaffney put her age at about thirty, and he was sure that she regarded her tweed skirt, jumper and flat shoes as sensible; and that the absence of make-up and the no-nonsense hair-style were exactly right for the office.

'I understand that you wish to speak to me?' She gazed at the two policemen haughtily, as though they were an unnecessary interruption in her day's schedule. Gaffney had decided to interview the girl on the grounds that a man's secretary was nearly as close to her boss as his wife; in some cases, much closer.

'Miss Farrell?'

'Yes.'

'It is "miss", is it?'

'Yes, of course.'

'Please sit down. I wanted to have a chat with you about Geoffrey Hodder.'

'I see.'

'How long were you his secretary, Miss Farrell?'

'Five years,' she said without hesitation. She sat upright, tensed, as though she didn't intend wasting too much time on this business.

'We – Chief Inspector Tipper and I – are investigating his death.' She nodded. 'So far we do not have a satisfactory explanation for it.'

'And you think I can help?' She spoke with what Tipper described as a cut-glass accent.

'I'm hoping that you may be able to shed a little light on his character. I gather that he was a rather secretive sort of person; kept himself very much to himself?'

She glanced from Gaffney to Tipper and back again. 'I would not have thought that strange, considering his job.'

'I'm not talking about professional reticence; that goes

without saying. No, I mean as an individual. Some people are very outgoing, but don't betray any secrets for all that— '

'You're not suggesting that Mr Hodder betrayed any secrets, surely, are you?' She looked suitably shocked and Gaffney realised that to attack a secretary's boss was one sure way to be denied any assistance.

'Not at all.' He would have liked a cigar, but was pretty certain that smoking would not meet with the girl's approval. 'I don't know how much you knew about the work he was engaged in . . . '

'Just about everything,' she said. 'I was his secretary.' There was a distinct edge of hostility in her voice.

'Miss Farrell, please don't misunderstand my motives. I am not out to attack Mr Hodder, just to discover the reason for his untimely death.'

'I still don't see how I can help,' she said, but sounded slightly mollified.

'Well to start with, we don't know the cause of his death—'

'D'you mean there hasn't been a post-mortem examination?'

'Yes, there has,' said Gaffney patiently, 'but the pathologist is undecided as to the cause, at least until he has made further tests.'

'D'you mean he might have been murdered?' A little of the cool reserve slipped.

'It is a possibility, yes.' Gaffney was becoming quite good at lying about Hodder's suicide.

'Good heavens,' she said in exactly the way that she might have taken the news that her old school had just lost an important hockey match.

Gaffney did not want her speculating on who might have killed Hodder; he was more interested in what had driven him to take his own life. Gently he steered her back. 'Did he seem at all depressed in recent weeks?'

She played briefly with a garnet ring on the middle finger of her right hand. 'Yes,' she said.

Gaffney waited until it became apparent that she was

not going to expand on that, at least not voluntarily. 'In what way?' he asked.

'Just wasn't himself. Didn't seem to have the sparkle any more.'

It seemed a strange word to use in respect of Hodder. 'Am I to deduce from that that he was quite a lively character then?'

For the first time since the interview had begun, she smiled; it transformed her whole face, and Gaffney noticed how attractive her brown eyes were. 'I wouldn't have said lively, no.' She paused again. 'But he was a very compassionate man; very sympathetic.'

'To everybody?'

'Oh no. In fact, he always gave the impression of being a little austere, particularly with his staff; the officers on his section, I mean. I think that they were a bit afraid of him. He was very demanding, and he didn't tolerate inefficiency. I've seen him get very cross when something's gone wrong.'

'Like the Dickson affair?'

'Exactly; and Nikitin and Gesschner, too.'

'Oh, you know about those.'

'Naturally. I was his secretary, as I said. A man doesn't have any secrets from his secretary.'

Gaffney took a leap into the unknown. 'You'd know about his marital problems, and his affaires with other women, then?'

He had expected a scandalised rebuttal, but she remained quite calm. 'Yes,' she said, 'and I'm probably the only one here who did.' She glanced quickly at Tipper before realigning her gaze on Gaffney. 'I hope that what I'm saying is in the strictest confidence,' she said. 'I'm only telling you now because he's dead, and it might help you to find out . . . ' She let the sentence tail off.

Gaffney decided that there was no harm in giving that assurance; Hodder was beyond the clutches of the vetting people now. 'In the strictest confidence, Miss Farrell.' He knew that if he had to breach that promise at some time in the future, he would just shrug his shoulders and get on with it; there wasn't much honour or morality in criminal investigation.

'He'd been married before, you know.'

'So I understand.'

'His first wife used to work here, before my time, of course. Then he got married to Julia, that's his present wife.' She stopped and looked momentarily sad. 'His widow, I suppose she is now.' Gaffney nodded. 'But that marriage was no more successful than the first. . . . '

'He told you that, did he?'

'Not at first, but I could work it out— '

'Just a minute, Miss Farrell. You say you were his secretary for five years.' She nodded. 'So that when you started, he'd already been married for five years or so, for the second time.'

'That's right. It was just after I came here that it started to get a bit rocky, so I gather.'

'And that was when he told you, was it?'

'No. Not immediately.'

'Forgive me for asking, but why should he tell you at all? With respect, you were only his secretary.'

She smiled with a schoolmistress-like tolerance. 'Some men will confide in their secretaries, when they will tell no one else. He was such a man, I suppose.'

'But so soon after your appointment?'

There was a silence for some time, and again she played absently with the garnet ring. Eventually she looked up. 'I was one of his affaires,' she said softly.

'I see.' Gaffney left it at that, hoping that she would explain in her own time. He was fascinated that a man with a wife who looked like Julia Hodder should be attracted to this plain girl sitting opposite him.

'He asked me to go to the theatre with him one day. He'd got two tickets apparently and was intending to take his wife, but she cried off. She rang him – I put the call through – and said that she didn't feel like going, and he should go on his own— '

'Did she tell you that?'

'No, but Geoffrey told me afterwards that's what she'd said. Anyway, he said it would be a shame to waste the ticket, and asked me if I'd like to go. He said he'd quite understand if I said no.'

'But you went?'

'Yes.'

'Why?'

'It was a play I particularly wanted to see, but couldn't get tickets for.'

'And that was all, was it? You just went to the theatre with him?'

'That was all then, yes. There was nothing romantic about it. We had a drink and a sandwich in a pub before the play started; I remember that because it was dirty and crowded. We had to eat our sandwiches standing up and wedged in a corner, and he kept apologising. He said that if he'd known he'd have booked a table at a restaurant.'

'Funny thing to say, wasn't it?'

'I don't see why.'

'Well if he had been intending to take his wife with him, surely he'd have done that anyway.'

'He mentioned that. He said they didn't bother. They always had supper when they got home.'

'Did you go out with him often after that?'

'No, not really. Five or six times, I suppose. Then it all came to a rather unsatisfactory end.'

'Oh?'

'The next time – after the visit to the theatre, I mean – he took me out for a meal. He said it was to make up for eating in a pub, before. But it was the time after that he really opened up. He told me all about his first wife, and what a bitch she'd been, and how he'd met his second wife. He told me all about the divorce too.'

'How long ago was all this, Miss Farrell?'

'Two years ago, I should think.' She paused. 'Yes, that would be about right.'

'What did he say about his second wife?'

'I know it sounds hackneyed, but he said that his wife

202

didn't understand him. They had little in common, it seemed; no mutual interests— '

'What were his interests?'

'Well the theatre, obviously, and music. He liked going to concerts, but she couldn't stand them. He also said that he thought that she might be having an affaire, and he didn't know what to do about it.'

Gaffney smiled. He was always amused by his own sex. He had met several men who thought it quite acceptable to have affaires but who regarded it as downright treachery if their wives did the same thing. 'And all this was two years ago, was it?'

'That's when it started, yes.'

'And when did it end? You said that it did?'

'Yes. It happened one evening, after another visit to the theatre. He took me home to my flat, in his car, and I invited him in for a drink— '

'Was that the first time you'd invited him in?'

'No. Probably about the second or third time. We were sitting down talking about something or other – I can't rightly remember now – when quite suddenly he asked me if I'd go to bed with him.' She looked away, her face reddening, not with the embarrassment of the proposition, but in its telling.

'What did you do?'

'I dropped my drink. It was a silly thing to do; I was so ... I was going to say shocked, but I wasn't. Quite honestly, I'd been expecting something like that to happen, but not as suddenly as that. There was nothing romantic about it; no soft lights and sweet music. He might just as well have been asking me if I wanted another drink, or if I'd take dictation.'

It was clear that she had not intended an innuendo in that last remark, and Gaffney kept a straight face. 'And did you sleep with him?'

'No. I asked him to leave ... ' She broke off, searching Gaffney's face for some trace of censure or cynicism. 'This is all very embarrassing, you know.'

'And was that the end of it?'

'Yes. I suddenly realised what I was getting into. I'd always been critical of girls who had affaires with their married bosses, and there I was on the brink of doing the same thing. And yet, the funny thing is that I might have done if he hadn't asked me straight out like that; it was so cold, so matter-of-fact. It made me feel sick, quite honestly; I didn't feel proud of myself and it was worse when I analysed it. I knew that that was what I'd been working towards. Afterwards, when I thought about it, over and over again, I knew that deep down I had wanted it to happen, wanted to go to bed with him. Then I realised that there was nothing in it of any permanence; he was into his second marriage, and probably it was his fault, not his wife's – either of his wives – and that I'd nearly become yet another girl he'd been to bed with.'

'Didn't that make life difficult for you in the office? You remained his secretary, obviously, and had to work with him every day, just as if nothing had happened.'

She nodded. 'Yes,' she said, 'and that was exactly what did happen. He never referred to it again. Never asked me out. Nothing. It was just as if we had never been out together anywhere. I was all set to ask for a transfer, but eventually I didn't bother.'

'And he didn't apologise?'

'No, not a word.' She looked serious. 'I suppose he thought that I was the one who ought to be doing the apologising.'

'You said earlier that you were one of his affaires. Was that a figure of speech, or did he have other women friends?'

'Oh yes. I didn't know for certain, but you can tell. When someone rings up and he's not here, a secretary will usually say something like, I'll get him to ring you, and take a number. The women in a man's life will never do that. They'll say it doesn't matter and that they'll ring later, but they'll never leave a name or a number.'

'I see,' said Gaffney, and thought it as well that chief superintendents didn't have secretaries. 'You don't know who any of these women were, then?'

She hesitated, thinking. 'No, I'm afraid not.'

'Have none of them telephoned since his death?'

'Only one; the current one, I suppose you'd call her.'

'What did you say?'

'I just told her that Mr Hodder had died.'

'What was the reaction?'

'Complete silence. She didn't say another word, just rang off.'

'And she's not telephoned since?'

'No.'

'Miss Farrell, you said earlier that Geoffrey Hodder was a compassionate and sympathetic man.' She nodded. 'And yet his treatment of you after your abortive affaire didn't seem like that; he ignored it, you say; made no reference to it.'

She smiled wistfully. 'You have to know Geoffrey to understand that sort of reaction. I think he was too embarrassed to mention it. I think he realised that he'd embarrassed me, and didn't know quite how to deal with the situation. It was very awkward, when you think about it; me still working as his secretary, if you see what I mean.'

'But he straightaway got himself involved with another woman, if your deduction about the phone calls is correct . . . '

'Yes, but I don't blame him for that. I think he was a man who needed women; not just for sex, but for companionship. He seemed to like talking to women, being with them. From what he said about Julia, she wasn't much of a wife to him.'

'Did he ever mention her after you and he stopped seeing each other – outside the office, I mean?'

She smiled. 'I know what you mean. No; that was the end of confidences of that sort. As I said before, it was just as though that little interlude hadn't occurred.' She relaxed slightly and crossed her legs. 'I suppose I was a bit hard on him.'

'Hard?'

'Yes. Throwing him out like that. I should have been a little more sympathetic, I suppose, but ... It was so gauche, just coming straight out with it like that; a bald proposition.'

'It strikes me, Miss Farrell, from what you've been saying,

that Geoffrey Hodder was one of those men who incited sympathy.'

She thought about that for a while. 'Yes, I suppose he was. Women tended to feel sorry for him; they wanted to mother him. But then, every once in a while, you could see a streak of hardness in him that negated it.'

'Such as?'

'The Dickson thing. He was absolutely furious that it had gone wrong. And obviously worried; worried sick.'

'What was the reaction of his team? People like Hughes and Selby and the others?'

'They generally seemed quite concerned, but only because of his uncharacteristic anger, I think. Not that you can ever tell with Mr Selby, of course.'

'Why of course?'

'He's a strange one. Never seems to have anything in common with anyone else in the office – a bit reclusive, really.'

'What did Geoffrey think of him, do you know?'

She shook her head. 'No, Geoffrey was very loyal to his people. He would never criticise them to anyone else.'

'Was Geoffrey angry with you? I mean did it spill over, this anger?'

'No. He was never angry with me, but then I was just a secretary. But you could tell. He didn't go out of the office for a day or two after Dickson went missing. And every time he walked up the corridor or went to the loo, he would ask, as soon as he got back, if the Director-General had phoned. To be perfectly honest, I think he was expecting to get the sack.'

'Did he drink much?' asked Gaffney, recalling what he had heard about Hodder's life-style before, in the army.

'Not that I know of,' she said. 'Certainly not in the office; no one does. But when we went out, he usually just had a gin and tonic, and a glass or so of wine with a meal. I've never seen him the worse for drink, but then I wouldn't expect to; it wasn't really in his character.'

'Even when the Dickson case went wrong?'

'No,' she said, 'not even then.'

'Did you ever meet Julia Hodder, Miss Farrell?'

'Only once. I was in Harrods one Saturday morning, doing some Christmas shopping. It was just before Christmas—' She broke off with a smile, 'It would be really, wouldn't it?'

Gaffney laughed. 'Some people, I'm told, do their Christmas shopping in the January sales. Somehow, I've never managed it.'

'It was rather embarrassing, actually. It was only a couple of weeks after I'd told him to leave my flat. I didn't really know what the outcome of that was going to be; I was still wondering about asking for a move. Anyway we all three came face to face . . . '

'And how did Geoffrey react to that?'

'Oh, he was the perfect gentleman. He introduced us, very formally. It was all very civilised. He just told Julia that I was his secretary, and she made some trite response like, We've spoken on the phone, and I said, Yes, I thought so, and how nice it was to meet the voice.' She smiled again. 'You know the sort of silly things you say on occasions like that?'

'And what did you think of Julia?'

'She was charming, and very attractive, too. Not at all like the picture I had of her, from what Geoffrey had told me. I was expecting a dragon, but she was well dressed and . . . and really beautiful. We stood chatting for about five minutes, talking about all the usual things, like how expensive everything was this year, and what a silly idea Christmas was, and so on. Then we split up and went our separate ways.'

'Did he mention it, afterwards?'

'No, not at all. I half expected him to ask me what I thought of her, or to say something about her having been pleased to have met me, but nothing. I suppose it was because it was that awkward period immediately after our splitting up. . . . '

'And you said nothing either, I presume?'

'No, I didn't. I didn't think it was a very good idea. I was still feeling a bit upset really, about his treatment of me; I didn't want to renew out intimate conversation. I just left it, and so did he.'

'And how long did your affaire with him last?'

'A matter of weeks, that's all.'

'And you say it was nearly two years since all this happened?'

'Yes.'

'So you've no way of knowing whether the marriage deteriorated even further? Or perhaps improved?'

'No. He never mentioned his wife again. I don't somehow think it improved, though, otherwise he wouldn't have continued to get phone calls from other women.'

'You're sure that they were other women, in the sense that they didn't work in the building?'

'Pretty sure. I know most of the women who regularly ring him up on business, and in any case they always say who they are and usually ask if he'll ring them back. No, they were definitely outsiders.' Quite suddenly, she said; 'Would you mind if I had a cigarette?'

'Good heavens no,' said Gaffney. 'I didn't realise you smoked.'

She opened her handbag and moved the contents around until she found a packet of cigarettes, and accepted a light from Gaffney.

'Were you at work the day before he died?' asked Gaffney.

'Yes, I was.'

'And did he seem any different? What I mean is, had there been any indications that he was getting more depressed, or more angry even?

She gazed levelly at Gaffney. 'Are you suggesting that he may have committed suicide?' she asked.

'It's one of the possibilities I have to consider, yes.'

'Oh! I hadn't thought of that. I'd imagined it to be an accident, or a heart attack, something like that. Frankly, I was astounded earlier on when you hinted that he might have been murdered.'

That came as no surprise to Gaffney. The news reports had carefully avoided any reference to the plastic bag that had been over Hodder's head when his body had been found; had merely stated that he had died in the toilets at Waterloo

208

Station. 'I was interested to know whether there had been any noticeable change in his demeanour.'

'No. He was still upset about the Dickson case, but he seemed quite all right the night before. He left the office at about half-past five, and said good night. He also said he'd see me in the morning, but he always said that.' She thought for a moment. 'Except on Fridays,' she added. 'Then he would always say something like, Have a nice weekend. That's what made it worse, I think. It was so unexpected. I couldn't believe it when I heard the next morning. It was so unlike Geoffrey to be late, or not to arrive. He always told me what he was doing.'

'And what d'you make of all that, Harry?'

'Comes as no surprise, sir, after what Hodder's military friends had to say about him, well two of them, anyway. What do we do now? Try and find these women of his?'

'What's the point?' asked Gaffney. 'What will they tell us? They'll tell us they knew him; tell us reluctantly, I suspect. And they'll either say they knew he was married or they didn't know. Either way we'll be no further forward, so what's the point?'

'I think you said at some stage of this enquiry, sir, that you never knew whether you were wasting your time until you'd wasted it. But I agree with you; there's not much point. What about Julia Hodder? Are you going to see her again, and put it to her?'

'Put what to her?'

'About her old man having it off with his secretary?'

'About him nearly having it off. I think we might do that, Harry, just to see what happens.'

Gaffney had intended to take Claire Wentworth with him again, and had told Julia Hodder so when he had telephoned to make the appointment; but only because she had asked. In the event, he changed his mind and took Tipper, considering, at the last minute, that Harry's penetrating and ruthless logic might be quite useful; provided that Julia didn't frighten him to death.

209

Her clothes reflected her expectation of the arrival of the woman officer again, and she wore a demure black dress, a combination of modesty and, Gaffney presumed, mourning.

'I am sorry to have to bother you again, Mrs Hodder . . . '

'It's no trouble,' she said, but her eyes were on Tipper as she spoke, and her right hand fluttered aimlessly near the high neck of her dress. 'I thought you said that you were bringing the young lady. . . . '

'That was my intention,' said Gaffney, declining to elaborate, 'but I've brought Mr Tipper instead.'

'Well,' she said, arranging herself in her usual seat in the centre of the settee. 'How can I help you?'

'I hope that my questions will not seem too irrelevant,' said Gaffney, 'but I am anxious to learn as much about your late husband as possible, in the hope that it may shed some light on his death.' She inclined her head to one side and folded her hands in her lap. Gaffney noticed that she was no longer wearing a wedding ring. 'I have been told that he was having an affaire, Mrs Hodder.'

'Oh?' There was a hint of a smile on her face. 'And who told you that?'

'I'm not at liberty to say.'

'Well I'll tell you. Caroline Farrell, his secretary.'

'You knew her, did you?'

'I met her once, in Harrods it was. She was having an affaire with my husband.'

'How did you know? Did he tell you?'

'He didn't have to. A woman can tell, in a variety of ways. A man will take a little more care about his appearance, and he'll suddenly start wearing after-shave to work when he's never done it before. Or he'll be especially solicitous to his wife, and bring her flowers when he hasn't done it since they got married.' She smiled. 'You can always tell.' She glanced at Tipper who smiled in return and nodded gravely. 'But in this case, I didn't need to take note of those things. I only had to look at her, at Caroline Farrell. I could see it in her eyes; absolute adulation.'

'She was his secretary,' said Gaffney. 'Most secretaries

seem to reserve that sort of look for their boss; either that or out-and-out contempt.'

'Ah, but that wasn't all,' said Julia triumphantly. 'I saw them together in the West End, going into a theatre.'

'Oh, I see,' said Gaffney. 'And who were you with?'

She gazed at him for some seconds before answering. 'You're really quite shrewd, Mr Gaffney,' she said. He wasn't quite sure whether that was meant to be a compliment or not. 'As a matter of fact you're right, but I'm not telling you who it was. But it served Geoffrey right anyway, because he had telephoned me earlier and said that something difficult had cropped up at the office and he would be late, very late.' She shrugged. 'I wasn't going to sit at home, so I telephoned someone in town and went up to meet him,'

'And the something difficult at the office was Caroline, was it?'

'Yes, but I didn't recognise her at first. When I met her in Harrods, she looked a typical Sloane. In fact, she looked dreadful. She was wearing some awful woolly hat, down over her ears, and one of those coats that people wear when they go to shoot pheasants. And no make-up. But when I saw her going into the theatre, she was really done up: elegant dress, high-heeled shoes, black stockings. And she was made-up, and her hair was loose – shoulder length.'

'This theatre trip; was it after you'd met her in Harrods?'

'Yes, two or three weeks afterwards. Why?'

'I just wondered. Did you tackle your husband about it, later on?'

She pouted and shook her head casually. 'No point,' she said. She leaned forward, frowning slightly. 'Look, Mr Gaffney, I'll be perfectly honest with you. Our marriage was at an end. We just lived in the same house, that's all. We went our own ways; it was quite amicable, really. We kept up the pretence, although I don't know why. When he rang me to say he was working late, I don't think for a moment that he expected me to believe it, but it was just for the sake of form. It was a bit childish in a way.'

211

'How long had this amicable sort of arrangement been going on, may I ask?'

'A long time.'

'What started it?'

'I did.'

'I'm sorry, I don't quite . . . '

'The mere fact that he, a married man with children, should have made the running almost as soon as I arrived here. And he was practised at it, too. If you have an affaire with a man who has never committed adultery before, he's shy, nervous, and worrying what'll happen if he gets caught. There was none of that with Geoffrey. He'd done it all before; he was smooth and accomplished. He knew all the tricks, all the devious things you have to do, like answering the phone when his wife's in the room and pretending that you're someone from the office. He was very good at that. I'm afraid that my husband was an old hand at deluding his wife, both of us in fact.' She smiled in a resigned way.

'How come that you got caught out by Elizabeth then, his first wife, if he was such an accomplished deceiver? And you were caught out, weren't you? Elizabeth said that she had a phone call and walked into your house, Raven Cottage, through the back door which had been left unlocked.'

Julia Hodder looked up with interest. 'So that's how she got in. I never did know; I must admit that I was a bit too taken aback to wonder.'

'Well did you lock the back door, or did you leave it to Geoffrey?'

She smiled. 'It's a long time ago, Mr Gaffney. I can't possibly remember after all this time. It must have been my fault. As I said, Geoffrey was very good at that sort of thing.'

'Did he tell you off about it afterwards?'

'Now you come to mention it, yes. He said it shouldn't have happened. Well I knew that; it was obvious it shouldn't have happened, but it did, and that was that.'

'Anyway, how does that have a bearing on his other affaires?'

'It was obvious to me when I sat down and thought about it. If a man can deceive his wife to have an affair with me, and when it's apparent that he's done it before, he's not going to stop just because he gets married for the second time.'

'But you married him just the same.'

'Yes, Mr Gaffney,' she said with a dreamy faraway look in her eyes. 'I married him just the same.'

'Did you ever think of leaving him, or he you?'

'Not really. We were both quite happy. As I said, we went our own ways. This is a comfortable house, and this is a nice village.' She swept a hand round the room. 'Why change it? Apart from anything else there was his job.'

'What did his job have to do with it?'

'Apparently the civil service are a bit funny about such things and he thought that a second divorce might cause problems.'

'What sort of problems?'

'Oh, I don't know, except that because of what he was doing – and I never knew precisely what that was – he had to be checked up on every so often. I can't remember what he called it now.'

'Positive vetting?'

'Yes, I do believe that was it. It always struck me as an unnecessary intrusion into one's private life, but I suppose it's something one has to live with these days.'

'And he told you nothing about his job?'

'I think you asked me that the last time you came down.' She held his gaze with her clear blue eyes. 'Other than that it was the Ministry of Defence, no, I have no idea what he did. I don't even know what he earned. Not that that mattered; I've some money of my own.'

'I see. Well thank you again, Mrs Hodder,' said Gaffney as he stood up.

'Are you going to be able to tell me what really happened to Geoffrey soon, Mr Gaffney?' she asked.

'I hope so.' At the door he paused. 'Mrs Hodder, do you know any of the other women with whom your husband had an affaire?'

She dropped her chin, as if deep in thought. Eventually she looked up. 'I'm afraid not,' she said. 'It's not the sort of question one asks, even in a marriage as loose as ours was.'

Gaffney nodded. He didn't believe her. Come to think of it, he hadn't believed much of what she had told him, except perhaps her account of her meeting with Caroline Farrell. The interesting thing about that was Julia Hodder claimed to have seen her husband taking his secretary to the theatre after the liaison was said by Caroline to have been over. It had to be that way round otherwise Julia would not have recognised Caroline Farrell. Either Julia Hodder or Caroline Farrell was lying. Gaffney knew that he would have to find out which of them it was. It was a depressing thought; he seemed to have been sidetracked into investigating adultery, but he didn't know at this stage where that might lead.

On the one hand, there was Julia Hodder openly acknowledging that her husband was having an affaire with his secretary, and appearing not to care; while on the other, Caroline Farrell stated that she had refused to go to bed with Geoffrey. Gaffney couldn't help feeling that it was all inconsequential rubbish, and probably had nothing to do with Hodder's death. Even less, he thought, was it likely to help him with his enquiries into discovering the leak he had been tasked to find.

Chapter Fifteen

'We're not making much progress, sir,' said Gaffney.

'What's your next move going to be then, John?' asked the DAC.

'With your approval, sir, to apply to the Secretary of State for intercept warrants for the five members of Hodder's team. We've interviewed them all, and they're boxing-and-coxing; closing ranks. I'm pretty sure that they won't think I'll apply for warrants, much less get them, but I reckon it's the only way to break this conspiracy of silence.'

'D'you think that's what it is?'

Gaffney shrugged. 'Difficult to say. I suspect that there's an element of resentment that police are investigating something they see as their preserve; on the other hand they might just be scared of the outcome.'

'Not without cause,' said the DAC quietly, 'but do you think that they are deliberately withholding information?'

'It's either that, or they really didn't know too much about it. It doesn't ring true, though. Hodder's the team-leader, and he forms up the usual five to assist, and then tells them nothing. I don't like it.'

'Do you think that intercepts will tell you anything? After all, the job's over – blown. I suppose if you'd put them on before friend Dickson did a runner, you might have learned something.' Logan looked doubtful. 'On the other hand, if they, or he, are professionals, I don't suppose you'd have learned anything. Nor, I suspect, will you now. Still if that's all you've got . . . '

'There is one glimmer, sir, and that's Selby; no one seems to fancy him too much. Maybe it's because he's unmarried, which makes them think he's a queer, or it could be his supercilious manner. Either way, he gets right up their noses. Probably nothing in it, other than a desire to shift the limelight somewhere else. The obvious ones aren't usually the ones who finish up in the dock.'

'Will warrants for the five be enough? Postal and telephone, presumably?'

Gaffney grinned. 'Enough to be going on with, sir,' he said.

'Right, John. Get your papers prepared and get them across the road. Incidentally, what about Hodder's wife – his second wife – d'you fancy her?'

'No, sir. At least, not as a suspect.'

Logan grinned. 'Like that, is it?'

Gaffney grinned too. 'She's some woman that, but I'm going to get Harry Tipper to do a few background enquiries. To be honest, I don't think she's anything but man-hungry; on her own admission she's put herself about a bit. Harry's got this theory that she's a high-class West End tom, a call-girl, but I doubt it somehow. Still, you never know. I'll let him find out; he likes proving me wrong, does Harry. It's interesting that she should have married Hodder; there's got to have been more to him than meets the eye. From what the military have told us about his Berlin days as a youngster, he was a bit of a goer. I'd like to find out more about him, but I suspect it's too late now.'

'What did his first wife have to say? You've seen her, presumably.'

'Yes, sir. She's bitter, not unnaturally; but I got the impression that her only regret is money, or lack of it. He left her in somewhat straitened circumstances; but it may be worth having another word with her, just to see if she'll open up a bit more.'

Logan nodded. 'I can see you're clutching at straws, John, and that's not a criticism; it's a bloody tough job. Still, you can only do your best.'

Gaffney laughed. 'Yes. An early arrest is expected, as they say – but not by me.'

'Well get your warrants, John, and see if they bring anything; and if you want them for anyone else, let me know,' said the DAC, cutting the end of a cigar.

To save time, Gaffney took the applications across to Queen Anne's Gate himself, having first ascertained that the Home Secretary was there; it had to be his signature and no one else's.

'If you care to wait, Mr Gaffney,' said the tall youthful-looking assistant secretary, 'I'll see if the Secretary of State will sign them now. There is, I gather, some urgency?'

'Yes,' said Gaffney.

A few moments later the assistant secretary reappeared. 'The Secretary of State would like a few words with you,' he said.

Gaffney stood up. 'Something wrong?'

'No, I don't think so.' The civil servant smiled. 'Follow me.'

The Home Secretary smiled benignly as he stood up. 'Mr Gaffney,' he said, 'I thought I'd take the opportunity of getting you to brief me on your progress so far, as you were here. You do have the time, do you?'

'Indeed, sir, yes.'

'Good, good. It'll take them a few moments to prepare the warrants anyway. Come and sit down.' The Home Secretary walked round his huge desk and indicated an armchair. 'Coffee – would you like coffee?'

'Thank you, sir, yes.' Gaffney lowered himself into the deep chair while the minister gave instructions to his secretary on the intercom.

'You will be aware that I instructed the Director-General to seek your assistance in this matter – ' Gaffney nodded. ' – but I understand that there has been an unexpected turn of events . . . '

'Yes,' said Gaffney. 'The death of Hodder. There is no doubt that it was suicide. What is not clear at this stage is the reason. The most obvious one is guilty conscience, I suppose – '

'Or a realisation that he held the responsibility, even though he was not instrumental in its cause, perhaps?'

Gaffney looked doubtful. 'I think that is taking vicarious responsibility to extremes, sir. He could just have resigned.'

The Home Secretary smiled a tight smile. 'Yes, I know all about vicarious responsibility,' he said. 'Maybe you're right. However, you want warrants for the five remaining members of the late Geoffrey Hodder's team?'

'Yes, sir. I've interviewed each of them, and they have little to say.'

'You mean they're deliberately withholding information?'

'I don't know – perhaps. On the other hand they may know nothing. The one thing that does come through is that Hodder appears to have told them very little about the latest operation. It's almost as if he feared a leak – suspected one of them maybe, but didn't know which one.'

The secretary came in, carrying a tray of coffee, and beneath her arm, a folder. Awkwardly, she put down the tray, and handed the folder to the Home Secretary. 'You're waiting for these, I understand, Home Secretary.'

The Home Secretary nodded. 'Thank you, yes. Just put them on the desk, will you?' He gestured to Gaffney to help himself to coffee, as the door closed behind the secretary.

'Well,' continued the minister, 'I hope that the warrants will give you a break.'

'So do I, sir. Incidentally, I have not released the fact that Hodder committed suicide. I'm letting everyone think that he might have been murdered. It may just provoke them into saying something that they wouldn't otherwise have done.'

'I see.' The Home Secretary looked blandly towards the big windows. 'I think that that is something I ought not to know.' He smiled. 'I'm rather surprised that I've not had a question about it yet. No doubt it will come. Still, that's not your problem, Mr Gaffney, is it?'

'Fortunately no, sir.'

'It needn't worry you, either. I seem to spend half my working day protecting the Metropolitan Police.' He put down his cup and saucer, and walked across to his desk. Taking out a gold fountain pen he signed the warrants.

'Miss Farrell, you said, when I last saw you, that your abortive affaire with Geoffrey Hodder was over when you met him and his wife in Harrods one Saturday morning.'

She gazed levelly at Gaffney, her eyes containing a trace of hostility. 'Did I?'

'Yes, you did. You said how embarrassing it had been, and then went on to recount the conversation – a rather trivial one, I recall – that you had had with them.'

'Yes, I remember.'

'But, Miss Farrell, I have a witness who claims to have seen you going to the theatre with him a week or two later.' Gaffney sat back and waited to see what reaction that would bring.

She took some time in lighting a cigarette, then dropped her lighter into her handbag before replying. 'What of it?'

'Is it true?'

'Yes, but why do you talk of a witness? You make it sound as though I've committed a crime.'

'Miss Farrell,' said Gaffney patiently. 'I am investigating the death of Geoffrey Hodder. I am also looking into the reasons why three recent cases in which he was involved appear to have gone wrong. At the moment, I am getting nowhere. Consequently, anything that might assist me has to be investigated.'

'And you think that my having an affaire with Geoffrey might be relevant?'

'I don't know, but I am always a little suspicious when I find that people are not telling me the truth. I am not concerned with morals; it doesn't matter to me whether you had an affaire with your boss or not, but if you're hiding something I want to know why.'

Suddenly she looked forlorn and vulnerable and tears started to well up in her brown eyes. 'I'm sorry,' she said, searching her handbag for a tissue. 'Yes, it's true.' She dabbed her eyes. 'It's something I'm not proud of.' She sniffed and took a deep breath. 'I'm thirty-two and unmarried. And suddenly Geoffrey wanted me. It was the first time in my life that anyone had ever wanted me. Of course I had an affaire with him.'

'So you didn't throw him out of your flat when you said you did?'

'Oh yes I did. But then I met his wife, on that Saturday, and I thought to myself, well, if he prefers me to her, I must have something.'

'So what happened next?'

'I apologised to him. I know that sounds a silly thing to have done, because it wasn't my fault; I didn't have anything to apologise for, but Geoffrey was the sort of man who somehow had that effect on people. And I knew it at the time, but I just couldn't help myself.' She put away her tissue. 'I suppose you think I'm very stupid.' Gaffney did, but he didn't say so. 'Geoffrey was in his office and I just went in and said that I was sorry about having been so short with him and that I didn't really mean it.'

'And what did he say?'

'He just smiled and said it was his fault and he shouldn't have been so blunt. Then he suggested a reconciliation dinner that evening. Afterwards we went to my flat . . . '

'And you made love?'

She looked down at the floor. 'Yes,' She spoke in a barely audible whisper. She looked up, and Gaffney saw that the tears had started to run down her face again. 'I loved him,' she said. 'He made me feel alive. He encouraged me to dress more fashionably.' She half smiled at the memory. 'Dowdy old me.'

'And how long did this go on?'

She waited some time before answering. 'Until he died,' she said finally.

'Did he ever mention marriage?'

'Yes, but only in a negative way. He said it was out of the question. He couldn't leave his wife. He'd done it before and if he did it again, the service might consider him to be unreliable.'

'And you believed him?' To Gaffney this seemed the ploy of a typical male wanting the best of both worlds.

'I made myself believe it. If I couldn't have marriage, my relationship with Geoffrey was the next best thing.'

'So the women who rang up, but never left a name, that was all untrue was it?'

'There were other women; I'm sure of that.'

'So you mean that he wasn't only deceiving his wife, but you too?'

'Yes, but I didn't mind. I couldn't very well, could I?' She smiled defensively. 'I'm not a raving beauty, and that was a marvellous interlude. But now it's over,' she said pensively, 'and I'm destined to become an old maid.'

Gaffney thought that that was probably true, and felt like telling her to go out and buy something sexy to wear, leave a button undone on her blouse and use some lipstick, but it was none of his business; he was trying to find if there was a leak. And that was all.

'I don't know about her,' said Tipper when they got back to the Yard.'

'What don't you know about her?' asked Gaffney.

'The Director-General didn't mention Hodder's secretary; that was your idea to interview her, sir. The point about her is that she was in the right place to know just about everything that was going on. Hodder took great care not to tell members of his team about the operation, but dowdy Miss Farrell, with her sympathy-evoking tears, she knew the bloody lot. That's the trouble with secretaries – they're invisible; no one thinks of them. The DG didn't mention her, nor Hodder or Carfax or any of the team.'

'What are you suggesting, Harry?'

'Well it's only a theory, but theories are all we seem to have at the moment. Supposing she's having it off with someone else— '

'Here we go,' murmured Gaffney.

'No seriously, guv'nor. It's happened before. Firstly, she was reluctant to tell us that she'd been having it off with Hodder.'

221

'That's understandable, I suppose.'

'It is if she's also shacking up with someone from say, the Russian Embassy at the same time, or another Dickson-like character, and feeding him all the information she's picking up in the office.'

'We can go on like this forever,' said Gaffney.

'And don't forget what Julia Hodder said about her being done up to the nines when she saw her out with her old man,' continued Tipper, refusing to be dissuaded from his idea. 'Perfect. Poor mouse-like, dowdy Miss Farrell in the office, but all tarted up when she's out with her fancy man.'

'Okay, Harry,' said Gaffney wearily. 'Just suppose for a moment that you're right; how are you going to prove it?'

'Surveillance?'

'Maybe, but even if you're right, she's going to be very careful now. She knows, as does everyone else, that the police are taking an interest in the missing three contacts. No one but a fool would carry on; they're going to wait until the heat's off. So I don't think that surveillance is the answer. On the other hand . . . '

'On the other hand what?'

'We could let Claire Wentworth have a talk to her, woman to woman. She might get a cough out of her.'

Tipper looked doubtful; he had no great faith in women detectives. 'Worth a try, I suppose,' he said reluctantly. 'But if she doesn't get anything, it'll put our Miss Farrell on the alert, and then we'll never get anything. Perhaps we ought to have a few more words with the five on the team. See what they knew about her. After all, they must all know Hodder's secretary.' He chuckled. 'Some might know her better than others.'

It was about ten days before the next interesting irregularity occurred. In addition to all the other duties he had taken on or had put upon him Harry Tipper was also responsible for examining the transcripts of the interceptions which were now in place on the mail and the telephones of the five remaining members of Geoffrey Hodder's team.

He wandered into Gaffney's office, reading a file. 'I think we've got something here, sir.'

''Bout time we got something, Harry. What is it?'

'This bloke Hughes – Patrick Hughes. Makes regular calls to a number in Hounslow. Goes out to a Miss Barbara Rigby, who lives at— ' He thumbed through the sheaf of papers in his hand. 'Got it: lives at 27 Paradise Court, Essex Road, Hounslow.'

'And?'

'And is a twenty-five year old air stewardess based on Heathrow. And she's single!' An evil smile appeared on Tipper's face as he sat down in one of Gaffney's easy chairs. 'Reading between the lines, he would appear to pay her a visit about twice a week, but rings her even more often than that. He also rings his wife from the office to explain that he's going to be detained on the job.'

'Fine turn of phrase this fellow's got,' said Gaffney.

Tipper grinned again. 'She works regular hours because she's on short-haul hops.'

'Sounds like it. But I'll bet The Office – as they're so fond of calling it – doesn't know anything about that.'

'It's a bit like juries on buggery cases,' said Tipper, thoughtfully. 'One half don't believe it – the other half are doing it.'

'Yes, well you'd know about things like that, wouldn't you, Harry?'

'Are you going to put it to him, guv'nor?'

Gaffney shook his head. 'Not until we know a bit more about her. Speak to our blokes at the airport – see if they've got a contact in the airline she works for. Then confirm that he's having it off with this bird – ' Tipper was about to say something, but Gaffney forestalled him. 'You know what I mean, Harry – no need to peer through the bedroom window.'

'Bedroom,' murmured Tipper. 'How old-fashioned.'

'Then,' continued Gaffney, ignoring Tipper's asides, 'we'll go and see the lady. After all, it might be perfectly innocent.' Tipper looked sceptical. 'The girl might be his sister, living under an assumed name,' added Gaffney with a grin.

'Well if the conversations are anything to go by, we can do him for incest,' said Tipper.

Gaffney shook his head. 'What an awful mind you've got, Harry. There could be something in it, but I suspect not. The sooner we get that out of the way the better.'

'Leave it to me, guv'nor,' said Tipper, 'I'll get someone to do it.'

The surveillance confirmed it. On at least two occasions in a week, Patrick Hughes made the journey to Hounslow, letting himself into Barbara Rigby's flat with his own key. Each time, he stayed for about an hour, and then went straight home.

Gaffney decided that he would interview the girl, and left a member of the surveillance team in position so that he could be certain that she was at home when he and Tipper called. That, he thought, would be better than telephoning her to make an appointment, and thus alerting her to the fact that the police were taking an interest in her.

They parked a short distance from Paradise Court and walked the rest of the way, Gaffney pausing only to dismiss the officer who had been keeping the flat under observation; he was fairly sure that no more fruitful information would be forthcoming from his continued presence.

The girl who answered the door was of medium height and slightly overweight in an attractive sort of way; chubby, but nicely rounded, as though she were constantly wrestling with the latest diet – and losing. But as Tipper later observed, she bulged in all the right places.

'Miss Barbara Rigby?'

She looked apprehensively at the two tall men. 'Yes.'

'We're police officers, Miss Rigby.' Gaffney produced his warrant card and held it up for her inspection. She glanced at it cursorily, but made no move to open the door wider. 'I wonder if we may come in?'

She still looked a little doubtful, but stepped back and opened the door. 'I'm afraid the flat's in a bit of mess,' she said, 'but I've only just got back from Venice.'

Thanks to a helpful security officer at the airline she

worked for, Gaffney knew that. 'Holiday?' he asked innocently.

'Oh no.' she shook her head. 'It wasn't a holiday. I work for an airline. I'm a stewardess.' She collected up some newspapers and magazines that were scattered about on the chairs and put them on top of a pile of records on a small table near the window. 'I'm sorry,' she said. 'I never seem to get time to tidy up.' She flicked a lock of blonde hair out of her eyes, and rather breathlessly invited them to sit down. 'Is it about the car?'

'The car?'

'Yes. Whenever I get mixed up with the police, it always seems to be something to do with my car.' She wrinkled her nose. 'I'm afraid I'm forever getting parking tickets.' She looked coy. 'And I've been stopped twice for speeding. I never seem to leave enough time to get to work, and working for an airline they tend to go without you if you're not there.'

'No, Miss Rigby,' said Gaffney, 'it's not about your car. I understand that Mr Patrick Hughes is a friend of yours?'

She looked alarmed. 'What's happened? Is he all right?'

Gaffney smiled. 'As far as I know, yes.'

'Oh,' she said, 'you quite worried me for a moment. I thought he'd had an accident or something.' She fanned her face with her hand and laughed. 'He's more than a friend – he's my fiancé.'

'Oh, I see.' It was only with difficulty that Gaffney kept his astonishment from showing.

She glanced briefly at Tipper and then looked at Gaffney again. 'Is that so strange? A lot of people get married, you know.' She laughed demurely.

'And when are you getting married?'

'We haven't fixed a date yet, but it won't be long. But why are you asking these questions?'

Gaffney hesitated. 'Mr Hughes is in what is called sensitive employment, Miss Rigby – '

'Oh, the civil service, you mean?'

' – and he has to be positively vetted.'

'Sounds like something you have done to a cat,' she

225

said. Then she giggled. 'Oh, I do hope not,' she added.

'Not quite.' Gaffney thought that he was going to have trouble getting this girl to take his enquiries seriously. 'But we do have to make certain enquiries about such people.'

'I suppose you want to know all about his bad habits, is that it?'

'If he has any, yes.'

She leaned back in her chair pretending to be thoughtful. 'Well . . . ' She drew the word out. 'He's always wanting me to go to bed with him.' She smiled. It had been said flatly, with no trace of embarrassment, as another woman might have said that her man spent all his spare time sticking stamps in an album. She crossed her legs so that the split skirt fell away; she made no attempt to adjust it. 'Not that I mind,' she said, closing her eyes briefly, and looking down with artificial modesty.

'As a matter of interest, do you know precisely what he does in the civil service?'

'No, not really,' she said airily. 'He never talks about it. But then I don't talk about my job either. We're usually much too busy doing other things to worry about our jobs.' Again she smiled, but this time she had sounded insincere, and a little nervous.

'Never mentioned what he does, or where he goes?' Gaffney hammered it home.

She shook her head, avoiding his gaze. 'I know he works in London, and I've got his telephone number at the office, but he's asked me never to use it – unless it's a real emergency.'

Like about ten minutes from now, thought Gaffney. 'Do you know which ministry he works in?'

'No – but you must know surely?'

'Yes, I do,' said Gaffney. 'I just wanted to see how much he talks about it to other people.'

'Does that include fiancées and wives, too?'

'Rather depends how much he trusts them, I suppose.'

'Are you saying he doesn't trust me, then?'

'No, not at all.' Gaffney smiled. 'Has he introduced you to many of his friends?'

She thought about that for a few moments. 'No,' she said. 'He hasn't introduced me to any. He said that all his friends were the people he worked with, and that they were all pretty uninteresting anyway.' She giggled again and shrugged her shoulders. 'Actually what he said was that he wouldn't trust any of his friends near me.' She uncrossed her legs and recrossed them the other way. The skirt remained parted, if anything showing a little more leg than before. 'Would you like a drink?' she asked suddenly. 'I've got a cocktail cabinet simply stuffed with duty-free.' Gaffney sensed tension behind the brittle gaiety and wondered what she was hiding.

'No thank you, Miss Rigby.'

She pouted. 'Oh, not on duty, eh?'

Gaffney didn't bother to tackle that old chestnut. 'You are aware I take it, Miss Rigby, that Mr Hughes is married?'

She sat up slowly and covered her knees, her bubbly demeanour dissipating instantly. 'I don't believe you. You're joking, aren't you?' She looked from one to the other, and shook her head. 'No – you're not joking,' she said, seeing no comfort in their solemn faces.

'I'm afraid not, no.'

With a long-drawn-out sigh, she pushed her hands up through her blonde hair. For some time there was silence in the room, broken only by the heavy beat of a stereo playing in a nearby flat. She took a deep breath and, gazing directly at Gaffney, said, 'The bastard – the absolute shit.'

'I take it you didn't know,' said Gaffney, and Tipper looked out of the window, willing himself not to laugh.

'No, I bloody well didn't.' She stood up and walked about the room, a latent bundle of human energy, waiting to explode. Gaffney thought that he wouldn't care to be Patrick Hughes the next time she spoke to him. Suddenly she stopped and turned. 'How long?' she asked.

'How long?'

'How long has he been married?'

Gaffney shrugged. 'About twelve years, I believe, I don't know precisely.'

'He told me he wasn't married,' she said bitterly.

'They do,' said Gaffney quietly.

'What?'

'You're not the first girl to have been taken in by a married man in that way, Miss Rigby.' He spoke sympathetically. She might be a flirt, but she had clearly had a raw deal. 'I'm sorry,' he said. 'I'm afraid I automatically assumed that you would know.'

'I'm not the sort of girl to have an affaire with a married man.'

Gaffney was not wholly convinced of that. 'Are you all right?' he asked. She appeared to be in a trance, but he didn't want to hear, later, that she had taken an overdose of drugs.

She nodded. 'Oh yes, I'm all right. I'm just shaking with bloody anger.'

'Are you sure he didn't tell you where he worked, Miss Rigby?'

She laughed, a short scornful laugh. 'He said he worked for MI5, but I didn't believe that for a minute. He was obviously trying to impress me. Silly of him really; he didn't need to.' She looked blankly beyond Gaffney. 'I loved him . . . I think.'

'And is that all he said?'

'He said he couldn't tell me what he did – it was all secret. I don't know why he bothered to make it all up.' She remained quiet for a while, then: 'He doesn't work for MI5, does he?'

'No,' said Gaffney, giving himself some licence in pre-judging what he saw as an inevitability.

She opened the front door. 'I'm sorry – it's been a shock.' She paused. 'I didn't even get your name.'

'It's Gaffney.' He spelt it for her.

She closed the door behind the detectives, walked through into the sitting room and sat down on the settee. Then she spent a long time staring into space.

'What a double-dyed bastard he turned out to be,' said Tipper, as they walked back to the car.

'If it's all true,' said Gaffney. 'Mind you, I don't altogether blame him; she was rather gorgeous. But she could also be a good actress. Assume for a moment that she's an agent – and she could be anything from Mossad to the KGB – and she had deliberately targeted Hughes. She gets him into bed and he tells her all she wants to know.'

'Mossad? Why would the Israelis want to know anything about Soviet spies, guv'nor, and that's what we're talking about.'

'Harry,' said Gaffney patiently. 'One of the things you learn very quickly in this unsavoury and dingy world of intelligence, is that all information has a price. That price is other information. If one agency picks something up that's no good to them, they'll trade it for something that is.'

'How very underhand,' said Tipper.

'Conversely,' continued Gaffney, 'she might just be a pawn, an unwitting pawn. Airports are good places for picking up information; there are foreigners everywhere. And you never know who's working for whom. Just suppose she tells another girl at the airport something that Hughes has told her. That girl tells another girl, who tells her bloke . . . '

'Blimey,' said Tipper, 'and I thought villains were bent.'

'There again,' said Gaffney with a smile, 'she might be shacked up with a bloke who's an agent— '

'As well as with Hughes, you mean?'

'As well as with Hughes. It's all happened before, Harry. Nothing's new in this game; there's a limited number of permutations.'

Tipper nodded. 'We'd better put a team on her, then; full background and surveillance.'

'Yes. I want to know everything about that young lady.'

'Be interesting to read the transcripts.'

'Of what?'

'Her next conversation with Hughes. She's going to be straight on the odey— '

'Straight on the what?'

'Odey, guv. Eau-de-Cologne: phone!'

Gaffney groaned. 'I do wish you'd speak English, now that

you're a Special Branch officer, Harry. Yes, she probably will, but it may not tell us anything.'

'But if she thought he was single . . . '

'And if she is an agent, she's going to work on the assumption – all the time – that his or her telephone is on intercept, and act accordingly.'

'Meaning what, sir?'

'Meaning that she might just try to salvage something. Put the arm on him: threaten to tell his wife unless he keeps on coming across with the goods. But it's all speculation until we know a bit more.'

'Do we pay him a visit – Hughes?'

'Certainly not.'

'But— '

'We wait,' said Gaffney. 'Right now, she's probably working out exactly what she's going to say to him. She'll remember my name because I purposely spelt it for her, and when he asks how she knows, she'll tell him. Then, Harry, he's going to panic, because he won't be quite sure whether we're doing some sort of vetting review, or whether it's a part of our wider investigation. Depends on what she says on the phone really . . . if she's kosher.'

'Now we're back to Mossad again,' murmured Tipper.

'Either way, he'll eventually come to see us.'

'You can be very nasty when the mood takes you, sir.'

'Yes,' said Gaffney, filling the car with cigar smoke.

Tipper coughed and opened a window.

Chapter Sixteen

Harry Tipper, being a very professional sort of policeman, always believed in doing as much as he possibly could seated at his desk. Only then did he leave the office and start making enquiries. He also believed, as a detective chief inspector, that he only did those things himself if he couldn't find anyone else to do them for him. Harry Tipper was a master of delegation.

Consequently the small team of officers which Gaffney had assembled for the Armitage–Dickson enquiry was now shaken out of its reverie and made to work. Which came as a bit of a nasty shock. But results were soon forthcoming.

The most important piece of information to a policeman making enquiries about anyone is that person's date of birth. These days, most people drive motor cars, and the easiest place to acquire this information is from the Driver and Vehicle Licensing Centre which for some inexplicable reason is situated in Swansea.

Detective Constable Richard Henley – one of the new Special Branch officers recruited by Gaffney and put straight to work – knocked on Tipper's door and entered nervously. 'I've got her date of birth, sir – 7th July 1952,' and he laid a piece of paper reverently on Tipper's desk.

'All right – just leave it. There's nothing clever about that. If there was, I'd've given it to someone clever to do.' Somewhat abashed, the young man turned to leave. 'Hold on,' said Tipper, 'I haven't finished with you yet. Get up to St Catherine's House and get a copy of her birth certificate.' He paused. 'You know where St Catherine's House is, lad?'

'No, sir.'

'Well find out,' said Tipper, 'you're a detective now.'

DC Henley left, hurriedly. He was beginning to realise that joining Special Branch was to be given a licence to kill time – not a licence to kill.

Tipper then sent for DC Bishop, another new entry, gave him Julia Hodder's date of birth, and told him to search every index known to man – quickly.

Despite constantly harassing his team, it was still some days before he was able to assemble even the barest of dossiers on Julia Hodder, née Simpson. And this he now presented to Gaffney.

'We are not a great deal further forward, sir. We have her date of birth, and we have a copy of her birth certificate.'

'What does that tell us, Harry?' asked Gaffney.

'She was born in the maternity hospital in Hammersmith – Queen Charlotte's – the daughter of George and Helen Simpson. They were living in Richmond at the time, and his occupation was shown as Colonial Service. I've had a marriage search done as well, but that contains no surprises. Geoffrey Hodder, divorced, married Julia Simpson, spinster, in 1978. His occupation was shown as civil servant, and the addresses tally. Passport Office confirm that she's got a passport, but then she would have, wouldn't she? The details on it match what we know. All other indexes searched – blank, nothing.'

'And you were the one who said he knew a few tricks,' said Gaffney, laughing.

'Guv'nor,' said Tipper, 'I haven't even started yet.'

There wasn't a Colonial Office any more and Tipper sought help from the Foreign and Commonwealth Office whose Security Department was accommodated in one of the little back streets of Westminster that seemed largely untouched by the modern world without.

'I'm Naylor,' said the tall, grey-haired man, rising from his desk. 'How can I help you, Chief Inspector?'

'I'm trying to trace someone who worked in the Colonial

232

Service in 1952,' said Tipper, flipping open his pocket book.

'Ah, well in that case you've come to the right place. You see, the Colonial Office was merged with the Commonwealth Relations Office in 1967, and then merged again to form the present Foreign and Commonwealth Office in 1968.' Naylor smiled. 'Complicated, isn't it?'

'Yes,' said Tipper. 'I have a delicate enquiry – ' He gazed levelly at Naylor. ' – a part of which is to attempt to trace a George Simpson who, in 1952, was in the Colonial Service, but was living in Richmond, Surrey, at the time.'

'Is that all the information you have?'

'He was married to Helen Simpson, née Gibson, and they had a daughter called Julia, born on – ' He paused to consult his pocket book again. ' – 7th July 1952.'

'Mmmm!' Naylor scribbled a few notes on a pad. 'The difficulty here, of course, Chief Inspector, is that when the offices were merged, we took over their records as they stood, but there was not a great deal of work done on them – not much point really, if you take my meaning. And they ran different systems to those of the Foreign Office.' He smiled again, benevolently. He was obviously a Foreign Office man. 'What exactly can I do to assist you?'

'I don't know,' said Tipper. 'Anything that you've got. Frankly, I don't know what I'm looking for; I'm just ferreting at the moment.'

'It's a long time ago, of course,' said Naylor, 'but I'll do what I can.'

Tipper gave him his telephone number at the Yard. 'Will it take long?'

'Difficult to say. There is obviously some urgency as far as you're concerned?'

'Yes indeed.'

'Have you any idea where he may have served?'

'Not really. But if it's any help, I understand that the daughter, Julia, worked for a charity in Africa until about ten or eleven years ago. It may be that he was in Africa. . . . Come to think of it, she said that she had been brought up

233

in Nigeria, and that her family were old Africa hands – that was the phrase she used. Is that any help?'

'At least it gives us a point of reference,' said Naylor. 'Old Africa hands, eh? That's not a phrase you hear too often now. Leave it with me, Chief Inspector. It may be that our man in Lagos can assist.'

'Fine,' said Tipper, 'but perhaps you could let me have anything as you get it, rather than wait for replies to telegrams.'

'I take it you've dealt with the Foreign Office before,' Naylor said with a smile. He stood up and extended his hand. 'I'll be in touch as soon as I've got anything at all.'

It took a mere ninety-six hours, which included what must have been an anguished weekend, for Patrick Hughes to come to Scotland Yard. He had telephoned Gaffney in the morning and asked if he could see him that evening.

He was not, however, at all contrite; he was very angry. 'What right have you got, going to see Miss Rigby and telling her I was married?'

'Every right, Mr Hughes,' said Gaffney. 'I am investigating, firstly a suspicious death, and secondly a serious leak in the service which currently employs you.' He made a point of emphasising the 'currently'.

'I don't see what it has to do with Geoffrey's untimely death.'

'I don't suppose you do, Mr Hughes, but then you're not the investigating officer, are you?'

'But— '

'Why didn't you declare this affaire you are having at the time of your positive vetting?' Gaffney didn't know that he hadn't but guessed that that was the case. He hadn't been allowed to see the vetting reports on any of the team, but didn't see why he should tell Hughes that.

'I – er – well . . . ' The bravado had gone as quickly as it had been contrived, and he stumbled into a half-hearted explanation. 'It doesn't affect my work,' he said eventually. 'What's it got to do with them if I don't get on with my wife? She's quite happy – we go our separate ways.'

'It is a question which is specifically put,' said Gaffney, who remembered his own positive vetting interview, and had been glad that he hadn't been having an affair with anyone at the time, and had been able, honestly, to answer in the negative.

'Yes, I know, but it's only relevant if they think that pressure is likely to be put on as a result of it.'

'And you think that in your case that is unlikely?'

'Yes. I said we go our separate ways.'

'Does that mean that your wife's also having an affair?'

As a proposition, that had clearly never occurred to him. At first he avoided the question. 'Look – I don't see what all this has to do— '

'Just answer the question, Mr Hughes,' said Gaffney sharply.

Hughes hesitated for a further moment. 'Quite frankly, no. To be honest, I can't imagine anyone wanting to have an affair with Shirley. Anyway, she's too tied up in her work.'

'Which is?'

'I beg your pardon?'

'What is your wife's work, Mr Hughes?'

'She's a social worker.'

'I see,' said Gaffney. Tipper sniffed. 'And she doesn't have time for affairs, even though you said that you each go your own way?'

Hughes looked down at his feet. 'It's not so much that,' he said. 'She's not the most attractive woman in the world. A bit of a bluestocking, as a matter of fact.'

'Does she know of your affair with Barbara Rigby?'

Hughes pondered on that for some time before answering. 'I shouldn't think so,' he said at length.

'And what would she have said if she had found out?'

'I don't know, really. I suppose that she would have been upset.'

'So your implied view that pressure couldn't be brought to bear upon you is a myth, yes?'

'I don't think it would have caused me to be disloyal,' said Hughes miserably.

'Disloyal to whom – apart from your wife, of course?' That did not please Hughes.

'To the state – to my country . . . '

'I see,' said Gaffney. 'So you can put all these little loyalties into convenient water-tight compartments, is that it?'

'Well there's loyalty and loyalty, isn't there?'

'There is? What about loyalty to Miss Rigby, then, who appeared to be under the impression that you were going to marry her, but whom you conveniently omitted to inform that you were already married? Is that another kind of loyalty that doesn't count?'

'No, but that's different. Anyway, I've had enough of this. My private life is my affair.'

'It strikes me that your private life is one long affaire,' said Gaffney dryly. 'But I shall decide when you've had enough of this. Right now, my inclination is to report the whole matter to the Director-General, and see what he wants to make of it.'

Hughes sat up, went red in the face, and started playing with one of the buttons on his jacket. 'There's no need for that, is there?'

'Mr Hughes.' Gaffney leaned forward on his desk, and stared at the man opposite him. 'Do you honestly think that anything I am doing on this enquiry will not be reported to the DG? The only thing that is likely to help you is if I can report to Sir Edward that you have been very co-operative.'

Deep down, Hughes had known all along that that would be the case, had been trying to convince himself that he could get away with it. He gripped his hands together in a tight bunch. 'What can I say?' he asked.

'For a start, you can tell me how it came about.'

'We met on a flight. I'd been out to Vienna – special job.' Gaffney wasn't interested in that – let him have his little secret. 'And she was the stewardess. We got talking and I invited her out to dinner one evening. It just blossomed from there.'

'Did she ever ask you if you were married?'

'Yes.'

'And?'

Hughes dithered, struggling with his conscience. 'I told her I was single.' He shuffled his feet. 'I didn't think it really mattered. It was never intended to be anything more than a one-night stand, but then it sort of got serious.'

'And what would you have done if we hadn't intervened?'

'I don't know. I did consider getting a divorce at one stage, but the more I thought about it, the more unlikely it seemed – I mean Barbara and I being married. She's not awfully intelligent, you know.'

Any sympathy that Gaffney might have had evaporated at that moment. Not only was Hughes a philanderer – he was also a snob, an insufferable, immoral snob. And the immorality didn't apply to his having an affaire – a lot of men did that, and women too for that matter, but it was the way of his having one, and his attitude towards the girl in Hounslow. Gaffney agreed with him; she wasn't very bright, but she deserved better than Hughes. 'How much did you tell her of your work, Mr Hughes?'

Hughes paled slightly. 'Nothing – absolutely nothing – I promise you.'

Tipper smiled. 'I suppose that would have been what you call a breach of security,' he said.

'She never asked what you did?' Gaffney again.

'No. I think I volunteered that I was a civil servant.'

'And she was happy with that, was she? Not very romantic, is it, being a civil servant? Miss Rigby's an air stewardess, goes to exotic places, and being rather unintelligent – I think that was what you said – wouldn't have been satisfied with that, surely? What did you lead her to believe? That you were a clerk in the DHSS? Surely not. You must have told her that you were something terribly dramatic.'

'I didn't. I assure you.' At last, Hughes was beginning to understand Gaffney's line of questioning.

'That isn't true, Mr Hughes. Let's go over it once more, shall we? You are on a flight from Vienna to London, and you meet this very attractive young lady. You chat her up, and she takes a liking to you – she's attracted to you. Here's a suave, well-educated man in his mid-thirties, just flown in from Vienna. There's nothing to that, is there? You do it all the time – a veritable man-about-town. You suggest dinner, and she accepts. You must be something out of the ordinary, yes? And then you tell her that you're a civil servant. And did she accept that? Or did she ask you what sort of civil servant you were? She surely didn't just nod and go on to talk about something else?'

'Honestly – I didn't tell her a thing.'

'And she didn't ask?' Gaffney gave him a long, penetrating stare.

'Well I might have hinted, I suppose.'

'Ah! And what did you hint, Mr Hughes, eh?'

Hughes fidgeted nervously. 'I think I might have said something about not being able to talk about my work – that it was hush-hush – something like that.'

'Why? Why not tell her that you were a clerk in the DHSS? After all that's a perfectly honourable calling, isn't it?'

'Yes, of course, but— '

'But not the sort of job to impress a nubile young lady who wasn't very intelligent, but who was willing to let you screw her just so long as she thought you were a bit of a mystery man.'

'No – I didn't have to impress her. We got on very well together— '

'In bed!'

'Yes – but that wasn't all. She was fun to be with, to talk to. . . . '

'And what did you talk about – when you weren't screwing, that is?' Gaffney was being deliberately coarse to try to goad this man.

'We . . . Well, I suppose we talked about television that we'd seen, and the places we'd been to . . . '

'Have you travelled very much, Mr Hughes?'

'A fair amount. There was one section I was in when I seemed to be forever getting on and off aircraft.'

238

'So you compared notes, discussed the hotels you'd been in; that sort of thing?'

'Well, yes.'

'And didn't she think it rather funny that a civil servant was gallivanting about all over the world? Doesn't exactly match the image of the chap who goes up on the eight fifty clutching an umbrella and a plastic, government-issue briefcase with his sandwiches in it, does it?'

'She never asked me.' Hughes's head was bowed now, his elbows resting on his knees.

'You're a liar, Mr Hughes. You told her you were with MI5, just to impress her, and you gave her the telephone number of the office, but made her swear never to use it. And all that so that she'd keep opening her legs for you.'

Hughes looked up, his hands clenched, and hate for Gaffney clear on his face. 'I— '

'Well?'

'Yes. Yes, damn you.' He rested his head on his hands.

'And you talk to me about loyalty . . . '

'Can I go now?'

'No,' said Gaffney. 'I haven't finished yet. Who is this girl?'

Hughes looked up sharply. 'What d'you mean? You know who she is. She's Barbara Rigby and she works for— '

'I know what she's told you, and I know what she's told me, but is it true?'

'But I . . . ' Hughes shot a panicky glance at Gaffney.

'You never bothered to find out, did you, because you were so bloody obsessed with her? She could be anyone. You didn't know, didn't care, just so long as you got your end away.'

'But I'm sure that she— '

'Sure, Mr Hughes? Sure what? That she really is an air stewardess, and that her name really is Barbara Rigby. How do you know? What enquiries have you made?'

'Well I— '

Gaffney raised his hand. 'You don't know at all. Does she work for the KGB? Does she have a controller who is rubbing his hands in some Iron Curtain embassy, delighted that an intelligence officer in MI5 has fallen for the oldest trick in the world?'

Hughes was now sweating profusely; his self-confidence, and the bombast with which he had entered the room, had drained away completely. Gaffney's questions had alarmed him to the point of open panic. He couldn't be sure whether this damned policeman knew something that he didn't, or was just provoking him. He opened his mouth to say something, but no sound came.

Relentlessly, Gaffney went on: 'I have a team of officers who are now spending a great deal of their valuable time investigating this woman's background, Mr Hughes, and do you know why? I'll tell you: because you think that you're so bloody clever. You imagine that because you're a so-called intelligence officer, you can do as you bloody well please, and that no one is bright enough to catch you at it.' Gaffney leaned back in his chair, and briefly surveyed the abject figure of Patrick Hughes. 'If I was you, Mr Hughes,' he said, 'I'd start to look around for a job: somehow I don't think you'll have your present one too much longer.'

'What will happen?' asked Hughes eventually.

Gaffney raised his eyebrows and sniffed. 'It's not up to me. It does reveal one thing though: your girl friend might not be very intelligent, but you are downright stupid.'

'Will my wife have to know?'

'Only if you finish up in the dock. Then it will all come out. But in that case, it won't really matter, will it? They tend to give rather long sentences for breaches of security.'

'I didn't tell her anything about the work I was doing, I promise you that.' Hughes's face was working nervously, and Gaffney could see that his self-control was all but gone. 'I didn't know anything about the Dickson job. All that I told you last time is true: Geoffrey didn't tell me anything.' He paused, staring at Gaffney with an expression of desperation.

'I have only your word for that, Mr Hughes,' said Gaffney, 'and so far, I haven't found that too reliable.'

'What are you going to do about him?' asked Tipper, when they had released Hughes from his torture.

'Report the whole thing to the DG, I suppose,' said Gaffney. 'But not yet. It's true that we don't know who Barbara Rigby is. Until we've got the results of that enquiry, we can't write him off. If it turns out that he's just an idiot who can't keep his mouth shut, then the DG can have him to do what he likes with. Incidentally, how is that enquiry going? Anywhere near a result yet?'

'I'll chase it up, guv'nor; we should be getting something fairly soon.' Tipper stifled a yawn. 'What d'you reckon the DG will do with him?'

'If it was left to me,' said Gaffney, 'I'd transfer him to the DHSS.'

'That didn't take long,' said Tipper. Secretly he thought that three days to find some records was tantamount to bone idleness, but he would profit nothing by saying so. He replaced the receiver and walked round to the FCO Security Department.

'It's not very much so far,' said Naylor, a modest smile on his face. He consulted a file on his desk. 'It appears that Mr and Mrs Simpson were killed in an air crash in 1975, in the Bight of Benin.' He looked up. 'That's just off the coast of Nigeria, south of Lagos.' His tone was slightly patronising.

'Yes, I know. Do you have any details?'

'They were returning from Calabar to Lagos. Been on holiday there.' He glanced up again. 'Quite a pleasant part that, you know – Calabar; the missionary Mary Slessor's buried there, as a matter of fact.'

'Really,' murmured Tipper.

'Yes – well.' He studied the file again. 'He was on the High Commission staff at Lagos. Private plane.' He was reading extracts from the file as they caught his eye. 'Just the two of them – and the pilot of course. Circling over the Bight before coming in to land at Ijeka Airport. No explanation – just went down. Tragedy really after a lifetime of service. He

241

was fifty-four; she was fifty. Tragic.' He shook his head.

'Anything about the daughter – Julia?'

'Nothing on here I'm afraid.'

'No indication that she had been informed – next of kin – nothing like that?'

'No – nothing. I've sent a signal to our man in Lagos, as I promised. He may be able to turn up something about this woman . . . ' He paused. 'Julia Simpson?'

'Yes – Hodder now.'

Naylor looked up sharply. 'I knew a Hodder – in Five.'

'Really?'

'I'll give you a ring if anything turns up.' Naylor closed the file and smiled benevolently.

'You're not going to believe this, sir. In fact, I don't believe it myself.' Tipper walked into Gaffney's office, holding the intercept file. 'But Selby's got a girl friend. Well, I presume it's a girl – might be a bloke, but if it is, he calls himself Rita.' He flopped down in one of Gaffney's chairs and opened the file, taking a photostat copy of a letter from it.

'Just because he looks like a poof doesn't necessarily make him one, Harry, despite the fact that you've convinced yourself he is. What does it say?'

'Well for a start there's no address on it – no sender's address that is, but it's pretty powerful stuff. Listen to this: "My dearest darling".' Tipper glanced at Gaffney. 'Not bad for openers, is it?'

'Get on with it, Harry.'

'Yes, right. "My dearest darling. How wonderful it was to see you on Thursday. Now, I've a big surprise for you! You-know-who is away in Sweden on business – until Tuesday. Five whole days!! So why don't you come down to Devon – at least for the weekend. We can have two days to ourselves. I don't suppose you can get any extra time off at such short notice, so come down on Saturday morning, or better still, Friday evening – in time for bed!! See you soon – love, love and lots more love, Rita." How's that grab you, guv'nor?' Tipper dropped the copy of the letter onto Gaffney's blotter.

242

'Well – there's a thing,' said Gaffney. 'Naughty, lucky, old Selby. Wonder who she is.'

'Or him,' said Tipper.

Gaffney laughed. 'That's a woman's writing, if I'm any judge. He never said anything about having a bird, did he?'

'We didn't ask,' said Tipper. 'More to the point, what are we going to do about it – anything?'

'Why should there be no sender's address, though, Harry?'

'She's married, isn't she? She says so. Not in as many words, but "you-know-who is in Sweden" – that's a dead give-away. So she doesn't put her address on it in case anyone else reads it – like nasty suspicious policemen who're doing a postal intercept.'

'He might have guessed – being in the trade – and warned her.'

'In that case, sir, he'd have told her not to write at all.'

'True, Harry, true. So he's having it off with a married woman. Like Hughes, not declared for vetting, I'll bet you.'

'You're probably right – well, it's a racing certainty – but are we going to waste all our time chasing blokes who are over the side?'

'As I've said before, Harry, we don't know we're wasting it until we've wasted it. At the moment, we've got nothing better to go on, and quite frankly, Selby is the most sussy of the lot.'

'Apart from Hodder. I mean, he's the one who topped himself, isn't he?'

'But there's not a shred of evidence to say that he killed himself because of the leak. We've just got to keep going until something turns up.'

Tipper shook his head. 'I don't think that Selby having it off with a married bird is going to be the answer, sir. He is single, after all.'

'But she's not, Harry. And that's where the pressure could come from. Supposing it had been discovered that he was having an affaire with a married woman. That could be used as a lever. You're probably right, and we're beginning to look like an expensive firm of private detectives, but until we know a little more about Rita – and Rita's husband – we can't dismiss it. We've nothing else.'

'There are the enquiries about Hodder, sir.'

'I know, Harry. But so far we've turned up nothing helpful about him. And the further away we get from his death, the less likely we are to find anything – that's my guess, anyway. In the meantime we'll have a look at Rita.'

'How? We've no idea who she is.'

'We'll find out, then. Set up a surveillance team and take him down to Devon.'

'But we don't even know when.'

'Yes we do.' Gaffney picked up the letter. 'She says come down on Saturday morning, or better still Friday evening. It's my bet that he'll get down there as quick as he can. My money's on Friday evening. Take him from his office and see what happens.'

'But we don't know how he's going to get there. He might go by train, but if he goes by car it's going to be one hell of a following job. It must be about two hundred miles.'

'Okay – so use a big team. Leap-frog with the vehicles. Use motor-cycles. Whatever's needed. Don't forget what the Commissioner told the DAC: we can have anything we want.'

'Yes, sir,' said Tipper, and looked at the ceiling.

Detective Constables Henley, Bishop and Cane stood in a row in front of Tipper's desk. Behind them was Detective Sergeant Ian Mackinnon, a half-grin on his face.

'Any of you know how many charities there are operating in Africa?'

The three new detectives glanced nervously at each other. Mackinnon continued to smile; he had been a Special Branch officer long enough not to be surprised by anything the governors came up with.

'No, sir,' said Cane. The other two shook their heads.

'You, skip?'

'No idea, guv'nor,' said Mackinnon, 'but I suspect that we're about to find out.'

'Dead right you are. Now then, I want you to list as many as you can discover – go to the Charities Commission, or some place like that. Most of these organisations are bound to have their headquarters in London; the British are suckers for giving away money – other people's money. Then I want enquiries made of all of them; find out whether they ever had a Julia Simpson working for them.' He looked at Henley. 'You've got her date of birth.' The DC nodded. 'Don't tell them why you want to know – well you don't know anyway, but spin them some fanny about missing persons; you know the drill.' He looked enquiringly at the sergeant.

'And if we find her?' asked Mackinnon.

'You won't. I know where she is. But if any of you find that she was working for them, let DS Mackinnon here know.' He switched his gaze back to the sergeant. 'Then you see the informant and get as much background as you can. And let me know, step by step.' The sergeant mumbled. 'What did you say?'

'I said it's going to be an interesting job, sir.'

'No it's not,' said Tipper, grinning, 'but when you're a DCI you'll be able to get someone to do these little jobs for you.'

'Barbara Rigby appears to be clean, sir,' said Tipper. He put a sheaf of papers on Gaffney's desk, and lowered himself wearily into the easy chair. 'That's the report.'

Gaffney glanced at the opening paragraph. 'What does it say?'

'Very briefly, born twenty-five years ago in Woodford, Essex. Went to a local comprehensive and got three indifferent CSEs. Left school at sixteen and got a job in the City as a clerk-typist. At eighteen, got a job with an airline based on Stansted. After two years at that, got a job with the same airline as a stewardess through the good offices of her manager.' He grinned. 'Moved to her present airline at Heathrow about three years ago. Has a reputation for putting herself about a bit; in short, she's anybody's.'

'That it?' asked Gaffney.

'More or less,' said Tipper. 'Likes men, discos and parties, in that order. Seems harmless enough. There's certainly nothing to indicate that she's anything more than she seems.'

'Just a bed-hopper?'

'That's about it, but that could make her dangerous. There again, none of the men she's been with seems to be interested in anything but her body; it's certainly not her brains. Incidentally there's a married police sergeant from the uniform branch at Heathrow on the rather lengthy list of her boy friends, past and present, that forms an appendix to that.' Tipper pointed at the report and laughed.

'Has he been interviewed?'

'Yes,' said Tipper, 'by me.'

'Any joy?'

'Not on his part, guv. I reminded him of that bit in the Discipline Code about a married officer consorting with a woman not his wife, whereby complaint was made. He didn't laugh.'

'Looks as though we can put that enquiry to bed, then.'

Tipper laughed. 'Unfortunate choice of phrase, sir, but yes, I reckon we can.'

Chapter Seventeen

It took three weeks to trace Julia Hodder's employment with an African-based charity. Three hard weeks of footslogging, frustrating and at times disappointing enquiry. It is one of the sad aspects of the influence of television that young men aspiring to the Criminal Investigation Department tend to think that all crime enquiries are naturally condensed into fifty-minute blocks. But as DCs Henley, Bishop and Cane discovered, such episodes in the romantic life of a detective took no account of the stairs – all charities, it seemed, had their offices on the top floors of old buildings that had no lifts – the unhelpfulness of some people, or the difficulty of parking a police car, detectives not being exempt from the vexations of driving in London.

'Yes,' said the woman who had introduced herself as the organiser, 'a Julia Simpson worked for us in Ethiopia about eleven years ago.' She had obligingly searched the records of her charity which, unlike some of the other organisations they had visited, were quite well ordered.

'Do you have a date of birth?' asked Bishop.

'Yes I do,' she said with a maternal smile. 'According to my list it was 7th July 1952. Is there anything else I can help you with?'

'No,' said Bishop, 'but I think my sergeant would like to come and talk to you.'

'Of course,' she said. 'We're always willing to help the police.' That bit was like television.

The follow-up was a disappointment. The woman confirmed what she had told Bishop. Had the young detective asked just

247

one or two more questions he could have saved Mackinnon a journey, but conscious of the strictures his chief inspector had placed upon him, he did not do so.

'I'm afraid that she's just a name in our records, Sergeant. There's no one here who would have known her. We're only the London administrators. I'm afraid you'd have to go to Ethiopia, and even then you might not find anyone who knew her. The people who work for charities tend to be a transient group. A lot of young people, you know – Americans mainly – it seems to be part of growing up these days.'

'Can you at least tell me how long she worked for you, then?'

The woman looked pensive. 'Just a moment,' she said, and crossed the room to a filing cabinet. After one or two false starts, she extracted a file. 'From the beginning of 1975 to about the middle of 1977, it looks like,' she said. 'But there's nothing here to say where she came from – or where she went.'

'A photograph, perhaps? Or anything to say that she lost both her parents in 1975?'

The woman closed the file, dropped it into the cabinet and shut the drawer. 'I'm sorry, no,' she said. 'I'm afraid our records are a bit sketchy. So often in this business you're living in the back of a truck, and you'd be surprised how often trucks – and records – get lost, blown up, burnt – so frequently in fact that it seems a waste of time ever putting things on paper.' She sat down at her desk again. 'We're accused of creating great mountains of paper here in London, but it doesn't help to feed the starving millions,' said the woman with a sigh. 'That's what our workers in the field tell us – they get a bit cross about it all at times.'

'I know the feeling,' said Mackinnon.

'A bloke called Naylor rang from the FCO, guv'nor,' said the reserve sergeant as Tipper came out of the lift at Scotland Yard. 'Says would you ring him back.'

Tipper preferred face-to-face enquiries once he was into an investigation; preliminairies were all right on the phone;

they could save a lot of time. He went back into the lift, rode to the ground floor and walked round to Naylor's office.

'I'm afraid we've drawn a blank on your Julia Simpson. I've just got a signal from the High Commission. None of the charities operating in Nigeria have heard of her.'

'I've got the answer to that,' said Tipper, 'or some of it – she spent a couple of years in Ethiopia apparently.'

'Oh good.' Naylor said it as though Ethiopia was the place to be, and Tipper thought he was about to get another little homily, this time on Addis Ababa. 'What they did say now . . . ' He rooted about among the papers on his desk and picked up the signal. 'What they did say was that there's a chap living just outside Brighton who was there with the Simpsons. The High Commissioner knows him personally it seems – retired now, of course, but he thought that he might be able to help. Rather good of him, really.'

'Very good of him,' said Tipper. There was no sarcasm in his comment; it was the sort of assistance that often helped to speed up an enquiry enormously. 'You have the name and address there, I hope?'

'There you are,' said Naylor, handing him a piece of paper. 'All written out for you.'

'Thank you,' said Tipper, 'you've been most helpful.' And he meant it.

It was about the most complicated surveillance operation that could have been staged. Following a vehicle for two hundred miles is extremely difficult, even for the most skilled of operatives. The least observant of drivers will notice when one particular car is following him, even if he glances in his rear-view mirror only occasionally. It was for this reason that Tipper arranged to have six vehicles of various types, none of which looked anything like a police car, and three motorcyclists standing by at three o'clock on Friday afternoon. Even so, Gaffney was beginning to have second thoughts, not because it could prove to be a futile operation, but because it was going to be a very expensive one. One of the quirks of police administration is that they'll swallow the costs of a success; but they make a terrible fuss if they think that money has been wasted.

The mobiles were not, however, needed for the first part of the observation. At five o'clock precisely, Selby left the grey, concrete pile that is the headquarters of MI5 and made his way through the side-streets of Mayfair until he reached Green Park tube station. There he caught the Piccadilly Line train and changed at South Kensington, waiting until a Wimbledon train arrived, which he boarded. It was apparent that Selby had no idea that he was being housed; nevertheless, to follow someone on the underground system, particularly during the rush-hour, is extremely difficult, the more so when he changes trains at a busy station.

At half-past five, Selby emerged from Fulham Broadway station and walked the short distance to his flat. His arrival was reported to control both by the team who had followed him and by the team which had been watching his flat since four o'clock. Now came the waiting. Gaffney and his officers still didn't know for sure whether Selby would stay in Fulham for the night, or travel down to Devon that evening. He certainly hadn't telephoned the mysterious Rita, at least from any of the phones being intercepted by Special Branch. Gaffney's guess was that Selby, despite his offhanded and languorous attitude, had been shrewd enough to make that call from a public telephone, if he had made it at all.

The short space of time which Selby spent in his flat almost caught the watchers by surprise. They estimated that he had been indoors exactly seven minutes before striding briskly from the building carrying a nylon holdall. A three-man team, adopting the usual ABC pattern, immediately covered him for the short walk to a lock-up garage, from which he drove, shortly afterwards, in a rather anonymous-looking Ford Cortina.

'Well at least he won't be going very fast in that, thank God,' said the policeman who was driving the souped-up transit van that was the first to fall in behind Selby's car. They were afraid that he might have owned a Porsche or something similar. That, on his wages, would have been interesting, but would also have made him extremely difficult to follow.

It was the first time that any of them had seen Selby's car, despite all the efforts that Tipper had made. There were certain things he would dearly like to have done to it to make it easier to follow, but he hadn't been able to. He briefed a motor-cyclist to undertake one of them at the earliest opportunity, which entailed that particular policeman stopping off at a DIY store and purchasing a hand-drill and a couple of slender bits. Following suspect vehicles in daylight was difficult enough, but following them at night was extremely hazardous for the surveillance drivers who tended to take risks in order not to lose their quarry. One set of rear lights looked much like another in the dark, particularly on a crowded motorway. And darkness regrettably ruled out the use of a helicopter.

Gaffney had decided to spend the evening sitting in the operations room in Special Branch at Scotland Yard, where he could listen to the transmissions. He had a feeling that the whole thing was a complete waste of time, but there was something about Selby that made him feel uneasy; something that didn't gel, even allowing for the fact that MI5 seemed to have more than its fair share of individualists. It was a view shared by the people he worked with; even Hughes and Craven, in their own way a little unusual, had not been very happy about him, although none of them was able to be specific. He didn't know what Selby's colleagues called it; but policemen called it gut-reaction.

It was rush-hour. That presented a plus – and a minus. The plus was that Selby couldn't go very fast; the minus was that the density of traffic made it impossible at times to get through to where you wanted to be. That, of course, was where the motor-cyclists came into their own.

The first report to reach Gaffney was that Selby was mobile and crossing Putney Bridge. A little while later they had him on the A316 Chertsey Road. 'Making for the M3 I should think,' said Gaffney.

'Sorry sir, do what?' The operator lifted one of his ear-phones.

Gaffney waved an apologetic hand, realising that he had distracted the man. 'Sorry,' he said, 'not you. I was talking to the skipper.' He turned to Claire Wentworth. 'M3!'

She nodded. 'I heard you, sir.'

It looked as though Gaffney was right and Selby was making for Devon. He was now clear of London's rush-hour traffic, but motorways presented problems of their own. He put on a spare set of headphones in time to hear the driver who was on Selby's tail saying that he wished he was still in traffic division. 'He's doing bloody ninety in that crate; he'll fall apart if he's not careful.' Gaffney took the headphones off again, preferring not to know what was going on; the consequences of a pile-up on the motorway, involving his surveillance team, were too horrific to contemplate, not only, he had to admit, because of the possible injuries to his men, but the certainty that it would blow the whole operation. Someone would be bound to ask if it had been worth it.

Later on, a motor-cyclist reported that Selby had stopped at Fleet services on the M3, and added that he'd fixed the lights. It was not until the following day that Gaffney found out what that meant; the motor-cyclist who had stopped to buy the drill had used it to make a small hole in Selby's rear lights. Following the Cortina had been considerably easier after that.

Selby left the M3 at Junction 8 and drove through Sutton Scotney on the A30. From then on, it was fairly straight-forward, with regular reports of his having passed through Yeovil, Honiton and Exeter, where he dropped south to Ashburton on the A38. Then, rather riskily, Gaffney thought, he crossed Dartmoor in pouring rain.

Just before midnight, Tipper telephoned the operations room and spoke to Gaffney: 'We've arrived, guv'nor. It's a pig of a place. There's nowhere to set up an obo, short of leaving a vehicle at each end of a fairly long country lane; and that'd stick out like a sore thumb.'

'Leave it, Harry,' said Gaffney. 'You won't learn anything else. Pull off the obo. Get the lads billeted for the night down there – the local old bill will know somewhere –

252

and I'll see you tomorrow. And thank the team; they've done bloody well.'

Gaffney dismissed his people at the Yard and went home. He just hoped that it had been worthwhile, but admitted to himself that he had probably achieved nothing more than to identify yet another adulterer.

Harry Tipper was back at Scotland Yard by noon. 'It was a non-starter from the obo point of view, sir. It's a large house – looks like an old farmhouse, converted, I should think. It's been nicely tarted up. But it's in a lane, south of Dartmoor, east of Tavistock. There isn't another house within sight. It's just outside a small village called Bere Watton.'

'It doesn't matter, Harry. I never intended that you should maintain observation once you got there. You did a bloody good job in taking him all that way, incidentally. I never thought you'd pull it off.'

Tipper chuckled. 'Piece of cake, guv,' he said. 'Mind you, it did get a bit hairy once or twice on that bloody A30. I think our blokes may have committed one or two offences of dangerous driving and failing to comply with traffic lights. Never mind; all in a good cause. What do we do now?'

'I'll get Devon and Cornwall Special Branch to make one or two enquiries – see if we can identify the mysterious Rita. Then we'll take it from there.'

'Are you going to 'front him with it?'

'Depends what we find out. If it's just a straightforward case of cherchez la femme, I don't think we'll bother.'

Tipper nodded. 'Selby's a complete prat in my book, sir, but I still don't see him as our man. Frankly, I don't think he's got the stomach for it.'

'We'll see, Harry, we'll see. Spies are funny creatures. They're often driven by ideology. Bit different from the criminal fraternity; I don't think I've ever met an ideological villain.'

The Special Branch of the Devon and Cornwall Constabulary is only a small unit compared with that of the Metropolitan

Police, but no less efficient. Detective Inspector Joe Partridge was the officer responsible for the investigation of subversive and related activities in the vast area which included Tavistock. Gaffney had had dealings with him in the past, and very helpful he had been, too.

'Joe?' There had been the usual difficulties of ensuring that Partridge was in an office that had a scrambler on the telephone so that Gaffney could talk with a reasonable measure of security. 'We've got a little job running up here that has put Tavistock in the frame.'

'Oh, right, sir. What can we do to help?' Partridge's soft Devon accent seemed to bring the freshness of the moors over the line and into Gaffney's office.

'It's a farmhouse on the edge of Dartmoor. A woman, first name Rita – no further particulars – lives there apparently. It's near a village called Bere Watton, and the house is called Tanglewood.'

'I've got that, sir. What d'you want us to do?'

'A few discreet enquiries, Joe, if you can, without alerting the occupant – or anyone else. Is that possible?'

'Don't you worry, sir – we'll find out what we can. Will I ring you back?'

'No, don't bother, Joe. I thought we'd have a run down next Tuesday. D'you think you'll have something by then?'

'Oh, I should think so.'

'Good. Well I'll see you at Tavistock nick on Tuesday. I might even let you buy me a pint of that lovely Devon cider.'

Partridge laughed. 'Don't want to drink that, sir, it rots your guts – better off with Scotch. See you on Tuesday.'

The constable on duty at the counter carefully examined Gaffney's warrant card and then Claire Wentworth's before conducting them to Joe Partridge's office.

'Bit keen on security, your bloke on the counter, Joe,' said Gaffney, smiling.

'Oh, him – he's a worry-guts,' said Partridge. He glanced appraisingly at Gaffney's companion. 'I don't think we've met.'

'DS Claire Wentworth, sir,' she said.

'Right, sit down. I'll just get some coffee organised and then I'll be right with you, sir.' Partridge went into the next office, returning minutes later with three mugs of coffee on a tin tray. 'Right then.' He drew a file across his desk. 'This house – Tanglewood – used to be Watton Farm, but some years back it was bought, and the farmland sold off. That's farmed by Jed Morgan now. I had a chat with him. There's quite a lot of land left round the house – about an acre, I suppose. He told me the house was refurbished, but he's never seen anyone there.'

'Who did the work – the refurbishment?'

'It wasn't locals, sir – least not local to Bere Watton. Could have been a firm from here in Tavistock, I suppose, but I can't find that out very easily without people wanting to know why. They're very nosey round here, sir – useful sometimes, but not always,' he added with a chuckle.

'D'you think the house is closed up, then?'

'It might be, I suppose. We've got a few houses like that around here. Rich folk from London own them and use them for holidays and the like – seems a waste to me, but no one's ever seen anyone there. Mind you, it is a bit remote. Anyhow, I popped out there to see what I could see—'

'Bit risky, wasn't it?'

'Not at all, sir. Happens down here all the time. People knock on doors asking for directions – that sort of thing. But there was no answer. I had a skirt round like, and it's well secure: couple of good mortise locks on the front door – solid as a rock it was – and locks on all the windows. I tell you what, sir, you wouldn't get in there in a hurry.' Partridge leaned back in his chair. 'So I took the helicopter out and had a look over it.' He smiled.

'Helicopter?' Gaffney looked surprised.

'Oh yes, sir, us country coppers have got a few strokes we can pull, you know. No, as a matter of fact, we do the occasional flight over the prison – routine security – so I cadged a lift over the weekend and got the pilot to take me round the house. It won't have surprised anyone, they're quite used to it round here – it doesn't even frighten the sheep any more.'

'Any luck?'

'No. I was hoping there might be a vehicle tucked away round the back – you can do a lot with an index number.' Gaffney nodded. 'But nothing,' continued Partridge. 'There's what looks like a covered swimming pool on the back of the house – either that or it's a conservatory – and there's trees and bushes all round the garden. Damned great garden it is, too, but you'd never see it from the outside. I suppose that's why they call it Tanglewood.'

'What about the electoral roll? Anything there?'

'No, sir. No names down for it. I had a word with the bloke who works in the electoral registration office at the town hall – ex-policeman, he is – and he never got the form back. He said he took a run out there, doing a follow-up, but got no answer. He put it down as empty. Probably means they're on a voters' list somewhere else. London, perhaps? If that's the case they could only be put on here for local elections, and I doubt they're going to be too worried about that. Half the buggers who live here aren't.'

'What about the rating department, Joe, did you try them?'

'Of course I did, sir.' Partridge grinned. 'Rates are paid by a Mrs Rita Hamilton, and sent to Tanglewood – and they're always paid prompt on the nail, in full. There's a telephone at the house, too – Bere Watton 142 is the number, but it's ex-directory. That goes out to Mrs Rita Hamilton, too. I checked with British Telecom. Again the bill's always paid by return, but there's not much on it, apparently – isn't used much. Mind you, that's no surprise. There's a few round here, still, who'd rather walk half a mile than use the phone.'

'So the mysterious Mrs Hamilton comes down here regularly, if only to deal with the bills. Yet no one's ever seen her. That's odd.'

'P'raps she comes down during the night,' said Partridge with a laugh. 'And down here night means any time after about half-past eight.'

'That's a pity. We'd come down in the hope of interviewing this mystery woman today.'

'Looks like you've had a wasted journey, sir.'

'No I haven't,' said Gaffney. 'You're going to buy me that pint of cider, now.'

Chapter Eighteen

Detective Sergeant Ian Mackinnon was put out at being excluded from what he saw as the mainstream of the enquiry. He knew that something was going on in Devon; Gaffney's briefing had told him that much. Detective Chief Inspector Tipper knew where the action was too, which was why Mackinnon, and not Tipper, found himself on the way to Brighton to interview some old duffer who had long since retired from the Foreign Office, whatever that had to do with anything. Mackinnon knew that background enquiries were vital to any investigation; he just wished that someone else could do them.

'Mr Marsh?'

'You must be the fellow from the Yard – telephoned me, eh? Come in, come in. Awful day. Let me take your brolly.'

Mackinnon followed him through to a comfortable room that was a combination of sitting room and study. It had a desk across one corner, and a whole wall lined with books in a high bookcase that rose to the ceiling. There were three or four armchairs, but the only sign of Marsh's African days was a pair of Ibo face masks on the wall over the fireplace.

'Rather good, aren't they? Cost five pounds Nigerian in Lagos market; charge you a fortune in London for those. Do sit down.' Without asking he crossed to a cabinet and poured two liberal measures of whisky into chunky crystal tumblers. One he put on the small table next to Mackinnon, together with a jug of water.

'Thank you.' It was only half-past eleven, but Mackinnon had read about old Africa hands.

'Excuse the muddle,' said Marsh, 'but my wife died a couple of years ago, and I can't be bothered with housework. Get a woman in once a week. Complains like mad, but clears it all up for me. Apart from anything else I'm trying to write my memoirs.' He waved a hand towards the desk which was covered with piles of paper. 'Not that anyone'll be interested now: Mau Mau, Rhodesia, Biafran war – all that stuff. Old hat, now. Never mind, keeps me occupied. Oh, did you want soda – I think I've got some somewhere.' He turned back towards his drinks cabinet.

'No – no, this is fine,' said Mackinnon.

'Always used to drink soda out there,' said Marsh. 'Never trust the water in those parts, take a tip from me. Yes,' he continued, lowering himself with some difficulty into a chair, and then interrupting himself: 'It's the arthritis, you know. This damned climate's no good for arthritis. Still I am seventy – not bad, I suppose. Yes – as I was saying, nobody's interested in yesterday. Too much going on. Chaps on the moon – that sort of thing. I was out there when the war was on – the Biafran war, I mean. Knew Jack Gowon quite well – good chap. Got chased out eventually, of course – they all do. And Colonel Ojukwu, the Biafran fellow – Chuk, we used to call him, never could pronounce his first name. He went too – well he went first, when he lost. Ran off to the Ivory Coast; never did know what happened to him after that. Lovely place, Nigeria, you know.'

Mackinnon took a sip of his whisky and gazed through the French doors into the garden; it was still raining. 'Do you live here alone, Mr Marsh?'

'Yes.' He chuckled. 'Shows, does it? Don't often get any-one to talk to. Say hallo to the postman when I see him, but it's no good trying to have a conversation with my cleaning woman; all she wants to talk about are those damned soap things on television. Half the time I think she's talking about her own family. Come to think of it, I think she does too.'

'I understand you knew George and Helen Simpson in Nigeria?' said Mackinnon. He had explained to Dudley Marsh on the telephone how he had come to have his name. Marsh had been delighted to think that someone was coming to talk to him about Africa.

'Yes, indeed. Good old stick, George Simpson. Lovely girl, Helen. Damned shame, getting killed like that. Only a few years to go for retirement, you know.' He suddenly looked sad, and glanced round the room. 'Still, I don't know that that's all it's cracked up to be. What did you want to know about old George, Mr – sorry, forgotten your name.'

'Mackinnon – Ian Mackinnon.'

'Which department are you, then?'

'Special Branch,' said Mackinnon. There seemed no point in hiding it.

'Thought so – Africa and all that. Met one of your chaps once. Came out to Nigeria with the Prime Minister – Harold Wilson that was – can't remember his name either. Hopeless with names.'

It wouldn't have meant anything in all probability. Mackinnon thought it unnecessary to tell Marsh that he had been at school when Harold Wilson was in Nigeria trying to stop the war. It was evident that Marsh, in common with a lot of people of his age, particularly those who had once led active lives, tended to telescope and confuse events which had occurred in the past.

'About four years younger than me, was George.' Marsh carried on. 'We overlapped by about a year, perhaps a bit less – can't remember now. He was an old Colonial Office chap, you know. I was Foreign Office through and through, but then we all got mixed up together. That was the socialists, you know. Hell of a mess. Still I suppose it's all settled itself down now; must be twenty years since that happened. Amazing the way time flies.'

Marsh droned on, plucking cameos out of his past, and occasionally smiling at some resuscitated memory. For about the tenth time since his arrival in Brighton, Mackinnon cursed his chief inspector for submitting him to the wanderings of this old fool. He was certain that nothing would come from the interview, had been from the start, and was wondering how quickly he could extricate himself.

'So when did you leave Nigeria, Mr Marsh?'

Marsh looked up at the ceiling. 'Middle of seventy-one, it must have been. Went off to Reykjavik. Damned silly – one extreme to the other. Didn't know a thing about Iceland, but that's the Diplomatic for you. Fascinating place, Iceland, you know.' He paused and stared at Mackinnon's glass. 'Have the other half?'

Mackinnon drained his glass. Why not? he thought. We shall get to the point eventually.

'I was there for the second cod war, of course. Should put that in my book, really. Make a nice contrast with Biafra – all quite gentlemanly – good chaps the old Icelanders.' Marsh stopped for long enough to take a swig of whisky. 'Not the same as Africa, though. It gets in your blood, Africa. George did the right thing – volunteered for a second tour.' He stared into his glass, looking for some rationale of life. 'Perhaps not, though,' he said, looking up at Mackinnon. 'Poor devil might still have been alive if he'd come home. Still, there we are.'

'Was the Simpsons' daughter working out there at that time?' asked Mackinnon.

Marsh was on his feet again. ''Nother drink, Mr er . . . ?'

'Not for me, thanks.'

'Think I'll just have a small one,' said Marsh, pouring a good inch of whisky into his tumbler. 'This rain gets into old bones, you know.'

'The daughter, Mr Marsh – you were saying about the Simpsons' daughter. . . . '

Marsh lowered himself carefully into his armchair again. 'Yes,' he said. 'I think you're right, they did have a daughter. Now let me see . . . I remember something about her.' He pinched the bridge of his nose and stared into his glass as if seeking the answer there.

'She worked in Africa, for a charity.' Mackinnon prompted him. 'Certainly in Ethiopia – but possibly in Nigeria, too.'

The old man nodded. 'Yes,' he said. 'There was something.' He relapsed into silence again, slowly shaking his head. 'There was something about that girl . . . ' He looked up sharply. 'No, it's no good – can't remember. If it comes to me I'll telephone

261

you. Leave me your number, young man, and I'll ring you if
it comes to me.'

Mackinnon thought it unlikely that he would ever hear
from Marsh again. Nevertheless, he wrote his name and
telephone number on a slip of paper and handed it to the
old man.

For a moment or two, Marsh studied it, then he folded it
carefully and put it on his desk, among all the other pieces
of paper. 'I do believe it's stopped raining,' he said.

It was two hundred miles from London to Tavistock, and
despite having police advanced drivers it still took Gaffney
and his team almost four hours to reach Bere Watton. They
had had to obtain a search warrant from the Bow Street
magistrate who had the unique power to issue warrants
for anywhere in the country. Gaffney had also tried to get
hold of an expert locksmith, but had given up in favour of
a sledge-hammer.

Detective Inspector Joe Partridge and two of his officers
were waiting at Tanglewood when they arrived. 'I've got a
locksmith standing by, sir,' he said, as Gaffney got out of his
car and stretched. 'He's at Tavistock. He doesn't know what
it's about, of course, but having had a look at those locks I
thought you might need him.'

Gaffney grinned. 'Well done, Joe,' he said. 'Get him out
here as soon as you can.' Gaffney surveyed the front door.
'But I reckon he'll have to be damned good to pick those.'
Partridge just grinned, walked back to the car and made a
call on the radio.

The locksmith, when he arrived by police car, carefully
examined the front door. He took off his cap, scratched his
head, and made a sucking noise through his teeth. Then he
stood up and slowly shook his head. 'Can't be done, sir,' he
said. 'Leastways, not in a hurry. Them's damned good locks.
I might do them, but I've got me doubts. It'd probably take
me an hour or more.' He shook his head again. 'I reckon your
best bet's to take the door in, sir. Mind you it'll make a mess
of it, but probably the easiest is to go for the hinges. Always

the weakest bit, the hinges. Pity about that – don't like being beaten.'

Gaffney shrugged. 'I knew it was too good to be true,' he said.

'On the other hand you might go through them panels,' said the locksmith helpfully. 'Often find the panels is weak, an' all.'

'Sorry about that, sir,' said Partridge. 'He's very good, but if he says it's no go, then that's it. I suppose you'll be needing a sledge-hammer?'

'Got one, Joe,' said Gaffney. 'Never go anywhere without one.' He grinned and looked across to one of the sergeants on his team, a tall, hefty-looking man. 'That's your speciality, isn't it?'

The sergeant nodded. 'I'll give it a go, guv,' he said, and walked back to the boot of his car.

It took about ten minutes of concerted hammering to smash the door in and effect an entry, during which time the remaining members of the team stood around making the sort of helpful comments of which only policemen are capable.

At last Gaffney was able to step over the threshold. As he did so he surveyed the damage that had been done to the door, and fervently hoped that it was all going to be worthwhile.

It was an unremarkable house and there was a mustiness about it that confirmed what Joe Partridge had said about the occupants not being seen by the locals. In the front of the house were a study and a dining room, and at the back, running the full width of the building, a sitting room, but what Partridge had believed to be a swimming pool turned out to be a large conservatory. Upstairs were three bedrooms, one about the size of the other two put together, and the only one with a made-up bed in it.

Gaffney despatched a detective sergeant to look outside at the back of the house, and to do a check of the outbuildings. He returned promptly to report that there was a barn under the trees, well hidden. Partridge went out and looked, and

263

told Gaffney that he hadn't been able to see it from the air. What was more interesting was the substantial lock on it. They didn't waste time trying to pick it; they sent for a pair of bolt-cutters.

Inside was a car. Gaffney looked at the number plate. 'Doesn't mean anything,' he said, 'but get someone to do a check.' He opened the boot; inside was a different set of plates.

'I'll check those too, sir,' said the sergeant.

'Don't bother. They belong to a Welsh milk-float.' The sergeant looked puzzled. 'This is the car Dickson escaped in.' He leaned back against the wall of the barn. 'And that's what I call evidence,' he said. 'Make a note in the action book: statement from the surveillance bloke, identifying this vehicle as the one he saw Dickson getting into at the Aldwych.'

'We haven't got an action book, sir,' said the sergeant.

'You have now, lad,' said Gaffney. He turned to Partridge. 'Right, now we take this place apart.' He breathed a sigh of relief; at least now the damage would be justified.

'We've tried to get into the loft, sir,' said a detective constable, appearing in the doorway of the sitting room. Gaffney was sitting in an armchair, not interfering, knowing that too many officers searching at the same time invariably got in each other's way. Gaffney, as the officer in charge, remained in one place so that his officers could consult him when necessary, and would know where to find him.

'What's the problem?'

'It's a heavy steel plate, sir, and it's locked in place.'

'Interesting,' said Gaffney. 'Try going through the ceiling in one of the bedrooms.'

'Won't that make a hell of a mess, sir?'

'Yes,' said Gaffney.

It was there, in the loft, that they found the transmitter and equipment for recording signals on tape which could then be broadcast in one very fast burst, making detection extremely difficult.

Gaffney returned to the sitting room from his inspection

264

of the loft just as another detective, who had been laboriously searching every book in the bookshelf there, gave a shout of triumph.

'What have you got there?'

'Currency, sir – a lot of it.'

Gaffney moved his feet off the heavy coffee table, and the newspaper which had been protecting it. 'Put it down there,' he said. 'Let's have a look at it.'

The detective spread out the high denomination notes of US dollars and French francs, and started counting. 'Excuse me, sir,' he said, reaching for the newspaper. He examined the foreign exchange column and did a few quick calculations. 'About ten grand's-worth in sterling equivalent, sir.'

'Not bad,' said Gaffney. 'Not bad at all.' He laughed. 'They don't change. It's beginning to look like a carbon-copy of the Portland job, and that was nearly thirty years ago.'

A detective constable showed Gaffney a small instrument he had found beneath the floorboards in the study, in a specially crafted trap.

'Good God!' said Gaffney. 'That's a microdot reader. You'll be finding one-time pads next.'

'These, sir?' asked the DC, and held up his other hand.

Gaffney laughed. 'I didn't think they still used them,' he said. 'Must be old stock.'

'Starting to look like Aladdin's cave, isn't it, sir?' said Partridge.

'Yes, Joe – we've certainly struck gold here. Several things now – '

'Yes, sir?'

'I'll need to get scenes-of-crime officers and photographers down from London. And fingerprints – the whole place has got to be fingerprinted. But most important of all, have something to eat.'

'Probably be better if we went into Tavistock for all that, sir,' said Partridge.

Gaffney hesitated. 'No, there's one thing I must do right now. How far's Plymouth Dockyard from here?'

'Plymouth, sir?' Partridge looked surprised. 'About fourteen miles, I suppose, but— '

'Can you lay on a car to get me there as soon as possible?'

'Yes, of course, sir.'

'Good, I want to use their secure government line to the Yard. While I'm on my way can you telephone them and ask them to get hold of Harry Tipper so that I can speak to him the moment I arrive?' He grinned. 'Otherwise we won't get breakfast till lunch-time.'

With the aid of blue lights, a two-tone horn and a skilful driver, Gaffney covered the fourteen miles in as many minutes, and when he strode into the office, an MOD policeman handed him the receiver.

'DCI Tipper's on the line, sir.'

Gaffney took the handset and yawned. He and his team had now been working for about twenty hours.

The Bow Street magistrate was not happy at having to suspend his sitting in the middle of a very heavy list. Still holding the note which Tipper had had passed up to him, he strode into his room. 'What is this all about, Chief Inspector?' he asked. 'I don't just suspend a sitting every time a police officer thinks he has something . . . what is it?' He paused to stare at the note through his half-glasses. '"Delicate and urgent" – well what's delicate and urgent about it?'

Tipper laid the form containing his information on the desk. 'I am seeking a warrant for the arrest of an MI5 officer for serious offences under the Official Secrets Act, sir,' he said. 'And we believe that there are other parties to the commission of those offences who we would not wish to have advanced notice of this man's arrest – presuming, of course, that you grant the warrant.'

The magistrate had the good grace to smile, and sat down at his desk. He read Tipper's information carefully; then he took a New Testament from a drawer and handed it to the chief inspector.

Tipper held the book in his right hand. 'I swear by Almighty God that I will true answer make to all such questions that the court may demand of me,' he said rapidly. He laid the book down. 'Harold Tipper, Detective Chief Inspector, Special Branch, New Scotland Yard.'

The magistrate nodded. 'Is this your information?'

'Yes, sir.'

'And is it true?'

'Yes, sir.'

The magistrate nodded again and signed the warrant. 'You don't need a warrant for this, you know.'

'I know, sir, but from my very first day in the force, I was always told that it's better to have a warrant than not.'

'So that the responsibility shifts from you to me, I suppose?'

'Exactly so,' said Tipper, picking up the warrant. 'Thank you, sir.'

'Don't mention it,' said the magistrate, 'and now, if you'll excuse me, Chief Inspector, I'll get back to my prostitutes.'

Fortunately, the Director–General of the Security Service was in his office that morning, and Tipper was shown there immediately he arrived from Bow Street.

'Mr Gaffney has asked me to see you, Sir Edward,' said Tipper when he had introduced himself and explained where he fitted into the investigation. 'He will, of course, see you himself the moment he gets back from Devon— '

'Devon,' said Griffin. 'What has Devon to do with it?'

Tipper told the DG about following Selby to Bere Watton and then repeated what Gaffney had told him on the telephone about the discoveries at Tanglewood. 'That's why I have a warrant for the arrest of Peter Selby,' he said finally.

For some moments, Griffin stared out of the window, a sad look on his face, before turning to Tipper. 'I had hoped it wouldn't come to this,' he said. 'I suppose that was hoping for too much. What d'you wish to do?'

'Is he in the building – Selby?'

'I don't know.' He sounded tired. 'But I can find out,' he said, reaching towards his intercom.

'If he is,' Tipper said, 'it might be better to have him come here, to this office . . . '

267

Griffin nodded and flicked down the switch. 'Ask Mr Selby to come and see me,' he said to his secretary.

It was less than five minutes later when the girl opened the door. 'Mr Selby's here, Sir Edward.'

There was an apprehensive expression on Selby's face when he entered the office, an expression which became more marked as he recognised Tipper.

'You wanted to see me, sir?'

Griffin did not reply, but waved a hand towards the policeman.

Tipper stood up. 'Peter Selby, I have a warrant for your arrest charging you with committing acts preparatory to the commission of an offence under the Official Secrets Act. Anything you say will be given in evidence.'

Selby's face went deathly white and he swayed slightly, reaching out for the back of one of Griffin's armchairs. 'What on earth are you talking about?' he asked, the words coming out softly, barely above a whisper.

'We can do this one of two ways,' said Tipper. 'Either you walk out of here quietly, with me, or if you want to make a fuss, you can be taken out in handcuffs – whichever you prefer.'

Selby turned to Griffin. 'Sir, this is a terrible mistake. You must know that. I'm not a traitor – I've done nothing wrong. Can't you help me?'

Sir Edward Griffin turned from staring out of the window, his face like granite. For a second or two he studied the abject figure of Selby. 'It's nothing to do with me,' he said coldly. 'It's a matter for the police.'

They walked down the stairs, to avoid the embarrassment of meeting people in the lift, and out of the main door. One of the Ministry of Defence policemen on duty there nodded. 'Hallo, Mr Selby,' he said. Selby ignored him; suddenly the police were on the other side – all of them.

They drove in silence to Rochester Row police station where Selby was placed in a cell in the secure interrogation unit. At one o'clock he was brought lunch. He didn't eat it.

* * *

The first thing that was handed to Gaffney on his return to Scotland Yard was a note asking him to telephone a detective inspector in the Special Branch unit at Heathrow Airport, urgently.

'I've got a bit of information about Barbara Rigby, sir.'

'What is it?' asked Gaffney.

'The security bloke from the airline she works for got it from one of his snouts. Apparently she was seen during a stopover in Vienna last month, having dinner with a steward from another airline.'

'Big deal,' said Gaffney. 'Which airline?'

'Aeroflot, sir.'

Chapter Nineteen

Gaffney and Tipper were already seated in the interview room when the haggard-looking Selby was brought in by two junior Special Branch officers.

'Sit down,' said Gaffney. He had a file on the table in front of him, but it remained closed. 'I've sent for some tea. I'm sure that you'd like a cup.'

Selby ignored the niceties. 'What the hell is this all about?' he asked. 'This – this man – ' He pointed at Tipper. ' – this man comes to my office and arrests me, in the presence of my own Director–General. He said something about committing offences under the OSA.' He was what Tipper described as white and spiteful. 'Well you'd better tell me what I'm supposed to have done, because I shall be getting on to my solicitor. I haven't done anything. It's – it's a false arrest – wrongful imprisonment; I think that's what it's called.'

'Mr Tipper tells me that he's already cautioned you, Mr Selby, but just so that there's no misunderstanding, I have to tell you that you are not obliged to say anything, but that anything you do say will be taken down in writing and may be put in evidence. Do you understand that?' He spoke softly, refusing to be ruffled by Selby's tirade.

Selby turned slightly sideways in his chair so that he was staring at the corner of the room to Gaffney's right, and folded his arms. It was the same display of truculence that had caused Tipper previously to liken him to a petulant schoolboy.

Gaffney took out a cigar and spent a little time lighting it. Blowing a cloud of smoke towards the ceiling, he said,

'You've got a few questions to answer – if you should wish to do so, of course.' He smiled benignly.

'I'm not answering any of your questions.' Selby continued to stare at the corner of the room. 'A man is innocent until proved guilty – isn't that what they say? And it's up to you to prove me guilty, which you won't be able to do.'

'Where did you go last weekend, Mr Selby?' Selby remained silent, as if he hadn't heard the question. 'All right, then,' continued Gaffney. 'Let me try it another way. Who is Mrs Rita Hamilton of Tanglewood, near Bere Watton in Devon? Not far from Tavistock, you'll recall.'

Selby swung round to face the two policemen. 'So that's it? That's what all this charade is about, eh?' His face was still pale, but now wore a half-sneering expression. 'Just because I'm having an affaire with a married woman, and I didn't tell those damned nosey parkers of vetting people, you drag me in here in the most embarrassing way possible. Well you won't get away with that. Just because I work for MI5 doesn't mean I don't have any rights, you know. I'd never tell the vetting people – ever! And do you know why? Because they revel in it. They love the filth; love asking questions about whether you've had sexual intercourse, and how many times, and do you ever do it in the back of a car. All that stuff. They love it – and they write it all down, and put it in your personal file. Well not on my personal file they don't. If I want to have an affaire, I'll have one. There's nothing wrong with it. Lots of men have affaires – married men sometimes. Even married men in MI5 probably. So what? That's not a crime, and certainly not a crime under the OSA. So you'd better think of something pretty good.'

'I have some photographs here, Mr Selby.' Gaffney tapped the file on the table with his forefinger. 'They are photographs which were taken at Tanglewood this morning.'

Selby glanced down at the file, a supercilious expression of condescension on his face. 'Really?'

They were large colour-prints, whole-plate in size. 'That's

the house, isn't it?' He handed over a photograph of the exterior. Selby left it on the table, affording it a mere cursory glance. 'And that, Mr Selby, is a photograph of the car in which Peter Dickson made his escape when police attempted to arrest him.'

Selby leaned across and pulled the print towards him. 'So you found it. Where?'

'In a locked barn in the grounds of the house in which you stayed last weekend. In the house itself we also found a transmitter, recording equipment, one-time pads, microdot readers, lots of foreign currency – in fact, Mr Selby, all manner of spying paraphernalia with which you, in the Security Service, will be more than familiar. Do you want to see the photographs of that, as well?'

Selby's arms dropped to his sides, hanging straight down by the chair. His jaw was slack and his face ashen. 'I don't believe you.'

Both Gaffney and Tipper knew that he did, that his expression of disbelief was just a formality, a cypher. 'Perhaps now you can understand why you were arrested, Mr Selby. So we'll start again. Last weekend you travelled down to Tanglewood. You left your flat at about twenty to six on the Friday evening and you drove to Devon – we can tell you your precise route if you're interested – and stayed at Tanglewood until Sunday afternoon when you returned to London. You stayed the weekend with Mrs Rita Hamilton who wrote to you to make the arrangements. I have a copy of her letter here.' He tapped the file again. 'On the other hand,' he continued mildly, 'I have to consider the possibility that Mrs Hamilton does not exist, that she is an invention of your imagination against a day such as this when, to coin a phrase, it all came on top, and you can, in all pretended innocence, blame a woman who has now conveniently disappeared.'

There was silence in the room, broken only by the hum of traffic from outside in Rochester Row, and further afield in Vauxhall Bridge Road. Gaffney knew better than to interrupt, than to press for an answer. He knew from long experience,

272

as did Tipper, that the response, when it came, would be the more valuable for its spontaneity.

At last Selby looked up from his long contemplation of the photographs. 'I love her,' he said. 'We're going to get married.'

Gaffney didn't say that he thought that unlikely, although he did recall that Houghton and Gee, two of those convicted in the Portland case, had waited until their release from prison to get married. 'How did you meet?'

'At a concert.' He paused as if recapturing the scene in his mind's eye. 'It was in Sussex, one of those country house music festivals. They're almost private really. This one was Monteverdi.' He glanced briefly at Tipper seeking sympathy and understanding for a liking of the obscure seventeenth-century composer; Tipper just nodded. 'She tipped wine over me, as a matter of fact.'

'I see,' said Gaffney.

'It was included,' said Selby humourlessly. Gaffney was tempted to make a frivolous remark. 'There was this table where you queued up. We both turned away from it at the same time, each holding a glass of red wine, and she tipped hers over me – accidentally, of course. She was so embarrassed.' He put a hand up to adjust his tie, but stopped halfway as he remembered that he wasn't wearing one; Tipper hadn't wanted him hanging himself before Gaffney had had a chance to talk to him, and certainly not with such an expensive tie. 'We got to talking – about the concert, the music – and we sat together for the remainder of the performance. The seats weren't reserved, you see.' He said that intensely, as though it were important.

'She was there alone, I take it?' asked Gaffney.

'Yes – yes, she was. Her husband doesn't like music very much – well, Johann Strauss, I think she said. . . . ' He spread his hands as if to indicate that Johann Strauss didn't really count as serious music; Tipper could almost hear Selby dismissing him as a café bandleader.

'Sussex seems a long way to travel from Devon for a concert.'

'Yes, it does.' Selby gave that some thought, doubtless finding it strange that inconvenience should ever be considered in the matter of Monteverdi concerts. 'I believe she said she was staying with a friend in town.'

'A man friend?'

'Of course not.' He spoke adamantly, but his ingenuous face indicated all too clearly that he hadn't thought of it before.

'Then what?'

'What do you mean – then what?'

'Well you presumably arranged to see her again.'

'Yes. I told her about another concert – it was about ten days later, at the Queen Elizabeth Hall. She said she hadn't heard about that one. Then she got out a little diary from her handbag and wrote it down. She said that she'd like to go, and would I mind if we went together. I said that would be fine, so I agreed to get the tickets, but she insisted on paying for hers. She said she wanted it to be all above-board – just a mutual interest in music, nothing more.'

'Did you know, at that time, that she was married?'

'Well no, not then; it was only much later that she mentioned him.'

'Was she wearing a wedding ring?'

Selby looked from one to the other, thoughtful. 'I didn't notice.' Tipper smiled. It was the first thing that he, and most other policemen he knew, looked for. 'I don't know.'

'So you met in London, ten days later, at the Queen Elizabeth?'

'Yes.'

'And you attended the concert, and then both went your separate ways?'

'Not quite. I invited her out to supper.'

'And she went?'

'Yes. But she insisted on paying for herself. She said it wasn't fair that I should pay as she had foist herself on me.'

'That would have made it quite a late evening – supper after a concert. Presumably she was staying in London again?'

274

'I suppose so. Yes, I think she said as much.'

'Who is this friend in London she stays with?'

'I don't know – I didn't ask.'

'And when did it start to get serious?'

'What d'you mean?'

'Mr Selby, you said just now that you're going to marry her. Not just on the basis of having wine thrown over you, and a couple of concerts, surely?'

'No.' Selby remained thoughtfully silent for a while. 'She mentioned that she was going to be in London the following weekend, to do some shopping.' He looked up guiltily. 'I invited her to my flat on the Saturday evening. I'd told her that I had quite a collection of Monteverdi, Praetorius too, and a particularly fine recording of the Allegri Miserere. . . . ' He shot a glance at Tipper, sitting to one side of, and slightly behind, Gaffney.

'And did she come to your flat?'

'Oh yes.' He gazed at Gaffney, but seemed to be looking beyond him, picturing the scene in his flat that evening. 'She's a very emotional person, you know, very affected by music.'

'You mean it turned her on, this early stuff?' It was Tipper who asked the harsh question.

Selby looked at him with distaste, but said nothing.

'What happened next?' asked Gaffney, but knew the answer.

'We made love – on the settee.' Selby's facial expression didn't change. It was just a statement of fact.

'And then she went home?'

'No. She stayed the night.'

'But wasn't she supposed to be staying with her friend?'

'Yes, but she asked if she could make a phone call.'

'I see. And what form did this phone call take – can you remember? Did it sound as though she was talking to a man – or a woman?'

Again Selby shook his head. It could have been a rejection of the idea that she might have been staying with another man, and two-timing her husband and him at the same time. 'I didn't hear what she said. The telephone's in the hall. I showed her where it was and went back into the sitting room and closed the door while she made her call.' The expression on his face said that it was impolite to eavesdrop on other people's telephone calls, and by implication to read other people's letters, even with a Home Secretary's warrant. 'She left after breakfast.'

'But you arranged to meet her again, I imagine?'

'Yes – well no, not exactly. She rang me at home a few nights later.'

'You'd given her your phone number, then?'

Selby glanced at Gaffney, the trace of a sneer on his face again, as though doubting the other's detective skills. 'It's on the dial of the phone. She must have noted it when she made the call.'

Gaffney nodded. 'So she came to the flat again?'

'Yes, it became quite a regular thing. She would ring me one evening to say that she would be there the following evening – when I got in from the office, of course.'

'Of course,' murmured Gaffney. 'But didn't you think this rather strange, Mr Selby? Here you have a married woman who lives in Devon, who spends an inordinate amount of time in London, and seemed to be able to spend the night with you whenever she felt like it.'

'Actually she didn't stay the night very often. I gave her a key to my flat and she would let herself in. She'd have supper ready for me when I got in, and then . . . '

'And then you would make love?' Selby nodded. 'And she'd go home?'

'Yes.'

'But not to Devon, obviously. What time did she usually leave your flat, after these little love-visits?'

'Usually about nine, maybe half-past.'

'Did she have a car? Or did she go by cab – or train, or what?'

'I've really no idea.' Selby spoke loftily, becoming bored with the whole business.

'Well you'd better think,' said Gaffney sharply. 'It's fairly evident that you have been consorting with a KGB agent, and

276

I'd venture to suggest that it may be in your best interests to give me as much assistance as you can.'

Selby looked shocked. It was obvious that despite the evidence which Gaffney had laid before him, he hadn't considered Rita Hamilton's status in terms as precise as that. Gaffney seriously wondered how he had held down his job or, for that matter, been able to secure it in the first place.

'Are you really saying, Mr Selby,' continued Gaffney, 'that you allowed her to leave your flat and walk the streets of Fulham fairly late at night, without a care about her welfare – this woman you say you love, and that you want to marry?'

'I remember now. She said she had a car.'

'Did you ever see it? Travel in it? What sort was it?'

'I don't know. I never saw it.'

'Now, you say that on these occasions she stayed with a friend in London. I mean, she must have done, mustn't she – she couldn't have travelled back to Devon at that time of night.' Selby nodded. 'But you insist that you have no idea of the address – or even vaguely where it was?'

'No.'

'Did she give you a telephone number?'

'No.'

'Not for the house in Devon?'

'No. She said it was too risky – her husband might answer the phone.'

'Ah yes – her husband. That brings me to my next point. How did she explain away her frequent absences to her husband? Did she volunteer an explanation for that?'

'She didn't say very much about him. She said he was something to do with import and export and had to travel abroad quite a lot.'

'But surely you must have discussed him with her when the question of marriage came up – your marriage to her, I mean.'

The trace of a smile appeared on Selby's face. 'Yes, we talked about him then. She used a strange word; she said the marriage was sterile. They no longer made love. She called it a marriage of convenience.'

'Presumably she saw no problems with obtaining a divorce?'

'No. She was quite sure that he was having an affaire, and she said it would probably be easy enough to prove it. But she didn't think it would come to that. She said she'd only have to ask her husband and he'd let her go.'

'All nice and neat, then. She would just hop out of one marriage and into another.'

'You make it sound sordid. It wasn't like that.'

'Adultery usually is sordid,' said Gaffney. 'But tell me about Devon. Why the decision to go down there?'

'She said that she didn't like coming to the flat – not so often. It made her feel dirty and deceitful.'

'But it was different in her own home?'

'I suppose so. I don't know, but she said she wanted to spend longer with me. I did too.' He paused to pour himself a glass of water from the carafe on the table. 'She suggested that I went down to Devon when her husband was away.' He sipped at the water. 'I wasn't awfully keen on that. I had this recurring thought that he would walk in on us; it made me feel uneasy. But she said that there was absolutely no danger. Her husband always rang her from the airport both on the way out and on the way in. She said that it was an unwritten agreement between them.'

'Did her husband know that she was having an affaire, then?'

'I don't know. I asked her that, but she just smiled and put her finger to her lips.'

'So you went to Devon?'

'Yes, she wrote to me to say that her husband was going to be in Sweden— ' He broke off. 'But then you know that, don't you?' Despite the fact that he had read other people's mail on dozens of occasions, he obviously still found it distasteful that someone else should have read his.

'Yes,' said Gaffney. 'Go on.'

'I went down there – which you also know. It was a blissful weekend.' A distant look came into Selby's eyes.

'Most of which you spent in bed, I take it?'

'Yes – we did.'

'Did she have a collection of Monteverdi, too?' asked

Tipper. He knew that there wasn't even a record-player in the house.

'I don't know. She certainly didn't play any music while I was there.'

'No, I didn't think so.'

Gaffney took up the questioning again. 'Did she know you worked for MI5?'

'Good heavens no!' Selby appeared horrified at the prospect.

'You mean you didn't tell her. That's not quite the same thing. I asked if she knew.'

Selby seemed momentarily puzzled by the question. 'She never mentioned it, if that's what you mean.'

'Did she ever ask what you did for a living?'

He considered that, and eventually said, 'No, I don't think she did.'

'Don't you find that strange?'

'Why should I?'

'Because you had discussed marriage. You said earlier that you were going to get married. That implies that you proposed to her, and that she accepted.'

'Yes, that's right.'

'But she never asked what your profession was. She never posed any questions about your income – whether you could keep her in a manner to which she was accustomed?'

'No.'

'And yet you must have realised, just from seeing that house in Devon, that there was a bit of money there somewhere. Did you not wonder about that?'

'I imagined that her husband was quite well off, yes.'

'But you didn't question her willingness to give all that up to come and live with you in a flat in Fulham which, with the best will in the world, Mr Selby, cannot be described as luxurious?'

'No.'

'If you'll forgive me for saying so,' said Gaffney, 'I think that you have been very naïve in all this. Did it not occur to you, as an officer of MI5, that you were being set up?'

279

'No, certainly not.' Selby reacted angrily. 'We fell in love, quite naturally.'

'This house in Devon. Where did you sleep? Presumably you slept with her.'

'Yes. There's a large bedroom, on the right at the top of the stairs. You obviously know it.' Gaffney nodded. 'We slept there.'

'And meals?'

'In the dining room. Where else?' There was still the odd trace of sarcasm in Selby's voice.

'You found nothing strange in the house? Nothing out of the ordinary?'

'No, not really.' He appeared to be thinking.

'And what of Mr Hamilton? Any trace of him?'

'No. I told you, he was in Sweden.'

'I know,' said Gaffney patiently. 'That's not what I meant. When a man lives in a house, there are usually traces of him. In the bathroom, for instance. After-shave, a dressing-gown. Suits in the wardrobe – that sort of thing.'

'I never looked.'

'You're not being very helpful, Mr Selby.'

'There was one thing. I was in the sitting room on the Sunday morning. We both were; we were having coffee. I walked over to the bookcase and started to browse. Rita looked up and asked me if I'd mind not touching the books. She said that they were her husband's, and he was very particular about them. She seemed quite worried, as though he might make a fuss if he came back and found any one of them out of place.'

'Didn't you think that strange?'

'Not really. I presumed that she had no interest in books, and that if he came back and found that they had been moved then he'd know that someone had been there; someone else, I mean.'

'Like a lover, perhaps?'

Selby spread his hands. 'I suppose so.'

'Did you go outside while you were there? In the garden; or the grounds, I suppose they were called.'

'No, I didn't. I suggested it, but Rita said it was all over-grown and uninteresting. I wasn't bothered; I'm not a garden person. That's one of the reasons why I live in a flat.'

'All in all then, you found nothing odd about the house?'

'No.' He adopted his supercilious expression again. 'But then you don't spend all your time looking for spies, do you?'

'Oh? I thought that's what you were paid for, Mr Selby.'

There was a light tap on the door, and a young detective entered the room silently. He handed a note to Tipper and left again. Tipper read the note and handed it to Gaffney.

'Interesting, but not surprising,' said Gaffney. He glanced at Selby. 'My officers have now found some photographic equipment, a Minox camera. For photographing documents, very likely. A real spies' nest, eh, Mr Selby?'

Selby looked uncomfortable. He knew that he was going to be hard pressed to explain how he, a professional intelligence officer, had spent a weekend in that house without realising what it was being used for, although without a dedicated and thorough search of the kind that Gaffney must have under-taken, nothing incriminating could possibly have been found; it was all too professionally secreted. But try convincing a sceptical English jury. Even if his counsel objected to every juror who was carrying a copy of the *Daily Telegraph*, he could still have a fight on. Even the liberal supporters of misguided civil servants who sent copies of innocuous memoranda to the newspapers would not be very sympathetically disposed to outright spying.

Gaffney returned to the thrust of his questioning. 'On the other hand, Mr Selby, I have to consider this proposition: that you have consorted with an agent of the Soviet Union; that, I think, is established to the satisfaction of all of us in this room. I am prepared to accept that you may have done so unwittingly, at least at the outset; nevertheless it's an indictment of your professional expertise. But I suggest that once you had formed a liaison with this woman, you then went on to disclose highly secret details of current MI5 operations. She must have rubbed her hands; it's the oldest ploy in the world, and you fell for it. It's called "pillow-talk". Once you realised that you were in over your head, you just had to keep on, didn't you?'

'Of course not; that would be a breach of security.' Selby said it as though he genuinely believed it; probably was so humourless that he couldn't see that as an understatement it came close to farce.

Gaffney laughed; the paradox of it amused him. 'Come now, Mr Selby. Rita Hamilton knew perfectly well that you worked for the Security Service, and you told her everything that she wanted to know; when you were in bed together, of course. You told her all about the Dickson affair— '

'I didn't know anything about the Dickson business.' Selby spoke with desperation. 'I told you that before; Geoffrey told us nothing.'

'What you said before, Mr Selby, was that Geoffrey Hodder told you that a Major Armitage from the MOD was passing classified material to a hostile intelligence officer.' Selby nodded dumbly. 'And that's what you told Mrs Hamilton. She in turn told the Kremlin using the transmitter which was installed not eight feet above the bed where you and she were making love. That was a cheap price for her to pay for your treachery, wasn't it?' Selby opened his mouth to protest, but Gaffney went on, relentlessly. 'That enabled the KGB to alert Dickson to the fact that MI5 knew all about him, and she – Mrs Hamilton – was instructed to make the usual arrangements. The result was that Dickson escaped, and was able to escape because you'd told Rita that he was under surveillance. We now know that he went straight down to Bere Watton— '

'Probably slept the night with Rita in the same bed,' said Tipper quietly in a spiteful aside. Selby looked sick.

'And all because of your obsession with a woman who deliberately set you up,' continued Gaffney, 'and conned you into believing that seventeenth-century music made her passionate. I'll bet she doesn't know Monteverdi from Monty Python.'

Selby's natural languidity finally deserted him; there was

almost uncontrolled panic in his face now. 'Are you crazy?' he asked, his voice rising. 'You've got no proof, none at all.'

Still Gaffney spoke mildly, his tone almost politely conversational. 'How long would it take us to get it? How many hours of interrogation, going over the same points, again and again? The hours of solitary confinement in between, and then the same questions, over and over again. You know the principles, don't you? You're in the trade. And eventually you'll crack, won't you? You'll tell me everything; everything I want to know. How much you told her; when you told her; and what you got in return.' He paused. 'Well we know one of the answers to that; sexual favours, but what else? A high price to pay for years in prison . . . ' Selby was ashen-faced now; he moaned slightly and Gaffney wondered if he were going to faint. 'Or was it ideological? Perhaps you deliberately sought a contact, and quite willingly gave information; no coercion at all, was that it? The sex was a bonus, maybe. Like Burgess, Maclean and Philby, were you? A great believer in the cause of Soviet supremacy, of world communism; is that you, Mr Selby? Are you really a closet communist? A latter-day Apostle?'

'No, I'm not!' Selby's voice had almost reached screaming pitch. 'I don't know, I didn't know.' He held his head in his hands, briefly, and then looked up, his face distorted with anguish. 'She was kind and sympathetic. She didn't ask me about my job; never mentioned it. I didn't even give her my office telephone number, and I certainly didn't tell her anything that was going on. I never mentioned Dickson, or Armitage. We just made love; it was wonderful, and unbelievable . . . '

Gaffney sighed. 'Selby, you're not convincing me. You're an intelligence officer; don't try to mislead me with all this nonsense about love. It's starry-eyed rubbish, and you know it.'

Selby seemed to recover his poise, although he was still very white about the face. 'You've got absolutely no proof. You can't keep me here, you know.' Suddenly he stood up, arms at his sides.

'Oh do sit down,' said Gaffney mildly, ignoring Selby's hysterical outburst. So far there wasn't much evidence that would justify his detention, but Gaffney was going to keep him just the same. He'd frightened him now, badly; that was obvious, and it might be productive to see what happened next, when he could confront Selby with Rita Hamilton. Then he would be able to see who accused whom. But they had to find Rita Hamilton first.

'Now we come to the point of all this, Mr Selby,' continued Gaffney. 'It is obviously a matter of great urgency and importance that we find Mrs Hamilton as soon as possible – and arrest her.'

Selby knew that that was the case, had tried to prevent himself from thinking it, stemming the very crystallisation of a concept that Gaffney had now put so graphically into words. 'Yes, I suppose so.' His hands, loosely linked, hung down between his knees, and his head was bowed.

'And you, Mr Selby, seem to be the only person to have seen her. Do you, by any chance, have a photograph of her?'

He shook his head absently. 'No.' Pause. 'I asked her for one, but she refused.'

'I'll bet she did,' said Tipper, half to himself.

'She said that she always looked awful in photographs.'

'I find it strange that, even so, you should not have a photograph of the woman you intend marrying.'

'Well I haven't.' There was a flash of anger, brought on in part by the hopelessness of the situation. His blissful happiness, the prospect of marriage to a woman he enjoyed and loved, all shattered in a single morning. 'You can search my flat if you don't believe me.'

'We did, this morning,' said Gaffney quietly.

A nervous tic appeared alongside Selby's nose. 'What right – I mean . . . ' The sentence faded. He knew what right they had. Suddenly it seemed he was without rights. 'How did you get in?'

'With your keys. We took them from you, together with your other possessions, if you remember.'

Selby nodded dumbly. He didn't remember. The morning's events were a jumbled blur – like a bad dream.

'Well in that case,' continued Gaffney, picking up his original question, 'perhaps you'll give us a description . . . ' He stopped. 'Better still . . . Harry, get hold of a photofit operator, as quick as possible. There should be one on stand-by at the Yard. We'll get Mr Selby to make up a picture.' He stood up and walked over to the shorthand writer who had been busily taking notes throughout the interrogations of Selby. 'Okay,' he said. 'You can take a break.'

'Thanks very much, sir.' The shorthand writer stood up and shook his right hand. He smiled ruefully. 'Cramp, sir.'

'S'what your right arm's for,' said Gaffney unsympathetically. 'While you're taking a breather perhaps you'd get some teas,' he added. Suddenly he stopped, driving the fist on his right hand into the palm of his left. 'Christ!' he said. He grabbed the DC's arm. 'Hang on here for a minute, with the prisoner.' He walked across to where Tipper was standing. 'Harry, come outside.'

In the corridor outside the interview room, Gaffney asked, 'Have we still got someone in Selby's flat?'

'Yes, sir. I left a DC in there. I suppose we could pull him out now we've finished the search. Anyway, we can always go back.'

'That's not what I was thinking of. Selby said that Rita Hamilton has got a set of his keys. She might turn up there, walk into the trap maybe.'

'It's a thought,' said Tipper doubtfully, 'but he also said that she rings him the day before coming.'

'Supposing she doesn't – just walks in. It's not a chance we can afford to take. Give that bloke a ring at Fulham, and send another bloke out there straightaway. If she turns up, nick her!'

Gaffney paced up and down the corridor smoking a cigar while Tipper was making his calls. He was now convinced that Selby was a naïve, innocent fool who had been taken in by this woman, whoever she was, because somehow she had known he was an MI5 officer. He had reached the exciting point that always came in a successful enquiry when everything was about to fall into place. Nevertheless, he had a worrying feeling in the pit of his stomach that Rita Hamilton was going to elude him. If she had been instrumental in arranging the escape of Nikitin, Gesschner and the man known as Dickson, sure as hell she was going to be able to fix her own disappearance. He wondered too what the Director-General of the Security Service was going to make of it all. For certain, he was going to be none too pleased with his man Selby. Even if he escaped prison – which he probably would – he'd certainly get the sack from MI5, just for being so bloody stupid.

'You're not going to like this, sir,' said Tipper, coming back into the corridor from the office where he had been telephoning. 'She's been and gone.'

'What?'

'Just before we finished talking to Selby apparently. I'm sure it's her. Turned up at the flat – just walked in, using her key. I don't know who was the more surprised.'

'What happened?'

'She and the DC came face to face in the sitting room. He told her he was a police officer and asked her who she was. She said something about being his daily.'

Gaffney laughed ironically. 'Daily what?'

'Our bold detective told her that Mr Selby was away, and was likely to be away for some time. In that case, she said, she wouldn't stay, and she left.'

'I'll bet she did. Just wait till I get my hands on that bloody DC,' said Gaffney angrily. 'Description? Did you get a description?'

'Of sorts,' said Tipper. 'In a nutshell, she sounds like the most expensively dressed cleaning lady in London. But be fair, guv'nor, he wasn't to know; you can hardly blame him . . .'

'Blame him,' said Gaffney, 'I'll bloody kill him. What the hell – Christ, Harry, he's a bloody detective, not a social worker. He's supposed to have brains, initiative. That's why we pay them so damned much.'

'Could have fooled me,' said Tipper. 'By the way, I forgot to mention it, but Joe Partridge is on the phone for you from the house.'

'What the hell does he want?' asked Gaffney, and swung into the office. He picked up the receiver. 'Joe? John Gaffney. Sorry to keep you. We've just had a bit of a crisis; well, a bloody balls-up, more like it. What can I do for you?'

'You know that coffee table in the sitting room, sir,' said Partridge. 'The one you kept your feet on?'

Gaffney chuckled. 'Yeah – what about it?'

'Well that heavy top was a cavity, beautifully made, and it contained two passports: one British in the name of Mrs Rita Hamilton; the other French, in the name of Madame Estelle Bisson. Each contained a photograph of the same woman, sir.'

'Ah,' said Gaffney. 'At last. Now we'll know what the damned woman looks like. Joe, have you got a fax machine at Tavistock?'

'Oh, bless you, sir, yes. We're quite up-to-date down here in darkest Devon.'

'Splendid. Listen, Joe, can you get those photographs faxed to me here at Rochester Row as soon as possible. Hang on, I'll get you the number.'

It was exactly thirty-two minutes before the photographs came through. Gaffney knew it was thirty-two minutes because he'd timed it; and smoked another cigar and consumed two more cups of canteen tea.

Impatiently he watched the print edging its way slowly through the fax machine until finally the complete photograph was in view. Then he stood upright, slowly, his lips pursed. 'Well I'll be damned,' he said.

287

Chapter Twenty

As soon as he had discovered Rita Hamilton's true identity, Gaffney had despatched a team of officers to her real address, knowing instinctively that she would not be there. The confirmation of her absence was passed to Gaffney by Detective Inspector Francis Wisley, who had spoken to some of the woman's neighbours. They had not seen her for a day or so, and her grey Volvo estate was missing; neither event was unusual.

Gaffney alerted the officers at Tanglewood. There was an outside chance that she might arrive there, and he told them to remove all outward signs of their presence, not that they could do very much about the smashed front door; but if she got that far she would not escape. The next, and only other, move that the police could make for the time being, was to send an urgent message to all ports and airports in the United Kingdom, and then sit and wait. Gaffney decided against bothering with Interpol; even if she were traced, the woman's lawyers would almost certainly rebut any attempt by the British to have her extradited, on the grounds that hers was a political offence.

Gaffney used the waiting time to see Sir Edward Griffin. He explained in greater detail than Tipper had done what had been found at Tanglewood, and gave him a résumé of the interrogation of Selby.

'Do you think he's implicated?' asked Griffin when he had listened to Gaffney's account.

From his pocket, Gaffney took a copy of the wanted notice which had been circulated to ports, and placed it on Griffin's desk. 'We have identified the woman,' he said, 'but Selby's adamant that he only knew her as Rita Hamilton.'

★ ★ ★

About sixteen million passengers travel through the port of Dover in a year, not all of them in the two million or so cars that go through there. The task of the police looking for the woman was, therefore, somewhat akin to seeking the proverbial needle in a haystack. Added to which, of course, it was by no means certain that she would go that way, assuming that she were going abroad at all. Anyway, the police were looking for a lot of other people at the same time.

Nonetheless, the information which had been received from Scotland Yard the previous evening was dutifully circulated to all the Special Branch officers on the early shift at the port. The task was made marginally easier by the knowledge that the woman was in possession of a grey Volvo estate, details of which had been passed to the staff of the ferry companies who checked the cars through, to Customs, to Immigration, and to the Harbour Board's own police.

Detective Constable Roberts was perched on a stool in the passport control office. For two hours now, he had watched the passports being presented to the immigration officer by an unending stream of people anxious to put the English Channel between themselves and the United Kingdom. For the most part they were ordinary families in the family car, and every thirty seconds or so, a handful of passports came up through the window of the small kiosk which was too hot in the summer and too cold in the winter.

Every once in a while, a foot-passenger – someone without a car – sneaked along the inside of the queue of vehicles and handed a passport through the hatch.

The woman placed her French passport firmly on the counter at the window, glancing casually towards the harbour wall. The immigration officer flipped through it, seeking the rectangular stamp that would show when she had landed in the United Kingdom. There wasn't one.

'When did you arrive, madame?'

She shook her head. *'Parlez français, s'il vous plaît.'*

289

The immigration officer obligingly switched to French and repeated the question.

The woman shrugged her shoulders. 'Perhaps six months ago. Why do you ask?'

'There is no stamp – no landing stamp – in your passport.'

She smiled. 'It is new,' she said. 'It was issued at our embassy in London. Here!' She turned the page and pointed to the issuing office stamp. *'Voilà!'* she said decisively.

The immigration officer smiled and nodded. Then he thumbed through the large book at his elbow. Of Madame Jeanne Giraud there was no trace. He placed a triangular stamp on the first blank page and handed the passport back.

Detective Constable Roberts now faced a predicament that confronts all policemen at some stage in their working lives. The conversation about the missing stamp and the renewal of the passport had given him an opportunity to study the woman's face. She bore a marked resemblance to the photograph of ... what was that damned woman's name? He opened his book of suspects; the copy of the message and the photograph were folded into the back. He studied it. The photograph was not good, having suffered the deterioration, first of the facsimile transmission, and second, the photocopier. Anyway, that woman – the one who had just gone through – was French. But it damned well looked like her. Then again she was a foot-passenger. He looked at the message once more; she was supposed to have a grey Volvo estate. He read the footnote to the message: "Wanted by Detective Chief Superintendent Gaffney, Special Branch, Metropolitan; detain but do not question." Must be serious – big stuff. It was not often that a detective chief superintendent in Special Branch wanted someone detained. What the hell was he to do? Let her go and regret it for ever more, or stop her and get done for wrongful arrest?

He looked across into the neighbouring booth. Perhaps he could unload it on to his sergeant. The sergeant wasn't there. Damn! That was it then.

He caught up with Madame Giraud just as she got to

the ramp of the ferry. 'Excuse me, madame.' She stopped and turned. 'I am a police officer,' he said.

She shrugged her shoulders. *'Ne comprends pas,'* she said.

'Police,' said Roberts, articulating the word as though speaking to someone who could only lip-read, and produced his warrant card.

'Police?' She repeated the word and shrugged again.

'You come with me,' said Roberts, and gesticulated with extravagant sign language.

She looked at the officer, then glanced around the huge arena of the ferry-port. In one direction lay the ship, and two crewmen standing on the ramp talking to a customs officer; in the other, the terminal buildings and the vast, sheer face of the white cliffs of Dover. There was nowhere to go. She shrugged again. 'Okay,' she said.

In the office, Roberts left a WDC with Madame Giraud and went into the detective inspector's office to tell him who he thought he had got in the outer room.

The DI walked to his door, opened it, and gazed at the woman. He closed the door again and walked back to his desk. 'What's she got to say for herself?'

'She only speaks French, sir.'

'Jesus Christ, Robby. Look at the bloody message: the wanted woman's English; and you tell me she only speaks French.'

'I think it's a try-on, sir.'

'Well for your sake I bloody hope so.' He pointed to the telephone on his desk. 'Get on the blower to this DCS in London. See what he's got to say. In the meantime, I'll get hold of Fred Birkinshaw, he speaks fluent frog – he can talk to her. He can even start to apologise for making her miss her boat, I suppose.'

Roberts began to feel less comfortable. He should have let the woman go. No one would have known, and he had to admit, now that she was in the office, that she looked less like the photograph than he first thought. 'Damn!' he said for about the tenth time, and dialled the number of New Scotland Yard.

Tipper was unimpressed. He'd already had a number of false alarms, and one bright spark at Heathrow Airport had even had an aircraft brought back after take-off, only to discover that his woman suspect was a respectable American, travelling with her husband, both of whom had vowed never to come to England again. In addition, the airline had promised to send the substantial bill for the recall of their aircraft to the Commissioner. Despite all that, Tipper listened patiently to Roberts's detailed description.

'What d'you want me to do, sir?' asked the unhappy Roberts.

'See what you can get from her,' said Tipper 'and ring me back.'

'But the message said not to question her, sir.'

'Do it!' said Tipper.

When Roberts returned to the outer office, Detective Sergeant Birkinshaw was engaged in deep conversation with the woman, but broke off immediately. 'Here,' he said, taking Roberts's arm and steering him towards the far side of the office, 'she's not best pleased with you, mate. Getting very uptight about missing her ferry, and wants to know what it's all about. She says she's done nothing wrong, and there's nothing wrong with her passport.'

'Oh Christ!' said Roberts.

'Well you're going to have to make up your mind, mate. Think of something to charge her with, or let her go. I'll tell you one thing though, for what it's worth: she's not French.'

'Not French?'

'Nope! Her accent's wrong, even if her passport does say she was born in Marseilles.'

'Excuse me, guv.' Birkinshaw and Roberts broke off their conversation. A Dover Harbour Board policeman stood in the doorway, his pocket book open.

'What is it, mate?' said Birkinshaw, walking across to him. 'Can't you see we're busy?'

'This car – this grey Volvo estate, guv.' The policeman pointed to his pocket book.

'Yeah, what about it?'

'It's in the long-stay car-park, guv.'

Two and a half hours later, Tipper walked into the Special
Branch office at Eastern Docks. 'Well, well, Mrs Hodder,' he
said. 'Fancy seeing you again.' He turned to the detective.
'Well done.'

'Nothing to it, sir,' said Birkinshaw, preening himself.

Julia Hodder was also taken to Rochester Row police station,
and lodged in a cell only a few feet away from that occupied
by Peter Selby, although neither knew of the other's presence
there.

Gaffney's men had searched the Hodders' house in Surrey
as a matter of routine. They hadn't expected to find anything incriminating and they weren't disappointed. Living
as the wife of an MI5 officer would have made it extremely
hazardous for Julia to leave anything lying about that her
husband might have found. The French passport which she
had used when she tried to leave the country had probably
been secreted somewhere else; might even have been in a
safety deposit box at the bank.

Gaffney and Tipper didn't interrogate her immediately;
they spent what little remained of the day in a hurriedly
convened conference with a senior official at the office of
the Director of Public Prosecutions. Sir Edward Griffin, the
Director-General of the Security Service, was there also, as
was Commander Frank Hussey of Special Branch.

During that time, both the DPP's man and Griffin spoke
on the telephone to the Attorney–General. Selby, an MI5
intelligence officer, had admitted to having an affaire with
Julia Hodder, believing her to be Rita Hamilton, or so he
said; and had stayed with her at Tanglewood, the house where
police had discovered spying paraphernalia. And finally, Julia
Hodder had been apprehended trying to leave the country on
a false passport.

The lawyer had already started to draft the offences for
which Julia Hodder could be arraigned under the Official
Secrets Acts, and other acts dealing with the acquisition and

uttering of forged or false passports, but in any case involving espionage there were always political considerations. The lawyer was concerned only with the legal aspects; Sir Edward Griffin's interest spread across the wider field of intelligence. The arbiter in all this was the Attorney–General, who had a foot in each camp, and without whose fiat a case of spying could not be brought to trial. He was essentially a lawyer, but he was also a politician; susceptible, therefore, to the blandishments of the intelligence community and, in the long term, the views of the Foreign Secretary and his advisers. And if a deal was thought to be to the overall advantage of Her Majesty's government, then the rule of law was conveniently forgone. It all hinged on what Julia Hodder had to say.

Peter Selby was another matter altogether. The Director of Public Prosecutions had ruled, some time ago, that proceedings should not be taken unless there was at least a fifty per cent chance of a conviction. So far, the lawyer had been unable to frame any charge upon which there was even a remote chance of securing such a conviction. Reluctantly, the assembled company were forced to agree that about all that could be proved against Selby was that he had been incredibly stupid. To date, stupidity had not been made a criminal offence. Which was probably as well for a lot of politicians, lawyers, civil servants, councillors, doctors, policemen, stockbrokers, business men . . . Again, it depended upon Julia Hodder and the extent to which she implicated Selby.

Detective Sergeant Mackinnon sat at his desk high in New Scotland Yard. Everything was happening around him, but still Harry Tipper would not release him from his mundane report-writing.

He let the phone ring three or four times before answering it, remembering the advice of an old Special Branch officer who would never answer it on the first ring. 'Let'em think you're busy, lad,' he would say.

He grabbed the handset impatiently. 'DS Mackinnon.'

'Oh, Mr er – it's— '

'Hallo, Mr Marsh.' Mackinnon recognised the ex-Foreign Office man's voice instantly. He also instantly regretted having answered it. Apart from being amazed that Dudley Marsh had found the piece of paper with his telephone number on it, he guessed that he was in for another lengthy period of irrelevant reminiscence. 'What can I do for you?'

'I've remembered about the Simpsons' daughter. . . . '

'And what's that, Mr Marsh?' Mackinnon lodged the handset in the crook of his neck and reached for the file and a pen.

'She's dead.'

Mackinnon threw down the pen and looked at the ceiling. A sergeant opposite grinned and Mackinnon mouthed the words, Why me? 'Dead, you say, Mr Marsh?'

'Yes, absolutely.'

'Perhaps you'd better tell me about it.' Mackinnon glanced at the clock then at the other sergeant. Putting his hand over the mouthpiece, he asked, 'Which boozer you going to, Pat?'

'Star,' said the sergeant. 'I'll get you one in.'

'Yes,' continued Marsh. 'Their daughter died in – now when was it? Must have been about 1954. They told me all about it one day. They were in London for a spell and the girl was born there. Old George should have gone off to Malaya, but there was all that terrorist trouble at the time, and he cried off, having a young baby and that, so they came out to Nigeria – that was his first tour. Kiddy caught some awful local bug and died. About two years old she was. Ironic, wasn't it? I mean going there because of the trouble in Malaya.'

'I think we're at cross-purposes here,' said Mackinnon. 'I didn't know they had two daughters. I'm talking about Julia.'

'So am I,' said Marsh. 'They only had the one. Biggest disappointment of Helen's life. They tried for another, you know. No good. Damn' shame, really.'

'Are you absolutely sure, Mr Marsh?'

'Certain. Why don't you check with the Foreign Office? Probably on a file somewhere. Very good with bits of paper, the Foreign Office.'

It took Mackinnon about fifteen minutes to get from Scotland Yard to Rochester Row police station, and a further five to explain in detail what he had been told by Dudley Marsh.

Gaffney immediately sent for Tipper. 'Your background enquiries on Julia Hodder look as though they've come up trumps, Harry. She wasn't Julia Simpson.'

'Eh?'

'The real Julia Simpson died at the age of two, in Lagos. Our Julia is bogus.'

Tipper held up his hands. 'Why in hell didn't the vetting people find that out? I'll bet that was my old guv'nor did that one.'

Gaffney laughed. 'Be fair, Harry. You find a birth certificate in St Catherine's House; you don't then trawl through the deaths to make sure she's still alive. Anyway, if she died in Africa, which is what Mackinnon's informant said, it won't be there.'

'It should be; in the consular section.'

'Even so, Harry, you don't expect to find that everyone up for vetting has adopted a dead person's identity.'

'It's slap-dash,' growled Tipper, unwilling to make allowances.

'Anyway, confirm it if you can. See your bloke at the Foreign Office; take Mackinnon with you, and he can explain more fully on the way. Better still, I should go to St Catherine's House first, if I was you; might save yourself a bit of time.'

'Dead?' said Naylor. 'But I thought you said you'd spoken to her.'

'That's what I thought,' said Tipper patiently. He knew this was going to be difficult to explain. 'I have interviewed a woman who purports to be Julia Simpson. I have seen a birth certificate for her, and I have seen her passport application. I can even tell you where she is right now. But my detective sergeant here – ' He indicated Mackinnon with a jerk of his thumb. 'My detective sergeant went to see your Dudley Marsh – the High Commissioner's friend – and he told him that Julia Simpson had died in Nigeria in 1954, aged two.'

'How extraordinary,' said Naylor. 'What d'you want me to do?'

'Is there any way of checking what Marsh said? To be fair, DS Mackinnon said he was a bit forgetful, and appeared to be rambling at times.'

'He kept telling me he was forgetful,' said Mackinnon, 'when he could remember.' He was only slightly mollified by his bit of information; still smarting that he seemed to have missed most of the action.

'He could have been mixing the Simpsons up with someone else,' continued Tipper. 'Or at least mixing their daughter up. Apart from anything else we've some loose confirmation that she was working for a charity in Ethiopia.'

'Or someone purporting to be?' Naylor smiled archly. He leaned back in his chair and tapped his teeth with a pencil. 'The normal procedure with births, deaths and marriages abroad is that they are registered with the consular section. A copy of the certificate goes to Somerset House— ' He paused. 'No, it's not there any more. . . . '

'St Catherine's House,' said Tipper.

'Ah yes, of course. Well it's sent there and lodged in the consular index or some such thing – it's separate from the United Kingdom indexes anyway.'

'Yes, I know all that,' said Tipper. 'We came via St Catherine's House on the way here. No trace. That's why we're here.'

'Mmmm! I see. Yes, well, they don't always get registered. The British abroad often don't bother. Causes a lot of problems with nationality subsequently, when it comes to getting passports – that sort of thing. Our people are always getting letters from the Home Office about it.'

'Really,' said Tipper. 'Fascinating.'

'Oh yes. Mind you, this fellow Simpson wouldn't have forgotten; well, I wouldn't have thought so, being in the

297

service. It could have been a slip-up in Lagos, of course.'
He reached across to his bookcase and selected a paperback
book. 'Let me see – 1954, you said?'

'When she died? Yes.'

'Mmm! No. I couldn't remember exactly when independ-
ence was. There was always a Royal hopping on a plane about
that time to do the flag-lowering thing.' He ran a finger down
the page. 'Ah! No, 1963, Nigeria. Still . . . ' He read to himself
for a while. 'There was a lot going on – autonomous regions,
then federation. It was jolly difficult for our chaps in those
days. Never quite knew what was what. Still, they shouldn't
have slipped up on something like that.' He replaced the book
carefully in its allotted place and swung round to face Tipper
again. 'I'll tell you what I'll do – ' He drew a pad towards
him and felt in his pocket for a pen. 'I'll shoot off a signal to
HE and get him to have one of his fellows poke about in the
basement, see if they can find anything. How would that be?'

'Thank you,' said Tipper. 'It is very important. I understand from one of my senior officers that the Prime Minister
is interested in the outcome of this enquiry.'

'Oh!' said Naylor, and stood up.

The signal, addressed to Gaffney of Handcuffs, was remark-
able for its brevity. It informed him that there was a record
of the death of an infant named Julia Simpson at the High
Commission. She had died on 15th September 1954. The
informant was George Simpson, a member of the Colonial
Service stationed at Lagos. It regretted that, according to
records, no copy of the entry had been forwarded to the
General Register Office in London at the time. A photostat
copy of the entry, said the message in conclusion, was being
forwarded by diplomatic pouch.

'Careless bastards,' said Tipper.

The next morning, Julia Hodder, wearing the white slacks
and black shirt in which she had been arrested, was brought
into the interview room. Gaffney and Tipper were waiting,
together with Ray Grierson, the deputy director of MI5,

whose task it was to sit in the corner and say nothing; just to listen; to hold a watching brief for the Security Service. Sir Edward Griffin had decided to send his deputy to undertake this rather mundane task, he had said, because of the 'serious implications for the service'.

For a whole hour beforehand, Gaffney, Tipper and Grierson had sifted the evidence, trying to deduce from it what had happened over the past ten years, and how Julia Hodder had succeeded so brilliantly in penetrating MI5. Finally, they had produced a summary which Gaffney was now going to use as a basis for his interrogation.

'What's your real name, Mrs Hodder?' asked Gaffney.

She looked sullenly at him, then at Tipper, and then pointedly turned to gaze briefly at Grierson; she knew instinctively who he was. She faced Gaffney again. 'I have nothing to say,' she said.

'Would you like a cigarette, Mrs Hodder?' Gaffney asked. He had noticed, when he had interviewed her previously, that she smoked; he had taken the trouble to buy a packet of her brand of cigarettes, and now laid it on the table. 'Coffee will be along in a moment.'

She hesitated, then reached out and took one. Gaffney met the end of her cigarette with the flame of his lighter. 'Thank you,' she said, and blew smoke into the air. 'But I still have nothing to say.'

Gaffney knew that this wasn't going to be easy, but he had plenty of time: days, weeks even, if necessary. 'In that case,' he said, 'I shall talk to you. Two or three days ago we searched the house at Bere Watton – Tanglewood.' There was no reaction; she continued to gaze coolly at him, smoking her cigarette. 'As you will probably realise, we found the transmitter, and quite a lot of other spying equipment. More important, we found the car in which Peter Dickson's escape was effected, just as he was about to be arrested. We also found two passports in the names of Mrs Rita Hamilton and Madame Estelle Bisson; each of which had a photograph of you in it. There was currency, too – a lot of currency, and some travellers' cheques. But then I am not telling you anything you don't already know, am I?' Still she said nothing. 'And we found a coded message that you had omitted to destroy, which gave you quite specific instructions to ensure that that car was disposed of immediately after it had been used. You failed to do that, Mrs Hodder – you failed to comply with orders, and as a result we now have possession of it, and were able to undertake a number of tests – tests which have given us valuable information.' It wasn't true; they had found a number of unidentified fingerprints, that was all. Not that it mattered. 'I don't think that your masters are going to be terribly happy with you, Mrs Hodder. If the director of the Chernobyl plant can get ten years in a labour camp for negligence, I tremor to think what you'll get for downright disobedience – if they ever get you back.'

For the first time, she looked slightly disconcerted, and stubbed her cigarette out with a little more determination than was in keeping with her character. 'You don't frighten me,' she said, but Gaffney reckoned that he had.

'And then,' continued Gaffney, as though she hadn't spoken, 'we come to Peter Selby.' There was a spark of interest, no more. 'We arrested him the day before yesterday, by the way; I should think he'll spend quite a long time in prison – poor Peter.' He waited, letting that sink in. 'He's been very forthcoming.'

She shrugged her shoulders, but she obviously hadn't liked that piece of information very much.

'Your three great successes were to ensure the escape of Nikitin, Gesschner and Dickson, each of whom is doubtless safely at home in the Soviet Union or wherever they belong.' It was true that recent information had come into the hands of MI5 that Nikitin was back in Moscow. Nothing had come from the East German liaison about Gesschner, and it was early days yet to get any intelligence on the whereabouts of Dickson. 'They have no doubt been given a great welcome.' He paused to light a cigar. 'Which is more than you will get, Mrs Hodder.' He pushed the packet of cigarettes across the table. 'Your people have long memories, and even after you've spent twenty-five years in an English women's prison

300

– which is probably what you'll get – they will still want to exact their revenge for your gross stupidity. They're like that, aren't they?' He carefully rolled the ash off his cigar. 'I think you'll die in prison, Mrs Hodder.'

She gently stubbed her half-smoked cigarette out in the ashtray. 'Can I see Peter?' There was no sign of emotion.

'Perhaps. It rather depends on you. We'll talk about it another time.' He stood up and banged on the interview room door. A WPC entered. 'You can put Mrs Hodder back in her cell now,' he said.

Chapter Twenty-One

They reassembled at four o'clock that afternoon. On Gaffney's instructions, a change of clothing had been brought from Surrey for Julia Hodder, and she now wore a plain black dress. Gaffney noticed that she was looking a little more strained than she had done earlier in the day.

'Peter Selby,' he began, concentrating on what he thought might be a weak spot in her reserve, 'was a mistake on your part, wasn't he?' She raised a quizzical eyebrow, but remained silent. 'He wasn't meant to feature in your arrangements at all. Your instructions were to come to this country and suborn Geoffrey Hodder. And you did. You were sexually attractive, glamorous, and younger than his wife. He was flattered that someone like you should be interested in him, let alone want him. You seduced him – and he was more than willing – and you succeeded in marrying him. To make certain of him, you even telephoned his wife one afternoon so that she could come and find you in bed with him ... and you left the back door open.' The briefest of smiles flitted across Julia's face. 'And you were patient. It was some considerable time before you started to extract information from him, well after the time when he might just have been suspicious, and perhaps start wondering. And you did it under the pretext of counselling him when he started to feel depressed. But it was you, Mrs Hodder, who sowed the seeds of that depression, that nervousness. By insidious methods you set him doubting his own abilities, sapping his confidence; very slowly you wore him down until he felt that he could do nothing, make no decisions, without consulting you. He discussed every operation with you, but for the first few years you didn't use that information, did you? That was clever, building his trust in you like that. But then you started; started passing that information to your masters in the Kremlin. You, or they, were even careful to pick a house at Bere Watton so that you could send your fast transmissions when helicopters were flying overhead on one of their routine checks of the prison, and so make detection much more difficult.' It was guess-work, all along the line, but it seemed logical to Gaffney.

'But the one thing you couldn't control was yourself. And that is what started the chain of events which resulted in your arrest.' Still she showed no reaction; just sat with a bland expression on her face. 'You couldn't resist other men, and Geoffrey couldn't resist other women; but there are different rules. Men think it's all right if they have affaires, but not if their wives do. It's unfair, but that's the way it is. When he found out about you and Dick Harris – and the others – he would have left you, but he couldn't afford to; he'd got no money, and he was still supporting his first wife. But he could – and did – stop sleeping with you. And that was too much for you. One of the things you said to me the second time we met was that you couldn't live without sex; that was not only true, it was your undoing.

'And then Geoffrey started to doubt your trustworthiness. Suddenly it came to him that you were the one person he'd told everything to. All about what he did; about Nikitin and Gesschner and Dickson, and God knows how much else that you'd wheedled out of him. And that terrified him. The poor devil didn't know what to do. How could he go to the Director-General and tell him that for the last ten years he'd been married to a KGB agent?' Gaffney walked to the door and turned on the lights, illuminating the high, white-walled room with a stark light. 'Now you were in a quandary; your source of information had suddenly dried up. Even so, your husband couldn't bring himself to report what he had discovered about you, despite being certain of his suspicions; instead, he killed himself. But during the anguished months leading up to his death, you had to find a new source of information. Geoffrey had told you all about his staff, their foibles and their problems, and Selby was the one that you chose as the most malleable: an aesthete, a single man – possibly a homosexual – and all round, a bit out of the ordinary.'

Julia Hodder remained completely in control of herself, and Gaffney was beginning to wonder whether he had got it all wrong. He certainly wasn't penetrating her ice-cold poise. Nevertheless, he persevered; he had no alternative. 'Then you embarked on an elaborate masquerade,' he continued, 'pretending to be Rita Hamilton. The risks were enormous, but you were desperate, because you had allowed your husband to find out about you. That sort of incompetence is unacceptable to your KGB masters, isn't it? But to your astonishment, Selby turned out not to be a homosexual; he proved to be an ardent lover, and that's when you made your biggest and final mistake. You broke all the rules; you took him to Bere Watton. I have asked myself why you did that, and there's only one answer: Selby had fallen head over heels in love with you.' Gaffney paused. 'And you with him. . . . '

For the first time since her arrest, she showed some emotion. 'It's true,' she said. 'He does love me, wants to marry me; and I want to marry him.'

'Then it's up to you, isn't it? You tell us what we want to know and you will be released: no trial, no prison.' This was the inducement that Gaffney had been authorised to offer, but only if she was prepared to talk. The DPP's man had argued long and hard in favour of the rule of law, but had eventually been beaten down, as is so often the case, in the face of what are euphemistically called 'intelligence interests'.

'I don't believe you.' Still Julia Hodder's face remained expressionless. 'British Intelligence doesn't work like that.'

Gaffney smiled. 'Oh, but it does, and you know it does. You've been a professional intelligence officer for long enough to know how the game's played. Your people are playing it all the time. Be frank with us and we'll give you a new identity, somewhere discreet and safe to live, and you can start a new life.'

She tossed her head. 'Huh! And be forever looking over my shoulder?'

'Or forever in prison – first a British one, then a Russian one. Do they put female prisoners in the Lubyanka, or do they go to labour camps too?' Gaffney paused, calculating. 'You're thirty-five now. Add twenty-five years' imprisonment here – that's sixty; a bit old to start work in a labour camp.' He sat back and waited. The methods he was using were downright coercive, and any evidence that resulted would be inadmissible in an English court; but he didn't want evidence, didn't need it. He was seeking intelligence, and that was a different matter altogether – that was always needed.

For minutes she sat in silence, gazing at a spot on the wall way above Gaffney's head. He prayed that no one would break the spell.

At last she spoke. 'What guarantees do I have?'

'None.' Gaffney spoke coldly. 'You're hardly in a position to demand any, but you don't have any real choice.'

Suddenly she smiled. 'I didn't really expect any,' she said. 'If our rôles had been reversed, I wouldn't have given you any.' For a moment, her decision hung in the air, apparently wavering. Gaffney held his breath. 'All right,' she said, 'supposing I tell you what you want to know. What happens then?'

'What you tell me will be assessed by the security authorities, and if it is found to be both accurate and helpful, the Attorney-General will consider withholding his fiat— '

She shook her head. 'I'm sorry, Mr Gaffney. I've no idea what you're talking about.'

'In all prosecutions under the Official Secrets Act, the Attorney-General has to give his fiat – his permission – for those proceedings. Without it, there is no prosecution.'

'I see.' She nodded.

'If that happens, then the authorities will arrange for you to be given a new identity and somewhere to live. And they will be in contact with you probably for the rest of your life.'

'Oh! Why is that?'

'Well primarily to protect you, but also to make sure you don't change your mind.'

'I shan't change my mind.'

'They all say that,' said Gaffney. 'The other thing we will make sure of is that you are not part of an elaborate plot.'

'And how will you do that?'

Gaffney smiled, but said nothing.

There was a pause while she mulled over the proposition. 'All right,' she said. 'What d'you want to know?'

'Who you are might be a good place to start; we know that you are not Julia Simpson, and never were.'

'My name is Alexandrina Belinska and I was born in Moscow in 1953 – 21st August, so you see I am only thirty-four.'

Gaffney nodded; that was probably quite important to her. 'Go on.'

'My father was a party official, so we had our own flat. No sharing.'

Gaffney looked across at the shorthand writer to satisfy himself that what she was saying was being taken down. Admittedly there was a tape-recorder running, but that was mechanical, and mechanical things could go wrong; shorthand writers tended not to.

'I finished school at sixteen,' she continued. 'And then I was selected for special training.'

'What sort of special training?'

'I was sent to learn English, thoroughly.'

'Yes, but for what purpose?'

'I wasn't told – and I didn't ask.'

'Yes, go on.' Gaffney glanced at Grierson, inviting him to participate in the conversation, but content – at least for the moment – he waved a hand of dismissal. 'Where did you go for this training?'

'Nikolayev – well, near there. It's on the Black Sea.'

'And what form did this training take?'

She looked across the room, up at the high, wired windows set in the wall near the ceiling. 'It was pretty awful. All the streets there are like English streets – are English streets, with

306

English cars and buses, and shops and post offices.' She darted a smile at him. 'And English policemen!' She became serious again. 'Everything is exactly as in an English town. I heard that Colonel Philby helped to design it, and gives advice every so often.' She smiled.

'Decent of him,' said Gaffney.

'But the worst part is in the dacha. Each of the students has his or her own dacha; it's a small villa. In every one of the rooms there is a television or a radio. You cannot turn them off. All day and all night they are on.'

'What do they broadcast?'

'All the English programmes. They are beamed on satellites, straight from England, then recorded and played back. Everything you see and hear, we see and hear. The first night you cannot sleep; the second night you are exhausted. But by the end of the first month, I knew that Harold Wilson was the Prime Minister, and that there was civil war in Northern Ireland. The opening of the Victoria Line was on television, and I knew all about *Coronation Street* and *Crossroads*. I watched *Panorama*, and saw all the party conferences. For three years I soaked up everything that you put out. All the time we used English money. . . . ' She broke off and laughed. 'It was much easier when you changed to decimal in 1971. Every newspaper was available to us, and we had to read them; they would test us – all the time, tests on language and customs and current affairs.'

'How long were you there, Mrs Hodder? You don't mind if I continue to call you that, do you? I don't think I could pronounce your real name.'

She smiled. 'I'm not very good at it either. It's a long time since I used it.' She leaned across the table and pointed to the cigarette packet. Gaffney nodded and gave her his lighter. She pulled deeply, inhaling the smoke. 'Three years I was there.'

'And then?'

'A year's illegal.'

Gaffney looked puzzled. 'A year's what?'

'A year here. I was an illegal immigrant, but with all the

307

right papers, not that you need them. I spent a year here in London, familiarising myself with your way of life – getting the feel of the place, I suppose you might say. Then I went back to Nikolayev for another year.'

'What was the purpose of that?'

'To iron out the problems. To learn how to look a police-man in the eye without feeling guilty; you know, the sort of thing you would never do in Russia. We had to make a list while we were here of all the things that worried us, that we found hard.'

'And what did you find hard? What were your problems?'

'Flirting with men. It is done differently here from the way it's done in Russia.'

Gaffney thought that she had learned well. 'And then what?'

'I went to Nigeria – to Lagos – to learn my life.'

'Your life?'

'Yes, learning to be Julia Simpson.'

'Tell me about it.'

'The authorities – the KGB that is – knew about her death in Nigeria, and they knew it wasn't in the records at St Catherine's House.'

'But it was in the High Commission in Lagos.'

'It was?' She looked shaken by that, shaken not only that the great impeccable KGB could have made such a mistake, but that they had put her at risk. 'It's been done before,' she said, as though that excused their incompetence, 'with Colonel Konon Molody, who your people knew as Gordon Arnold Lonsdale.' Gaffney nodded. 'I had to learn all about Julia, and my parents, George and Helen, who were conveni-ently killed in an air crash in 1975. I familiarised myself with where I was supposed to have been brought up. Then I went to Ethiopia and did some relief work with a charity, building up my life story all the time.'

'Had it been decided at that time what you were going to do?'

'I don't know. One does not ask. But while I was there I was given my orders and a very full briefing on Geoffrey.'

'By whom?' Grierson spoke for the first time. 'Can you remember the name?'

'Kuprin,' she said, turning to face the MI5 officer. 'Colonel Alexis Kuprin – he was the military attaché at the Soviet Embassy in Addis.' She spoke without hesitation, instantly recalling the man's rank, name and post.

'Where did you receive this briefing? In the embassy?'

She laughed scornfully. 'Of course not. What would an English relief worker be doing going into the Soviet Embassy in Addis Ababa? No, it was specially arranged – in a safe house.'

'Where was it? Can you recall the address?'

'Yes. It was Harar Street, number 17.' She paused to take another cigarette – this time without asking – and light it. 'But it's no longer there. Since the revolution things in Ethiopia are much easier for us.' She spoke contemptuously, implying that Grierson should have known that.

'What were your instructions – in relation to Geoffrey?' asked Gaffney. 'That you should come to England and seduce him?'

'Yes. It was all exactly as you said.' Her blue eyes looked straight into his, unwavering.

'Were you aware of what he did – what he was?'

'Of course. It was a thorough briefing.'

'Please go on.'

'I came to England, to Surrey. I was given exact details. I bought Raven Cottage and got to work.' Gaffney smiled at her businesslike approach. 'It was easier than I'd hoped. When I saw Elizabeth, I knew it was going to be a pushover.' For the first time, she looked a little sympathetic. 'Poor old Geoffrey.' She wrinkled her nose. 'He didn't stand a chance, really,' and she laughed.

'I can imagine,' murmured Gaffney. Grierson frowned; he didn't enjoy flippant remarks about his late colleague.

'The one thing that my training hadn't prepared me for, though, was the hostility of English women.' She smiled at the memory. 'They were so unkind. But things got better when I married. They didn't seem to mind me so much then.'

309

'As a matter of interest, what would have happened if you'd become pregnant? Would you have had the child?'

'That would not have been possible.' She frowned slightly, a wistful expression. 'I had to be sterilised before leaving for duty abroad. It's not considered quite proper for majors in the KGB to have babies – especially when they're on active service.' The frown disappeared and she smiled again.

'No, I suppose not.' It was difficult for Gaffney, despite his experience, to visualise this attractive woman opposite him as a KGB major. 'How easy was it for you to extract information from your husband? Or was it very difficult?'

'At first, yes, very hard. So I didn't try. I waited for about six years— '

'Six years!'

She looked at him patiently. 'Of course. When you have invested so much time in an operation – a creation – you don't rush it, only to fall at the first fence. There was always plenty of time. We were not in a hurry for anything.'

'No, I suppose not.' Gaffney couldn't help admiring the girl's professionalism.

'Then Geoffrey was promoted – that would have been about two or three years ago. . . . ' Behind Julia, Grierson nodded at Gaffney. 'He began to feel the strain. Quite frankly, I think it was a mistake. He wasn't up to it. It happens in Russia, too, you know. People get over-promoted. What's that lovely expression? Promoted to the level of their incompetence. Well that was poor Geoffrey. Not unnaturally I took advantage of that. It was a long, slow process, but it paid off in the end. I could see he was worried. So, carefully and gently, I got him to confide in me, in a way that wouldn't make him suspicious. It meant making some sacrifices, of course— '

'Oh?' Gaffney raised an eyebrow.

'Oh yes. I could have prevented the arrest of the man you knew as Charles Godfrey, but I had to let you have him. It was all part of building Geoffrey's confidence in me, so that in the end he would tell me everything. And he did. Unfortunately, he told me so much that he began to realise. It was a pity about Peter Dickson – coming so soon after Nikitin

310

and Gesschner. If it had stopped there – at least for a while –
I might have got away with it. But Major Armitage was such
a gift – and Peter Dickson so valuable an operator – that I
really had no choice.' She shrugged her shoulders so that it
opened the front of her dress a little more. Gaffney smiled
inwardly, pleased to have official confirmation that his trap
had been so successful.

'You say that he began to suspect?'

'More than that. He knew. He was really frightened by
the Dickson disappearance. I've never seen him in such a
state – a nervous wreck. And after that interview with you
at Scotland Yard, Mr Gaffney, I think he knew that there
was going to be trouble. It was like a blinding glimpse of
the obvious. He asked me outright if I was an agent.'

'And what did you say?'

'I denied it, of course. What else could I do?'

'Obviously you were going to have to do something.'

'Obviously.' Suddenly her face was very stern, possessed of
a steel-like quality that lent her features a frightening, almost
compelling attraction. 'I was going to have him liquidated.'
Even Gaffney, with all his experience, was staggered at her
coolness, at the cold matter-of-fact solution to a problem.
She betrayed no emotion at the prospect of disposing of a
man with whom she had lived for nigh on ten years. 'It was
him or me,' she said.

Gaffney tapped Tipper's foot under the table, a signal
for him to take over the interrogation. With several murder
investigations under his belt, Tipper was a natural for dealing
with murder, attempted murder, threats to murder and conspiracy to murder. 'What plans did you make?' he asked.

She smiled at him, and again he felt uncomfortable. Whoever had trained her in the subtle art of seduction had done
a good job. 'None. I just thought about it. And that's not
a crime, is it?' She continued to gaze unwaveringly at him.
'I didn't have to. The next morning he went to work and
committed suicide.' She switched her gaze back to Gaffney.
'You did say it was suicide, didn't you?'

Gaffney nodded. 'Yes, it was.' He felt Tipper's foot touch

his. Tipper was out of his depth and wasn't afraid to say so. He'd spent a professional lifetime interrogating prisoners against whom there was some sanction: usually a charge for a serious offence. This gentler persuasion was not his medium. 'How did you get on to Selby?' asked Gaffney.

'You seem to know that already,' she said, and smiled. 'Geoffrey told me about him, as you suspected. He told me about all the people he worked with.' She shot a glance over her shoulder at Grierson. 'But Peter seemed the best. From what Geoffrey said, he was different: he loved music and the arts. And he was single. I'd already decided that Geoffrey had served his purpose, and he was becoming a danger to me. It was time for a change.' She was chain-smoking now. 'I got my controller to find out more about Selby.'

Grierson looked as though he were about to ask a question. Gaffney knew what the question was, but he had no intention of allowing it to upset the flow. The identity of Julia Hodder's controller would come later: another day in all probability. He shook his head briefly. 'How did your controller find out more?'

She spread her hands in a gesture of ignorance. 'I don't know.' She spoke sharply, implying that a professional like Gaffney should know. 'I presume he had him followed: I don't really know. Anyway, I was told that he went to concerts, always by himself, and that he was very keen on Monteverdi. Then one day I got a telephone call from my controller to say that Peter was going to a concert at a country house in Sussex that evening. So I went too; and I bumped into him, literally, and emptied my glass of wine over him.' She smiled at the memory. 'It was him who apologised.'

'Was that part of your course in how to seduce men?' asked Gaffney, smiling also.

'No.' She looked serious. 'It just seemed like a good idea at the time.'

'And so you went on to develop a relationship with Selby in exactly the same sort of way that you had done with Geoffrey Hodder – yes?'

'That was the intention, certainly, but it didn't work out quite like that.'

'Oh?' Gaffney had a brief glimpse of sadness, perhaps the only time he was to see the real Julia behind the mask of the KGB agent.

'It all went wrong.'

'How so?'

'I fell in love with him.' She looked first at Tipper, assessing, with feminine intuition, a greater degree of sympathy there than in Gaffney. 'KGB officers aren't supposed to do that. But Peter was the first person I'd ever met who was artistic, kind and loving . . . and sympathetic. I'd never experienced any of that before – never.' She looked down at the floor, playing with the wedding ring that once again adorned her finger.

'Whatever made you take him down to Bere Watton?' It was the one error that Julia had made that had intrigued Gaffney from the moment he had discovered what Tanglewood was being used for. It was the enigma: the one mistake that a professional of her calibre should never have made.

She shook her head, doubting briefly her own capability. 'I should never have done that. But what else could I do? I couldn't have taken him to Surrey; he would have found out immediately who I really was. Anyway there were all those eyes watching. And they have long memories; I could almost hear them saying that Julia Hodder's single again – watch your husbands. I couldn't have made a move without the whole village knowing and watching and wondering. I suppose I moved too quickly. If I had spoken to my controller, I could have had him set up a new place, a new identity. But with Peter working for MI5, I knew, deep down, that it would be short-lived: a passing happiness. And that was what I wanted most of all. I was tired of the whole business. I wanted to be a real wife; a family was out of the question, of course; I told you that.' Again the brief look of sadness. 'But at least I had hoped for something out of life.'

'How did you engineer the escape of Nikitin, Gesschner and Dickson?' Gaffney thought that it was time to bring her back to the mainstream of the enquiry. There would be time for self-pity later on.

The brittle professional took over again. 'It was easy. I arranged for them to go to Bere Watton. They stayed there for a month or two, and then they flew out in the ordinary way, through Heathrow; with new identities. Nikitin and Dickson went to Moscow, via Delhi or Geneva, and Gesschner went to Berlin. It is very simple, you know.'

'Then why didn't you do the same thing?'

She smiled at the naïveté of the question. 'I couldn't very well go to Tanglewood, could I? It was in the hands of the police.'

'How did you know that? It wasn't in the papers, or on television.'

'I guessed what had happened. It was pure luck, too, but I went to Peter's flat in Fulham. I met your policeman; a nice young man, very attractive.' She smiled; Gaffney looked sour. 'The fact that he was a policeman and there in Peter's flat was a danger signal, and when he told me that Peter was away and wouldn't be coming back for some time, I knew that something had gone wrong – badly wrong.'

'But why Dover? You were making for France, weren't you?'

She nodded. 'That was my second mistake. I was pretty sure that Peter couldn't be in too much trouble. He hadn't told me anything – that would have come later, perhaps – and he certainly couldn't have suspected anything about Tanglewood; that was too well disguised—'

'So long as he didn't read the books,' said Gaffney drily.

She laughed at that and reached across for Gaffney's lighter. 'I had this idea that I would go to France and wait for him, and that we could settle down there and be happy.' Her face puckered momentarily and Gaffney thought that she was going to cry. 'An impossible dream. There would have been no chance, not with his job. When you discovered Tanglewood, I knew in my heart that it was all over. But I still hoped – hopelessly. But he would never have trusted me, not after Geoffrey. And you can't build a happy marriage on suspicion.' She suddenly looked very sad. 'Not that I would know,' she said.

'I am instructed by the Director of Public Prosecutions to offer no evidence against Major James Armitage, sir,' said counsel.

The magistrate mumbled something incomprehensible, and quite probably uncomplimentary. Then he looked up at Armitage, standing in the dock of No 1 Court. 'You are discharged,' he said grudgingly. He would never understand the machinations of the Security Service as long as he lived. 'Next,' he said, surveying the brassy prostitute who now stood in the dock.

It was a whole week before John Gaffney received the note. A week during which Julia Hodder's communist upbringing, her adherence to the ideology of the Soviet Union – ingrained since birth – and her KGB training struggled with her love for Peter Selby and her new-found loyalty to a country she had at first despised, but had since grown to cherish.

It was a week during which she sat in her cell at Rochester Row, emerging daily for a debriefing with Grierson, and waiting for the decision of the Security Service whether or not to recommend that the Attorney-General should waive the prosecution.

She waited and wondered and worried. Worried that, after all, they would imprison her and throw away the key. It was what the KGB would have done. At first, her training rejected absolutely what she was contemplating. No matter what they did, she should not betray her own. But she knew that if she didn't, she would never be safe from them, perhaps not even then. If they ever got her back they would cremate her alive; that was the rule and she knew the rules.

It was that thought, more than anything else, which caused her to write the note.

Gaffney stood in the doorway of the cell. 'You wanted to see me?'

She was sitting tightly bunched, legs crossed, left hand

cupping her right elbow, and exhaling cigarette smoke in nervous little puffs. 'I wanted to tell you the name of my controller.' She looked directly at Gaffney. 'It's John Carfax.'

'Really?' Gaffney's mind immediately attempted to assess this latest twist, trying to estimate if it was a further example of Soviet disinformation from a woman he had never trusted; a bid perhaps to salvage something for the KGB from the wreckage. 'But why?' he asked. 'Why should the KGB have two spies in MI5?'

She smiled impishly. 'Mr Gaffney,' she said, 'you can never have too many spies in an organisation like MI5. Carfax is due to retire next month. The KGB are great planners; I was put in position ten years ago to cater for his going. Then Geoffrey killed himself. . . . ' A brief sadness crossed her face, but it was the look of the professional at a plan gone wrong.

'So you went after Peter Selby as a replacement?'

She nodded. 'As you say, I went after Peter Selby.' She stared pensively at the floor. 'I'd allowed for everything but my own emotions.'

'But he's still here – Carfax; why didn't he escape as soon as you were arrested?'

She smiled tolerantly. 'You have to know the KGB to know the answer to that, Mr Gaffney. Do not be taken in by Mr Gorbachev and his *glasnost*; nothing has changed. When I was a child, I belonged to the *Komsomol*, the communist youth organisation.' There was a faraway look in her eyes. 'We wore white skirts and white blouses with a red, triangular scarf, and from the very first we swore to love the Soviet Union, to live, to study and to fight according to the teachings of Lenin and the Communist Party. John Carfax would not imagine for one moment that I would betray him; that, in the KGB, is unthinkable. It would certainly never have occurred to him that I would trade information for freedom.' She stood up and paced the cell. 'He knows that there is no freedom. I will either die in prison; or I will die out there.' She gestured briefly at the high, wired window, then turned to face Gaffney, a brittle smile on her face. 'There aren't many options for a spy, are there?'

It came as no great surprise to Gaffney to learn, six months later, that a widow called Margaret Donaldson had been found dead in her house in Inverness, or to learn that the Procurator–Fiscal's report to the Crown Agent stated that she had committed suicide. But Gaffney, and the few others who knew that Margaret Donaldson was Julia Hodder's cover-name, wondered. . . .